NORMAN HALL

THE AWAKENING

The Sequel to *Good Girl*

Copyright © Norman Hall 2019

Norman Hall has asserted his right to be identified as the author of this Work in accordance with the Copyright, Designs and Patents Act 1988.

ISBN 9781091270633

Cover image – Kristin Bryant
https://www.coroflot.com/kristinbryant

Copy-editor – Nicky Taylor
https://www.nickytayloreditorial.com

*For all the Jessica Anne Khalids
in the world.*

AUTHOR'S PREFACE

The Awakening is the sequel to my debut novel, *Good Girl*, published earlier this year. If you haven't read *Good Girl* then I suggest you do so, because the two novels go together.

However, I appreciate you may have just stumbled across *The Awakening* and, if you have, you might be confused if you don't know what happened before.

So, for those who haven't read *Good Girl* and want to dive straight in, I have provided a short reprise. Those who have can skip the next bit.

REPRISE OF *GOOD GIRL*

In the first novel, we are introduced to Jessica Anne Khalid, twenty-three years old and destitute. Abused as a teenager by her father, and seeking sanctuary from a torrid life at home, she falls under the spell of Pakistani cab driver Mohammed Khalid, marries him at seventeen and, at eighteen, gives birth to daughter Leila. She is yet to discover that Mo is not only a member of a child sex-grooming gang, he is also a drug dealer and inveterate gambler.

Over time, Mo's nefarious activities get him into serious debt and, with it, trouble. Fearing for his life, he flees to Pakistan, taking four-year-old Leila with him and leaving Jess with all his debts. With no family, and now faced with eviction and bankruptcy, Jess abandons what little she has left and disappears.

After two or three weeks spent sleeping rough, she finds a job with accommodation in a canal-side pub. She assumes a new identity as "Alice", but the lecherous landlord, Dave, has designs on her, and his unwelcome advances turn eventually to sexual assault. Traumatised by the behaviour of yet another man, she flees, unaware she is pregnant with twins.

While Jess's life lurches from crisis to crisis, seventy-year-old retired army officer Peter Jeffries is still coming to terms with the twin tragedies of losing his young wife to leukaemia and the disappearance of his daughter, Lisa. Lisa had found it impossible to cope with her mother's premature death and sought solace by taking a gap-year in Nepal, but goes missing after being caught up in a severe earthquake. Peter blames himself for Lisa's disappearance, believing he failed to show her the love and support she needed. Having travelled to Nepal in a futile bid to find her, he now presumes her dead.

When Jess and Peter meet by chance, she unwittingly takes on the role of surrogate daughter, unaware that she bears a striking resemblance to Lisa. Peter believes he has been blessed with a second chance and resolves to make amends for his failings with his own daughter. When Jess confesses her terrible past and he realises that she too has lost someone she loves, Peter secretly resolves to find Leila and return her to her mother.

Three years pass and, weakened by long-term illness, Peter receives the news that Leila has finally been found. But before Leila can be reunited with Jess, Peter dies, leaving Jess and her daughters everything in his will, unaware that his own daughter, Lisa, is in fact still alive.

So now, read on ...

THE AWAKENING

CHAPTER 1

Sujay Bahadur Gurung stood patiently on the edge of the trail, gaze fixed on the lone figure standing on a ridge a hundred metres away.

As ever, and almost since the beginning of time, the towering presence of 7,227-metre-high Langtang Lirung loomed large over the valley, and he saw that even now, the evidence of the mayhem and destruction the mountain had rained down upon the old village of Langtang remained indelible. A vast area of barren rock and scree sloped three kilometres down from its peak and spread itself across the valley, beneath which still lay the ruins of a small town and the bodies of most of its inhabitants. It was a stark and poignant reminder of the scale of the disaster and the annihilation of a community that, even after five years, not a single shrub, weed, sprig or blade of grass could permeate the blanket of stone.

The sole building to have survived the landslide, protected from the millions of tons of falling rock by an overhanging cliff, still stood as a sentinel, marking the grave of Langtang like a giant tombstone.

Sujay had been here many times before and wondered if, when and how this cruel manifestation of death might eventually spawn new life and perhaps gradually ease the pain of the past. Nature had been slow on the uptake, it appeared to him. In contrast, and despite the magnitude of the disaster, man's indomitable spirit had been resolute, and every time he came, he saw that the new village of Langtang, sited two hundred metres away under the protection of solid cliffs at the base of the mountain, had grown yet another hut, shack or barn.

There were new teahouses too, servicing the steadily increasing number of trekkers, some returning to a site they had visited in the past, others simply there out of morbid curiosity; sightseers of the infamous. But for whatever reason they came, all were welcome. They brought their money; income the new population of Langtang badly needed.

Sujay lowered his charge's rucksack to the ground. This visit was especially poignant for him, almost a repeat of the trip he'd made five years ago with the elderly Colonel Jeffries, although the circumstances could not be more different. He was still coming to terms with the consequences of his journey to England four months previously and remained unsure where they would lead.

He watched the young woman standing motionless on the ridge, hands in the pockets of her stylish and expensive red trekking jacket, staring out across the valley at the desolation below her. The likeness was remarkable and the circumstances bizarre, and he would like to know more about her and her motivation in coming here, but there would be plenty of time for that in the days ahead. He was not naturally inquisitive about his clients, being unremittingly courteous and respectful of their privacy, but the situation was highly unusual. He'd played a significant part in a saga that, for him, still held many unanswered questions.

But for now, as ever, the focus of his attention was the journey ahead and the distance they still had to travel. He checked his watch: 1.15 p.m. He would give her another minute or two before they rejoined the trail. They'd stop for lunch soon and then it would be three more hours to the place where they'd spend their third night. Perhaps she might be more inclined to unburden some of her thoughts now she'd been to see for herself.

The young woman standing alone on the ridge overlooking the Langtang Valley examined the desolate landscape that stretched out below her and she felt a wave of dismay and sadness rising from within. She tried to imagine what force of nature could possibly, without warning, have brought the entire side of a mountain down onto the heads of the unsuspecting villagers and at such speed that afforded them no time to get to safety. It was beyond her comprehension.

She saw figures moving around in the new settlement to the east and felt wonder at their resilience, awe at their determination to start again, admiration for their refusal to give up. She wondered who they were and how they lived their lives.

She thought of Peter standing here and the despair he must have felt looking down on the same scene, realising that his beloved Lisa was in all probability somewhere down there under the rubble and gone forever. She could hear him, even now.

"I have to believe she's dead. But I can't be certain. I just hope wherever she is, she's at peace."

She swallowed deeply and choked back a tear as she recalled his words back in the garden at Chalton. But the tear was not for Lisa. It was for Peter. *If only he were with me now.* She looked down at her feet and noticed footprints made by hiking boots just like hers, and she wondered whether any of them were Peter's. It was five years ago. Surely not?

Jessica Anne Jeffries drew a deep breath of cool Himalayan air through her nostrils, held it for a moment and, with eyes closed, exhaled slowly until her lungs were empty. She remained motionless for a few seconds until her body demanded oxygen, so she opened her mouth and, with eyes glassy and moist, began to breathe normally again. Her moment of contemplation was interrupted by a plaintive call coming from a hundred metres away.

"Miss Jess, I think we must be going now!"

Jess turned her head at the sound and saw Sujay's arm held high, hat in his hand, waving at her. She waved back in acknowledgement. It was not over. Not by a long way. The search for the truth had started four months ago, the day Leila had returned, and she would not rest until she knew. She took a last look at the valley and walked slowly back to the trail, where her Nepalese guide was waiting for her.

CHAPTER 2

The day Leila came home was the happiest day of Jess's life. After her daughter had been taken, it seemed to Jess that all life had stopped. In the aftermath of Leila's disappearance five years previously, all the other elements that made up Jess's miserable world had quickly unravelled, and although it seemed at the time there was little hope of ever seeing her daughter, giving up had never been an option. The determination to carry on, regardless of any hope of success, eventually led her down the path that reunited her with Leila.

When the hugs and kisses and tears and euphoria in the garden subsided, they all went indoors for tea and celebrations. Sophie and Lucy were thrilled to meet their new sister, even though they couldn't properly comprehend what that meant or who she was. They shrieked and screamed with delight and ran around the house as if possessed, and Leila, despite being five years older than them, joined in the games with gusto. Jess was similarly hyperactive, constantly jumping up from the kitchen table to see where the girls had gone and what they were up to, seemingly unable to let Leila out of her sight for more than a minute or two.

She repeatedly led them back into the kitchen and sat them down with the adults, who calmly sipped tea amidst the chaos, but within seconds the girls were off again, chasing each other from room to room, clutching their favourite teddies and shouting at the top of their high-pitched voices.

Jess had a thousand things to ask, but her brain was still buzzing from Michael's revelations earlier that afternoon. She babbled incoherently, throwing questions at him without waiting for answers, until he decided she was not in a fit state to absorb any information, nor would she be for some time to come.

"Jess," he said in his distinctive, calm and rational manner, his comforting voice somehow rising above the mayhem that was going on around them. "I suggest you take some time to let the dust settle. Get to know your daughter again. None of us can appreciate the trauma she may have experienced over the last four or five years and how that might manifest itself in the coming days." Jess looked up towards the kitchen doorway that led to the hall. She could still hear the girls playing and their squeals echoing around the house. The feverish and edgy manner she'd been unable to moderate slowly relaxed as Michael continued.

"You should be prepared for some emotional fallout as Leila adjusts to her new surroundings. Remember that only twenty-four hours ago she was immersed in the madness of Kathmandu with people she didn't know and little understanding of what was happening to her." Jess lowered her eyes as new and darker thoughts began to whirl around inside her head. Emma moved to the chair next to her and took her hand. It was cold and shaking.

"I shall have to get used to calling you Jess in future," she said with a kindly smile. "Unless, of course, you prefer otherwise."

Jess looked up at her ruefully.

"No. That's fine, either will do. The twins think I'm Alice. That was the only name Peter ever used, so I guess I'll be stuck with it for a while yet." But as she spoke, it began to dawn on her that the road ahead might be fraught with difficulties. It was tempting to think that now, all was right with the world, and this was another exciting new beginning on a journey that would take them who knows where? Despite her elation, she knew that she needed Peter's towering strength to help her more than ever, and realised how terribly she missed him. But Peter was gone, and whatever she had to do, she would have to do it herself.

"You know, Jess," said Emma. "We were never blessed with children and sometimes it's been a matter of great regret, for me at least." She turned to Michael who smiled fondly back at her. "It never happened for us. It wasn't to be. But despite all the bad things that happened to you, I hope you'll appreciate how lucky you are and that you've so much to look forward to. And of that, I confess to being insanely jealous." Jess looked up at her, worried for a moment that, for the first time ever, Emma might be about to weep all over her. "We'll be here to help you in any way we can. Be in no doubt about that." Jess flung her arms around her, and Emma stiffened slightly but then gently patted Jess's back in response.

"We are going to leave you to it," announced Michael, putting his mug down and getting to his feet. "I'll come back in a few days and we'll have a chat about things, but if you need anything, anything at all, just call. Any hour of the day or night. Promise?"

"Promise," said Jess, and she stood up just as Lucy ran into the kitchen.

"Mummy! Mummy! Leila's caught a mouse!"

"Oh my God!" gasped Emma, leaping up from her chair, nervously clutching the pearls around her neck. "Michael! Go and deal with it immediately!" Michael shrugged, giving the impression that in this particular matter he might be somewhat out of his comfort zone.

"Don't worry about it," said Jess calmly, pleased they had all been brought back down to earth, at least for a moment. "We get them now and again. I think it's time we got ourselves a cat." Michael sighed with apparent relief; his pest control services might not be required. But Emma wasn't convinced the danger had passed and she was right, as usual, as Leila came bounding into the kitchen, hands clasped together, with Sophie in hot pursuit.

Leila stopped in front of the women as Emma leaned back instinctively, lips pursed, eyes wide in trepidation. Leila held up her hands and, with a smile of delight, opened them to reveal a small brown furry animal sitting up in the palm of one hand, whiskers twitching and tiny chest heaving. But it was only for a second as Emma, having feared the worst, whimpered and recoiled, her sudden movement spurring the rodent into action. It leapt a foot in the air out of Leila's hand, and landed on the kitchen table, hopping and skipping down to the far end as fast as its little legs could carry it.

Emma's terror was complete. She screamed like a banshee and the twins joined in, running in circles around the table, squealing with excitement, and then crawling underneath it in pursuit of the mouse.

"Michael! Michael!" Emma shrieked at her husband who remained calm but unclear as to what he should do, as his wife hopped manically from one foot to the other. Without making a sound Leila dropped to the floor and joined the twins under the table, but within a second they all reappeared, charging out of the kitchen and continuing the chase down the hallway. "Oh ... Oh!" moaned Emma, still shaking and twitching, and it was Jess's turn to comfort her with a hand on the shoulder.

"They're harmless," she said, hands on hips. "Nothing to worry about."

"Michael! Go out there and check it's gone." Michael, dutiful as ever, did his wife's bidding. He was back in a moment.

"They've all gone upstairs. Quick, while the coast is clear." He winked at Jess as Emma tottered out of the kitchen on tiptoes, holding her skirt up above her knees. Jess went up to him and threw her arms round his neck.

"Thank you," she said quietly in his ear, "for everything."

"I'll call you tomorrow. Don't hesitate," he ordered, pointing at her as he shuffled backwards out to the hallway.

"I won't."

"Michael!" Jess heard Emma's summons from the other end of the hall and she smiled before she heard the main door shut with a loud thud, and for a moment the silence engulfed her. Then came the distant cries from upstairs, summoning, impatient, demanding.

"Mummy! Mummy! *Mummy!*" She shook her head and put her brain back into gear.

"Coming," she shouted and set off at a run.

CHAPTER 3

The mouse game continued for another half hour before Jess finally ushered the poor creature into a jam jar and deposited it outside, where it swiftly disappeared into the undergrowth.

She'd lost track of time and when she realised it was 5.30 p.m. she took the twins upstairs for a bath. As usual, they monopolised her attention, but she hugged, kissed and stroked Leila's hair continuously, if only to remind herself that she was real, and between embraces, Leila clung on tightly to Jess's skirt and it was a comfort to them both.

The twins cavorted and splashed around in the warm water with their floating toys and Leila helped in such a way that suggested she had done this before. But, curiously, she had said very little since her arrival, and although Jess spoke to her constantly, her daughter responded mainly with a smile and a nod or shake of the head. She'd said the odd word to the twins while they were playing, but Jess couldn't understand them and after a while, realised, with some sadness, that Leila probably understood and spoke Urdu better than English.

Bath time over, and with the twins in pyjamas, she sat them all down at the kitchen table and prepared a dinner of roast chicken and vegetables. Once their food had been chopped up for them, the twins were adept at using a spoon to feed themselves, but before she could do the same for Leila, she was greedily shovelling the food into her mouth with her right hand. *It's going to take time.*

***

There having been no warning of Leila's arrival, there had been no preparations nor any sleeping arrangements made. The twins slept in Jess's room, in their own beds, as they'd done since they were born, and as she couldn't allow Leila to be by herself, she decided that, at least for the time being, Leila would sleep with her in her bed. Jess thought it strange that in a house as big as Chalton Manor they should all share one room, but she would have it no other way.

Having put the twins to bed, she ran the bath again and, together in the bathroom, she tried to help Leila undress, the way she had always done before. But to her dismay, Leila resisted, and after a moment she left her alone, hovering outside the open door for fifteen minutes until she heard the water draining away. Jess went back in with a warm bath towel and as Leila stepped out of the bath, dropped to her knees and wrapped it around her, massaging her briskly. Leila giggled and squirmed, this time pleased at the attention.

"Turn round," she said playfully, and when there was no reaction she smiled and twirled a finger in the air, whereupon Leila made a brief sound of recognition and spun one hundred and eighty degrees. Jess rubbed the towel over her shoulders and down her back. She gasped in shock.

Long, pale horizontal marks spanned the gap between her shoulder blades, several extending down her back and onto her buttocks. Jess clamped a hand over her mouth to stifle a cry, spun Leila round again and clasped her daughter to her chest, one hand behind her head pulling it into her neck. Leila clung on without making a sound, and Jess tightened her hold as her tears fell onto the bath towel she still gripped in her free hand. Tears of horror, tears of rage, tears of guilt, but also tears of joy that her beloved Leila was finally back with her, safe in her arms.

She held her for a few moments while she gathered her composure, released her hold and forced a smile through her tears. She swept Leila's hair away from her eyes, rubbed her face and kissed her gently on the forehead.

"You're safe now," she whispered. She slipped one of her own tee shirts over Leila's head. "Come on," she said and led her into the bedroom by the hand.

The twins were oblivious to the world, exhausted by the exertions of the day, and they didn't stir as Jess pulled back the covers for Leila to climb into bed. Jess drew the duvet up to her chin, leaned over and kissed her again, before walking around to the other side. She lay on the top of the bed next to her, fully clothed.

For the first time in five years Jess watched her daughter slowly drift off to sleep. She lay awake, unable to take her eyes off her, occasionally dabbing at a stray tear provoked by the myriad thoughts, memories and emotions that threatened to overwhelm her, and there she stayed until the sun rose again.

***

Despite her best intentions, Jess dozed off from time to time, waking randomly with a start, fearing it had all been a dream but then realising it was all for real.

When she climbed off the bed at six thirty the next morning, all three girls were still asleep, so she kissed each one of them on the head and slipped quietly into the shower, leaving the bathroom door open so she could see any movement. But there was none.

She dressed in jeans and tee shirt and went downstairs into the kitchen to make herself some tea. She was tired but also excited and nervous as to what the day would bring, and she sat alone at the kitchen table cradling her mug in both hands in contemplation. Leila had arrived with little more than the clothes she was wearing and a small canvas bag that contained a couple of tee shirts and some underwear. A shopping expedition would be necessary.

After a few moments, she heard a shuffling noise behind her and turned to see Leila, yawning and stretching, arms folded behind her head. "Mummy?" the little girl said quietly, and Jess rushed to her and hugged her again in joy.

"Hello, darling, did you have a nice sleep?" Leila looked at her blankly for a moment before nodding. "Come on, let's go and get the little ones up," she said, and hand in hand they went back upstairs to wake the twins.

***

Michael rang later that morning from his office to check everything was okay. Having spent most of the night awake, Jess's mind had been running through all the questions she wanted to ask and she started firing them at him incoherently. He suggested they put a date in the diary to meet and promised to answer all her questions as best he could, as well as go through a few administrative matters. They agreed a date for the following week.

Emma called soon after. Jess explained that she would need to get Leila some new clothes and Emma insisted she drive over immediately and take them shopping in Oxford. Peter had driven them everywhere before, so Jess had never learnt to drive and didn't have a licence. She now knew this was something she'd have to attend to if she was not to rely on others in future. Clothes bought and lunch eaten, Emma dropped them all back at the Manor at 3.00 p.m.

The girls ran upstairs with a bundle of shopping bags, squealing and shouting, and Jess, exhausted but happy, slumped down on a kitchen chair with a cup of tea. Another day almost over. She wondered how she would cope, yet knowing somehow she would.

CHAPTER 4

Jess sat opposite Michael at the same table in the same meeting room in which Peter had, four years previously, revealed his intention to change his will in favour of "Alice". And in that very room, he had instructed Michael to start the process of tracking down Leila and bringing her home.

Jess felt nervous and fidgety for two reasons. Firstly, she had agreed to meet Michael in his office "so as not to be disturbed or distracted," he had said, which meant that, much against her instincts, she'd had to leave her precious daughters in Emma's care for a couple of hours. She had no doubts about Emma's good intentions, nor that her girls would be safe, but she did have concerns that Emma's nerves might be tested to their limits if the girls were their usual hyperactive selves. It was simply being parted from them that she found difficult to bear.

Secondly, she remained confused about her current position and apprehensive of the future. And although she had many questions about how and why Peter had done what he had, and how Leila had been found, she was not entirely sure she wanted to know the answers.

"We have a few things to get through," said Michael by way of introduction, and Jess nodded without quite knowing what he meant. Michael in his office, wearing a suit, speaking like a lawyer, seemed to her a far more forbidding animal than the man they all knew as "Uncle Mikey".

"Why did Peter do it?" blurted out Jess. She still felt unworthy of his kindness but also harboured some bitterness that he had never told her, and now he was gone, there was no chance of explaining.

"Do you mean clearing all the debt, changing the will or finding Leila?"

"All of it."

Michael sat back in his chair.

"Well, the debt part was relatively quick and easy. The notices had gone out and all your creditors were lined up at the County Court so it could be settled in one fell swoop. There was a complication with a couple of rather unpleasant characters who had bought a debt from who knows where; a legacy of Mo's drug dealing."

Jess was instantly transported back to Wellingford five years earlier.

"Oh God! I remember two evil guys who used to frighten me to death."

"Quite. Well, they were made an offer and persuaded to desist." Jess frowned, not fully understanding what he meant, but Michael was clearly not going to elaborate, as he moved on swiftly.

"As regards his will, I have to be honest with you, Jess, and say that when Peter came here to explain his plans, I tried to talk him out of it. Not, you'll understand, because I thought he was wrong; in fact, I think it was the noblest of gestures and I was full of admiration for him. I simply wanted him to be sure he was doing the right thing for the right reasons. You will have known that he wasn't a well man, and together with the heartbreak of losing Lisa, I feared he might not be thinking straight." He paused for a moment. "I also thought that he had become a little obsessed with you and the fear that you might leave him had clouded his judgement."

"It never crossed my mind to walk away once he'd told me about Lisa."

"But when he told me that he didn't want you to know about the will, I knew then that his motives were totally altruistic. You remained free to make your own future as you saw fit, without influence from him or any financial incentive, while he could make certain that, for as long as you remained with him, you and the twins would always be provided for. I assume that if you had decided to leave him, he'd have thought again, but we'll never know." She looked pensive as he continued. "I also have to say, Jess, that I hadn't known you very long when Peter came to see me, and when he told me you were pregnant too, I may have formed, shall we say, a less than charitable view of your character."

"You thought I was a gold-digger," she shot back.

"It was a possibility I couldn't ignore."

"I guess Emma thought so too."

"She had her doubts from the moment you met, but I hope you'll believe me when I say we've come to love you a great deal and, as we've already said, we'll always be there for you. For your sake and Peter's."

Jess chided herself for being riled at Michael's honesty and had to accept that from their point of view, her circumstances had been, at best, questionable.

"Thank you. I really am grateful to you both. I'm just still a little … wound up."

"The other thing is, of course, he had no one else left. He was profoundly affected by Janica's death and, try as he might, he couldn't seem to console Lisa. When she disappeared from his life too, he truly was a lost soul."

"He said he regretted never having told her that he loved her." Jess recalled the agony she felt when Peter had related his story in the garden.

"Peter blamed himself for driving Lisa away. It was entirely irrational but he'd talked himself into it and, grieving as he was, on two levels, he would not be persuaded otherwise. You have to remember, Peter wasn't a man to show his emotions, at least not in the affectionate sense. It seemed to him that his wife and daughter were such soul mates, he was quite content to take a back seat. They never wanted for anything. He provided for them. He would have died for them and he showed them as much love as anyone could; he was just never very good at saying it. Janica knew him. It was one of the things that attracted her most – his stoic Britishness, his matter-of-factness, his calm under fire. God knows he had needed that in the past." Jess nodded in understanding, but her sadness was evident.

"But Lisa had problems of her own. She was totally reliant on Janica, at least on an emotional level. Living at Chalton meant she didn't have any friends locally and had to travel a fair distance to school. Janica may have been her mum but she was also her best friend and there were only twenty years between them, so the bond was especially strong."

Jess wondered how strong the bond between her and Leila might become, and the sobering thought occurred to her that there were only seventeen years between them; she could be a grandmother at thirty-four at this rate.

"Lisa even called her mum by her Christian name. We always thought it was a bit weird and modern, but it reflected how close they were. It took fifteen months after diagnosis for Janica to succumb to the cancer, during which time Peter and Lisa had to watch her slowly fade away, and when she died, Lisa's whole world imploded. She virtually closed down, wanted to die herself, and the more Peter tried desperately to encourage her and shake her out of her despond, the worse he made it."

"Oh God," said Jess. "It must have been terrible for them both."

"Lisa had to get away from Chalton. From the constant reminders of life with Janica. She had to have a complete break, which is why she went travelling. She read something about Buddhism at university and decided Nepal was the place to be. A place of escape, both physically and mentally."

"Yes. Peter told me where she went, but not why."

"He would have agreed to anything by then. Anything that would help her, as they say, find herself. He thought Nepal was intrinsically peaceful and benign, and going with a friend from university somehow made it more acceptable. It started off fine and Peter was encouraged. He could sense the old Lisa coming out of her shell. Motivated and enthusiastic. Keen to explore and discover new places and meet new people, and in the early days they seemed to talk more on the phone than they ever did at home."

"And then they lost touch."

"Peter was sanguine about that. He didn't want to pester her, and the fact is, mobile phones don't work so well in remote parts of the Himalayas, so he was not surprised when the calls dried up. He didn't need to speak to her; he just needed to know she was safe. He was torn between the need to know and the desire to leave her be." Michael sighed. "Well. You know what happened next."

"Yes. The earthquake in Nepal didn't register with me at the time. It was so far away from reality as I knew it and I suppose I had other things on my mind, with Mo running away and taking Leila."

Michael nodded.

"Peter was beside himself. He made frantic attempts to find out where she was and whether she was okay. There was nothing he could find out from here. No news, good or bad. Nothing. He flew out there himself to look for her and …"

"He discovered that Lisa had died at Langtang."

Michael nodded.

"He was a beaten man. There was nothing left for him. Just memories, a misplaced guilt and a profound sense of self-loathing. He was finished. Ready to drop. Ready to be taken as soon as his good lord called, and the sooner the better, as far as he was concerned." He looked at her and smiled. "And then … you turned up."

She nodded in understanding.

"And then I turned up. Sodden, weak, feeble, pathetic … and pregnant. Although I didn't know that at the time."

"Did he ever show you a photograph of Lisa?" asked Michael carefully. Jess shifted in her chair. She still felt guilty she'd intruded on Peter's private grief when she'd inadvertently seen the picture and had never told him that she had. She hadn't meant to pry, but it would have taken a monumental exercise of self-will not to have turned over that picture frame when she stumbled over it, especially as at the time she herself was having doubts about Peter's intentions. And recalling those doubts – doubts about a man who'd put unlimited resources behind finding her daughter when his own was lost; a man who'd given her and her children everything, unconditionally, without her knowledge, without asking anything in return – she was suddenly overwhelmed with shame and sadness. But she told the truth, always.

"No, he never showed me." She looked up at Michael. "But I found a photograph of Lisa and Janica in a drawer full of sweaters." She shrugged. "I was just tidying, doing my job, and there it was."

"So you know …"

"That we could have been twins? Yes." She shook her head. She needed to explain and she felt herself becoming more animated. "This was before I knew she was dead. At the time, I almost freaked. I thought that maybe Lisa had run away. Run away from him for the wrong reasons. For the same reasons I ran away from my father. It was just too awful to contemplate. The parallels were there and unmistakeable. I was a substitute. A replacement Lisa. And I didn't know what he intended. Despite his kindness towards me, and the fact that, up until then, he'd never once touched me, other than to shake my hand when we first met, I was frightened. And confused. It took me a few days before I plucked up the courage to ask him, and when he told me all about her, I was mortified. Not just because of the pain he had clearly suffered but because I had doubted him. But, to my shame, I was also relieved."

"There's no shame in that," said Michael gently. "How could you possibly have known?"

"I don't think I trusted anyone back then," she said, the sorrow and regret evident in her voice. "Peter restored that faith. He trusted me when he had no reason to do so and every reason to do otherwise. It was an act of pure selflessness."

"That was the way he was, Jess."

"And now he's gone." She couldn't stop the tears forming again. Michael passed her a tissue from a box on the table and she wiped her eyes and nose. She took a sip of water from a crystal glass. "And Leila?" she sobbed. "Why did he spend the next three years and countless thousands searching for someone he'd never met, or even knew existed?"

"Oh, he knew she existed. You told him so. That was all he needed. I confess, the lawyer in me checked with Births. I'm sorry."

"No, no – don't be," she said quickly. Michael leaned forward to get closer to her.

"He had already lost his daughter, so he knew what it was like, even though the circumstances were very different. He even said to me that he thought your suffering had been worse than his and he made it his mission to put things right for you in the way he had been unable to do for himself or his family. And it gave him a goal. Something to live for. And despite his poor health, he far outlived the consultant's prognosis. He was never in any doubt that she could be tracked down and brought home, although none of us could have known how long it would take."

"But he never once said anything to me about it."

"He didn't want to give you false hope, despite his own optimism, especially when you had your hands full with the twins. It would have been a dreadful torment for you to experience the numerous false alarms, dashed hopes, constant wondering. He knew you had to focus on Sophie and Lucy, and if, in the end, he was wrong, then you'd be no worse off. But if he was right …"

"And he was."

"Yes, he was."

"And so … how did you find her?"

Michael sat back again and sighed.

"Well, I didn't actually do much other than coordinate matters and manage the expenses. I put some feelers out with contacts of mine in India, who in turn had contacts in Pakistan. But progress was slow and nothing happened for a very long time, so Peter suggested we use two of his men, Jackson and Rutherford. Ex-soldiers. SAS. They'd worked with Peter in Kosovo back in '98 and he said they were the best, although they'd since left the service and were, shall we say, freelancers. By the way, these were the same guys who, er, negotiated with your evil debt collectors."

Jess swallowed, remembering the blood-stained baseball bat, tried to imagine the encounter and what might have happened but then shuddered at the thought.

"But they had their own contacts, especially in Asia; they'd served in Afghanistan, had the odd skirmish with the Taliban on and around the border with Pakistan and basically knew their way around." Jess was listening intently, and one of the questions that had always plagued her came to the fore.

"I never understood why he took her. Mo. He was never that close to her, and although I knew he and his mates had abused other girls, he never hurt Leila because she never left my sight. I never believed he would do that to her anyway, but there was no logic in taking her back to Pakistan when he could have found thousands of vulnerable girls already out there. And he'd have had to buy her a ticket when I know he had no money. He'd have had barely enough to buy his own. Was it too simple to believe he just loved her?" Jess didn't know that Peter had wondered much the same, but his conclusion had been less charitable. "So why take her to Pakistan?" Michael took a breath before he replied.

"He didn't."

The words hit her like a bombshell and her jaw dropped, but she was unable to utter more than a single word.

"What?"

"He didn't take her to Pakistan with him."

"Then …?"

"He sold her. Here in the UK."

"Oh my God!" she clasped a hand over her mouth in astonishment and then, still searching for explanations, said "but ... how can that happen ... here?"

"I'm afraid people trafficking is not confined to bringing the vulnerable in from poor parts of the world. It works in all directions." But she was still confused.

"But ... Leila came back wearing traditional dress and speaking Urdu. She can barely understand English."

"Oh yes, she was in Lahore when we eventually found her."

"Now I really don't understand," she said in exasperation, sitting back and putting her hand to a forehead that was beginning to throb. Michael noticed.

"Would you like some paracetamol?"

"No ... no. I'm fine, thanks. I just don't get it."

"Let me explain."

***

Mohammed Khalid stood outside the huge wrought-iron gates, staring through the bars at the daunting Georgian mansion standing proud and floodlit at the end of a short, curving drive. He felt a tug on his left hand and looked down at his four-year-old daughter who was looking back up at him, kicking her feet on the ground in boredom.

"What?" he said gruffly.

"Where's Mummy?" said the little girl for the fourth time in the past half hour.

"She's in that big house," said Mo, hoping that would finally shut her up. He was nervous and apprehensive and the last thing he wanted was any more aggro from the kid. She'd moaned and whinged at him from the moment he'd picked her up from pre-school, bundled her into his car and driven to London. *Where's Mummy? Where's Mummy?* She had kept on at him until he'd lost it and shouted at her and she'd started crying. Then, mercifully, she'd stopped, only the occasional whimper indicating she was there at all, strapped into the child seat in the back of the Passat.

He'd parked in a resident's bay in a street around the corner, but it was after seven and he'd only be ten minutes or so, he judged, so he'd risk being clamped. And if he had to abandon the car here and use the train for the last leg then so be it. Here or Heathrow, it hardly mattered.

The gates remained steadfastly shut and he noticed two cameras pointing down at him from the top of the stone pillars either side of the gate. *They must have seen us, we're on time. What are they waiting for?*

He spotted a panel of buttons on the right pillar and decided he'd have to press one of them. He examined it closely. A numerical keypad, a small flat panel with a Wi-Fi logo on it and a slot illuminated by a dim blue flashing light and what looked like a small speaker. But then he saw what he was looking for: a large chrome button at the bottom, bearing the words "Call for Assistance".

Mouth dry, heart beating a little faster and still gripping Leila's hand tightly, he looked around, instinctively checking there was no one watching him, and reached out tentatively for the button. Before his finger got there, the gates snapped open with a loud crack.

"Aah!" He jumped back in shock, but he noticed one of the gates beginning to swing inwards, followed by the other, and he breathed a sigh of relief. He jumped again at the sound of a disembodied, strangulated voice emanating from the speaker.

"Approach the house slowly. Stay on the drive." And then there was another click. Mo led his daughter slowly up the driveway, step by step, looking left and right, expecting at any moment someone would leap out of the darkness and attack him.

It was only a hundred feet or so to the house and Mo took note of the cars parked at an angle on either side – on the right, a black Range Rover, on the left, a white Porsche Carrera, and next to it, also black, a Mercedes S Class. His, hers and theirs, he thought. As he got nearer, the drive split and swung around the house to the right and down a slope, disappearing from view. Underground garage, he guessed, with no doubt more luxury hardware inside.

He dragged Leila along, her little legs taking four paces for every one of his, and reached the bottom of a flight of eight stone steps that led up to a huge oak-panelled double door beneath a large portico, the area bathed in a bright yellow glow.

As they climbed the steps, two men in dark suits stepped into view from either side of the door. They were smartly dressed with white shirts, black ties and shiny shoes, and their hands were crossed in front of them, as if they were waiting patiently for something or someone.

Mo looked at each of them anxiously, curious that, given the darkness, they both wore sunglasses. Ray-Ban Aviators with gold frames. He stopped when he got to the top step and the man on his right spoke.

"Take off your jacket."

Mo hesitated for only a second, until the man stepped towards him and he quickly released Leila's hand. He shrugged off his bomber jacket as Leila looked up at the second man who was standing still, watching, her little neck straining backwards to take in his height. "Hold out your arms," said man number one, demonstrating the pose the visitor was required to adopt. Mo copied the move, his jacket dangling from his right hand.

The man stepped forward and frisked Mo roughly; neck, shoulders, around his back and chest, up and down his legs, inside and out, and lifted his trousers above the ankle feeling over his socks and shoes, the whole procedure watched intently by the man on his left. He checked Mo's jacket pockets and, satisfied, turned to Leila and dropped to his haunches in front of her. She burst into tears.

"Quiet, Leila!" hissed Mo and she stopped momentarily. The man spun her around one hundred and eighty degrees and ran his hand down the back of her coat, before turning her back round, whereupon her face creased up and she started to wail again.

"Okay," said the first man and Mo grabbed the hand of his still weeping child and gave it a tug.

"Shh!"

The second man spoke into his lapel and instantly one half of the oak door swung inwards. He gestured towards the open doorway with a nod of the head and Mo dragged Leila through into a large entrance hall, brilliantly lit by an enormous sparkling chandelier.

The floor was chequerboard marble, and two matching staircases curved up each side of the wall ahead of him to meet on a galleried landing on the first floor. The walls were adorned with giant oil paintings, the ceiling featured ornate plaster coving and, above the chandelier, a huge plaster rose.

Between the staircases, a sculpted archway revealed a wide corridor extending into the distance and, at the far end, a floor-to-ceiling stained glass window. The door thudded closed behind him, the sound echoing around the entrance hall. Mo turned to see man number one had stepped in behind him and had resumed his stance, legs apart, his hands crossed in front.

"Mr Khalid," said a voice from nowhere, and Mo turned to see a tall, impeccably dressed Asian in his late fifties strolling into the entrance hall from a room to his left.

"Yes," said Mo, swallowing deeply and trying not to show his fear. The Asian stepped forward and looked down at Leila with some disdain, but before he could say anything more, they were both distracted by the sound of heels click-clacking on the marble floor. A woman was hurrying towards them from the corridor ahead. Forty-something, big hair, big earrings, dressed in black silk trousers over high heels and a cream silk blouse with cashmere scarf, her neck and hands dripping expensive jewellery, the pungent scent of her perfume arriving long before she did.

"Let me see! Let me see!" she said excitedly as she trotted up to where Leila stood, completely ignoring Mo and dropping down to her haunches in front of her. "Oh, sweetheart!" Mo thought she sounded American. "Aren't you just the most beautiful girl in the world?" she gushed at the little girl, whose eyes widened and nose twitched at the sight and smell of the woman squatting in front of her. The woman took Leila's hand in hers and tried to stroke her face with the other, but Leila turned her head away. "Aw sweetie, come on now. Say hello to Mama." Leila said nothing and the woman's smile dropped.

"Mahmoud!" she snapped. The Asian let out a deep sigh.

"That will be all, Khalid. You may go." And before Mo could respond, the woman had taken Leila's hand out of his and dragged her off down the corridor, heels echoing as she went. Leila turned her head around as she trotted along behind, propelled at speed by the woman gripping her hand.

"Daddy?" she called out, and for a second Mo felt a surge of remorse until the woman and his daughter disappeared into a room to the right and he quickly remembered his business was not yet complete. But he suddenly noticed with alarm that the Asian man had turned and was disappearing back into the room from whence he had come. Mo was about to take a step forward and call out when he was stopped dead by a large yellow padded envelope slapping into his chest.

Mo looked down stupidly at the envelope and then to his right at the man in Ray-Bans who was holding it. He took the envelope and slowly looked inside. He scanned the contents, eyes darting around a dozen neat bundles of notes. He had planned his negotiating strategy well in advance, deciding he would take his time and ensure every penny was there before he released Leila to anyone, keep them waiting until he was satisfied; run the show, so to speak. But it hadn't gone according to plan. He knew when he was totally out of his depth, and it was now.

He did some quick mental arithmetic; twenties, looked like fifty in a bundle, a dozen bundles, twelve grand! He only asked for ten! But then he noticed something else and began to protest.

"These are dollars! I said ten grand Sterling."

"So? You've got twelve grand US. Same thing."

"No it's not!"

But the man stepped forward and Mo flinched, sweat forming on his temples.

"I suggest you leave," said the man in the Ray-Bans. "Now." The threat was clear and the menace which accompanied it, unmistakeable. Mo turned and, gripping the envelope tightly, stomped out of the open door past the second man, down the steps to the driveway, fumbling to put his jacket on as he disappeared into the night and beyond.

***

"Mo was in a lot of trouble, as you well know. He was being hounded by some very nasty people for money he owed both through gambling losses and a drugs deal that went badly wrong. The stuff he was peddling was, shall we say, substandard. We learnt that from your friendly debt collectors. He had to get away and so he sought refuge in Karachi where his parents still had family. He'd been planning his escape for a while but needed the money for his fare, so he sold Leila to a rich couple in North London who wanted a mixed-race girl." Jess was totally absorbed trying to keep up; her mind was racing but she didn't want to interrupt his flow.

"He was a Pakistani businessman with political connections in Islamabad, and his wife, a Canadian socialite from a publishing dynasty. He already had three teenage sons from a previous marriage, but she wanted a daughter and, well, she was told she couldn't have kids. He wasn't interested in having a daughter but he wanted to shut his wife up, so he bought her one." The questions were amassing in her head and she couldn't stop them spilling out.

"But why couldn't they just adopt?"

"Because they'd have had to wait and jump through all sorts of hoops, and people like that don't like to wait when the problem can be solved instantly with a sum of money that means nothing to them."

"How do you know all this?"

"Mo told us."

"When?"

"After we tracked him down in Karachi."

"Why would you believe him?"

"Well at the time, we didn't, but then Jackson was quite confident that Mo had every incentive to tell the truth, and subsequently, it turned out he was right."

"Jackson?"

"The, er, SAS man."

"What incentive?"

"Let's not go there, Jess."

"Oh God." She wondered what they might have done to Mo but then to her dismay realised she didn't much care. A window had been opened onto a world she knew nothing about, and it frightened her. Michael went on.

"So, we'd spent two years tracking down Mo in Pakistan, and when we did find him he kept us on the hook for several weeks pretending he still had her in order to extract more money, when the reality was Leila had been in St John's Wood all the time."

"But how did someone like Mo come across this couple in the first place?"

"Through his driving contacts. One of their many staff was a driver and he was a friend of a friend. Mahmoud Kayani – that's the husband – had an entourage of security men and this driver chap used to ferry them all around in a bulletproof Range Rover. It's a dodgy business being a rich, expat Asian with aspirations of a political comeback, especially when the government back home doesn't want you." Jess struggled to imagine such a situation. It was an alien world to her. "The driver overheard the wife nagging her husband about having a child, so he knew what they wanted, saw an opportunity and set it all up." Jess was calculating the timeline in her head and frowned.

"You mean that, from the time I left home, all the way through to after the twins were born, Leila was living fifty miles away in London with these rich folk?"

"Yes. And long after that, too." She rubbed her forehead and moaned. All that stuff with the police and the Home Office and the Pakistan Embassy, all a waste of time. She remembered sitting on the train to London, distraught, broken, staring aimlessly out of the carriage window, believing Leila to be thousands of miles away when, in reality, she could have been playing in a garden not a hundred yards from where she sat. The thought of it tormented her. And then she returned to the same question that had puzzled her earlier.

"But you still haven't told me how she got to Lahore."

"We turned our attention to the Kayanis, and we watched them in London for six months but never got sight of Leila. We guessed they just kept her indoors; a trophy child for the wife. But from time to time we also considered the whole thing might be a wild goose chase. Until we had a breakthrough. Rutherford managed to make contact with the driver and he pretty much confirmed Leila was there. But before we could do anything, they packed up and returned to Islamabad, leaving their sons at school in England. Mahmoud Kayani had a political bandwagon rolling and he obviously decided the time was right to make his play."

"And they took Leila with them?"

"Well, the problem was we never managed to see any evidence of her in London, so we had to assume that, if they did have her, she'd have gone with them, so we had to regroup and start again in Pakistan."

Jess thought back to that time, when she had her hands full with Sophie and Lucy, looking after Peter and Peter's house, living a relatively peaceful existence at Chalton, and all the while, this intense and dangerous operation spanning continents was underway, instigated and funded by Peter, managed by Michael, all on her behalf, and she, completely oblivious to it. Michael was talking again and she listened.

"The good thing was they weren't difficult to find. He was high profile, always in the news, making speeches and organising demonstrations and rallies and being interviewed on TV, but always surrounded by big guys in dark glasses and sharp suits, and this made him virtually inaccessible.

"But money always talks in that part of the world, and through a local contact, Jackson got in with one of the staff at the Kayanis' mansion on the banks of Rawal Lake in Rawalpindi, which is close to the capital. He confirmed they had a daughter but her name wasn't Leila, it was Hilja." Jess looked puzzled "It means quiet, calm," explained Michael. "But he said the weird thing was the girl wasn't quiet or calm at all. She apparently threw tantrums and had screaming fits and smashed expensive ornaments, and neither the mother nor her staff could control her." Leila was fighting back against her captors, thought Jess proudly, but then decided she was probably fantasising. Michael paused.

"Go on," urged Jess. Michael took a breath.

"He said Kayani sahib did not tolerate disobedience in his household, especially from a girl, regardless of age, and beat her with his belt until she was quiet; like her name." The words slammed into Jess and she gasped.

"Michael! She has scars on her back! Leila has scars all over her. Oh, Michael. This man beat my baby?" Michael's face filled with sorrow and he nodded.

"I guess so. I'm sorry." Jess wrapped her arms around her chest and swayed back and forth in her chair, unable to shake off the image of a little girl being sold to these ghastly people and then being tortured by this monster. *Her little girl. What would she have been thinking? Where's Mummy?*

Why has Mummy left me? Would she have been crying for her? The thoughts were unthinkable. But it might explain how reserved Leila was, even with her, and why she said so little. She wiped her hand across face, her eyes red and moist.

"Do you want to take a break?" said Michael, apparently concerned that all this was getting too much for her. "I can organise a sandwich."

Jess lifted her chin defiantly. "No, I'm not hungry," she said and then smiled at him, grateful for the consideration. "Thank you."

Michael put down his fountain pen and put both arms on the desk in front of him.

"Jess, I know this is painful for you, hearing all this stuff, but you've got to remember, there is a happy ending to the story. I urge you to concentrate on the present. You and Leila are back together again, and that wouldn't have happened if you hadn't done what you did."

"You mean, run away and abandon her?"

"You didn't abandon her. You were as much a victim in all this as she was. There was nothing you could have done and I know it's hard to comprehend, but ultimately, it was all for the best."

He was right, thought Jess. It was very hard to comprehend. A bizarre sequence of events, some planned, some serendipitous, all unforeseen. Actions and reactions by people totally unknown and unrelated to each other. And although evil was the instigator of the nightmare, good came out of it all in the end, because despite all the evil in the world, there was much more that was good. Jess gathered her thoughts and spoke rationally.

"So, she's in a luxurious prison in Rawalpindi, a plaything of the rich and famous, a pet puppy subjected to the occasional whipping. What happens next?"

"Jackson and Rutherford take it in turns to watch the Kayanis for any sign of Leila, but it's very unproductive and time-consuming. They can't get near the house because it's in extensive grounds protected by high-level security and patrolled by armed guards and dogs. They try and follow them wherever they go, but he travels in a convoy of black Range Rovers with guys armed to the teeth, so they have to be careful they're not spotted, because that's exactly what the bodyguards are trained to do, albeit for different reasons.

"Mrs Kayani goes out from time to time but never with any children in tow and always with her own guards and a couple of women. Ladies in waiting, I suppose. Eventually Jackson rents a top-floor apartment on the other side of the lake and, using a telescope, he and Rutherford take turns watching the back of the house. It's six weeks before they spot her."

Jess sat up, straining her imagination to picture the scene, like something from an espionage movie.

"She's playing on a swing in the back garden, surrounded by razor wire; not, you understand, to keep her in, but to keep others out."

"But how could they be sure it was Leila?"

"From the crumpled photograph you once showed Peter. He scanned and emailed it to me without your knowledge." Jess was past being surprised at anything they did.

"They thought they might try and snatch her from the lakeside but knew that would only be possible at night, and she would never have been let out there after dark. But one night, Jackson's watching TV in the apartment and there's an item about Kayani on the campaign trail in Lahore. He's flown there in his private helicopter and his wife has gone too to support him and she's there, on the tarmac behind him, holding hands with a little girl."

"Leila!"

"He's putting out the family-man image and, for once, Leila's useful to him. Jackson calls Rutherford and tells him to get down to Lahore and see what he can do, so Rutherford races two hundred miles down to Lahore in a beat-up old Honda, figuring this may be their best chance. Jackson tells him they're staying in the Luxus Grand, so he checks himself in.

"Well, Kayani sahib is hosting a grand reception for all his cronies and acolytes, and Mrs Kayani is there too." She thought Michael looked like he was beginning to enjoy this. Maybe the worst was over and the good news was about to break.

"All his goons are down there watching the private function room apart from one left outside their suite. Rutherford gets the chap to, er, step aside" – Jess closed her eyes, trying not to think about what may have happened – "and he talks himself into the room in his best Urdu. The only one in there is one of Mrs Kayani's female servants. He gets her to hand over her phone and locks her in the toilet. He finds Leila in one of the bedrooms."

Jess is biting her fingernails, there, in the hotel room, seeing her daughter, willing nothing to go wrong, even though she knows by now that everything goes right.

"Leila neither screams nor resists Rutherford, so he picks her up, calmly carries her down the stairs and out of a side entrance into a taxi." Jess breathes a sigh of relief and knows it's irrational, but she feels calm. For a moment.

"Then all hell breaks loose. The chap guarding the suite raises the alarm and somehow the entire Pakistani state security apparatus is mobilised. Within a couple of hours, train stations, border crossings and airports are teeming with soldiers and police, and roadblocks are set up on all main roads out of town. Kayani doesn't know what's going on but accuses his opponents of kidnapping. He probably sees it as an opportunity to make some political capital, and as he never wanted Leila anyway, he's not bothered if he gets her back or not.

"Meanwhile Rutherford's already crossed the Indian border, mingling with all the crowds at Wagah – that's where India and Pakistan hold that flamboyant ceremony – and they've got another taxi and driven thirty miles to Amritsar, where he has a safe house." Jess was now dizzy with place names, numbers and the whirlwind of events and just wished it all would end.

"But it's all over the regional news and has spread into India, where the government there is supporting Kayani in his bid to be prime minister of their biggest enemy, so now the Indians are looking for her too. So he lays low in Amritsar for a few days with his Sikh girlfriend, Juneeta—"

"He has a girlfriend in India?" asked Jess in astonishment.

"And I think in one or two other places around the world," added Michael. Jess was beginning to wonder at this ex-SAS soldier, mercenary, womanising, globe-trotting renegade. Was there no end to his talents? And why would he be motivated to risk his life rescuing an eight-year-old child for her bankrupt mother? But she knew, of course: money. Peter's money.

"He called me from there and told me Leila was fine but that it was going to be tricky getting her out of India because of the publicity."

"But she's my daughter!" shouted Jess. "Why couldn't you just announce that she'd been found and was being returned to her mother?" It seemed so simple. "It could easily be proved."

Michael sighed.

"Jess, if we'd done that, we'd have got nowhere. We'd have got bogged down in international politics. You may have been relieved to know she was alive and where she was, but you'd never get to see her, and the likelihood is the Kayanis would be able to concoct whatever 'proof' they needed she was theirs. The only real way is DNA testing. Do you really think we'd be able to demand DNA samples from Leila to prove parentage, especially when one of the real parents is unwilling to come forward?"

Michael was right, of course. It would have been futile and unbearably painful to try. Failure was virtually guaranteed.

"No, we made the decision to" – he hesitated, trying to choose his words carefully but electing to use the only ones that were true – "kidnap her back. It was the only way." Jess nodded and Michael went on.

"Anyway, thousands of pilgrims were returning home from some festival at Amritsar so Rutherford used it as a cover to get them on a bus going to Dharamshala which is a town in the foothills of the Himalayas. The bus went the long way round, dropping off people from many towns and villages along the way, and it took them two days to get there. But he knew he'd never be able to fly her out of India because India has very tight security, and he decided Nepal was by far the better option.

"The Nepalese are, for a fee, far more relaxed about who comes in and out. They wouldn't have covered a news story emanating from Pakistan and are not that pally with India either. Added to which Rutherford had spent several years in Nepal with the Gurkhas and had many contacts there, so he knew that if he could get her to Kathmandu, he could get her out."

Jess had no conception of the difficulty travelling in these remote places, the distances involved or the time it may have taken. She remained utterly bewildered by the whole saga but knew that as well as Peter and Michael, she owed a huge debt of gratitude to Jackson and Rutherford, regardless of how well they'd been paid. But she couldn't imagine how Leila might have felt being dragged along by a strange man in a strange place, living from day to day, constantly moving, constantly hiding.

"And did you get regular updates about where they were, and how they were?"

"Yes, every few days or so, but we lost contact once they crossed into Nepal and were in the Himalayas. But I had met Rutherford so I was quite confident they'd be okay. He eventually called me when they got to Pokhara and I called Peter and told him." Michael suddenly stopped.

Jess sensed something was wrong. She thought back. There had been no change in Peter at that time. No change in his attitude or his demeanour, no lightening of his mood and certainly no announcement. She would have thought that in the face of such remarkable news, he'd have been moved to say something to her.

"When did you tell him?" she asked tentatively. Michael was silent for a moment, trying not to meet her eyes.

"It was the day he died."

"Oh no!" she gasped and then whispered, almost to herself, "in the garden." She shook her head, remembering the moment with utmost clarity, skipping over the lawn with the twins to fetch Grandad. Seeing him from a distance, inert, knowing something wasn't right. Telling the twins to stay where they were and hold hands. Knowing he'd gone. Not knowing that Michael's call had been the trigger. "I killed him," she whispered, her anguish raw and absolute.

"No, Jess, you kept him alive." She looked up at him, tears in her eyes again. "Peter had been on borrowed time for years. It was the search for Leila and your love and care that kept him going for as long as he did. Once he found out we'd got her back, he could finally let go and be reunited with Lisa. He had done for you what he had never been able to do for himself: get your daughter back. He did it, and his work was done." Jess slumped forward onto the desk and buried her head in her arms, her shoulders heaving as she wept. Michael got up and walked around, crouching down to put an arm around her.

"I told you. It was all he ever wanted."

"Oh God," she wailed, "I can't bear it."

"Yes you can, Jess. You're as strong as they come." They remained quiet for a moment or two in contemplation until she eventually composed herself and he went back to his seat.

"And then she was home," she murmured.

"Yes, it took a few days to forge a passport for her, and she and Rutherford flew back to London last week."

She suddenly had an urge to see this man, Rutherford, and Jackson for that matter. They seemed to have moved heaven and earth, put themselves in danger, worked tirelessly and patiently on the task of rescuing her daughter from an impossible situation, for someone they had never met. It had to be more than money. Whatever they were, they had to be good people, or they'd have given up long ago, money or no money. And if Peter had known them and asked them, then they must be good people. She knew that. She felt beholden, especially to Rutherford.

"What happened to him? When can I see him? To thank him?"

"I'm afraid I don't know. He didn't hang around at Heathrow. Said he was off to Malta to see someone."

"Another girlfriend?" she asked smiling, while wiping her face for the umpteenth time that day.

"Probably," laughed Michael. But Jess was still processing the facts and a thought hit her.

"Michael. What about the Kayanis?"

"What about them?"

"Well. What if they decide to try and get Leila back? What if they use their power and their money to find her and demand we give her back?"

"They won't."

"But how can you be so sure?"

"A couple of weeks after Rutherford got Leila out, Kayani was at a rally in Islamabad, riding an open-topped truck with his guards, waving to the crowd. Someone lobbed a grenade and he was killed." She was now so numb with each revelation she could barely respond.

"Oh, my. But what about the wife? She was the one who wanted Leila in the first place. Won't she come looking?"

"No. She's gone back to Canada. She's marrying a newspaper tycoon. She'll have lost interest."

"How? Why?"

"Well, during the trip across the Himalayas, when Leila was with Rutherford, she told him a few things. He speaks

Urdu, remember? She said that she spent most of her time with the servants, helping them look after their own children. Mrs Kayani didn't pay her any attention after a while."

"A puppy for Christmas," said Jess absently.

"Quite." Michael looked at his watch. "Come on. I'll buy you some lunch."

"Thanks, Michael, but I'd like to get back and see the girls if that's okay."

"Yes, of course. We do have a few other things to talk about, but they can wait for now. I'll get Sandy to run you home." He stood up and walked around the desk and held out his hands. She took them in hers and stood in front of him.

"Michael. I owe you so much."

"No, Jess. I was just the middleman. Peter did it all."

"And what about Jackson and Rutherford?"

"Oh, they're probably keeping busy somewhere. Just a job to them. I'll call you and we can reconvene in a couple of days." She nodded and then threw her arms round his neck.

"Thank you."

***

When she'd gone, Michael walked over to the window and stood looking out onto the market square. He remembered Peter standing in the same spot, issuing instructions to change his will in favour of this strange girl who called herself Alice and bore a striking resemblance to Lisa, insisting he spare no expense in finding Alice's daughter and stubbornly refusing to be talked out of any of it. He had insisted Leila was still alive, and although he could not possibly have known for certain, he was right. Right about it all, apart from one thing. One key detail. How things would have turned out differently had he known.

He was relieved that Jess had asked to adjourn their discussion. It had let him off the hook, for a while at least. They had lots of administrative stuff to deal with – briefing her on her assets, her change of name, Leila's identity, her marriage to Mo – and all that could be dealt with fairly easily.

But one outstanding matter still caused him great difficulty and he wrestled with his conscience. He was faced with a dilemma and he'd still not worked out what to do about it. It was whether Jess needed to know. Either way, there was a risk, and he had to assess the risk before he said anything else. Not even Emma knew. Only him. It was a burden that weighed heavily, and he suddenly felt his age.

CHAPTER 5

Jess waved at the small car receding down the driveway and let herself into the house. Her house. Chalton Manor. She still couldn't quite come to terms with it. In her mind it would always be Peter's house and it seemed ridiculous for her to live here alone with three young children. They'd be much better off in something more modest. She would talk to Michael about it, but there was no rush; there were other priorities. She stepped into the hallway and was met by Emma who came striding out of the kitchen, looking flustered.

"Jess. Thank goodness you're back! I'm at my wits end!"

"Why. What's happened?" said Jess in alarm, regretting she had left them alone.

"Oh. Nothing's happened," said Emma and Jess relaxed. "I'm just worn out. How on earth do you manage it? I mean where do you get the energy from? They've had me playing all sorts of silly games. The kitchen and drawing room are strewn with debris, toys everywhere. Goodness me, I need a stiff drink!" They were interrupted by a familiar squealing as the twins, followed by Leila, met them in the hallway.

"Mummy! Mummy!" shrieked Sophie and Lucy in unison as they jumped up and down, tugging Jess's skirt. Jess put a hand on each head and rubbed their hair.

"Have you been good for Auntie Emma?" she asked and they nodded excitedly as Leila strolled in behind them. "Hello, darling. I've missed you. I've missed you all," she said, giving them each a hug in turn. Leila remained quiet but smiled and held out her hand. Jess took it and Leila led her into the kitchen, followed by Emma and the twins.

The kitchen table was covered in newspaper and littered with green stalks, leaves and petals, and on it stood a small vase filled with flowers from the garden.

"We've been flower arranging," said Emma with some satisfaction. "I am afraid we raided some of Peter's …" She paused for moment to reflect. "I mean, your flower beds. I'm sorry, I keep forgetting."

"It's okay," said Jess with a sad smile. She kept forgetting too.

"Leila seems to have some expertise in this field. She did that mostly herself."

"That's beautiful, sweetheart."

"Flowers … for … you … Mummy." Leila said it slowly and deliberately. Jess put a hand on her head, pulled her closer and hugged her again.

"Well, I must be off," announced Emma with a flourish.

"Thank you so much for looking after them."

"Anytime," said Emma, and Jess gave her a knowing smile. Emma glided out of the kitchen and let herself out.

"Come on! Let's tidy up and have some lunch."

By 7 p.m. the twins were fast asleep in bed. Leila had quickly assumed primary responsibility for bath times and although Jess never left them unattended, she allowed Leila to take control and do most of it herself. To her great relief, Sophie and Lucy seemed totally at ease with their new sister and Leila in return was undemanding and, as far as Jess could tell, assimilating well to her new environment. One day, there would be stories to tell.

The grandfather clock in the hallway struck 8.00 p.m. as Jess and Leila snuggled up on the drawing room sofa, reading a picture book.

"Okay, young lady. I think it's your bedtime." She closed the book and kissed her daughter's head. "We're going to have to get you sorted out at school soon. Would you like that?" Leila nodded. Jess was acutely aware that Leila's

English was still rudimentary. No doubt the Kayani woman had spoken English to her in the early days, but if she had been left in the company of disinterested servants and other kids, then Urdu would have been their main language. She hoped that, like most young children, Leila would quickly adapt, that her current reticence in speaking simply reflected unfamiliarity with the words and was not symptomatic of any underlying disorder or latent trauma. It would take time, but they had lots of that.

She took Leila upstairs and together they checked on the twins. She let Leila run a bath and get ready for bed by herself and then lay on the bed next to her, as usual, until she was sure she was asleep. She checked the baby alarm and went back downstairs.

She sat in the kitchen with a cup of tea, the house virtually silent but for the hum of the central heating boiler and the occasional rustle of the trees outside the kitchen window. The house was cavernous, its size now strangely oppressive, and without the towering presence of Peter, she couldn't help but feel vulnerable again.

Michael and Emma had insisted they would help in any way they could, and she believed them and was grateful. But she was also realistic enough to know that, over time, contact would dwindle, and she had to learn to look after her family by herself. Michael and Emma had their own lives to lead, and although Emma had clearly expressed sadness that they'd never had a family, she'd moved on many years ago. It seemed unlikely to Jess that she'd want to engage with someone else's on a regular basis. Jess smiled to herself recalling Emma's relief at her return that afternoon. The last thing Emma wanted was to be first on call for childcare, whatever she may have said.

She thought again about her conversation with Michael and Leila's incredible journey from the moment she'd been taken from pre-school in Wellingford, shipped halfway around the world and back again. Five years had passed. She felt a wave of anger rising inside her and tried to suppress it.

She'd never forgotten Leila in the years she'd been gone, but had never imagined she would ever see her again.

She wondered what had happened to Mo, how she could have been so stupid to fall under his spell and how she failed to foresee the disaster that would unfold. She put it out of her mind. She had to live in the present. She would talk to Michael about selling Chalton and finding somewhere smaller and more manageable. She yawned and rested her forehead on her arms, and soon, she drifted off.

***

She's in her tent, on the mattress, on the ground, listening to the dogs barking in the night and the rustle of the trees and she's cold and hungry and tearful and wondering when this will ever end and then it's raining and the tent has a leak and it's dripping on her sleeping bag so she tries to move over to avoid it but the water is rising and she has to get out and she wrestles herself out of the sleeping bag and fumbles with the circular zip of the tent flap and when it releases she looks outside but she's floating on water, bobbing up and down and moving faster and faster and there's a rush of water into the tent and the sound of it is getting louder and louder and it's the sound of the weir and she tries to get out and then she can hear screaming, "Mummy, Mummy!" and it keeps coming, "Mummy, Mummy!" and she's flailing around in the water trying to stay afloat and there's a thunderclap and a flash and she feels herself sinking and someone's still screaming. "Mummy, Mummy!"

***

"Mummy, Mummy!" The screaming of the baby alarm woke her. She pushed back violently on her chair, knocking it to the floor, and raced out of the kitchen, down the hall and bounded up the spiral staircase, two at a time. She swung around the banister on the first floor and dashed down the corridor, the screams getting louder and the thunderous crashes more frequent.

She burst into the bedroom, almost tripping over one of the bedside tables which lay upended on the floor, the table lamp alongside it, extinguished. She flicked the main light switch and saw the twins standing up on their beds, jumping up and down as if on trampolines, screaming and crying in panic. She saw books lying all over the floor along with ornaments from the mantelpiece, and as she noticed Leila was missing from the bed, sounds of crashing came from the bathroom. She leapt over the debris and into the en suite. She pulled the light cord.

Leila was standing in the bath, bottle of shampoo in hand, ready to throw it onto the floor where several other bottles, soap bars, toothpaste and make-up containers lay strewn, covered in a thick layer of talc.

"Leila!" she cried, dodging a flying shampoo bottle which hit the wall mirror with a loud crack and fell into the washbasin below. She raced forward and plucked her demented daughter out of the bath. Her face and hair were covered in a cocktail of talcum powder and shampoo, her eyes streaming with tears that left vertical streaks down each cheek and her hands and arms flailed at Jess's back as if trying to beat her off. "Leila! Leila! Ssh! It's okay. It's okay. I'm here. Mummy's here!" she hugged her and swayed from side to side and after a second or two, Leila's struggling subsided and she went limp in her arms.

Jess carried her back into the bedroom where the twins were still crying although now sitting down on their beds, rubbing their eyes. She laid Leila down on her bed and brushed her sticky, powdery hair back off her face, then rushed over to the little ones and hugged them both together.

"Sophie, Lucy, it's okay, Leila's just had a bad dream. She's okay now. Come on, lie down and go to sleep," she said gently, but she knew it would take time for the twins to settle down again. She looked around. The room looked a mess, especially in the bright light, so she switched on the other bedside lamp and turned off the main light. She restored the upturned bedside table and lamp to their rightful positions and then returned to attend to the twins whose tears had now subsided to a snuffling murmur. She laid them down and covered them with a blanket, and they remained quiet as she climbed back onto the bed next to Leila.

Her daughter was lying still, on her side, eyes wide open, breathing deeply through her mouth, her cheeks still streaked with shampoo, talc and make-up. Jess went back into the en suite, found a flannel and ran it under the warm tap, being careful not to contaminate it with the glass fragments in the basin. She sat on the bed and dabbed her daughter's face gently to remove the mess, talking to her, consoling her, and when she had done the best she could, snuggled up next to her and held her closely. Within a minute or two, Leila's breathing settled down and she drifted off to sleep.

Jess lay there with her, with all her children, heart still beating irregularly from the exertion and the fright and the panic, and there she stayed till morning.

CHAPTER 6

Jess could only assume Leila's nightmare had been caused by her time away in Pakistan. Michael had said she'd been rebellious, throwing things and no doubt giving the Kayani woman cause to think again about her trophy child, although a consequence of Leila's behaviour had been vicious punishment at the hands of her monstrous husband. There was no simple solution. Time was what they needed and she had no idea how long it would take for Leila to forget or at least get over her ordeal, if she ever could.

By morning, the children were almost back to normal and Leila even allowed Jess to help her wash in one of the spare bathrooms, the en suite being temporarily out of commission. It took Jess most of the morning to clean up the bedroom and bathroom, and she called one of the handymen Peter had used to come and replace the broken mirror.

For the rest of that week, they all went upstairs together, and while the girls slept, Jess filled her time sitting on the chaise longue reading from Peter's extensive collection of books. But she realised this wasn't sustainable and began to wonder how she'd continue to cope alone in a huge house with three demanding children.

The twins would soon celebrate their fourth birthday and be ready for pre-school, and although Jess still had recurring fears about letting them out of her sight, especially after what had happened to Leila, she knew she'd have to loosen the reins at some point. Similarly, she could not know what, if any, education Leila had had whilst away, and she needed to go to school. She wasn't sure when the new autumn term started at Chalton Primary, but guessed it was only weeks away, so she resolved to make an appointment with the head teacher and take the girls there to meet her as soon as possible.

***

The following week, Michael rang and suggested they meet again to go through some administrative issues. Much to Emma's relief, Michael agreed to come over to Chalton so that Jess didn't have to be parted from the girls. He brought his PA Sandy with him and, having had three children of her own, she was adept at keeping the girls occupied while Jess and Michael were in discussion.

Michael explained that Peter's estate amounted to approximately six million pounds, half of which was tied up in Chalton Manor, the remainder spread over a wide range of investments that included bonds, shares and cash. Peter's army pension had died with him but there were plenty of assets to generate a reasonable income, and even if some or all of them had to be liquidated, Michael estimated she could easily live off them for fifty years or so without having to sell the house.

Jess had never heard of so much money. She'd always assumed Peter was comfortably off but had never considered what that might amount to. There was no elation; the money meant nothing to her without Peter, but she took comfort from the fact that, as Peter had intended, they would all be provided for. Nor did she fully understand all the terminology and felt quite bewildered when Michael was trying to explain, but he assured her he would continue to manage her affairs until such time as she became more familiar with them and could do it herself. The one asset she knew only too well was Chalton Manor.

"Michael, I don't think we can go on living here indefinitely. The place is far too big, costs too much to heat and maintain, and we don't use more than two or three rooms. We'd be much better off in a small, three-bedroomed cottage or something like that. I'm sad to think of giving up Peter's house, but it'll always be Peter's house to me and I think one day soon, the kids and I will need to have a place we can really call home. I am quite happy to stay in the area, but if we are going to move, I will need some help. Sorry."

"I quite understand," said Michael. "It'll take a while to arrange everything, three to six months maybe, but I'll get Edward Ross, one of my junior partners, on it. What about all the contents?" Jess looked in dismay around the dining room where they sat at the large mahogany table.

"Gosh. I hadn't thought about that."

"Don't worry, I am sure we can find a home for them somehow."

"I really am very grateful to you, you know."

"You're family, Jess."

***

They agreed she'd need to take driving lessons and get a car, and she'd need childcare from time to time. Leila would enrol at Chalton Primary and start the following month. Sophie and Lucy would go to pre-school classes in the same building. Although school was just a mile away, in the village, Jess needed to get her own transport as soon as possible.

Michael had already helped her open her own account at the bank and funded it from the balance of Peter's client account held at his practice. It still had surplus funds left over from the search for Leila. The will had to go through probate, so he explained it would be a while before all Peter's assets were transferred into her name.

Michael had assumed that she would want Leila's surname changed to Jeffries and he had brought the requisite forms for Jess to sign. The twins had been born Jeffries, their birth certificates indicating, at Jess's request, "father unknown". Jess was more than happy for the respective fathers to be expunged from her memory.

"And I want my marriage annulled," she declared. She had had no reason to think about it before, but as all the facts had become clear, it took on a new significance. Mo's behaviour had been even worse than she'd assumed at the time and she didn't want any further connection between him and her family.

"That won't be necessary," said Michael.

"Why not? I want all links severed."

"You weren't actually married to Mo, Jess." She looked at him, uncomprehending. He was simply wrong.

"Yes I was! One of those religious people, an Imam, did it. There were witnesses. Family."

"You were married under Sharia law but it was never registered. Under British law, your marriage to Mo doesn't exist." She sighed and shook her head. She shouldn't be surprised at anything any more.

"Oh well, that figures. It wasn't much of a marriage anyway. He was never home and when he was, it was just to—" She broke off, unwilling to complete the sentence. Michael averted his eyes and she saw something in his look, his awkward body language. And then it dawned on her.

"I wasn't the only one, was I? He had others."

His silence was all the confirmation she needed. Michael shifted in his seat, but then nodded.

"Under Sharia law, a husband can have up to four wives at any one time."

She shook her head, no longer astonished at her own naivety.

"It all fits. He wanted boys. Sons, not daughters. So he had several of us. We were just slaves; well, I was."

"I'm sorry."

"No. Don't be. It makes it all the easier to cope with. Knowing all the facts."

Michael sighed.

"That's about it, Jess. Everything is in hand. I'll get back to you as and when I need signatures or have something to report. If you need anything in the meantime and I'm not available, just call Sandy."

"Okay, thanks." And then as an afterthought she asked. "Michael, why don't you and Emma come over on Sunday for lunch; that is, if Emma can bear it." They both laughed. "It's the least I can do for all the help you've been."

"We'd love to," said Michael.

***

Michael drove Sandy back to the office and then went home. Yet again, he'd failed to confront potentially the biggest issue of all. He'd spent many hours agonising over it and hadn't come to a firm conclusion. But Jess's expressed desire to sell Chalton Manor had tipped the balance. It was a game changer. It seemed to him inevitable that he would now have to divulge to Jess one last crucial piece of information. It was his duty, but he could not possibly imagine how she would take it.

CHAPTER 7

After a couple of weeks of relative peace and tranquillity at Chalton Manor, Jess made the decision to move the girls into the adjoining bedroom. Leila had had no recurrence of her nightmare and, for her own sake, she needed to get more sleep simply so she could function properly. The two rooms had a connecting door that she could leave open at night, so she'd always be on hand, and she'd be able to decorate the girls' new room in a style more suitable for children, with no hard objects. Despite her express intention to move, she couldn't tell how long that might take and judged that the money spent on the conversion was worthwhile, even for the limited time they had left.

The girls loved their new private space, with new beds and soft furnishings, pink carpet and curtains and wallpaper illustrated with their favourite cartoon characters. They continued to share the en-suite bathroom, but the new arrangement gave Jess some breathing space, the girls a new and exciting place to stay and their first taste of independence. Despite this, and in the early days, Leila often slipped back into Jess's bed during the night, but as time wore on, the frequency diminished.

Sandy's eighteen-year-old daughter Keira was drafted in to provide childcare from time to time while Jess took driving lessons, and she quickly passed her test. By the end of August, a brand new Range Rover stood in the drive of Chalton Manor. Jess had been aghast at the cost, but Michael assured her she could easily afford it and it meant she could trade in Peter's old Land Rover in part exchange. Emma had convinced her that, despite its size, it was a sensible choice and offered maximum protection for her family.

The car proved to be most liberating and they were able to go anywhere and do anything by themselves, without resorting to help from others. Above all, life appeared to have taken on a semblance of routine and normality that Jess had not known since Peter had died. She knew her next challenge would be to cope with the transition that came with the children's schooling.

She could not have been more wrong.

CHAPTER 8

It was a warm and sunny afternoon, three months to the day since Peter had died, and Jess and the girls were at home. The children seemed settled, happy and playful, and she had every reason to be optimistic about the future.

Thanks to Peter their financial security was assured, although she'd have traded it all in an instant to have him back. His death had left a gaping hole in her world and she mourned him desperately; her biggest regret was that he'd died before he could see her beloved Leila, their emotional reunion the culmination of his remaining life's work.

She stared out of the kitchen window, watching the girls playing in the garden, then looked at her watch. Michael was late. He'd phoned her to say that probate had been granted, and he'd give her an update on the transfer of assets. He needed some final signatures, after which his work was complete. It was unlike him not to be on time, but she had no other pressing engagements so it mattered little. Then, the doorbell rang.

"Hello, Michael," she said as he stepped into the hallway and kissed her on both cheeks. "No Emma?"

"No. She has a lot on, what with the book club, golf, bridge and all that other stuff she fills her time with." Jess could only imagine what it would be like having time to fill and had little concept or knowledge of the activities in which Emma seemed to be engaged.

"Do the girls still terrify her?" she asked smiling.

"Oh no, it's not that," he said, attempting to reassure her, but she gave him a wry smile to show she wasn't convinced. "Well, not all that."

"Would you like some tea?"

They had tea and cake in the kitchen while Michael shuffled some papers, briefed her on a range of issues that went over her head and got her to sign various documents she didn't understand. But she sensed something different in his demeanour. Michael had always been calm and articulate, measured and unflappable. Over the years, that was the man she had come to know. She had total faith in him and trusted him completely, so to find him distracted and hesitant was unusual. She found it slightly unnerving that Michael, of all people, should have something on his mind. Something was bothering him.

"It's all done, Jess," he said, but he sounded tired and it disturbed her.

"I guess the next step is to think about selling the house and moving somewhere smaller," she said tentatively, but instead of responding, he walked over to the kitchen window, removed his glasses and tucked them into the pocket of his tweed jacket.

"Shall we go for a walk?" he said after a moment, without turning, watching the girls running around on the grass.

"What is it, Michael?"

"Come on, I need some fresh air."

They sat on the patio. The same place she and Peter often sat; the place where she'd finally plucked up the courage to ask him about Lisa and the place where the terrible truth about his own loss had been revealed.

Jess sat back on her chair, arms folded, watching the girls, subdued, a sense of foreboding growing in her mind. She had been through enough to recognise the signs. She was no longer the naïve, innocent, exploitable young woman whose unremitting trust in others had lured her into being systematically and persistently abused. She had learnt life the hard way, and if everything now appeared stable, secure and predictable, then it was most likely an illusion; a precursor to another difficult challenge. The challenges would always be there and she would deal with them, provided she knew what they were. Michael shifted in his seat and leant forward, but she refused to meet his eyes.

"Jess, there's something I haven't told you," he said finally. "All that stuff about Peter and Leila was true, every word of it." She continued to stare blankly into space, looking but not seeing, her mind wrestling with conflicting emotions, her face grim, her mouth set and closed. "But there's something else. Something Peter didn't know and something I only found out myself a week after he died." She remained stiff and immobile but her breathing started to increase in intensity.

"I didn't tell you before because it seemed to serve no purpose. I've agonised over what to do for a while now, but having gone through all Peter's affairs and dealt with his estate, it's become clear to me that, now, you really do need to know."

She turned her head sharply to look at him, defiant, challenging him to speak, to continue, to say what he had to say, despite the large part of her dreading the outcome. He took a deep breath.

"Lisa … is alive."

She didn't react for a second but when she did, it was a simple snort, a short burst of air through her nostrils. She looked back to see her daughters running around, squealing as usual, the sounds of happiness mingling with the birdsong and the faint rustle of wind through the trees. And then the sounds of the past returned, the echoes rising in volume and intensity and her vision losing focus, blurring, reality dissolving all around her.

"I have to assume she's dead. But I don't know for certain. I just hope wherever she is, she's at peace."

"I'm sorry that—"

"How?" she snapped, a new reality forming, demanding she adapt. Instantly. She looked at him again but he seemed lost for words and avoided her eyes. "How do you know?"

she demanded, her voice rising in intensity. He took a moment and she waited, patient, but unrelenting.

"I saw her."

"Where?"

"She was at the funeral."

"What funeral? Peter's funeral?" Her eyes were wide, the shock profound and absolute. He nodded.

"She was standing at the other end of the graveyard, looking on."

She felt a panic begin to take hold and twisted in her chair to try and keep control of her shaking body. She struggled to process the image.

"But ... how do you know it was Lisa?" she demanded.

"I wasn't sure at first, and then she turned and walked off."

"So, it could have been anybody!"

"No," he answered quickly. "She came to see me the next day. In my office."

"What!?" Jess could barely contain her anger. Anger at the betrayal, the deceit. But also the anger of frustration, confusion and fear, and the shame of her own conflicting and irrational thoughts, and she wanted to lash out at something or someone and Michael was the only target. She put both hands over her eyes and rubbed them vigorously, and when she lowered them and turned to look at him, all she could see was sorrow and regret.

"She was with a Nepalese chap, Sujay. He was the one who took Peter to Langtang. He was the one who eventually found her."

"And when was that?" she demanded, her voice clipped, chin up, eyes wet, the defiance contained but resolute.

"I got a call from Sujay the week after Peter died. He said they were coming back to see him but hadn't been able to make contact and so had called me. I spoke to Lisa then and had to give her the bad news. She was too late. I told her not to come, at least not until after the funeral, but she insisted. Wanted to pay her respects."

"Pay her respects?" asked Jess, incredulous, the words laced with bitterness and irony. He nodded. She released the tirade. "What does she know about respect? She had everything going for her, a wonderful father who would have done anything for her. She takes herself off on a self-indulgent, rich girl's jaunt – to what, 'find herself'? – because she's a bit upset, and he doesn't know where she is or whether she's safe. She jets off to the other side of the world, totally ignores him, and all the while he's left here, alone in this decrepit pile with his grief, thinking it's all his fault. She doesn't once think of letting him know she's all right, even when he travels all the way to Nepal to try and find her? She lets him think he's responsible for getting his own daughter killed and leaves the guilt to fester and eat away at him? For five years? What kind of respect is that? What happened, did she run out of money?" She knew she sounded truculent and irrational, but she couldn't help it.

"It's not as simple as that, Jess."

"Oh, really?"

"No." They sat quietly for a moment. Jess crossed her arms tightly across her chest and sat back in her chair. Her rage subsided, replaced by a steely determination. She had been here before, in one way or another. "I'd quite like to explain," he said gently.

"What's there to explain?" She couldn't keep the bitterness out of her voice.

"Nothing has changed, Jess." She looked straight at him.

"Do you mind leaving us alone now, for a while." She said it calmly, back in control. He tried again.

"It changes nothing."

She nodded, but she knew and she didn't need to be told by anyone.

"It changes everything, Michael."

CHAPTER 9

She lay in bed, wide awake. It was 10.30 p.m., the kids long since fed, bathed and put to bed in their own room, and the house was quiet. The door between her room and the girls' was open, as usual, so she would hear any disturbance. It was always possible Leila might come and visit her during the night if she happened to wake up and feel the need to be comforted. Jess would welcome it. She needed some comfort herself.

But for the moment she was consumed by her own thoughts and they prevented sleep. She regretted being angry at Michael. It was sheer impulse, a reaction to his shocking and unexpected announcement, and it had destabilised her. Just when she thought life was settling down to something approaching normality, it seemed her world had been turned on its head all over again.

Having thought about it all evening, she understood she couldn't blame Michael for Lisa's reappearance. It must have come as a huge shock to him too and she knew she needed to apologise for her behaviour towards him, especially after everything he'd done for her. But he had said that he'd thought long and hard before telling her and decided ultimately that she needed to know. Why did she need to know? Was he simply trying to share the burden of knowledge? It was inconceivable that Michael, an experienced lawyer, the soul of discretion and dispassionate guardian of his clients' affairs, should feel the need to unburden himself of a secret like that, for no obvious reason. After all, he'd insisted nothing would change. But at the same time, his revelation undermined that very notion.

She had also been angry with Lisa for putting Peter through so much torment and pain. Michael had said it wasn't that simple and she hadn't given him the chance to explain. How complicated could it be? She couldn't help thinking what might have happened if Lisa had reappeared at any time prior to Peter's death. In her first few weeks at Chalton, she'd always assumed Lisa would return one day and it was only after Peter had told her the full tragic story that they both were able to move on and make a new life together. From that moment on, time had started to heal the wounds.

Jess would never have wished Lisa dead. She would have done anything to make Peter happy, and if that meant welcoming Lisa home at any time, she would have gladly done it and stepped aside and left her to take her rightful place alongside her father. Whatever had driven Lisa to remain hidden and incommunicado, oblivious or otherwise to her father's pain, all would have been forgiven and forgotten amidst the euphoria and joy he would surely have felt at seeing her again.

And what did Lisa know of the will? Michael had referred only to a meeting they had in his office the day after the funeral. What did they discuss? What did Lisa know about her and her children? Had Lisa seen them in the graveyard, made any connection, seen the resemblance, drawn any conclusions or made any comments about her? And where was she now? Was she likely to show up here at any time?

It was impossible for her to unravel the mystery. There were too many questions. She would have to go and see Michael and talk to him. He said nothing had changed. But for her, and Sophie and Lucy and Leila, everything had changed. She knew what she had to do.

***

Sandy showed Jess into Michael's office and he greeted her warmly but reservedly. She had called Sandy at home during breakfast and asked if Michael was available to see her that day, and if so, whether Keira could pop over to Chalton and look after the kids for a couple of hours. He was and she could.

"Morning, Jess. How are you?" He kissed her on both cheeks and, without waiting for a reply, said, "Please, sit down. Would you like some coffee?" Jess sat down nervously, contrition the first item on her agenda.

"No. Thanks very much. And thanks for seeing me so promptly." It was too polite. It was not the way they were. It was not the way she wanted them to be.

"I'm sorry about yesterday—"

"No! I'm sorry. I shouldn't have been so stroppy." She smiled sheepishly at him and he smiled back.

"It's perfectly understandable. It must have been a great shock."

"Yes. But I know it wasn't your fault. I was just, well, a bit confused and, I suppose, worried. Worried that everything was going to come crashing down again."

"Nothing's going to come crashing down," he said gently and calmly, but she wasn't listening.

"You know, I couldn't have done any of this without you and I'll never be able to thank you enough for what you did to get Leila back. And Emma too. You've been wonderful to me and I had no right to take it out on you."

He sighed.

"Jess, I know you're grateful, but just to see you and the girls happy and content is thanks enough. I know for a fact that this is what Peter wanted, and it was an honour and a privilege to be able to help him. And help you too."

She nodded. Friends again.

"Maybe I could have some tea?"

He smiled and picked up the phone.

"Sandy, could we have two teas, please? Thanks." She picked a handkerchief from her bag to blow her nose and he took the opportunity to try again.

"You know, there's nothing to worry about. Nothing is going to change."

"I know. You said that. But then why did you tell me? If I didn't need to know before, why do I need to know now?"

He sat back in his chair.

"It was always debatable in my mind. I just got to the point where, on balance, it seemed to be the right thing to do."

"Does Emma know?"

"She didn't, but she does now. She's as shocked as you are."

"Did anyone know?"

"Sandy showed them into my office that day, but she didn't know who she was. She wasn't with me when Lisa went missing."

"Them? Here, in this office?"

"Lisa and Sujay."

"The guide? He was here too?"

"Yes."

"So no one knew but you?"

"No." He sounded regretful.

"So, what tipped the balance? What made you say something?" There was a tap on the door. It opened and Sandy came in and put a tray down on the side table next to Michael's desk.

"Thanks Sandy." Sandy smiled at Jess and gave her a wink before closing the door behind her as she left.

"I need to give you the background. The context." He passed over a cup and saucer and she took a sip. She held the saucer in both hands as he spoke.

"As we now know, Lisa wasn't killed at Langtang. She was there, but she was very lucky. Legend has it that the entire population was wiped out, but it turns out a few villagers did survive and Lisa was one of them. She was the only Westerner to get out, but she was badly injured. No help arrived for days, according to Sujay, by which time she had already managed to drag herself out from beneath the rubble and crawl her way up to a ridge and onto a trail that was rarely used. She said she didn't remember the rest, but eventually woke up in a place called Chumtang, some thirty miles to the north, being attended to by some women villagers. Sujay assumed she must have been picked up by a mule train. He said they only went that way once a month, so she was very lucky indeed."

"Oh God, how awful."

"Quite."

"So how long was she there?"

"Four years."

"Four years?" Jess almost spilt her tea. *How could she have been there four years?* She couldn't comprehend it. "How bad was she?"

"Well, I don't really know. She had some broken bones, apparently. She certainly walks with a limp and she has a terrible scar down one side of her face. Beyond that I can't tell."

Jess still didn't understand.

"So, assuming she recovered after, say, a few months, why did she stay out of sight? Why didn't she try and get word back to Peter that she was okay?" Her anger was coming to the fore again. She couldn't help thinking of Peter's despair and hopelessness at losing her. She didn't stop to think Lisa may have had a reason.

"Because she didn't know who she was."

"I don't understand."

"She lost her memory. Retrograde amnesia. Presumably brought on by a blow to the head and the trauma of the disaster. She lost all her possessions in the landslide. All she had were the clothes she was wearing at the time. She didn't even know her own name, never mind where she was born or where she'd come from." Jess's mouth dropped open as she tried to imagine the state she'd been in. "And because she had no ID, the villagers didn't know who she was either. They just took care of her. They called her 'Alisha'. Quite appropriate, actually." Jess looked puzzled. "It means 'Protected by God'."

Jess took another sip of tea and then put the cup and saucer down on the desk. Her head was beginning to hurt. Was it possible Lisa had lived in a remote Himalayan village for four years with complete loss of memory? If so, then she'd misjudged her greatly and she suddenly felt pangs of guilt for doubting the girl. She tried to imagine her situation, recovering from her injuries, knowing nothing about her past, oblivious to what may have been going on back home, and both she and Peter, each unaware that at one point they were only thirty miles apart. And then, two or three months later, when he's given up all hope, she comes walking back into his life. But this time it's not Lisa, it's Lisa's double, and Alice has a story similar to his, but the roles are reversed. The parallels were stark and extraordinary. Too extraordinary to contemplate. But something wasn't right.

"But she must have found out who she was eventually, or how else could she have come back?"

"She told me that as time went by, fragments of her memory returned. Initially not enough to know who her father was or where she was from – but her time at Langtang as a teacher; the kids in her class; the earthquake itself; the landslide. Word eventually got back to Kathmandu that a Western girl was living in Chumtang. A survivor of Langtang. Sujay got to hear about it and put two and two together. He trekked all the way up there to check it out. He found her and between them, they filled in the blanks. Eventually, he persuaded her to come back."

"Persuaded? Why did she need persuading?" Her frustration was growing again.

"Well, I can't be sure. But it may have been something to do with her Buddhism."

"What do you mean?"

"I mean that I knew she had shown some interest in it at university. She said so before she went. Said it helped her to cope with Janica's death and she wanted to know more. That's why she went to Nepal in the first place."

"Religion? Religion took her to Nepal and stopped her coming back?"

"It's not quite religion, Jess. More a way of life. I'm by no means an expert, but I think it may have had a profound influence on her judgement." Jess shook her head, trying to work it all out.

"So, let me run through this again. She goes off to Nepal to get over the loss of her mum, becomes a Buddhist, gets caught in the disaster, loses her memory for a few years and then, when she gets it back, decides it's better to stay there as a Buddhist than get in touch with her family?"

"I don't pretend to understand it any more than you, Jess," said Michael ruefully. "That's just what she said."

"So what did make her come back?"

"Sujay." She shook her head again. "Sujay explained to her that Peter had come to try and find her after the earthquake. That Peter had visited Langtang, had probably stood on the same ridge she'd crawled along in her battered state and that he'd finally gone home utterly despondent and broken. She said she knew then that he loved her."

The words came back instantly.

"I loved her dearly. I can't bear to think she may not have known that."

Jess exhaled slowly and fought the wave of emotion building inside her.

"Oh God. I can't bear it," she whispered as Michael continued.

"But of course, Sujay hadn't seen Peter for years. Didn't know where he was or even whether he was still alive. Had no idea you existed, and even if he had, it wouldn't have stopped him. He was just doing his duty. Finishing a job he'd started years previously. Reuniting a parent with a lost child." *The parallels.* They must have got back to

Kathmandu about the same time as Leila." She let out a nervous laugh. An involuntary puff of air. *They could have passed each other in the street.*

"It took him a day or so to find out that I was the contact. He got through to me the week after Peter died." Her mind was still whirling from the revelations, revising opinions and judgements, getting closer to Lisa by the moment; beginning to understand.

"I spoke to Lisa and I have to say she didn't sound like the Lisa I knew. But she was able to give me enough personal detail to convince me she was who she claimed. I told her there was nothing here for her, it was too late, and she was remarkably composed. Not at all upset or traumatised. Just matter of fact. Accepting. But she insisted she wanted to come back anyway."

"Why?"

"As I said, she wanted to pay her respects. She may have been a Buddhist, but she was still Peter's daughter. I thought I had persuaded her to wait till after the funeral. Let the dust settle a bit. So I was surprised to see her there. But she kept a low profile. In truth I had no idea how I was going to handle it when she learnt about you, or even saw you. That's why I wanted to delay things until I had time to brief you. The last thing you needed at the funeral was to see Lisa, your double, apparently risen from the grave."

"That would have been, er, difficult," she nodded. "But how could they afford the flights? She couldn't have had any money. Who paid for them to come over here in the first place?" Michael looked uncharacteristically awkward and shifted in his seat.

"Er, you did, indirectly. I knew Peter wouldn't have hesitated, so I used Leila's fighting fund. I'm sorry, a technical breach of trust. I hope you'll forgive me."

"Of course. There's nothing to forgive." She smiled at him, thinking how honourable and upstanding he was, and in that way at least, just like Peter. She missed Peter terribly, but she still had Michael. "So where is she now? When can I see her?"

"You can't. She and Sujay flew back to Kathmandu almost immediately."

"But why?"

"That's where her life is."

"But did you explain to her about the will? Did you explain to her about me?" Michael sighed.

"I explained to her that, because Peter was convinced she had died in Langtang, he'd made other arrangements in his will. I didn't feel the need to go any further than that and she didn't press me to."

"But surely, she must have realised there was a fortune here that belonged to her?"

"Once belonged to her," he corrected her gently.

"Well, it's the same thing," she protested, but then wondered why she was saying it at all.

"No, it's not Jess. Peter's will was his and his alone. He changed it in full cognisance of the facts, as he saw them. He was of sound mind and body, more or less, and although, as I said to you before, I challenged him on it, I had no doubt whatsoever of his sanity or his rationale."

"So, she just walked away? Lisa just went back home to an impoverished life in a tiny village in the Himalayas?" It sounded even more implausible when she said it out loud.

"Yes."

"But why?"

"Because she's a Buddhist. I looked it up. They have no interest in wealth, assets, belongings or any physical possessions. They believe that the pursuit of wealth cannot bring happiness and ultimately leads only to suffering. Their whole lives are dedicated to the avoidance of suffering and the quest for nirvana. Spiritual enlightenment. Awakening. As I said, I'm not an expert." He waved a hand in the air. Jess exhaled slowly.

Michael may not be an expert on Buddhism, she thought, but he was far better informed than she was. She had no complaint about the principles of Buddhism, at least as far as he had explained them. She had lived a meagre existence most of her life, had been destitute twice before she met Peter and didn't feel particularly euphoric about her inheritance, other than it gave her peace of mind for her children.

She did have to admit, though, given the choice between destitution and wealth, she would choose the latter, but again, only in as much as it allowed her to provide adequately for the ones she loved. And in that sense, she knew exactly where her priorities lay, as did Lisa. *Or was it Alisha?* She made a mental note to look up Buddhism and learn a bit more. But then the original question came back. She reiterated the facts.

"So, if Lisa had no interest in the will, had no idea who I was or that I even existed, only wanted to see where her father was buried and go home again, back to her primitive life in Nepal, and I had no idea she existed either, and in fact, no one but you had any idea she was still alive … why did you tell me?"

"Because I felt I had to."

"But you said nothing had changed. Lisa's gone back. She'll probably never return and we can all go back to our lives as if nothing has happened."

"It was selling the house that made me think."

"Made you think what?" She could feel her frustration bubbling to the surface again. Frustration at not being clever enough to work it out for herself. Frustration at having to rely on others to spell out what may be obvious to them, but was never obvious to her.

"I said nothing has changed. The will is the will and, as far as I'm concerned, Peter's wishes have been carried out properly and in total accord with his instructions."

"So?" *Get to the point.*

"There is a tiny chance, an infinitesimal chance, that one day, Lisa may get bored where she is, renounce Buddhism, seek to regain all the trappings of Western culture, and come home and challenge the will. Jess frowned.

"Can she do that?"

"She may be able to make the case that, due to Peter suffering the trauma of her disappearance and supposed death, and his increasingly poor health, none of which was her fault, he could not have been of sound mind, and therefore not fit to change his will. Furthermore, she could easily argue that if Peter had known then what we know now, he would never have cut her out in the first place. Which is undoubtedly true."

Jess thought about this for a moment. Michael was outlining a scenario in which Lisa might take back what she believed to be rightfully hers. Everything Peter had given to her would be taken away. Taken away from her children too.

"How tiny?" she asked.

"Virtually non-existent. And if even if she did, we'd fight her and it could drag on for years. And even if a court eventually found in her favour, she wouldn't get it all. Any court would give maximum consideration to the children he had willingly cared and provided for. It would not be difficult to show that even if he had left Lisa as the primary beneficiary of his will, he would have made provision for you and the children too."

It sounded inconceivable that Lisa, from what little she knew of her and her actions so far, would change her mind and return. But it still worried her. She could not live with a cloud hanging over her, not even for a few years, even if it was so unlikely to materialise. She needed to know; she needed security.

"So, if it's that unlikely, why mention it."

"The house was the trigger. It's reasonable to suppose Lisa might have some emotional attachment to the house, having grown up and lived there with her parents. If anything, it's the one thing that might prey on her mind. If we sell the house too soon, before we are absolutely sure she's not coming back, then it would make it all the more difficult to unravel the mess afterwards."

"So what you're saying is, I have to stay there a while, living in fear of Lisa coming back at any time and claiming her inheritance?"

"Not living in fear, Jess. Just being prudent."

She thought about it. She didn't care about the house or the money, or the will, or Lisa. She just cared about her children. She never expected anything from Peter, nor he from her. *What would Peter have wanted?* She cared about that. Peter's estate was rightfully Lisa's. There was no other way to look at it.

Michael was talking as a lawyer again.

"I thought of asking her to sign a waiver, relinquishing any right she may have had to challenge the will, but she'd have needed independent advice and that would have taken time. And even if she had agreed to it, any independent lawyer would have smelt blood and fought for her to get their hands on a slice. And she just wanted to get away. Get back home. Her home. As I said, everything points to the fact that nothing will ever happen. But I had a duty to brief you there was a risk, however small it might be."

"I understand," said Jess, quiet, still thinking. There was a moment when neither of them spoke. But her mind was racing.

"I'll tell Edward to stand down on the house. At least for a month or two." She heard him but it didn't register. She had already decided.

"I'm going to see her."

"Sorry?" Michael thought he'd misheard.

"I'm going to see her. Lisa. Alisha."

"You can't," he said, shaking his head. She looked at him and he seemed flustered for the first time ever.

"Why not?"

"Well, you've no passport for a start."

"I'll get one."

"And go to Nepal? By yourself?" She smiled. He was sounding like Peter.

"Yes." She was calm and resolute.

"To do what?"

"To find out the truth for myself. To tell her about me and Peter. And to tell her it's all here for her if she wants it."

"Jess! You can't do that," he blustered.

"You've already said that."

"But how are you going to find her?" protested Michael.

"Sujay. I'll find Sujay and he can take me."

"But what about the kids? Who's going to look after them?" She had already thought of that. She knew what she had to do. She looked straight at him and she was sure she saw him swallow deeply.

"I'm going, Michael. I'm going to find Lisa."

CHAPTER 10

Leila and the twins rushed into the hallway as the door closed behind her with a great thud. Leila got there first and Jess lifted her up high and hugged her, and then dropped to her knees to kiss Lucy and then Sophie, and the four of them joined in a group hug.

Jess's thoughts had been in turmoil after her conversation with Michael, and as she drove the Range Rover back from Hareton, her head had been spinning with the arrangements she needed to make. Michael had done his best to talk her out of it, but she was resolute and in control.

"Get me a passport, Michael, or I'll get a new lawyer. And can you ask Sandy to look at flights and timings and hotels?"

She didn't know which of them was more surprised by her new-found confidence and assertiveness.

Keira sauntered out of the kitchen.

"Hi, Jess," she said with a big smile, relaxed in a way Emma had obviously found impossible in the same circumstances.

"Hi, Keira, have they been good?"

"Good as gold. Haven't you?" she said, addressing the girls who were jumping up and down.

"Yes!" squealed Sophie and Lucy in unison as ever, and Leila nodded enthusiastically.

"They're just a joy to be with. I'm going to have a dozen when the time's right," she gushed. *You're only eighteen!* Jess almost articulated her thoughts but stopped herself. She was in no position to offer advice to young women on the best time to have babies.

"I'm really grateful," she said, fishing in her purse. She drew out fifty pounds and thrust it at Keira. *Fifty pounds. Three days' interest for a loan shark. Once the difference between life and death; now, just pocket money.*

"Gosh. That's too much for having fun."

"No, please take it. I'll need you again soon."

"Cool!"

"I need to talk to your mum, see if you have space to take the girls in for a while. I have to go away. Just for a couple of weeks."

"Oh yeah," said Keira, "we've got four bedrooms and two of them are spare. That would be awesome!"

"When are you back at uni?"

"Not for another month."

"Great, that fits in quite well. Provided your mum and dad are happy. I'll call her."

"Brilliant! Okay, if you don't need anything else, I'll be off." Keira flung her arm around Jess and kissed her, dropped down and hugged each of the girls in turn and then, plucking her crash helmet and jacket off the coat rack, waved back at them. "Bye, girls." She let herself out of the front door, and a second later Jess heard the scooter fire up with a pop and a crackle and then whizz off down the drive.

"Come on, you lot. Let's have some lunch."

CHAPTER 11

Jessica Anne Khalid had never had a passport. She'd never been out of the country. She would have gone after Mo to Pakistan in search of Leila, but that needed a passport and that cost money which she didn't have, never mind the airfare. But a whole new world opened up for Jess Jeffries the day she decided to go to Nepal.

She sat in her Business Class seat on the Emirates flight to Kathmandu, via Dubai, and watched her fellow travellers boarding, slowly filling up all the vacant seats, many of them dragging carry-on luggage, most of them making their way to the economy section behind her. She was fascinated by the cross-section of humanity: white people, black people, Asians, Orientals, businessmen, backpackers, women and children, all ages, all shapes and sizes and all, apart from her, it seemed, knowing what they were doing because, in all likelihood, they had done it all before.

She sensed envious eyes on her from the economy passengers shuffling past her seat, no doubt wondering who had paid for her expensive fare. *Rich kid? Sugar daddy?* Well, either or both, she might have to concede.

Michael and Emma had taken her to the airport, and after a lengthy list of instructions from Michael, numerous dos and don'ts from Emma and a tearful farewell, they left her at the Business Class check-in desk. She was treated like royalty and a personal representative escorted her to the executive lounge where, remarkably, all the food and drink was free and plentiful. She was totally bewildered and thoroughly excited.

She watched her fellow Business Class passengers, fascinated. An Arab, resplendent in white thaub and keffiyeh, a woman in black abaya and hijab, exotic women in designer clothing dripping jewellery, and sharp-suited businessmen in crisp white shirts with laptops and tablet computers.

She foraged around in the pockets and compartments of her seat. A blanket, a pillow, a bag containing socks, earplugs, black eye mask and flat black slippers; another containing headphones and a leather vanity case filled with luxury toiletries. A tall, elegant flight attendant stopped by her seat, bearing a tray of drinks.

"Good evening, Miss Jeffries," she said pleasantly. *How does she know my name?* "Would you care for a drink? We have mineral water, fruit juice or champagne." Jess hesitated, unsure of what to say.

"Er, how much is that?" she asked. The woman smiled.

"It's complimentary, madam." *Complimentary? Madam?* Jess raised her eyebrows and beamed.

"Champagne, please. If that's okay?"

"Of course." The woman placed a small glass bowl of mixed nuts, a padded paper mat and a fizzing champagne flute on the console next to her. Jess turned her head surreptitiously to see what everyone else was having and noticed the Arabs were on orange juice and the businessmen on water. But, she spotted with relief, one middle-aged woman with obviously dyed hair, sunglasses and copious amounts of gold jewellery was holding a flute like hers. She looked around to see if anyone was watching and took a sip. It was cold, sparkly and glorious.

"Menu, Miss Jeffries?" Jess was taken by surprise, accidentally inhaling champagne through her nose, and looked up, coughing and spluttering. Another exotic goddess was standing over her holding out a stiff booklet, her make-up rich and dense, her teeth sparkling white and her smile as perfectly formed as her figure.

"Thank you," said Jess after a moment, recovering her composure. The woman walked on to the next seat and Jess opened the booklet. There were no prices. *It's complimentary, madam!* She giggled with delight and sat back in her seat.

She barely noticed take-off, the huge A380 betraying little sensation of movement, and in no time it was dark outside so there was nothing to see through the window. But there was plenty to keep her entertained on board; a three-course meal with wine, films and flight information on her personal screen, people constantly moving around and the flight attendants patrolling the aisles, seeing to their every need. She even had time for a sleep, once she had worked out which buttons turned her seat into a bed.

But three hours into the flight, movement in the cabin settled down and the lights were dimmed, leaving just the glow of one or two personal reading lights to punctuate the gloom. She decided she would find the toilet so got out of her seat and headed back down the plane towards the bulkhead separating Business from Economy. The cubicles on her side were occupied so she crossed over to the other aisle. She found the washroom, discovered how everything worked and used all the supplies, including the fragrant soap, hand lotion and complimentary perfume.

But when she exited, she turned the wrong way and was halfway down the opposite aisle before realising her mistake. As she retraced her steps, her eyes fell on a middle-aged man, forty or fifty, sitting in the last row of Business Class. His head was back, eyes closed, and he appeared to be asleep. He was scruffily dressed in jeans and crumpled shirt and she could see he was unshaven and his hair unkempt. *Not your typical Business Class passenger.* She chided herself for her unwitting snobbery. As if he could read her mind, his eyes suddenly opened and he gave her a warm smile. She felt herself blushing and moved on swiftly around the bulkhead and back to her seat.

The landing was as smooth and uneventful as take-off. Jess stuffed the vanity bag in her rucksack and followed the other passengers off the plane, accepting the best wishes from the flight attendants, all of whom looked as perfect and fresh as they had seven hours earlier. Her connecting flight wouldn't leave for a couple of hours so she gaped through the windows of some of the designer shops in Dubai airport and then went to the executive lounge to freshen up.

She called Keira from the lounge.

"Jess, you only left this morning!"

"I know, but I can't help it."

"They're fine. They're gorgeous. Don't worry, we'll look after them."

An hour later she boarded the Boeing 777 for the four-hour flight to Kathmandu, noticing with some disdain the plane was not quite up to the same standard as the previous one. Then she laughed at herself for being so fussy. *Look at you now, international traveller!*

She tucked into the food, but stayed off the wine. She was already feeling tired and knew it would be mid-morning when they landed, and she didn't want to arrive with a hangover, however mild.

She spotted one or two of her fellow passengers from the London flight, including the scruffy guy in the jeans, but thought nothing of it. There was no reason to think she was the only person travelling from London to Nepal. *Maybe he's an explorer or mountain climber?*

The plane landed and taxied to its gate. She disembarked, and in the heat and dust and sweat and filth and noise of Tribhuvan International Airport, Kathmandu, Federal Democratic Republic of Nepal, her luxurious journey abruptly ended.

She needed a visa, readily available from one of the many desks, provided she fill in a form, get in a queue and hand over forty dollars and a photo. Sandy had said the easiest way to get one was on arrival, although having queued for thirty minutes in the increasing humidity, she was not so sure.

The visa desks were each manned by three or four mainly middle-aged Nepalese, each tasked with shuffling, stamping, folding and stapling bits of paper, the most senior one handling the cash. Eventually, she handed over her money and documents, and after much theatre, jabbering and gesticulation, she was given a receipt which she then had to take to another queue to get the visa.

The people queuing comprised mostly trekkers and backpackers; young and old alike, all kitted out, like her, in walking boots, tee shirts and cargo pants or shorts, all with a rucksack hanging from one shoulder. But there were also some conventionally dressed tourists, mostly European, all engaged in the visa ritual.

And then it was on to the passport queue where the visa, issued not more than a few minutes previously, was examined closely by severe-looking men in military-type uniforms, before being stamped ceremoniously and the holder waved through. Jess noticed a similarly chaotic process at the local immigration queues, where ethnic Nepalese waited impatiently to flash their passports and get home from their work in India or elsewhere.

But the humidity and cacophony in arrivals was nothing compared to the baggage hall, where chaos reigned. Kit bags, tent bags, suitcases and capacious rucksacks, no doubt stuffed full with fleeces, jackets and sundry all-weather gear, vied for space on the rickety carousels along with large cardboard boxes wrapped in clear plastic, boasting flat screen TVs, computers or similar pieces of electronic hardware. And to make space on the overloaded machinery, men in yellow tee shirts pulled items off the moving conveyor and tossed them onto the floor where they piled up like dead bodies, their owners clambering over each other like vultures to get to their belongings.

Jess looked left and right amongst the pile, searching in vain for her bag, unable to get close to the carousel, jostled and pushed by people of all ages, shapes and sizes, gripping her carry-on, beginning to despair of ever seeing hers appear.

And then it did. A brand new North Face soft bag with her readily identifiable label flew on top of a pile of others, and she launched herself into the throng, grabbing one of the handles and hauling it to safety before it could be buried.

She staggered over to the exit, relieved it was all over, and the crowds thinned in the corridor as people made their way out. But it wasn't over. Another security check. Men in military uniforms, some with machine guns, checking baggage tags with baggage receipts.

Then out through automatic sliding doors to the main concourse where the madness increased ten-fold. Hundreds of men, shouting, waving their arms around, some holding up cards bearing names of myriad nationalities scrawled in felt tip, others with official travel company signs, all shrieking at her and everyone else, while others tried to take her bags off her. "Taxi, miss. Me take bag. Good taxi."

She clung on to her bags, trying to be polite.

"No, thank you! No, thank you!" she said while being pushed and shoved in all directions, the heat and dust increasing as she staggered and fought her way closer to the outside doors. And then, above the cacophony, a sound she recognised.

"Miss Jess! Miss Jess!" A Nepalese man grabbed her arm and pushed his way through the dense crowd of bodies, dragging her behind him to the relative safety of the fresh air outside.

"Oh God! What a nightmare," said Jess, doubled up, trying to catch her breath, wheezing and sweating in the heat and immediately wondering if this air was fresh, what did they do for pollution?

"Miss Jess? Welcome to Kathmandu." She looked up. Sujay Bahadur Gurung held out a hand, smiling broadly, still clutching a handwritten sign reading "Jeffries", which she hadn't noticed before.

"Sujay?" she gasped, still struggling for breath as her throat and lungs tingled from an acrid substance in the air she couldn't identify, but guessed was simply something burning.

"Yes, Ma'am."

"How did you find me?" she said, still panting.

"It's my job." It sounded a simple enough answer to a stupid question. "Come. Let me take your bags." With no perceivable effort he slung both of them over his shoulder and gestured to the car park opposite. He stayed beside her and held her arm as he dragged her across the road, holding up his hand from time to time to stop the traffic amidst the blast of horns while engines rattled and roared and black smoke billowed all around them.

"Is it always like this?" she shouted, shielding her eyes from the sun.

"Oh, no. This is a quiet day," he laughed.

They reached the car park and he helped her into the back of an open minibus. He slid the side door shut and got into the front seat next to the driver. "This is Mitesh, my brother." Mitesh turned and gave her a crooked grin, pressing his palms together.

"Namaste."

Without waiting for a response, he turned and rammed the stick into gear and, with lots of engine revving and horn blasting, inched the minibus out of the car park and into the traffic.

"Is it your first time in Kathmandu?" asked Sujay.

"Yes." *Nobody comes here twice, surely?*

"We have thirty minutes to your hotel. It's only two kilometres, but" – he shrugged – "you know ... traffic." She looked out of the dusty, dirty window. The roads and streets and pavements were crowded, heaving with cars and scooters and bicycles, carts pulled by horses, carts pushed by people, people moving in all directions, people just sitting around on their haunches on the pavement, skinny dogs trotting about, dodging the traffic, stray mules chewing languidly on dusty, dried-up vegetation and small fires burning everywhere, spewing out noxious black smoke.

Randomly sited and vertically challenged telegraph poles supported an impossibly knotted mass of wires, with hundreds of cables snaking out in all directions like tangled spaghetti. She stared at the buildings, their state of dilapidation leaving her unsure as to whether they were still under construction or being torn down. She had never seen anything like it.

"Dwarika's is an excellent hotel," said Sujay. "Very fine. The best place to stay in Kathmandu." He nodded to himself in satisfaction. She felt a degree of comfort in that, but wondered why, if it was only two kilometres away, there was not yet any evidence that the dereliction she could see all around her might magically transform into luxury accommodation. Then the penny dropped, or so she thought.

"It looks like it's taking time for things to be rebuilt after the earthquake."

"Oh, no. This area was not affected." She didn't know whether to feel shame or embarrassment at her faux pas or to laugh out loud. *Welcome to Kathmandu!*

***

The street was lined with windowless buildings, some propped up on bamboo stilts, some without roofs, the shops at ground level open to the dust and filth blown around by the relentless traffic and the endless crowds going about their business.

The minibus suddenly veered across the pavement through an archway and came to rest in front of two giant oak doors. Sujay jumped out and slid the door open. Jess hesitated. *This can't be it.*

"Come, Miss Jess. We are here. Dwarika's." He took her hand and she stepped down gingerly from the bus. A porter in smart uniform rushed forward and stood to attention.

"Namaste," he said, hands pressed together in front of his nose.

"Namaste," she replied and made a feeble attempt to emulate the greeting with her hands as he ushered her through the doors. She looked around for her bags and saw another similarly dressed porter following behind carrying them, Sujay at his side. She walked slowly on – and into paradise.

An oasis of calm and serenity opened up before her. Fountains trickled and splashed all around, marigolds sprung from raised beds and huge terracotta pots. Trees sprouted from gaps amongst the flagstones beneath her feet and swallows swooped above her head, chirping and tweeting, as if serenading the weary traveller with their unique welcome. In contrast to the mayhem outside, it seemed like she'd stepped through a portal into another world.

She looked up and around and she could see the hotel was built around four sides of a giant courtyard. Guests in smart clothes sat outside a restaurant, some eating lunch or just having a drink. Across the courtyard striped parasols and loungers were arranged around a swimming pool, from which could be heard the occasional splash and whoop of delight.

Two beautiful young women in traditional costume approached her and one of them placed a garland made from fresh marigolds around her neck, then stepped back and pressed her palms together.

"Namaste," she said, while her colleague offered Jess a tray with a single glass of orange-coloured fruit juice.

"Thank you. Namaste," said Jess, loving it already. The women bowed and stepped aside, gesturing towards the reception desk which was set in an open-air lounge furnished with soft leather sofas and black teak carved tables.

"Miss Jess?" she turned and saw Sujay was behind her. "Would you like to check in now? Then perhaps you might like some lunch or perhaps go to your room to rest?" Jess didn't know what she wanted; she was so dizzy with sensory overload. But he led her over to the desk where a handsome young man in a fine suit looked up and greeted her.

"Namaste, Miss Jeffries. Welcome to Dwarika's."

"Thank you," she said grinning foolishly, still sipping the delicious drink.

"Your room is ready. May I have your passport and a credit card, please?" He smiled politely as she fumbled in the leg pocket of her cargo trousers and pulled out the requisite items.

"Thank you." He swiped the card and handed the passport over to a female colleague who disappeared into the office. "You may collect your passport later." He thrust a white sheet of paper in front of her, marking three places with a cross. "Please sign here, here and here." She did as asked and he handed her a large bronze key. "You are in room 601. The lift is by the swimming pool. Your bags have already been taken there. Please enjoy your stay." He bowed stiffly and she nodded, still grinning.

"This is some place." she said to Sujay.

"The best hotel in Kathmandu," he repeated. "I suggest you go to your room. Have shower, or take bath, have some rest. I will come back at 5 p.m. and we can talk more then."

"Thanks, Sujay." He started to walk away but she called after him.

"Sujay?" He stopped and turned.

"I know it's your job, but how did you spot me in that crowd? At the airport."

He smiled.

"I just look for the twin sister of Miss Alisha."

CHAPTER 12

She pushed the heavy key into the lock and turned, the mechanism responding with a loud clunk. The door swung open and she stepped tentatively into the room. It was huge. Floor-to-ceiling windows dressed in translucent nets and heavy ornate curtains hung at two sides. A king-sized bed piled high with colourful cushions, elaborately carved wooden furniture and a three-seater sofa sat on a floor tiled with terracotta, adorned in places by the occasional thick rug. A bowl of exotic fruit lay on the coffee table alongside two bottles of mineral water.

The room opened out into a bathroom area dominated by a central double-width bath, seemingly carved out of a single block of black stone. A large porcelain sink with antique brass taps was set into a mahogany cabinet, next to which were a toilet and bidet and a separate wet area with a shower enclosure tiled in the same black stone.

She walked over to a window and pulled back the nets. She could see people down in the courtyard and by the pool, and across the rooftops, the crazy panorama of Kathmandu with its ramshackle architecture and myriad smoke trails drifting inexorably into the deep blue sky.

She plucked her phone out of her pocket and dialled.

"Keira?"

"Jess. Hello. Are you there?"

"Yes. I'm here. What time is it?"

"It's just gone nine." Jess looked at her phone which read 14.52 and thought it a bit weird she was five-and-three-quarter hours ahead. No matter.

"How's everyone?"

"Hold on." There was a pause and she heard Keira calling in the background, the slap-slap of tiny feet, the unmistakeable squeal and the breathless enthusiasm of the little people she loved.

"Hello, Mummy!" Her face lit up.

"Hello, Sophie."

"Hello, Mummy!" A second, similar voice chimed in.

"Hello, Lucy. Are you having a nice time with Keira?"

"Yes!" They shouted in unison.

"Are you being good?"

"Yes! We're making fairies!" And before Jess could say anything else, they were gone, their shrieking and squealing receding into the distance.

"They're fine. We're having a great time. We're making fairy cakes." Jess laughed at the image; the kitchen a bombsite, no doubt, the girls with sticky fingers and flour in their hair.

"How's Leila?"

"Oh, she's sitting quietly on the sofa reading a book." Jess's amusement waned a little as she tried to imagine the scene.

"Can you put her on?" She heard Keira whisper something and then her elder daughter's voice, calm, detached, withdrawn.

"Hello?"

"Hello, darling," she said, trying to sound happy and enthused, attempting to suppress the dark feelings rising inside her. *Stop it! You know Leila never says very much.* She asked the same question. "Are you having a nice time with Keira?"

"Yes." Cold. Disengaged.

"Well, I'm missing you lots and I promise I'll be back very soon." But there was no response. "Leila?"

"Why have you gone away?" It sounded plaintive and disconsolate, yet accusatory. Judgemental. Jess tried to maintain her composure, but almost immediately she felt it cracking.

"Oh, Leila." *How do I explain?* "It's just a few days, baby. I'll be back before you know it." But her heart was bursting and, without warning, the tears came. "Leila? Leila?"

"She's okay, Jess. Believe me," said Keira, wise beyond her years.

"Keep telling her, Keira. Keep telling her I'm coming back. I can't bear it if she might think I've left her again." She wiped a cheek with the back of her hand.

"I will. Don't worry. Go and do what you have to do and get back here. We're all missing you."

She dozed for a while then showered and dressed in a white linen shirt and jeans. Down in the reception area, Sujay was waiting for her.

"Hello, Miss Jess. Are you refreshed?"

"Yes thanks, Sujay. Are you hungry? Would you like to have some dinner?" She didn't feel terribly hungry, but thought it only polite to ask.

"Oh no. Thank you. My wife will be waiting for me at home. She will be cooking something. Perhaps we can take some tea? Lemon and ginger?" She nodded and he shouted something unintelligible to a passing waiter who bowed and scurried off.

They sat on sofas opposite each other and Sujay spread a map out on the table between them, sliding it around so they both could read.

"We are here in Kathmandu," he said leaning over the table, pointing at the spot. "Tomorrow we take a bus up here to Syapru Besi" – his finger tracked a winding road north-west and then north – "which is about one hundred and forty kilometres."

"Oh, not that far then."

"Yes, Miss Jess, but—"

"Jess," she jumped in and he nodded, smiling.

"But this is not your M1. The road is very winding and not very smooth, and it will take about seven or eight hours."

"Oh. Okay." She felt a little stupid. She still had a lot to learn.

"And then we have to walk east and follow the route of the Langtang Khola, that's the river, to Langtang, which is about thirty kilometres and will take us about three days."

"There are no roads, then?"

"No," he laughed. "No roads. Just trails. And then we pick up the trail that goes north-east across the mountains almost to the border with China. To the village of Chumtang. And this is another three days."

"Lisa … Alisha is in Chumtang?"

"Yes."

"Have you warned her we are coming?"

"It's not possible. There is no phone signal there."

"So how do you know she'll be there?" Sujay sat upright and smiled at her.

"She will be there. This is her home. There is no reason for her to leave and nowhere for her to go." Jess frowned. It was going to take them a week to get there, so presumably a week to get back. That's two weeks, plus a day or more in Chumtang. She was going to miss her flight back.

"Is there not a quicker way? I can't be away for more than two weeks." She didn't mean to sound agitated, but despite having been away for only a few hours, all she could think of was Leila and the girls; especially Leila. She'd been gone less than a day and already felt homesick; guilty she had rushed off and left her. Left them all. She began to regret ever starting out on this mad adventure. She'd never imagined it would be so difficult. *They tried to tell me.*

"No. I am sorry. If we walk for longer each day we can get back, maybe, but remember we have to think about the altitude. How are you at walking at altitude?" Jess looked at him without knowing how to respond. *Altitude?* Before she could say anything, the waiter brought the tea and set it down on the table.

"We're not doing any mountain climbing, are we?" she asked, unable to conceal the consternation she felt. She had visions of ice and snow and pickaxes and ropes. It was inconceivable. It was impossible.

"No, no, no. The walking is not too difficult. But the trails go up and down and we will get to four thousand five hundred metres at the highest point. You may not be able to go too fast and you may get a headache."

"Oh, I can manage a headache," said Jess, her mind put at ease. Or so she thought.

"Yes, but you might feel sick too. Sick and a headache. It's called altitude sickness and it is not good. If you get altitude sickness and it's severe, then you may not be able to carry on." Jess couldn't quite grasp the concept so decided the best thing was to dismiss it.

"I'll be okay."

"Jess. Neither you nor I know whether you will be okay. It affects different people in different ways. It does not matter if you are old or young, fit or not fit. Anyone can get altitude sickness and there is no medicine you can take to stop it, once it starts, apart from paracetamol or ibuprofen. If you get it bad and you don't descend immediately, then you could die." She looked at him in horror. *Stupid. Stupid. Stupid. Go home now. Leave it!* She took a sip of tea. The lemon and ginger somehow felt invigorating. Medicinal. She lifted her head and banished the negative thoughts.

"Well, then. We shall have to see. There's only one way to find out." She was pleased she hadn't done any research on altitude sickness before she came, or she might not have come at all. She trusted Sujay. Trusted he'd keep her safe, and if, for some reason, she couldn't get to see Lisa after all, then at least she'd tried. There was no giving up. Not yet.

"Okay. Do you have good walking boots?"

"Yes."

"Do you have sleeping bag and warm clothes?"

"Yes. All my stuff is new."

"Okay, then. I suggest you get some food and go to bed early and have a good sleep. I will be back tomorrow. We leave at eight." He folded up the map and they both stood up.

"Sujay?" she said, still clutching her teacup. "I'm not Lisa's twin sister."

"You are her sister though?"

"No." She looked at him and he frowned, obviously confused. *Who wouldn't be?* "We've never met before."

"You are not a relative?"

"I knew her father."

"Colonel Peter?"

"Yes."

"Colonel Peter had two identical daughters, but you are not sisters?" She could see this would take time.

"I'll tell you along the way."

***

She had dinner in the Krishnarpan, one of five choices of restaurant within the hotel, notable for its traditional Nepali cuisine. She sat on a cushion on the floor at the end of a long table, invited to join a group of adventurers from England the night before their flight to Pokhara and the start of their trek to the Annapurna Sanctuary. She chatted with a middle-aged couple who were on their eight or ninth trek and their third visit to the hotel, and they managed to give her some reassurance that, in all probability, she'd be fine at altitude. Just take it easy, they said. *Bistari* – slowly, not too fast. *If they can do it, I can do it.*

The woman expressed surprise and concern that she was travelling alone with a guide and was curious to understand the reason for the trip, but Jess remained non-committal, something in which she was well practised.

She ate samaya bajee, a mixed hors d'ouevres, then dal bhat, a traditional vegetable curry with lentils and rice, and finished off with fresh fruit. She declined the wine, determined to keep a clear head, but it was well after midnight before she could make her excuses and return to her room.

She rang home again before going to bed. She'd calculated it was around 7.00 p.m. UK time.

"How's Leila?"

"Oh, you know Leila, Jess. She keeps herself to herself."

Like mother like daughter.

"But she's not … unhappy?"

"No. She bathed the twins and put them to bed. She's up there now, reading them a story."

"Is she now?" Jess was pleased if it meant Leila's reading was getting better and proud her eldest seemed confident enough to assume responsibility for looking after the twins.

"Yes – oh, wait a minute, here she is. Leila, it's Mummy." There was a short pause while the phone changed hands. Jess's eyes darted around in anticipation.

"Hello?" Again, no emotion. No warmth. *Like mother like daughter.*

"Hello, darling. I hear you've been working very hard."

"I have given Sophie and Lucy a bath and I have read them a story and now they are fast asleep," she said proudly.

"Well done!"

"I will look after them for you, Mummy. So you don't have to worry about us." Jess choked back a tear.

"Love you, darling."

"Love you, Mummy."

"Bye, sweetie. Can I speak to Keira, please?"

There was another pause while Keira came back on the line.

"Hi."

"I'm leaving early tomorrow. I don't think I'll get much of a signal for a while, so I won't be able to call."

"We're okay, Jess. Honest. Call us when you get a chance."

"I will. Bye."

She ended the call and stared out of the bedroom window at the dim, sporadic lights of Kathmandu and over the rooftops in the direction of the mountains to the north.

Peter might have had the same view, she thought. Five years ago, he was preparing for a similar journey, at least as far as Langtang, but with little hope of finding Lisa alive. However difficult the trip might be for her physically, she wasn't burdened by the same mental pressure as Peter. She wasn't alone in the world. She had a family waiting for her and she would get back to them just as soon as she could.

She would find Lisa for him and she would tell her, and she would try to put things right. It was the least she could do.

CHAPTER 13

She presented herself at reception at eight o'clock sharp. Sujay was waiting for her, in a dark green shirt, the pockets and sleeves adorned with several badges denoting Nepal, the Himalayas and the logo of his employer, Everest Tours. He wore khaki cargo trousers that had pockets in each leg, over well-worn boots that looked to Jess more like trainers. He held a grey floppy hat that looked familiar.

"Morning, Sujay," she said, excited but apprehensive, laying her bulging rucksack on the floor.

"Good morning, Jess. I hope you had a good evening."

"The food was wonderful, but I confess I didn't sleep much, thinking about the trip."

"Well today you don't have to do much except sit on the bus. You can maybe sleep some. Have you had breakfast?"

"Yes."

"Have you checked out?"

"They said I don't need to. They'll move my big bag out of the room and keep it till I get back and then I'll check out the day I leave." He looked at her rucksack and gestured towards it with his hat.

"May I?"

"Yes, of course." Sujay picked it up, then set it back down on the floor. She looked at him.

"This is too heavy."

"What do you mean? It's perfectly okay. You don't have to carry it. I can manage."

"I'm sorry but when you are walking up a steep hill at four thousand metres you will say 'thank you, Sujay, for making me bring a lighter bag'."

"But I need everything in there." She didn't want to argue with him before they'd even set off, but she'd taken great care in choosing her inventory and even greater care packing it.

"You don't need the mattress. We'll be staying in village teahouses. They have beds. That's two kilogrammes."

"Oh, okay," she said. News to her.

"How many clothes do you have?"

"Er, I have a change of clothes for just about every day, that's about twelve of everything," she said, satisfied with her forward planning.

"You only need two or three at the most." She looked at him as if he were mad.

"But am I going to be able to do any washing?"

He laughed.

"You won't. Trust me, you won't want to and you won't need to."

"Will I get a shower?"

He made a rocking gesture with his hand. "Maybe. Maybe not."

She could tell he was beginning to enjoy this and felt her frustration growing. "What else do you have? Snacks, energy bars, cutlery, extra shoes …?" She looked increasingly uncomfortable as he continued to reel off the list. "Evening wear, pyjamas, hats, Swiss army knife, tin cup, head torch, extra batteries, medicines, toiletries?"

He stopped and she lifted her head to look at him.

"You forgot the gas bottle and burner," she said, and they both laughed. "Oh, Sujay!" She felt such an idiot, such an amateur, but she knew he knew best.

"Trust me, Jess. You are going somewhere where you need very little other than warm clothing and water. Everything else we can get along the way. How much water do you have?"

"I brought two bottles from the room and got a third from reception."

"Two litres is enough. We can buy in villages along the way. Water is very heavy. If you carry too much weight, it will be very difficult for you."

"What about these sticks?" she said, pointing to the two light alloy telescopic poles strapped to her rucksack.

"Yes. You will need these."

She gave in. She asked reception for a laundry bag and decanted most of the contents of her rucksack into it while he watched. He almost bent over double laughing when he saw her lift out a brightly coloured kimono style garment. "You have a dressing gown?"

"It's silk!" she shot back, "It doesn't take up any space!" but then snorted and threw it into the laundry bag in mock rage.

"Can I keep my toothbrush?" She held it up as if threatening to strike him with it.

"Toothbrush is okay."

"Towel?"

"Towel is okay."

She tied down the straps and handed the rucksack to him.

"Satisfied?" He took it and smiled. He was satisfied.

She handed the laundry bag to the man at reception and Sujay led her through the hotel courtyard and out of the large oak doors. She felt a little conspicuous in her brand new white artificial fibre trekking shirt, black cargo pants and shiny new boots, but no more so than any other European trekker ready to set off on their first journey. She now had only one change of trousers and two changes of shirt and underwear. As well as these, her red hiking jacket, a micro fleece and one set of thermals, rolled up and stuffed in the top of the rucksack, completed her wardrobe.

She looked at the front of her shirt, which already had a small dirty streak on it near the waistline. She tried to rub it off but just made it worse and she wished now that she hadn't picked white. She wondered how bedraggled she'd look the day she got back.

Mitesh was waiting for them in the minibus. They climbed aboard and she watched out of the grubby, dusty window as paradise receded into the distance and they were swallowed up in the madness and mayhem of Kathmandu.

***

The journey out of the city centre was slow and tedious such that within the first hour they'd only travelled twelve kilometres, the endless streams of traffic and the inevitable jams severely hampering progress.

Between animated bursts of conversation with Mitesh, Sujay tried to draw her attention to various points of interest, but Jess was taking little notice of him, captivated instead by the sights and sounds and smells of the city as viewed through the minibus windows. The relentless human activity on this alien urban landscape fascinated her, and at every turn, junction or stopping point, some unusual ritual was acted out, people going about their business, as they did everywhere else in the world, in the name of survival.

The traffic began to ease as the density of buildings decreased and soon she caught glimpses of greenery and open fields. They turned onto the Prithvi Highway and as the road twisted and turned and they gradually gained altitude, dense forest appeared on either side, the air wafting in through the open window becoming noticeably cleaner and cooler.

Jess stretched out on the bench seat with her head on her rucksack and tried to doze, but as the road was bumpy and the minibus noisy, she couldn't get any sleep. Sujay and Mitesh kept up their relentless chatter and she wondered how they could find so much to talk about for so long. But she managed to filter out most of the noise, and as the bus rattled and the road swung her left and right and left again, she thought of Chalton, the green fields of England and wondered how her girls were doing five thousand miles away.

After three hours, they'd covered more than half the distance, but as Sujay had explained, the further they travelled, the worse the road became and the rougher the journey would be. An hour later, they reached the Betrawoti river where it met and joined the Trishuli river at Betrawoti Bazaar.

"We will take a break now and have some lunch," said Sujay. Mitesh pulled the bus into a roadside café where other larger buses had stopped, and she could see many passengers milling around the car park. Nepalese, old and young alike, carrying bags and children, trekkers with rucksacks and walking poles accompanied by porters in tee shirts, tracksuits and soft trainers. Brightly coloured but dilapidated old buses, luggage piled high on their roofs, were parked haphazardly around the broken concrete ground that served as a car park.

They went indoors and queued cafeteria-style for steaming hot food; noodles, rice, vegetables, and the ubiquitous dal bhat slopped out with ladles into large plastic bowls. They seated themselves amidst the transient throng and deafening chatter that echoed around this most basic of restaurants, and Sujay and Mitesh gorged on a huge plate of noodles. Jess did her best to join in but was not particularly hungry and she left half of hers for the boys to finish.

That afternoon, the bus zigzagged its way steadily up the increasingly narrow and precipitous road, engine screaming and gears crunching, both men shouting and gesticulating to other drivers on either side of the road. And amidst the cacophony of horns and plumes of black smoke, the seemingly endless convoy of buses meandered and crawled their way up the mountain towards their mutual destination.

The road quickly worsened, degenerating into a single track strewn with small rocks and potholes. Jess looked out of the right-hand window. With mounting fear she realised they were travelling along a cliff edge with no barriers and, despite Mitesh's constant wrestling with the wheel in an attempt to find a smooth path, the bus rolled and pitched alarmingly, throwing its occupants from side to side, forcing her to grip anything she could to steady herself.

Finally, by four o'clock they reached their destination: Syapru Besi, 1,500 metres above sea level and the starting point for trekkers to the Langtang Valley. The bus pulled into a parking area alongside three others and Sujay helped her down.

"This is where we start," he said, and she stretched her aching back and legs. Mitesh passed down their rucksacks, jabbered something to Sujay in Nepali and got back behind the wheel.

"Where's he going?" asked Jess, suddenly anxious.

"He has to go back to Kathmandu."

"What, now?"

"Yes. He has work there tomorrow."

Jess couldn't hide her astonishment and was immediately concerned for him.

"But it'll be after midnight when he gets back. And along that road, he'll kill himself!"

"No. No. He is a good driver. He has two or three hours of light, and remember, it's all downhill." Sujay laughed. "He'll be back by nine thirty." Jess looked at him and shook her head. *Maniacs.* She noticed one or two buses continuing on up the road.

"Where are they going?"

"Border is just fifteen kilometres. Chinese migrant workers returning home. Are you ready to go?" She lifted her rucksack over one shoulder.

"Where's the hotel? I really need a shower."

"We don't stay here tonight. We start the walk now. We have time to get to the Vishna Lodge before dark. It's about two hours from here." Jess groaned.

"Must we?"

"You want to be back as soon as possible, then best we don't waste time." He pulled his grey floppy hat out of his pocket and put it on his head. She recognised it immediately. It was the same one Peter wore when they were on the boat. She thought of him standing here with Sujay, five years ago, in the same hat, ready to go off in search of Lisa. Could he ever have imagined that one day, a strange girl bearing an impossible likeness to his missing daughter would be here now, retracing his steps? The difference was that, unlike Peter, Jess knew Lisa was alive and where she was.

The air was noticeably cooler now and the combination of altitude and the weakening afternoon sun made her shiver. She pulled a red micro fleece out of her rucksack and put it on. To the west, she looked out across the valley at the terraced rice fields that stretched down the steep slopes in front of her and out of sight. The mountains on the other side were dark apart from their tips, which still glowed from the last rays of the setting sun, and large black birds of prey circled lazily above them, silhouetted against the darkening sky. They were already higher than the highest point in the UK and still had much higher to climb.

Another group of trekkers had set off ahead. The start of an adventure for them, but for her, it wasn't just an adventure. It was a mission.

CHAPTER 14

Sujay led the way up the main road for about two hundred yards to a police station where he presented their permits, explaining to her that as this was a national park, entry was strictly controlled. They turned right onto a path, passing a large rock which bore the legend "Langtang 30 km" in smudged blue paint.

A number of trekkers were up ahead, already putting distance between them, and others overtook as they started their ascent, tracking the route of the Langtang Khola, the river that fell away below them as they climbed higher with each step.

She tried to step up her pace, fearing that she was holding him up. "Bistari, Jess" said Sujay. "There is no need to rush."

"I'm fine," she said, but her breathing had already deepened from the exertion and they had only been going for fifteen minutes. "How will I know if I'm getting altitude sickness?"

"You probably won't feel anything below two thousand metres," he said but then smiled at her. "After that, you will know. The lodge is at about two thousand five hundred. We have plenty of time to get there before dark. Bistari!"

He deliberately slowed his pace, taking long slow strides while she trotted along dutifully behind him, and soon they were alone with the trees and the mountains and the fresh air, the last vestiges of sun warming their backs as it gradually slipped behind the mountains to the west.

She kept her head down in concentration, focusing on a path worn down by thousands of walking boots but still rough and stony. When eventually she did look up, she noticed Sujay was fifty yards ahead and she increased her pace to try and close the gap. Her legs shut down in protest. In an instant, the ache that had been growing steadily in her thighs was superseded by a dull numbness, the signals from her brain failing to get through to her feet, and she halted, unable to make her legs move.

She heard herself gasping for breath, and from nowhere an invisible vice seemed to clamp itself across her chest, tightening inexorably, constricting the airflow to her lungs. She bent forward and rested her forehead on her walking sticks, feeling a distant throb forming in her head.

"Jess? Are you okay?" Sujay had trotted back and was standing next to her.

"Yes," she panted, meaning "no", her lungs desperately attempting to suck in huge breaths through ever-narrowing tubes. "What – height – are – we?" she gasped.

"Oh, just under two thousand." Her faced creased up.

"What?"

"You'll be fine. We just go a bit more slowly. You have to acclimatise." She lifted her head and looked at him sceptically, unable to speak. *Acclimatise? We've been going less than an hour and I'm finished already!* She felt a wave of despair and leant forward to rest her weight on her walking poles. "Your breath will come back in a minute." He was right. As quickly as it came, the debilitating sensation subsided.

"How am I going to do this for six days at over twice the height?" she complained, cursing herself for her weakness.

"You will be okay. After a couple of days it will be much easier."

"A couple of days?"

"Yes. We just go slowly. You will get used to it. Believe me." She shrugged and tried to move her feet. They obeyed.

They went step by step, slowly and surely, and the path flattened out. Jess got her second wind and started to stride out. "Bistari," he said again and she slowed down. They got into a rhythm and, as he'd predicted, it got easier. As soon as she started to feel the ache in her thighs, she stopped for a moment and moderated her breathing.

They climbed higher and higher, and to her relief the path descended at one point and they were able to increase their pace.

"That's better. It's a lot easier going down," she said, almost beginning to enjoy it.

"I am afraid we are only going down to go up again."

"What? Oh, don't tell me that! How can that be?"

"There are a lot of ups and downs. That's why it takes so long. It's only twenty kilometres in a straight line, but thirty when you take in all the bends and contours."

She soon realised why they'd been descending. A steel rope suspension bridge spanned the rushing waters of the Langtang Khola, swollen by the rainy season that was now coming to an end. Sujay led her across and she moved nervously, sticks in one hand, the other tightly gripping the twisted steel handrail, while the bridge swayed and wobbled under her feet. She chose her steps carefully, concentrating her attention on where she placed each foot, the gaps in the wooden slats providing a glimpse of the foaming water a hundred feet below her that pummelled the rocks and boulders lining the riverbed. After five minutes of terror, she stepped onto solid ground at the other side, exhausted and relieved.

"Phew! Are there any more like that?"

"Just one or two. That's why we have to descend to cross the river, otherwise the bridge would be one or two kilometres long. You would not want to walk across a two-kilometre suspension bridge," he laughed. "Now, we climb. Bistari!"

He set off again and they climbed through dense forest of maple, bamboo and oak, the air filled by a continuous chorus of chirping and screeching amidst the rustle of the trees. She stopped to listen and caught a glimpse of something moving rapidly from branch to branch high above her. "Langur monkeys," he said. "There are many of them here, but don't worry, they won't come near us."

Jess was beginning to feel more comfortable now. She maintained a steady pace, and although it felt painfully slow, Sujay insisted it was the only way.

"That's why I said three days. Some people can do it in half that time, but it is more sensible to go slowly, otherwise you risk not getting there at all. Besides, we get to enjoy the scenery."

"Did you bring Peter this way?" she asked.

"Yes. Colonel Peter and I came along this path five years ago."

"Was he as slow as me?" she laughed, wishing he were here now and wondering if he was watching.

"He was slow. But he was not as young as you are and I think he was not so fit either."

"Is that right? Well I'm not feeling so young and fit at the moment," she said between breaths, stretching out each arm in turn, propelling herself forward on her poles.

"We have one more hour to the Vishna and then we can rest." Jess couldn't help but notice Sujay looked totally relaxed trudging uphill at altitude. She judged he was in his thirties and guessed he must have done this trek a hundred times already. She felt feeble and inadequate next to him, a pathetic European out of her depth, but she thought he was probably used to that. She had to accept this was his job, his backyard, and, after years of experience, he was bound to find it easy. A stroll in the park. Literally.

"Have you ever been to England?" she asked him.

"Only once," he said and then she cursed herself for her stupidity. *Must be the altitude.*

"Of course. The funeral. You came over with Alisha." She was careful to get her name right.

"Yes. She asked me to go with her."

"But you knew by then Peter had died?"

"Yes. We knew that. She did not feel strong enough to come alone, and as I knew her father, she said I should come too."

"I didn't see you there," she asked not so innocently, and felt a pang of conscience that she was putting questions to someone who had no obligation to provide any answers.

"Miss Alisha did not want anyone to know. She wanted to be there and say goodbye to her father but not to interrupt anything." Jess couldn't resist probing further.

"Did you see me?"

"No. We saw some people but they were all at a distance and walking away. I just thought they were all family members."

"What about two little girls? Did you see them?" She looked at him and he appeared to be thinking about the question.

"No. I was worrying about Miss Alisha. Worrying how she might be upset."

"And was she?"

"Not very. But then she is a Buddhist."

"Are you a Buddhist?"

"No," he smiled. "I am Hindu."

"Are you" – she hesitated, not sure how or even whether to ask the question – "friendly with Alisha?" He didn't flinch.

"Yes. We are friends. But I am not her boyfriend. I am married. I have two children," he said with pride. "A boy age six and a girl age two." Jess smiled.

"I have three children," she said, and she realised how proud she was too and how much she was missing them. Sujay stopped to look at her and she was grateful for the opportunity to take a rest.

"You have three?" he said, shaking his head in astonishment. "But you are not old enough!"

"I'm twenty-eight." She smiled, suddenly feeling a little abashed but nonetheless touched by his remark.

"And how old are your children?"

"Leila is nine and the twins are four."

"Oh my. You were a young mother. And your husband? How old is he?" Jess sighed. She suddenly feared if she were not careful, she might become the subject of the conversation.

"I don't have a husband. He left."

"I'm sorry." Sujay looked embarrassed.

"No. Don't be. It's okay." She was quick to try and reassure him. "We are all better off without him." That was certainly true. But then she thought for moment. *I wonder where Mo is now? Seems like a lifetime ago.* But she wanted to get back to Lisa. Alisha. She started walking again.

"So, when you found Alisha, that was the first time you'd met?"

"Yes."

"How did you know it was her?"

"Colonel Peter gave me a photograph. I always kept it. I pray to the god Vishnu that she is found one day. And he answer my prayer." Jess knew nothing of Hindu gods and hadn't heard the name, but before she could ask, Sujay continued. "Vishnu is the preserver of life. He shows compassion and kindness to all living things. This is similar to Buddhist."

"But how were you sure that the girl you heard about was actually Lisa? Alisha?"

"I was sure."

Jess frowned, unable to understand or rationalise his certainty. There were forces and beliefs at work here she simply didn't understand. Faith. Something she had neither recognised nor acknowledged existed, until she met Peter. Back then, they'd each embraced faith in their own way, even if they weren't aware of it.

They reached the top of the rise where the trail swung sharply left, and in the rapidly diminishing light, the vista opened up before them. Directly ahead and across the valley on the mountain opposite stood a few buildings scattered randomly across the hillside.

"There." Sujay pointed. "Village of Lamchi. This is where the Vishna Lodge is. About thirty minutes." She smiled at him and nodded. They set off again, buoyed and encouraged the end was in sight.

As darkness descended, they climbed the last few steps up the stone path to Lamchi and within minutes were standing in a courtyard outside a row of raised terraced huts, each with a bright blue painted door and small, green-framed windows. A few porters sat around, some smoking, some chewing, and several trekkers were outside their huts, attending to washing and rucksacks, one or two crossing the courtyard to the buildings opposite.

The courtyard was separated from the huts by a walkway and railing along which thin ropes, strung between wooden pillars that supported a pitched roof, were adorned with various items of clothing, drying in the evening air. Opposite the huts was a larger, well-lit building from which emanated the sound of revelry; tired and hungry trekkers laughing and discussing the highlights of their day over noodles and soup, dal bhat and beer. The canteen.

"Welcome to the Vishna Lodge," said Sujay. "We call this a teahouse. It is typical accommodation for all the travellers who visit here. Wait here, I will find the key for your room." He wandered off to another building next to the canteen and emerged a few minutes later with a large key on an even larger wooden fob. "Number six," he said, pointing to one of the huts, and she followed him up a few steps and onto the walkway, stopping outside a locked door that sported a large number six crudely painted in white. He unlocked the door and stood aside.

She stepped into a cold, gloomy and vaguely damp room with a flagstone floor, a tiny window on the far wall and sparsely furnished with a double bed and a small pine table. The floor looked damp and dirty, the window encrusted with cobwebs and filth, and a single light bulb dangled from the ceiling on the end of a twisted cord. The front window that looked out onto the walkway was similarly decrepit with smeared, cracked glass, and grey net curtains hung limply on each side. An electrical plug socket and switch precariously fixed to the door jamb were fed by a chaotic trail of wiring. She looked at the double bed.

"Where are you sleeping?" she asked, suddenly nervous.

"I sleep with the guides and porters over in the main building," he said, giving no indication that he may have understood what she might be thinking. She felt guilty, but relieved and then concerned for him.

"Can I not pay for a room for you?"

"No, no." He smiled. "Thank you. But we are used to sleeping all together. They are my friends and we will have a good laugh and maybe a little rum later." He winked at her and she nodded, content. He flicked on the light switch and the dirty bulb cast a dim yellow glow across the room. "There is a toilet and shower at the end of the building. If you want a shower then it's best to do it now. The water is heated by solar and it will not be hot in the morning."

"Thanks." The thought of a hot shower was good. He looked at his watch.

"It is now six thirty. I see you in the restaurant at seven. Okay?"

"Okay. Thanks." She dropped her rucksack on the bed and he backed out of the door, closing it behind him. She sat down on the bed; it was hard and unforgiving, and she noticed that for the first time since they'd left Syapru Besi, she felt cold. She shivered and rubbed her arms. *Shower!*

The shower and toilet were together in a large cubicle, lit by another yellow light bulb. The toilet was a simple ceramic floor plate with ridged sides and a hole in the centre. Next to it, and fed by a hosepipe poking through the back wall, was a large blue plastic bin full of water, a clear plastic jug tied to its rim by an orange nylon cord.

A cracked basin with a single wobbly tap was loosely fixed to the right-hand wall, and on the opposite side, a white plastic box with two dials hung crookedly and precariously.

A threadbare flexi hose sprouted from the box, culminating in a small, battered showerhead that lay forlorn on the wet floor next to a central drain hole.

She shivered in the cold. The temperature had dropped quickly when the sun went down and she thought it close to freezing but removed her boots and socks and stripped off, hanging her clothes and towel on a spare nail, careful not to dangle anything on the wet floor.

She picked up the showerhead and examined the controls, turning one of them slowly anti-clockwise. The box hummed into life and a jet of freezing water spurted out onto her leg, making her squeal in shock. Pointing the head down at the drain hole, she fumbled with each control until, eventually, something approaching warm water appeared, quickly learning that the balance of pressure and temperature was a tricky compromise.

With nowhere to mount the showerhead, she squatted on the floor, held the hose in one hand and moved the head around, directing the miserly trickle all over her. She found a thin bar of used soap on a tray next to the shower box, picked off some encrusted black hairs and used it to wash herself, but decided not to wet her hair, as she wasn't certain how it would dry.

Three minutes was enough, and sensing the temperature of the water dropping, she turned it off and hastily dried herself with her towel. She slipped her clothes back on and, carrying her boots and socks, trotted swiftly back to her hut in bare feet.

She felt clean but frozen, her breath condensing in the cold air as she stripped off again and quickly put on her thermal underwear. By the time she was fully dressed the chill in her body began to subside. Outside, she draped her towel over one of the suspended lines and walked briskly across to the canteen.

A blast of heat and steam cosseted her like a warm blanket. The brightly lit room had several rows of long tables strewn with plates, beer cans and maps. Around it, in animated conversation, trekkers of varying nationalities sat on long wooden benches, joshing good-naturedly with each other, laughing loudly in shared bonhomie, while porters in puffer jackets and woolly hats handed out steaming plates of food passed to them through a hatch to the kitchen.

Through the hatch, Jess could see men in mixed garb, flamboyantly banging woks and metal spatulas, shouting and arguing with each other amidst the occasional surge and flash of flame from the gas-fired ranges.

Sujay appeared and handed her a steaming mug of lemon and ginger tea, heavily sweetened with honey. He found her a space next to a group of Canadian women, and she sipped her tea, feeling the warmth trickle through her body.

"Hi!" said the loudest Canadian, rattling off the names of her friends, who all nodded, smiled or extended a hand, their names forgotten the moment they were introduced. "We're from Edmonton, Alberta. I guess you can tell? Where are you from?"

"England," she said, hands clasped around her mug.

Sujay was back.

"Can I get you some food? Some dal bhat and chapatti, maybe?" Jess was in no mood to choose and just nodded.

"Are you by yourself?" asked the loud Canadian whose name, Jess recalled, was Nancy.

"Yes. But I have a guide," she said jerking a thumb at Sujay's back as he approached the kitchen hatch.

"Aw. Shame you're alone. You wanna join our group?"

She smiled broadly but they both knew she was just being polite.

"Thanks. But I think we're probably going a different way."

"Where you headed?"

"Chumtang." Jess felt pleased with herself she'd remembered. It made her sound knowledgeable.

"Never heard of it. What's there?"

And from nowhere, she heard herself say, "My sister."

***

Sujay had told her, "Don't sleep with all your clothes on. You will be warm enough in your sleeping bag with just your base layer." And despite all instincts to the contrary, she followed his advice.

The room had been like an icebox but he'd given her a hot-water bottle, and having clasped it to her middle for a few minutes, she kicked it down to the bottom of the sleeping bag where her feet now luxuriated in its warmth.

She had no way of communicating with home. As expected, there was no mobile signal, and the Wi-Fi was down, so she couldn't use her phone for anything other than to take one or two photos of the Canadians. They exchanged email addresses, pledging to keep in touch. She thought it unlikely they would, but they'd been good fun, very friendly and welcoming. The shared experience of adventure, she thought.

She thought again about the days ahead. *What will happen when I meet Lisa? Alisha?* Alisha presumably didn't know Jess existed, any more than she knew Lisa had been alive. How would she react? How would she be able to explain?

She had run through a speech in her head, but she knew that when the time came to deliver it, it would all come out differently. There was no escaping the fact that her arrival in Chumtang would come as a shock, but she was coming in the spirit of friendship. She was coming to square the circle, just as Peter had for her.

She had no idea of the time. Everything was quiet outside, the last trekker long since turned in. "Breakfast is at six thirty tomorrow," Sujay had told her, "and then we climb to three thousand metres." She needed to sleep, and she did.

CHAPTER 15

Jess stopped, flicked off the straps of her rucksack and lowered it to the ground along with her walking poles. The morning sun was warm on her face and she decided that as well as the trekking jacket she'd removed earlier, she could dispense with the fleece.

The morning had started misty and cool, but within an hour the mist began to dissipate and the temperature rose steadily. Like everyone else, she'd been woken by the cockerel, a shrill crowing that obviated the need for an alarm clock, but had then lain for a while, curled up in her sleeping bag, listening to the sound of people stirring outside, putting off the moment when she would inevitably have to expose herself to the cold morning air.

Her hot-water bottle had some residual warmth so she used its contents to wash her hands and face, and after a quick breakfast of hot tea and porridge, they set off along with some of the other trekkers on the slow climb to Saramlang. As usual, they were overtaken and left bringing up the rear. Before long, they were alone with the mountain views and the sounds of the Himalayas.

"Bistari," he had said for umpteenth time and she felt as if she was finally becoming acclimatised to the altitude.

"How high are we now?" she asked, without breaking her rhythm, slow though it was.

"I think about 2,700 metres." A long way from their peak, she thought, but surely by then she'd be a seasoned trekker? "We walk for the whole day and stay in another teahouse tonight. We should be in Langtang by lunch tomorrow."

"Are we staying in Langtang?" she asked. She couldn't dispel the fear that, if there had been a landslide there once, there could be another. She knew it was irrational, but what would Peter think if, having lost one daughter in Langtang, another might suffer the same fate? She brushed the thought aside. *There is no such thing as fate.*

"No. We will carry on. The tourist trail ends there and we go on along the Chumtang mule trail. All the other tourists and trekkers will return the same way.

"Did you and Peter get any further than Langtang?"

"No. We did not know Miss Alisha was alive then."

It was a sobering thought. So near and yet so far. In the absence of memory or identification, Lisa, just like Leila, may as well have been a stone's throw away. And if, by some stroke of good fortune, Lisa had been found, Jess wouldn't be here now and Leila wouldn't be safe at home. It was too complicated to unravel and consider the possibilities, too disturbing to consider alternative hypotheses. Whatever had happened, had happened, and there could be no regrets.

"Had you been to Chumtang before?"

"No. There is no reason to go there. It is not on the tourist trail. I just went once to find Miss Alisha."

"And now you're taking me there to find her again?"

"It is my job," he smiled at her.

They walked on, the mountains ahead of them, towering and majestic, reaching into the clear blue sky, amidst the constant rush of waterfalls cascading down from their left, disappearing beneath their feet and under the trail on their journey to the river far below. At times, they crossed over the rushing water on handmade bridges built from logs and branches. Sujay stopped and pointed at a giant peak to the north-east.

"Langtang Lirung," he said. "It is over seven thousand metres." Its snow-capped peak was visible above layers of thin cloud. She had never seen anything like it before other than in books or on TV, and for once she understood the true meaning of awesome.

By 1 p.m., they had reached the village of Tandhola. There were no teahouses here but Sujay approached one of the small houses adjoining the path and climbed up the stone steps to the open door. Three small children with dirty faces and ragged clothes ran barefoot to meet him and he greeted them fondly. A middle-aged woman emerged from the house, squinting in the sunlight, wiping her hands on a tea towel. She and Sujay talked excitedly for two or three minutes while chickens ran around their feet and a large cow bellowed from the adjacent barn.

"Come!" he called to Jess with a wave. She mounted the steps and the children ran up as if to greet her, but stopped and eyed her with a mixture of curiosity and disdain. "We take some lunch now," he said and disappeared inside.

Jess followed him into the house. It was dark and it took a moment for her eyes to adjust, but a shaft of light through a roof window revealed a large room with three beds at one end, a pine table and chairs in the middle and large, brightly coloured cushions scattered haphazardly on the floor. An open fire set against one wall was home to several blackened pots and pans, one of them steaming, and next to it stood a rudimentary kitchen cabinet with Formica worktop, on which lay vegetables in various stages of preparation, including a pile of chopped greens that resembled cabbage. And on top of a tall mahogany dresser that seemed incongruous in its surroundings, and which was laden with mismatched crockery, sat a small black and white TV that chattered and squawked, its fuzzy picture swirling with lines of horizontal interference.

"Namaste," said the woman with a wide grin, her hands pressed together in traditional pose, her parted lips exposing several missing teeth.

"Namaste," Jess reciprocated. The woman wore a bright red cardigan with yellow hoops over a buttoned-up grey shirt, a heavy dark blue skirt that almost reached the ground, heavy striped socks and battered plastic sandals. Her black hair was tied back in a knot and her skin was brown and gnarled. Jess thought she looked in her fifties but then realised with shock that unless she was the childrens' grandmother, she could be no more than thirty-five.

"Please, sit down," said Sujay, and the woman returned to her stove. Jess dropped her rucksack and sat on a chair, noticing the children standing in the doorway were watching her studiously. She smiled at them but getting no response, foraged in the top of her rucksack and brought out a packet of boiled sweets. The kids' eyes lit up and they ran over, plunged a hand in turn into the bag and ran outside squealing with delight. She looked up at Sujay who was watching her.

"Sorry," she said, "excess weight." But it made him laugh and she laughed with him.

They feasted on stir-fried vegetables, rice, chapattis and tea, although the woman declined to join them, continuing to chop and cook, attend to her stove and bring them plate after plate of steaming food whilst maintaining, without drawing breath it seemed, her interminable dialogue with Sujay.

When they'd eaten all they could, Sujay got up abruptly.

"Time to go."

"What about clearing up?" she asked, her housekeeping instincts kicking in.

"No. She will do that." But Jess felt uncomfortable.

"Can I give her something?"

"Yes. You can give her." She got her purse from her rucksack and pulled out a ten dollar note.

"Is this okay?" she asked him, looking for guidance.

"It is too much. Two dollars will be enough. If you give her ten dollars, then every time I bring people here she will expect ten dollars." Jess understood the logic but shook her head in dismay. Two dollars for a three-course lunch for two was an insult, she thought. She had to believe he knew best, but it didn't make her feel any better. She wandered over to the woman who put her hands together again and smiled at her expectantly.

"What's 'thank you'?" she called.

"Dhanyavada," he said.

Jess put her hands together. "Dhanyavada," she repeated and took the woman's hands, thrusting two dollars into it.

"Dhanyavada," said the woman and stepped back, clearly happy with her pittance. Jess turned and saw the kids were back. She fished out a handful of sweets from her bag. The children stepped forward, hands raised, and she dropped three of the paper-wrapped sweets into each. They beamed and ran off into the sunshine, shouting and laughing.

They marched on into the afternoon sun stopping only to drink from their water bottles, the colour of the mountains changing gradually from green and yellow to a rich, dark ochre in the fading light.

"How much time do you spend away from your family?" she asked him at one point.

"Maybe two weeks or three weeks. It depends on the group I am taking. Then I have one or two days at home before I go off again."

"You must miss them," she said, knowing herself how it felt to miss the girls.

"Yes, of course. But I must work."

"Does your wife work?"

"She does some laundry and cleaning, but mostly she looks after our children."

"Must be very hard for you."

"No," he said without rancour. "It's what we have to do."

"Where did you meet your wife?" she asked, curious to understand the path of true love in Nepal.

"She was given to me. It was an arranged marriage." Jess sighed, but mainly at her own ignorance. She'd been in Nepal only a couple of days and had already learnt a lot about their way of life, their attitudes, their hospitality, their faith, their work ethic and their poverty. She wished she could live up to their example.

"But you do love her?"

"Of course!"

***

She lay in her sleeping bag in her room in the teahouse at Saramlang, hot-water bottle at her feet, the bag pulled over her head, still wearing her thermal hat.

Her head was thumping. By mid-afternoon they'd reached 3,400 metres when the headache had started. She'd tried to ignore it, but it wouldn't go away and got worse as they climbed higher until it felt like a sledgehammer pounding her skull.

Sujay gave her a maximum strength ibuprofen but it did little more than take the edge off the pain. To make matters worse, she felt vaguely nauseous and didn't want to eat anything for supper, but Sujay insisted she try some plain boiled rice and she did her best to get it down. He convinced her that she needed the energy but she was beaten by the smell of fried eggs and dal bhat in the busy canteen and begged to be allowed an early night.

In the circumstances, she had neither the will nor the energy to take a shower. Instead, she had another pill and a cup of sweet lemon and ginger tea and climbed into her bed, praying the discomfort would soon go away. At this moment, in this place, she thought, personal hygiene was of little consequence to her or anyone else.

She was much better the next day, although she felt as if she had a hangover and approached the day's climb with some trepidation.

"Today we climb to 3,700 metres, then back down to 3,500 metres," he said to her over a breakfast she didn't want. He tried to encourage her. "You must eat some porridge." She knew it was for her own good, but it looked like gruel and had the texture of lumpy wallpaper paste. But she forced it down and to her relief, it stayed down.

The weather was fine and sunny when they set off though the temperature was just a few degrees above freezing, and she remained wrapped up in her warm clothing until around 10 a.m. when she could start divesting herself of some of the outer layers.

She said little on the way up the trail, concentrating on her breathing, refraining from overexertion, desperately hoping the nausea and headache would remain at bay. They did.

They stopped and sat on a boulder and she drank the previously boiled water from her bottle.

"Yuck!" she grimaced. "Why can't we just drink the water from all these springs and waterfalls? It's everywhere." She gestured around her at the fast-flowing water, crystal clear and cold as ice.

"It might be okay, but might not," he said. "You cannot take the risk. We have our own special bacteria here in Nepal that your English stomach will probably not like. So you have to drink the boiled water." She nodded. She knew he was right, of course; she just felt like moaning. She was tired, her legs ached and her head was thick, but she was thankful the nausea was gone.

"How much further?" she said, taking another swig.

"Thirty minutes." *Everything in Nepal is thirty minutes away!*

"Are you sure?"

He grinned, rocking one hand from side to side. "Thirty minutes-ish."

It was forty-five. And then she was there. On that ridge. Looking down as Peter had, broken and defeated, as perhaps

Lisa had in her battered state, broken and bloodied, but alive. Looking down on the desolation of Langtang.

"Jess, I think we must be going now!"

CHAPTER 16

Over the previous few years, a new village at Langtang had gradually established itself, born out of the perseverance of a few determined survivors and supported by the ever-increasing number of tourists who, for whatever reason, began to return to the area. Jess and Sujay followed the trail down to the village, descending to a sign that greeted their arrival, proudly proclaiming the altitude: 3,500 metres.

Amongst the new dwellings, numerous teahouses and restaurants had sprung up, the village's notoriety one of the factors in its renaissance. For all the trekkers milling around the central area, this was the end of the line. The place to rest, take some pictures, take a sombre stroll amongst the few visible remains of the old village, maybe even pay their respects, before wending their way back along the same trail, back to Syapru Besi.

They sat outside in the cool sunshine sipping lemon and ginger tea and eating a slice of pizza. *Pizza! I've come all this distance, to the very edge of civilisation, and they've got pizza.* She had to laugh. It was a poignant reminder of her own world and, as she did in every spare moment, she imagined the girls at home with Keira, laughing and playing, and craved the day would soon come when she could get back to them.

"It's very busy here," she said between bites.

"Yes. It gets more and more busy each time. It's good."

"But we're not staying?"

"No, we have to move on. There are no more villages or teahouses between here and Chumtang, but I know a place we can stay." She sat back in the chair and exhaled loudly, rubbing her stomach. He looked at her half-eaten pizza. "You must eat." It sounded like an instruction.

"Oh, Sujay. I can't eat any more. I'm full," she complained. It had sounded like a nag, but she knew he meant it for the best.

"We go to four thousand metres. You need the energy."

"Okay, okay," she said in mock exasperation and reluctantly resumed her lunch. A woman she recognised walked over, fully tooled up, rucksack on her back, ready to go.

"Hi Jess!"

"Oh, hi Nancy."

"You made it then?" The other Canadian girls wandered up behind her.

"Yes. Just about, but we've a way to go yet."

"Aw well, we're about to head back. Have a good trip. Say hi to your sis!"

The group waved at her as they filed past and before long they were small specks on the trail behind them.

"Sujay?" He turned to her as she spoke. "Lisa. Alisha. Does she really look like me?"

"Very much. You look like the same person. You are the same height and have the same hair colour. But she has a big scar on her face."

"Was that because of the ... accident."

"Yes. The landslide. I don't know what happened to her. I mean, how she hurt herself. She does not walk very well. Sometimes she has a stick. She could not walk like you do." He paused for a moment.

"But you are not the same person. You are a happy person." Jess tried to rationalise his comment. *I'm a happy person?* She'd never had cause to consider it but had to accept that, yes, she probably was happy; at least, as happy as she could be. She may have had some difficulties over the years, but then, she imagined, didn't everyone? But she'd come through it all and now there was much to look forward to. "You always have a smile," he said, "even when you are angry." She put on a look of mock indignation and he laughed at her.

"I'm never angry!" she protested, leaning over to slap his arm, and he clutched it, grimacing, as if hurt. She sat back and they were quiet for a moment.

"Are you a happy person?" she asked him gently, still curious about him.

"Yes. I am a happy person." He stretched out an arm, looked around and then pointed to the immense Langtang Lirung towering over them. "How could I not be happy? Here. In my country. Look." She turned her head and had to agree that, even after just a few days, she had become entranced by the Himalayas.

"But what about Alisha."

"She is Buddhist." Jess frowned. She didn't understand.

"Does that mean she can't be happy?"

"She seeks a different kind of happiness, and she has not found it yet."

"How will she know when she finds it?"

"She will know." Jess felt she was no clearer. She wanted to be prepared for when they eventually met. She had the advantage over Lisa. She knew she was coming, knew that they were lookalikes, knew who her father was and knew who she was. But Lisa, Alisha, was totally in the dark. What on earth would Alisha do when she saw her and heard the truth? The more she thought about it, the more she worried that maybe this had been a big mistake. She should have let things be.

She'd been told Alisha was content, living in her remote paradise, free from the cares and worries of the modern world, oblivious to the thoughts and emotions that rattled around Jess's head as a matter of routine. And now she was going to open up old wounds, disrupt the girl's very existence and introduce potentially serious complications. For what? For whom? For her own peace of mind? Her own gratification? She couldn't say. Maybe it was the altitude fogging her brain.

"How will she react when she sees me?" She looked at him closely, trying to see into his mind, anticipating the response but wary of hearing the answer. He took a moment and it made her feel uneasy.

"She will welcome you. She will give you everything she has, if you want it. And she will do everything in her power to ease your suffering."

CHAPTER 17

They plodded slowly uphill on the north-east trail out of the village, heading for the Chinese border, leaving Langtang and all the other trekkers behind. The landscape was bleak and devoid of trees, and across the valley she could see the rice terraces cascading down the hillside and, randomly dotted amongst them, a hut topped off with the inevitable feathery plume of white smoke.

Sujay walked a step or two in front of her, leading her on, and, watching his back, she could not stop thinking about what he had said. *My suffering? What does he mean? I'm not suffering.* Maybe it was just a poor choice of words, the meaning lost in translation. She certainly had a lot on her mind but it centred mainly on whether she was doing the right thing and what she was trying to achieve, and that amounted to no more than a minor torment in the scheme of things. Natural reticence in the face of the unknown. Her trip may not achieve anything other than to put minds at rest. *Whose?*

Or was this diminutive Nepali simply demonstrating his innate perspicacity? His ability to see through the façade and focus on the core; identify the truth, the truth being that she felt an obligation. That she felt undeserving and privileged, especially here amongst some of the poorest people she had ever met, and she owed that privilege to someone she could never thank; someone to whom she could never repay the kindness in any way, other than to do what she was doing now. Seeking out the closest thing to Peter she could find, pour out her heart and express her gratitude; salve her conscience. Ease her suffering.

The sickness returned. It started with a distant, sporadic throb every minute or so, gradually increasing in frequency and severity until it became synchronous with every step, so that every time she put a foot down, a hammer struck in her forehead. He gave her an ibuprofen and she drank deeply from her bottle, but the boiled, sanitised water tasted rank and adulterated and merely exacerbated the nausea building inside her.

It was late afternoon and cold. The sky was a mass of grey and, without any direct sun, the temperature had dropped to just above freezing, so they were both wrapped up in fleeces and jackets, her thermal hat pulled down over her ears. They had been climbing steadily for over two hours, and after a particularly steep section, her thighs burnt from the build-up of lactic acid. She stopped for breath and let the pain in her legs subside. She leaned forward on her poles, resting her pounding forehead on the back of her gloved hands, the thump-thump of her heartbeat echoing in her ears, swallowing ominously, trying to suppress the inevitable.

"Sujay?"

"Yes, Jess?"

"Thank you – for making me – bring – a lighter bag." She affected a grin despite her discomfort and he laughed. She'd remembered his comment back at Dwarika's.

"How much further?" she gasped.

"Oh. Thirty minutes or so," he said, and had she not felt so ill, she would have laughed out loud at the utter predictability of the answer. She looked up at him with a wry smile and snorted, but without warning, lost control of her stomach, projecting a stream of vomit over a clump of thorny shrubs that bordered the trail.

"Ugh!" She coughed and spluttered and vomited again; lunch, breakfast, last night's dinner, she couldn't tell, but it kept coming, and as it did, the pounding in her forehead and temples intensified to the point where she thought her head might explode. She dropped to her knees and let go of her poles, her body tipped forward, supported by both hands pressed flat onto the dirt. "Oh God!" she wailed and convulsed once more, but this time there was just bile. She was empty. She stayed there for a moment, head bursting, chest heaving, gasping for breath, and then flopped back on her bottom, head between her knees. After a few minutes, the breathing stabilised, the headache subsided to a manageable rhythmic throb and she wrapped her arms over her woolly hat in a futile attempt to stop her brains rattling.

"Are you okay?" He was crouching down in front of her and it sounded like the stupidest question she'd ever heard, but she had no energy to counter it and no desire to converse; she just wanted to die. But she found the strength to lift her head. Her neck muscles screamed in protest, and the pounding in her head briefly returned until she opened her eyes. "Look at me," he said, pointing two fingers at his own eyes, and she obeyed, as best she could. He examined her pupils and she watched him intently for a moment until he smiled at her. "You're okay," he said, getting to his feet.

She looked at him, her jaw dropping open in amazement, and then put her head back between her legs and moaned.

"When you are ready."

He helped her to her feet and handed her the discarded walking poles.

"Thank you," she said, the weariness in her voice heavy and resigned. She noticed he had strapped her rucksack to his chest. She wanted to protest but knew it was futile. He put one hand on her back and helped her take the first step.

It took another hour, but she got there. The little stone house was much like the one they had been in the previous day. A wood fire burnt strongly in a brick fireplace built into a corner alcove, and a woman busied herself next to it, chopping vegetables on a wooden board with a large meat cleaver. A baby, barely one year old, sat on the floor on a goatskin rug, looking bewildered, sucking on a sugary stick, while Sujay sat on some cushions next to a man who puffed periodically on a clay pipe, filling the air with an acrid and curiously pungent aroma. The men seemed to be engaged in discussing important worldly matters, and although she couldn't understand anything they said, she found the sound strangely comforting, curled up and dozing as she was on the threadbare mattress behind them.

The woman had given her lemon and ginger tea sweetened with lots of honey and she'd taken two full-strength paracetamol which seemed to have done the trick. To her astonishment, she actually felt hungry, and the smell of frying food wafted around the room, teasing her senses and making her salivate.

They sat cross-legged on the floor and ate from wooden bowls using chopsticks. Noodles, with shredded vegetables, doused in a thick black sauce that came out of a bottle. Sujay and the man topped theirs off with a virulent red sauce and it looked to her like a trial of strength as to who could eat the most chillies. They drank tea, their cups constantly refilled from a huge teapot, and it tasted different from the tea she had got used to.

"This is Chinese influence," he explained.

After dinner, the men opened a plastic bottle and poured a clear liquid into two shot glasses before downing it in a single gulp.

"You like to try?" he said.

"What is it?" She was not at all sure she wanted try and was worried about the consequences for her recently consumed dinner.

"Rice wine. Home-made." Their host poured out a measure and Sujay handed her the glass, which she sniffed tentatively.

"I hold you responsible for this," she said, and they all watched as she put her lips to the glass and then threw her head back, swallowing in one. The fiery liquid burnt her throat and she gasped in pain, massaging her neck with her spare hand. The men slapped their thighs and bellowed in laughter, while the woman, sitting quietly, breast-feeding her baby, looked on in amusement.

"More?"

"No!" she said, and thrust the shot glass back at Sujay. "Thank you." But as hideous as the rice wine tasted, she felt a glow of warmth inside her and a delicious drowsiness take hold. She looked around but could see no door other than the one through which they had originally entered. Nor had she had noticed any other buildings, but then she'd been weak and tired at the time. "Er, Sujay, where do we sleep? Is there another room?" she asked, fearing she already knew the answer.

"We sleep here."

"Where?"

"Here." He gestured around the room.

"Where?" she persisted.

"You sleep here on this mattress and we pull this curtain across and we sleep over there." He pointed to three wooden benches arranged on two sides at the other end of the room.

"But this is their bed," she objected.

"That's okay. You are their guest." She felt bad about it but it was pointless arguing and she had other things on her mind. She leant close to his ear.

"Where's the toilet?" she whispered, feeling stupid because, in all probability, the man and woman wouldn't understand what she was saying. But the man immediately said something unintelligible and waved in the air. Sujay laughed.

"Come. I show you. Put your jacket on." He grabbed a head torch, led her outside into the freezing night air and down the steps to the trail. On the opposite side of the path, a wooden structure like a tiny garden shed on stilts was built into the hillside. He shone the light on it. "Here." He gave her the torch and she stepped onto a plank that bridged the gap between the path and the shed-like structure and onto the narrow walkway around it. She turned back to him, perplexed.

"The door's around the other side," he pointed. She stepped gingerly along the walkway and around to the opposite side. There was no door. The shed was open to the air, facing out across a valley that was invisible in the black of the night. The hut contained a wooden box topped with an inset black plastic toilet seat. She shone the torch over the seat, but there was nothing but a black hole, and twenty or thirty feet down, the torchlight revealed a swathe of accumulated effluent strewn across the rocks, grass and shrubbery below. She groaned but got herself organised and sat there, entranced by the millions of stars twinkling above her, imagining how spectacular the view might be in daylight.

She fished in her pocket and used a wet wipe but then was at a loss to know what to do with it, deciding eventually there was no other choice than to drop it down the hole.

Back inside the hut, the curtain had been hung around her bedroom area and the woman brought her a bowl of warm water and a white flannel. Behind the curtain, she stripped off to her underwear and rubbed herself all over with the warm flannel, leaving her feeling surprisingly refreshed and relatively fragrant. She put her thermals back on and peeked through a gap in the curtain. The man and woman were curled up on the benches, fast asleep, the baby snuggled up to the woman's chest, her husband snoring loudly. Sujay was on the third bench, fully clothed, sleeping bag rolled up under his head, clearly still awake.

"We're up at six," he said. "Goodnight."

"Goodnight, Sujay."

The fire continued to glow in the corner and the room was still warm as she wrestled herself into her sleeping bag and closed her eyes; as ever, alone with her thoughts.

CHAPTER 18

She looked back at the Chinese couple and waved at them as she and Sujay set off along the trail on the penultimate leg of their journey to Chumtang.

They had feasted on rice and eggs and tea for breakfast and she had tried to give them twenty dollars, but Sujay said dollars were of little use to them and so she gave them two thousand rupees instead. Sujay had snorted a little but she pointed out that as he was unlikely to bring other Western visitors here, it could do no harm, and she desperately wanted to show them her gratitude. Despite the relatively large sum of money, they seemed unmoved, but they took it graciously and bowed.

"We have another day's walk and one more night and then we shall be in Chumtang by tomorrow afternoon." They'd only been walking for a few days but to her it seemed like months, so far removed was she from her own environment. But the weather was fine, the trail flat if not descending gradually, and she felt fortified by the food and rest. When they'd started out, the temperature had been barely above freezing so they'd wrapped up warm, but soon she was able to discard her fleece.

"It is easy now. There are one or two inclines but we are coming down to three thousand five hundred metres." She was grateful to hear it. She couldn't bear a repeat of yesterday, but then she was reminded she'd have to come back in a few days and run that gauntlet again.

She hadn't showered since the first day, but as Sujay had warned her at the outset, normal standards of personal hygiene didn't apply out here and, in truth, she felt no ill effects from wearing the same clothes and washing with little more than a tiny wet wipe, and last night's self-administered bed bath had been positively luxurious. It was a revelation to her that, out in the wild, the most basic of items could seem so important.

Peter had never got this far. He'd turned back at Langtang, convinced that no one could have survived, equally convinced that, even if Lisa had somehow beaten the odds, she would have let someone know. Cried for help. She wondered how he might have fared at over four thousand metres but it was an academic thought. The extraordinary thing was Lisa had come this way, with broken bones and a blank memory, apparently transported on the back of a mule. Two and a half days from Langtang, not counting her excruciatingly painful resurrection from the rubble. From her initial disparaging comments about Lisa's apparent conduct and assumed motivations, she had built up more than a little respect for this person she had never met, and her admiration grew with every step. Lisa was probably an extraordinary person. But then, after all, she was a Jeffries.

By late morning, they had descended to three thousand metres and, in comparison to the previous day, the air was rich and clear, so she could breathe normally and enjoy the scenery. They dropped below the tree line and the trail swung left and right, up and down, across raging streams; and, as always, the valley on their right afforded spectacular views of the mountains when visible through the gaps in the trees.

They reached a small plateau where the course of the trail swung round to the left but widened out on the right to an area the size of a small car park. The trees on the right had disappeared, having at some time in the past slipped down the mountainside, and the gap they left gave an uninterrupted view of the peaks in the distance.

Three men stood at the extreme right-hand edge, some thirty feet away, one of them holding the reins of a brown, heavily laden mule, all three smoking. They stood, heads down, scuffing their feet on the ground, a spare hand lazily stuffed in a tracksuit trouser pocket.

Sujay stopped for a split second but she had already looked across, and seeing one of the men look up, she waved at them.

"Namaste!" she called.

"Keep going," he said tersely and quickened his pace.

"What is it?" She sensed something in the tone of his voice and could see his eyes focused on the men as he walked.

"Chinese. Keep going. Don't look at them." But as he spoke, two of them exchanged words, flicked away their cigarettes and sauntered across to their right, closing the distance, on course to intercept them on the path ahead. Sujay stopped twelve feet away from the men and held an arm out to his side, indicating she should wait.

Jess stood behind him and to one side, studying the men and feeling increasingly apprehensive. They were dressed in filthy sweatshirts, tracksuit bottoms and battered trainers, and the shorter of the two had a long leather scabbard, housing a machete, dangling from his belt. The taller one stepped forward and said something in Chinese. Sujay replied curtly in the same language. She had no idea what they were saying but it disturbed her. The exchange was repeated, this time with a little more urgency. Until now, she hadn't seen Sujay look so tense and she began to feel frightened.

The tall one said something and in response, Sujay launched into an extensive diatribe. The two Chinese men slowly separated and as the taller one approached, hands in pockets, the other went wide, disappearing from her peripheral vision. The conversation became more animated and aggressive, and Sujay stepped forward in an attempt to reinforce whatever point he was trying to make, gesticulating with both hands. Jess remained rooted to the spot, not knowing what to do but feeling her heart race. She twisted her neck to see the shorter Chinese man standing motionless twelve feet behind her, smirking.

When Sujay and the tall one were just two feet apart, Sujay lifted one arm again and shouted as if to wave the man away. In response, the man removed his hand from his pocket and poked Sujay in the stomach with a swift punching movement.

Sujay flinched and Jess ran forward.

"Sujay!" she cried as he took a few steps back, slowly at first, but then his backward motion gathered pace and he lost balance, falling backwards, a hand pressed against his middle. She saw the puzzled expression on his face and the blood oozing out between his fingers. She looked up in horror at the tall guy, who held a long thin blade in his right hand, glistening red. He casually wiped it on his trousers, closed the blade and slipped it into his pocket. "Sujay!" she screamed again and dropped to her knees beside him as he slowly lay back on the ground.

The second Chinese man was on her in a second, grabbing her from behind by her rucksack, and as the taller one shouted instructions he dragged her kicking and struggling across the open area towards the edge, one hand gripping her hair tightly. He stopped a few feet from the cliff edge, arm round her throat as she continued to struggle, trying to get free of his grip. She could see over the side. It was a sheer drop and from her angle she couldn't see the bottom. The tall one arrived in front of her.

The two of them jabbered excitedly, laughing and sneering while the third man simply watched from a distance, holding onto the mule. The tall one took a step forward and roughly tore at the clasps of her rucksack, grinning at her, open-mouthed. He stank of tobacco, garlic and sweat, and she saw what few teeth he had left were either black or yellow.

The one holding her pulled off her rucksack and threw it on the ground, resuming his grip around her neck, while the tall one yanked down the zip on her jacket and ripped it open. His partner pulled the jacket down off her shoulders, pinning her arms behind her. The man in front felt around in the inside pockets of her jacket and pulled out her iPhone, squealed in triumph and held it aloft like a trophy, before slipping it into the back pocket of his trousers.

She screamed but he grabbed her mouth with one hand and squeezed tightly, stifling the cry, while the man behind slipped his spare hand round to her chest and roughly groped her through her white tee shirt, laughing and grunting lasciviously.

The tall one barked an order and the groping stopped. She shook with fear, feeling hands on her shoulders, pressing her down, forcing her to her knees, the guy crouching behind her, gripping her tightly round the neck. He resumed his groping and grunting as the tall one looked down and sneered at her. She saw both his hands had disappeared down the inside of his tracksuit pants, and he was working them up and down vigorously. He inched forward, pulled his hands out and tugged his trousers to the ground, his phallus springing upwards to attention.

He held himself in one hand and put his other behind her head, gripping and tugging her hair with such force she shouted out in pain; and then she knew. They had already killed Sujay. They were going to rape her and then they were going to kill her and throw her over the edge. She screamed with all the power in her lungs and the tall one screamed along with her, as if mocking her. She opened her eyes to look at him in defiance, her teeth bared in rage. Whatever happened next she was going to hurt him.

He put one hand behind her head, pulling it towards the other gripping his phallus, and only then did she notice he had a third, larger hand around his testicles, the knuckles white with pressure. *He has three hands?*

The tall man's scream intensified. The neck of his sweatshirt had tightened and appeared to be choking him. He released her hair, moving his free hand up to his neck to try and relieve the pressure on his windpipe. She watched his eyeballs bulge and then he self-levitated, canted his body at an angle and launched himself over the edge as if fired from a catapult, his arms windmilling in space, his feet tied together by the pants around his ankles, his screams disappearing into the abyss to end abruptly with a thud.

She turned her head to follow his trajectory and then caught a shadow of movement in front of her, but within a fraction of a second she felt a violent push in the back and was propelled forward. With her arms still constrained by her jacket, and unable to break her fall, she hit the dust face first, her forehead colliding with a small stone. She blacked out.

The bandit holding the foreign devil bitch from behind had been so engrossed in his groping he was slow to notice his colleague's acrobatics, but he heard his screams and then screamed himself when he saw a figure the size of a bear standing above him. He pushed the bitch forward and leapt to his feet, whipping out his machete, and with a banshee cry, lifted it behind his head and lunged at his attacker, swinging the blade down with maximum force.

"Aieeeeeeee ....!"

His assailant easily caught the machete arm by the wrist, pulled it down and swung his body around, smashing the elbow of his free arm into the bandit's face, breaking both nose and left cheekbone, causing an instant explosion of blood, teeth and gristle. The bandit screamed again as his machete arm was twisted around behind him, the weapon dropping from his hand. His opponent swung round again and brought his elbow down with maximum force on the upturned arm, cleanly snapping the joint. The bandit fell to his knees, still screaming, his face caked in blood and gore. The bear-man grabbed him, one hand on the trouser belt, the other around the neck of his sweatshirt, and with a short run and a hefty swing of both arms launched him, still screaming, into space after his colleague.

The third bandit had watched in terror as within the space of just twenty seconds, the bear-man despatched both his colleagues. He leapt astride the mule, kicking frantically with his legs and whipping its flanks with the reins in a desperate attempt to escape. The mule grunted and whinnied under the onslaught of blows, but trotted off down the trail at a speed of its own choosing. The bandit looked back, fearful the bear-man might pursue him, but saw him crawl over to the foreign devil bitch lying prostrate.

Jess felt hands on her shoulders again. She was stunned by the fall and only semi-conscious, but she understood enough to know what was happening and summoned up reserves of energy to cry out again. "No! No! Get off me! Get off me!"

She flailed her arms around as she felt someone pulling her up to her knees and reached behind, managing to find flesh and dig a nail in, tearing at her attacker's face with all her might. But he grabbed her hands and held them like a vice.

"Jess … Jess! It's okay. Stop! It's okay. You're okay."

What …? A man's voice. English. He knows my name! How does he know my name?

"What …?" she mumbled.

"It's okay," he said again, and she relaxed a little, but her chest was thumping, her body heaving with the exertion and one of her legs twitched involuntarily. She felt a body behind her, holding her steady, cradling her, and she lay back, panting, her cheeks streaked with dust and tears. "Stay still. Just stay calm. You're okay now." The voice was mature, gentle, warm and comforting. She wondered whether she had died but then opened her eyes a little, and as the fog cleared she managed to focus on something she recognised. Someone lying on the ground twenty feet away.

"Sujay!" She wrestled herself free and promptly fell over, got up again, and half ran, half crawled to where her guide was lying motionless. He looked calm. One hand still held his stomach and his face was serene, almost smiling, but she noticed one of her own hands was sticky from the blood on the ground and he was lying in a pool of it. "Sujay?" She touched his cheek but had no idea what else to do. She sensed someone beside her. A big man was kneeling next to them, pulling at a rucksack that was neither hers nor Sujay's.

"Unbutton his shirt," he instructed her calmly as he foraged inside, and for a moment she didn't understand him. "Do it!" he shouted, and startled into action, she fumbled with his buttons, carefully moved the bloodied hand to his side and opened up his shirt. He wore a green tee shirt underneath, stained with a large circular patch of blood and at the centre, a small vertical tear. The man grabbed the hem of the tee shirt and ran a knife up to his neck, exposing a brown, shiny, hairless chest and yet more blood. He flipped the top off a large plastic bottle of water and tipped it over Sujay's belly, and as the blood cleared away, she could see a one-inch vertical incision in his stomach, four inches to the left of his umbilicus. The man pulled a chrome hip flask out of an inside pocket

"This is going to hurt, buddy," he said as he splashed amber liquid over the wound. Sujay's face creased up in pain but he remained still. The bleeding stopped for a second or two but then resumed almost immediately, pulsating out of the slit.

"Press it together! With your fingers. Press it together to stop it bleeding," he barked at her and she mutely complied, Sujay wincing with pain at the pressure as she struggled to stop her hands slipping in his blood.

"Sorry!" she pleaded forgiveness. "Sorry."

The guy dabbed at the wound with a white pad and then attached two large strips of surgical tape across his middle, either side of the wound, pulling it tight.

"Move your hands." He slapped another white pad over the slit and stuck down some more tape to secure it. "Have you got any more of those white shirts?" he said, nodding at her.

"What do you mean ..." she mumbled, still confused and largely incoherent. He looked irritated. "Yes!" she said, suddenly comprehending, and turned her head to look for her rucksack. She spotted it over by the cliff edge and raced over to it. She was back in a few seconds, ripping open the flap and rummaging around inside. She pulled out the shirt which was clean and hadn't been worn. He took it off her and he ripped it open with his knife, spreading it out into one large piece of cloth.

"Now. I'm going to roll him a bit, you're going to slide this behind his back and then I'll roll him the other way."

"Okay," she said, beginning to feel a little less useless as he handed her the mutilated shirt.

"Ready?" She nodded. He rolled Sujay onto his left side and he moaned. She tucked herself under his arm and laid her shirt out on the ground, leaving enough cloth to reach around to his front. He then leant over Sujay and pulled him the other way, and this time he cried out in pain. Jess retrieved the other end of the shirt and he rolled Sujay onto his back. He pulled the two ends together tightly and knotted them on one side. A small patch of blood appeared through the layers of bandage.

"That'll have to do for now." He reached into his pocket and pulled out a chunky black phone. A smallish brick with stubby aerial. She looked at him almost in contempt.

"That's not going to work! You won't get a signal around here!" *Not on that old thing. It's not even a smartphone!* He ignored her, punched some buttons that bleeped in response and put it to his ear. To her astonishment, someone must have answered because he said something unintelligible, something that sounded like the language Sujay used. She fished around in her jacket for her phone but it was gone. Then she remembered. It would be down at the bottom of the mountain in the pocket of a dead Chinaman.

The guy looked up to the sky and gave some more instructions, answers to a few questions, then nodded. "*Jaldi karo. Alavida.*" Hurry. Bye. He clicked off.

"How did you do that? On that?" she said, amazed. He looked it, dumbly.

"Satphone."

"What?" *Satphone? Satellite phone? Wow!* She looked up at the sky, expecting to see a spaceship or other such flying object hovering overhead. There was none.

"Sujay? Sujay," he said leaning over. "There's a chopper coming to get you out. But there's no room for it to land here so we're going to have to get you to an open space. Do you understand?" Sujay rocked his head a little from side to side, delirious and weak from the loss of blood.

"How are we going to do that?" Jess asked, the panic beginning to return.

"I'm going to carry him. You're going to carry the bags."

He looked at her closely for the first time. "You've got a nasty scrape on your head. Let me fix that." She lifted her hand up to her face and felt around, feeling broken skin above her left eyebrow, and she winced. He pulled out a sachet from his bag, ripped it open and dabbed it gently on the wound. She winced again and drew back. "Still," he ordered, and she looked straight at him for the first time, watching him as he concentrated on his work. He looked familiar somehow. She'd seen him before. She noticed he was bleeding from a scratch on the cheek.

"You're bleeding too."

"Don't worry about it."

"I'm not worrying … Oh God! Did I do that?" He smiled and then it came to her. *The scruffy guy on the plane. How?*

"You. You were on the plane. The flight from London. And Dubai." He said nothing. He unwrapped another soft pad and taped it to her skin. "Who are you?" she challenged him. "What are you doing here?" He didn't respond. "Who are you?" she was shouting, shaking in confusion.

"Simon," he said, holding out a hand. "How do you do." She looked dumbly at his huge, calloused hand and shook it limply, but then frowned when something else suddenly came to her.

"How do you know my name?"

"Not now, Jess." Her face creased with frustration. "Let's get Sujay sorted out. Up you get." She snorted and stood up. "Turn around." He held out his rucksack for her to put her arms through. It was heavier than her own, but then he was obviously stronger. He attached all three bags to her, front and back, tugging at the straps and slapping the load with the flat of his hand when he'd finished. She stepped back to steady herself. "How's that? Can you manage?"

"I think so." He dropped to his knees next to Sujay. His breathing was shallow and his eyes were closed. "He's lost a lot of blood, but I guess he's a pretty strong chap. We've got about half-an-hour before the chopper gets here." *Thirty minutes – no kidding.* "We need to get him away from the trees. Sujay, I'm going to lift you up now, okay?"

Jess watched, feeling impotent and useless and fearing the worst as Simon squatted in front of Sujay, slipping one arm under his knees and another under his waist. He took a deep breath and keeping his back straight, just like a weightlifter, slowly straightened his legs. Sujay moaned as Simon reached vertical, one of Sujay's arms left dangling.

"Phew! He's only a little chap but he's got plenty of muscle on him. Eighty-five kilos, I reckon." Jess heard the strain in his voice and wondered how on earth they were going to get very far like that. "Let's go." Simon took a few faltering steps but soon got into a rhythm and started plodding slowly along the trail, with Jess and her three rucksacks following behind.

***

Mercifully, the trail went downhill, albeit only slightly, and although progress was painfully slow, they walked for ten minutes without saying anything. Jess still felt numb with shock; the reality of the assault she'd just endured hadn't yet hit her, and she remained confused about Simon's presence. *He came from nowhere, but he saved us!* She realised she hadn't proffered any thanks for what he'd done nor for what he was doing now, but the hideous episode with those vile Chinese guys had reawakened the suspicions she used to have about men. In her short time in Nepal she'd been lured into believing that all people were considerate, thoughtful, hospitable and well meaning, but in an instant that illusion had been shattered, roundly trashed in as extreme a way imaginable.

For the moment, Simon was their saviour. It troubled her that, despite all the evidence in his favour, she was once again looking for sinister intent. They came across some large, round boulders, two feet high, and Simon stopped.

"Need to take a break." He did his best not to show the exertion but she wasn't fooled. In the last few minutes, he'd walked with an increasingly wide gait, staggered a little from time to time and now had sweat on his brow. In contrast, she felt fine, and despite her load, she'd managed well. And with every step, they descended into richer air.

He sat down on a boulder and rested Sujay on his lap. Jess leant over them and touched Sujay's face. He was breathing but unconscious and his skin was cold and clammy.

"He's very cold."

"Not a lot I can do about that." He wheezed, taking in deep breaths and grimacing

"I know! I'm just saying." And she was suddenly annoyed at herself for sounding irritable. She was just desperately worried. He smiled at her, and although she was not ready to drop her guard, she felt the need to salve her conscience. "How are you feeling?" she asked him.

"Aw, well. You know. I've had worse." He let out a small chuckle. "Do you need a hand with those bags?" She frowned and looked at him as if he were mad, then realised the question was meant in jest. She couldn't stop herself smiling, just a little.

"No, thanks. You've got your hands full."

He looked up at the clear blue sky.

"Chopper should be here soon."

"How come it's so quick?"

"From Kathmandu to here in a straight line with no obstacles …?"

"But how are they going to know where we are?"

"GPS on the satphone." She felt stupid again.

"Oh. So you called up an air ambulance, just like that?"

"Air force, actually, or Nepalese Army Air Service, to give its proper title."

"The Air Force?"

"Yep. They've got nothing better to do," he said and he winked at her, so she turned away, unwilling to show any reaction. She knew he was being flippant, probably just to make light of the situation and make her feel better, but deep down she was still shaking. The entire expedition had been disrupted in the most violent and unimaginable way. She'd seen her friend almost stabbed to death in front of her and she had been subjected to a terrifying assault by two vicious thugs who'd then been thrown to their deaths by the guy sitting next to her. And all she knew was that his name was Simon. Or he said it was. And he had a hotline to the Nepalese Air Force! It all seemed so unreal. "Come on, buddy," he said to Sujay's comatose form, and stood up with a grunt. She noticed the blood patch on Sujay's middle had spread, leaving a six-inch diameter dark red stain on her nice white shirt and also on Simon's.

They trudged on for another ten minutes and she began to feel hot, but she was trussed up by the rucksacks and buckles and decided it was the lesser of two evils to continue on rather than try and remove her jacket. Simon was plodding on, step by step, slowly and methodically. She heard Sujay talking to her – *"Bistari!"* – and she felt a wave of apprehension and grief. *Don't die – what am I going to say to your wife and children?*

She thought about her girls and how reckless she'd been, leaving them and almost getting herself killed. Michael had tried to warn her. If only she'd listened. If only she'd thought through the implications, considered the risks before flying halfway around the world to this wilderness.

She kept replaying the events in her head, and she shuddered. Her mind wouldn't let her shake them off. What might have happened? "*It didn't. Get on with it!*" Peter's voice came through loud and clear, cutting through her febrile imagination. Simon had stopped again.

"What is it?"

"Down there." He jerked his head, nodding towards a stretch of land that had opened up to their right. It was peppered with rocks and boulders, but largely green with coarse grass and shrubs. A fast-flowing stream zigzagged its way through the rocks, making a bid to escape down the mountain. Most important of all, there were no trees. "We need to get down there."

The ground fell away sharply to the right of the trail and there was a twelve-foot drop before the gradient levelled out. Simon carefully stepped over to the edge, looking for a secure way down, but there was none. Just rocks and scree and spiky, thorny shrubs awaited them. But he had no choice. He tried to go sideways, testing the ground for a safe foothold but his right foot slid away from him and he almost dropped Sujay. He managed to regain his balance and she called down to him.

"Can I help?" she asked, the agitation evident in her voice as she anxiously watched him struggling with his load.

"Maybe," he said, panting with the effort. "Go ahead of me. I can't see where I'm going."

She jumped down and around in front of him, and although her feet slid on the loose scree, she and her accumulated baggage weighed relatively little so she had no difficulty keeping her feet.

Simon lifted Sujay against his chest, fearing he was beginning to slip, and repositioned his arms to make them more secure and comfortable. Sujay moaned. *At least he's still alive.*

"Okay. Guide me."

Jess felt her heart begin to race. He'd given her responsibility for advising him where to go and she didn't know what to do, what to tell him. She started to panic with indecision.

"Right foot. Down. Down. Back." His right foot pressed against solid rock. His left one followed.

"Left foot. Forward. Up a little." He took another step and brought his right foot alongside.

"Now. Big step. Right foot. Down, down, down …" She could see he was slipping, craning his neck over Sujay's body as if to see where his foot was going. But his legs were growing steadily apart, reaching the point of no return. Then he struck something solid and pulled his left leg down, grimacing.

"Next bit's easy. Three steps forward." She backed down the slope, arms outstretched as if ready to catch them, as if that were remotely possible. They were halfway there. He twisted his head upwards, one ear to the sky.

"Chopper!"

She jerked her head up, looking around desperately, searching for the evidence, hearing nothing but the birds and the ever-present tinkling of water and the sound of scree and gravel, moving beneath her feet. But then, she sensed a distant hum that quickly developed into a bass drone and then a rapidly approaching whup-whupping sound that within just ten seconds was fifty feet above them. A red and gold monster hovering above their heads, engines roaring, their deafening noise shaking the ground beneath them, throwing up clouds of dust.

"Right foot down!" she shouted, but it was pointless. No one could hear anything amidst the infernal cacophony. He stepped down gingerly, twisting each foot to test its hold, and she held out both hands in a symbolic gesture of support, willing him down safely. One step after another. "Almost there!" And then the slope was behind them and they were picking their steps amongst the boulders to a tiny patch of flat dirt next to the rushing stream. Simon dropped to his knees and lowered Sujay onto the ground. He sat back and put his hands on his hips, gasping for breath.

She leaned over Sujay and stroked his face. He opened his eyes a crack and she thought for a moment he was smiling. She smiled back at him, fighting off the tears, and looked around. Simon was on his feet, shading his eyes and staring up at the Indian-built HAL that maintained its position, blowing dust all around them.

She looked to the sky and saw someone in a white helmet and blue flight suit sitting in the open hatchway of the chopper, his feet resting on a flatbed suspended from wires attached to a rail above his head. Simon waved at him, and as the stretcher began to descend slowly, the guy in the blue suit stood casually on it, holding onto the one of the wires. It seemed to take forever, but eventually, Simon was able to grab the edge and guide it to the ground. The airman unhooked himself and the four wires from the stretcher, and the cables drifted away as the chopper adjusted its position. The two men clasped a hand in the air, picked up the stretcher and moved it to where Sujay lay.

"Okay?" shouted Simon, and with him at Sujay's head and the airman at his feet, they lifted his limp body onto the stretcher. The airman pulled at two thick canvas straps, one across Sujay's chest and another across his thighs, tightening them, and together the men carried the stretcher back to its landing spot. The chopper roared again, resuming its position, and they re-attached the cables. The airman climbed onto the stretcher and hooked himself on, then spoke into his helmet mic and waved one finger around in the air in a circular motion. The stretcher lifted and within a couple of minutes it was back in position by the hatch. He climbed in, swung the stretcher through ninety degrees and pulled it inside.

The chopper hovered in position for a moment or two and Jess looked at it in consternation.

"What's he waiting for?" she screamed in Simon's ear.

"He's sending a chair down," he shouted back, shielding his eyes from the dust kicked up by the rotor blades.

"What for?"

"So we can get you up." She looked at him and took a step back, shaking her head.

"No!" He opened his palms and gave her a bemused look. "No! I'm not going. Tell them to get Sujay back."

"Jess! For Christ's sake. It's over!"

"No! It's not over," she shouted at him, straining her head forward, defying him to challenge her. "I'm going to Chumtang."

"How?" he shouted back

"On that path," she screamed, aimlessly jerking a thumb over her shoulder and then pointing at her feet, "on these legs, carrying this bag." She slapped the rucksack on her chest. She was exhausted and dirty and afraid, deafened by the noise, blinded by the dust, and she was angry at everyone and everything.

He looked over his shoulder and saw the chair had reached the ground. He walked towards her and she backed away, her eyes fierce, her expression determined and immovable. He held out a hand.

"No! I'm not going back!"

"He needs his bag." Confused for a moment, she hastily untied the straps holding Sujay's bag to hers. She held it out to him, arms extended, expecting a trick. Expecting to be scooped up and bundled into the chair and whisked upwards before she had time to resist. He took the rucksack at arm's length and tied it to the chair, then stood back and waved the chopper away. The airman in the blue flight suit waved back at him and the HAL wheeled around. Within thirty seconds, all sight and sound of it had disappeared.

She stood, still laden with two rucksacks attached front and back, simmering, fists clenched by her side. She watched him trudge over to the stream, kneel down and splash the icy cold water over his head. He cupped his hands, filled them with the crystal-clear water and drank heavily, repeating the exercise twice more. She relaxed and wandered over, subdued.

"He says that's not good for you. It's dangerous." He looked up at her open-mouthed, squinting in the afternoon sun, a huge smile forming, revealing strong white teeth. In the context of what had happened that day, it sounded the most ridiculous thing to say and she broke into a smile.

"Story of my life," he said.

"Can you untie me?"

He got to his feet and helped her release the rucksacks, and within a second or two she was relieved of her burden. She slipped off her jacket and rubbed each shoulder. Hot and sweaty, she knelt down by the stream and did what he did. The water was freezing and glorious; clear and fresh and wonderful, and she doused her forearms, head and hair, before plunging her face under the surface and scooping up a mouthful of the sweetest natural mineral water in the world, swallowing it with a loud gulp.

"Don't blame me if you throw up," he said, knowing it was unlikely. "I'm done giving piggybacks for the day." Jess rubbed her forehead and felt the tape over her eyebrow, an unwelcome reminder of their ordeal.

He sat on a boulder, chewing on a cereal bar. It was gone in two bites. "Want one?" She nodded and sat down next to him. He fished two more out of his rucksack and handed her one.

"Sujay wouldn't let me bring these. Too heavy."

"Not if you eat them."

She looked at him as if he were stupid.

"They're the same weight whether you eat them or not," she said, taking a bite, strangely relieved to be engaged in frivolous chitchat.

"Not after a while." She laughed at him. He took a swig from his bottle, freshly filled from the stream, and then passed it over. She drank the clear, sweet water and handed it back.

"Better than the boiled stuff."

"The best."

She finished her cereal bar and scrunched up the wrapper. She hesitated for a moment and then decided she needed to say something.

"I didn't thank you for what you did."

He shrugged.

"That's okay. Glad I could be of assistance."

"Where did you come from?"

"Oh, I just heard a commotion."

She was not convinced.

"We haven't seen anyone since we left Langtang apart from those guys, and all of a sudden you just appear from nowhere, walking along the same path as us?" She watched him mull something over.

"I've been following you for a while."

"What?"

"I've been following you since you left Kathmandu … well, London actually." She turned to face him. She didn't know whether to be angry or afraid, but she was definitely disturbed.

"Why?"

"Someone asked me to."

"Who?"

"Michael Goodman."

She shook her head to try and clear her mind

"Michael? But …"

"He was worried about you. Thought you might need a bit of protection." He sounded matter of fact but there was a hint of regret, mild discomfort at the subterfuge. Jess thought through his last statement and she felt her anger rising again.

"Did Sujay know?"

"No. Well, at least, I don't think so. If he did, he didn't show it."

"So, all the while we've been travelling, staying in teahouses and ramshackle farmers' huts, you've been sneaking around behind us, watching."

"Hardly sneaking."

"Well what would you call it?" She was angry at the deception, the presumption and, most of all, the manipulation. Angry that people couldn't leave well alone, couldn't trust her to make her own decisions. "I'll kill him when I get back."

"Why? Because he was right?" He said it so calmly she glared at him, because she knew he was right and she knew Michael was right too. She stood up and stomped over to the stream, arms crossed, angry at herself now, and that made it worse. She felt a hand on her shoulder. "Jess?"

"I'm okay. It's okay. I'm sorry." She wiped a hand across her nose and sniffed. "I'd be dead at the bottom of that cliff if you hadn't been there. I know that."

"I reckon it's just a bit of delayed reaction," he said, squeezing her shoulder, trying to console her.

"Yeah. I think you might be right. Oh God! Who were those guys?" She shuddered again at the thought.

"Bandits. Robbers, thieves and murderers. It's rare around here but we are close to the border. They probably just come over on a fishing expedition, see who or what they can plunder, and scoot back. They're pretty unassailable. The Nepalese aren't going to police around here and the Chinese aren't going to lose any sleep over it. No different from a thousand other places in the world. You were just in the wrong place at the wrong time." She turned to look at him, noticing for the first time he was tall; well over six feet, dark hair flecked with grey, brown eyes and greying stubble. Late forties, she guessed, or more.

"And you were in the right place."

"See how it all balances out?" He was being flippant again and she knew he was just trying to make light of it.

"Do you think Sujay is going to be all right?"

"He's got a good chance, I reckon. It was quite a clean wound, and provided the knife didn't hit anything critical, his biggest worry is blood loss. But that's easy to fix if they get to him quickly." She went quiet for a minute and then said, almost absently.

"You killed those men."

"'fraid so. Apart from the one that got away."

"I've never seen anything like that before."

"Bugs. Vermin. Pest control. Nothing more than that." He turned away, clearly not wanting to prolong the conversation. She knelt down by the stream and splashed water on her face again. "Okay!" he announced. "If we're going to Chumtang, we'd better get started. I, er, assume you know the way?"

"Mm ..." She spluttered and waved an arm aimlessly. "I guess we just ... follow the path?" He looked at her, eyebrows raised.

"Well, you'd better lead on."

CHAPTER 19

They clambered back up the slope and onto the trail. Jess took a moment to look back up the track in the direction from which they had come and then noticed Simon had already set off ahead, so she quickly followed him.

She noticed immediately his pace was quicker than Sujay's but was relieved to discover she was becoming acclimatised and suffering no ill effects. They walked in silence and soon she found herself immersed once more in the magnificence of the Himalayas. There was no one to be seen, the wilderness complete apart from the vultures, buzzards and eagles circling high above them and the occasional group of yak or tahr grazing on steep slopes across the valley.

Stream upon stream tumbled down the mountains and cliffs to their left, carving through the rocks, rushing under makeshift bridges fashioned from tree trunks and rope. She had no idea whether they were headed in the right direction, but the path hadn't split at any stage so she assumed that until it did, they couldn't go wrong. In addition, she felt safe and secure with Simon, content to place her trust in him, and he had already more than adequately demonstrated his survival techniques. And if the worst came to the worst, there was always the satphone to call up a chopper and get them home.

"Where did you learn to speak Nepalese?"

"Spent a couple of years here with the Gurkhas, training them."

"You're army then?"

"Not any more. Gave that up a long time ago."

"So, what do you do now?"

"Oh, this and that. A bit of private security, you know." She didn't know and sensed it was not something he was going to talk about readily, so she decided not to push it. *Maybe the less you know, the better.* But she tried again anyway.

"But you obviously have friends in the Nepalese Air Service?"

"I've got friends everywhere." He smiled at her and she took the hint.

"You haven't been to Chumtang before?"

"No. It's a bit off the beaten track, but it's a reasonably big village and they do lots of trade with China because it's so close to the border."

"How do you know?"

"Looked it up. Didn't you?"

"I didn't know where I was going. Sujay showed me on a map and I just followed him. But how did you know?"

He laughed.

"Michael. When he set it up with Sujay, he wanted to know exactly where you were going and what you were doing and how long it would take. And then he briefed me."

"And how do you know Michael?" He gave her a look that suggested she should stop asking so many questions, but she waited and he sighed.

"Just google it. Private security offering invisible protection service to young women travelling in the Himalayan wilderness. Discretion assured." He shrugged, and they trudged on, side by side, picking their way between the stones and thorny shrubs that littered the trail, the afternoon sun warming their backs as they continued to head north-east.

"Do you know why I'm going to Chumtang?"

"Yes," he said casually, "but do you know what you'll find when you get there?" She stopped in her tracks. He kept going.

***

By 5 p.m. the light was beginning to fade and the temperature had dropped to just above freezing, the sun having disappeared behind the mountains an hour before. Just like Sujay on previous days, Simon showed no signs of fatigue, but Jess was feeling tired. Her legs ached, she was hungry and the chill was beginning to permeate her jacket and fleece. She stopped and called to Simon, who had consistently been five yards ahead of her for the last couple of hours.

"How much further?" He stopped and turned around.

"What? Do you mean to the Chumtang Hilton?" She hung her head and sighed. She was in no mood for jokes. He walked back to where she stood, bent double, forehead resting on her poles. "I don't think we'll get there tonight. Sujay's plan was always to get there by tomorrow."

"So, what do we do?" She was suddenly alarmed. Whatever Simon was, he was not Sujay; and Sujay was an expert at his own job, in his own country. Sujay had been this way before, more than once, so he'd know exactly where they were and would have made plans to provide shelter, just as he'd done before. Simon was thinking the same thing and she had read his mind.

"Well, I assume he must have known there was somewhere around here to bed down. It can't be far away; we just haven't found it yet." His insouciance annoyed her and she looked at him in dismay. But she couldn't moan at him, after all he had done. All she wanted to do was lie down. "Come on, I bet it's just around the next bend." He turned and set off again. She shook her head and followed meekly behind.

***

It was. A single farmhouse set back on one side of the trail with another small wooden shed-like structure opposite and below them, rice terraces stretching down the mountain and out of sight. The ubiquitous plume of white smoke drifted up from the roof of the hut and she could already smell the stir-fried vegetables and taste the lemon and ginger tea.

She stayed on the trail as Simon climbed the steps to the front door and rapped a couple of times, but there was no answer. He looked around at her and tried again.

"Namaste!" he called once, then again. There was a click and shout from their left.

"*Ni shi shui!*" Who are you?

A man stood by the side of the house, pointing his rifle. Simon instinctively raised his hands. Jess stepped back and the rifle swung towards her. She shrieked. The man shouted. "*Zou kai!*" Go away!

"He's Chinese," said Simon and it filled her with dread. "It's okay, he's just a bit nervous." *He's a bit nervous!* Simon broke into Chinese, speaking softly and steadily, gesturing down the trail where they had come from and pointing up to where they were going, and after a few moments, the man lowered his rifle. He barked something that sounded overly aggressive and it worried her, but he then waved at the tiny wooden structure opposite. Simon nodded and reached carefully into his inside pocket and brought out some money. He handed it to the man who snatched at it, barked again and waved him away. Simon bowed and came back down the steps to where she was standing.

"He says we can sleep in the barn." She turned her head to look. It was dark and featureless and there was no smoke coming out of the roof. Her heart sank. "He doesn't want us in the house. Foreign devils." He shrugged. "Might have been different if Sujay had been here."

"Didn't you tell him?"

"What? About Sujay?"

"Yes."

"I guess if I'd said we had a Nepalese guide with us but he got stabbed and had to be airlifted out, it might have got a bit lost in translation."

She sighed and looked at the shed.

"Oh, great."

"Come on. It'll be fine. Just think how good the Chumtang Hilton's going to feel tomorrow. They've got a swimming pool and a sauna and jacuzzi."

"Have they?" Her eyes lit up. He looked at her, impassive, staring, and it gave him away. She slapped his arm in anger. "Stupid!" He chortled, rubbed his arm and put on a pained expression.

"Come, madam, allow me to show you to your suite," he said, grinning, and to her total annoyance, she couldn't stop herself grinning back at him.

The barn was about three metres square, little bigger than a large garden shed, and housed a range of scythes, hoes, spades and other farming tools, together with a number of white plastic tubs, some open, stacked and empty, some closed with lids, all emblazoned with Chinese writing. The floor was stone, covered with a layer of straw, and the air bore a pungent smell; a heady cocktail of manure, ammonia and tar.

A workbench with a vice and a few other tools lined one side below a filthy, cracked window and, incongruous amongst the farming paraphernalia, an aged mattress stood vertically on its end against the opposite wall. Some of the yellow foam padding had burst out of rips in the seams and it featured brown and yellow streaks; stains of indeterminate provenance.

"En suite over there" – he pointed to a corner – "space-saving bed—"

"Enough!" she said, desperately trying not to encourage his puerile behaviour. "I thought this was the loo." Then, looking puzzled, said. "So, where is the loo?"

"Er, I think it's wherever you want it to be. Outside."

"Oh …"

"Look, it could be worse. At least we've got a roof." He dragged the mattress and laid it on the floor. "Here. Take a seat. I'll be back in a minute."

"Where are you going?" she said, suddenly alarmed.

"Don't worry. I'll be right back." He disappeared out the door, pulling it closed behind him, and she unfastened her rucksack. She sat down on the mattress and drew her knees up towards her, wrapping her arms around them and resting her head. She must have dropped off, because the sound of the door being kicked open startled her awake. Simon came in backwards and then turned, a steaming bowl in each hand.

"God, you terrified the life out of me!"

"Just been down the local takeaway. Noodles, vegetables, chilli sauce." She gaped at him, open-mouthed in delight.

"My hero." He passed her a bowl.

"Bunch up." She shuffled along the mattress as he sat down beside her, pulling two sets of chopsticks out of his top pocket.

They shovelled the hot food in without speaking, grunting and murmuring and slurping the noodles as they went down.

"White wine, madam?" He passed her a bottle of Himalayan spring water and she took a large swig. She passed it back and he did the same.

"How did you manage that? What did you say to him?"

"The old boy's fine. Just as long as you ply him with rupees and stay out of his house."

"Thanks. What would I do without you?"

"All part of the service."

Darkness descended quickly and they sat there in the light of their head torches, talking about Sujay, Kathmandu, England and, inevitably, her daughters.

"Would you like to call home?" he said.

"Do you mind?"

"No. Not at all. I think we might get a signal."

"I thought it used satellites."

"It does, but it depends on the satellite coming around."

"I'll pay for the call," she said. It would be expensive and she was anxious not to appear presumptuous.

"Er, you already are." She looked at him, puzzled, then she laughed.

"And I suppose I'm paying for you, too?"

"I suppose."

"Give me that phone!" She snatched it out of his hand but she was smiling. "What do I do?"

"Just dial as normal." She waited and it rang, and rang, and when it rang four times, Sandy's voice cut in.

"Answerphone," she said. "Hi Sandy and Keira, just checking everything's okay. I guess you're out somewhere. No idea what time it is, but I'm fine and hope you are too. Please give a big hug to the girls. Call you tomorrow. Bye." She ended the call and handed the phone back. She noticed he was looking at her and she ventured a personal question. "Do you have any family to call?" But she was fairly certain of the answer.

"Nope." She wanted to ask why. She wanted to know more about him and wanted to chat, but whenever she'd got close he'd either changed the subject or walked away. There was nowhere to walk to now, but she didn't feel brave enough to press him any harder. He got to his feet.

"Where are you going?" she said, trying to suppress the sudden apprehension in her voice.

"To give you a bit of privacy. Best get some sleep."

"Wait! Where will you go?"

"He's got another hut round the back. Not quite as salubrious as this one, but it'll do. Goodnight." He picked up his rucksack and opened the door.

"No!" she almost shouted, her fear rising. "Please ... don't leave me." He stopped and turned round and laid his rucksack on the floor.

"Are you sure?"

"I don't want to be alone." She felt awkward, cowardly, embarrassed at her helplessness. But the memory was only a few hours old, still raw, and she was fatigued. Alone, in the cold darkness of the night, her mind would never let her rest. It would taunt her and terrorise her.

"Okay. Neither do I." He said it with a smile but she knew he didn't mean it. She knew he'd said it just to make her feel better. He'd be one of those who always preferred to be alone, whenever possible, so there was no one to ask awkward questions. And in that moment, Peter's voice echoed in her head.

"I'll have you know, I'm a founder member of MYOBS – The Mind Your Own Business Society!"

Simon. Another member.

"Thanks." She got to her feet and rummaged around in her rucksack, pulling out her sleeping bag and laying it on the mattress by the shed wall. She unzipped her jacket and then noticed he was still standing there, watching, looking awkward. She twirled a finger in the air, smiling. "Turn round."

"Oh. Yes. Sorry." He turned to face the door and she stripped to her thermals, climbed into the sleeping bag taking her outer clothing with her to keep it warm, and pulled the zip all the way up so that only her face was visible.

"Okay." He turned back, studiously avoiding eye contact, and took off his jacket. She saw the brown dried bloodstain on his shirt. He sensed her eyes on him, and twirled a finger.

"Turn round." She grinned at him and then turned on her side, facing the wooden planks of the shed wall, pulling the sleeping bag over her head. She closed her eyes and listened intently. Listened to the rustle of heavy fabric, the buckles unclipped from the rucksack, the whoosh of his sleeping bag, the rasp of its long, heavy zip and the sound of undressing, imagining each item in turn: fleece, shirt, belt, boots, trousers, and she smiled wickedly to herself. She felt his weight on the mattress next to her and his fumbling with the zip and heard it slide all the way up. The head torch clicked off and they lay still in a silence that would be absolute but for their own barely discernible breathing.

"Are you warm enough?" he asked in a whisper and her eyes darted around in the blackness.

"Yes. Thank you," she whispered back. She felt him roll over on his side, facing the opposite way.

"If you get cold, just move closer. Okay?"

"Okay."

"Why are we whispering?"

"You started it."

But she felt warm and safe and secure. She smiled to herself, and despite the horrors of the day, she was still smiling when she fell asleep.

CHAPTER 20

She didn't hear him get up, get dressed or leave the shed, but she heard him come back, carrying tea in tin mugs. Not lemon and ginger this time; green tea with large leaves like floating seaweed and with a distinctively smoky aroma. She sat up and leaned back against the wall, sipping the brew.

"Sleep well?" he asked her. He looked bright and alert and in control.

"Fine, thanks. Can't wait for the swimming pool, though."

"Well, as soon as you're ready, we'll be off. No breakfast, I'm afraid. Mr Grumpy's not in the mood. But I've got a chewy bar."

"Perfect."

"He says it's only about three or four hours to Chumtang, so we'll be there in plenty of time for lunch. I'll leave you to get showered and dressed and do your make-up."

"Out! And close the door behind you!"

***

Despite having nothing more than a mug of smoky tea and a small cereal bar inside her, Jess felt fit, energised and motivated. He set a steady pace but she kept up with him without difficulty, even having the energy to speak from time to time, although he seemed to have no inclination to start a conversation.

She'd been thinking about what she might say to Lisa when she saw her, and she approached it with some trepidation. She was excited but fearful, stimulated but wary, and, like any long wait, she just wanted it to be over. But she also wanted to talk with him and decided it best to steer clear of personal questions.

"You know I'm coming all this way to see someone I've never met?"

"Yes. Colonel Jeffries's daughter." He said it in a way that suggested he was familiar with the Jeffries and it took her by surprise.

"Do you know her?"

"Not really. I met her once, about twenty years ago. She was just a kid."

"But you met her father?"

"Oh yeah." Jess shook her head in frustration.

"Why didn't you say anything?"

"About what?"

"That you knew Peter."

"You didn't ask."

"Well, I'm asking now." *Do you take lessons at being irritating, or were you born like that?*

"I was in Kosovo with him, back in '98. He was our commanding officer. Hero of the Falklands. Top bloke, the colonel."

"Did you know Janica?"

"Sure did. We all knew Janica. We all lusted over Janica." She wasn't quite sure she liked the inference but noticed for the first time he'd lowered his guard a little. "Can't believe she went off with the old boy. But then again, he was something else."

How handsome he must have been, she thought, especially in uniform. She looked at Simon and realised he'd have been her age back then, and she tried to imagine him as a young soldier. It wasn't hard.

"But she was smitten and so was he, so we withdrew gracefully. Went to the wedding and everything." Jess suddenly wondered where all the photographs were. There were none at home, at least none she'd found. Surely Peter wouldn't have destroyed them? She made a mental note to search everywhere; the loft maybe? *Yes, when I get back. Before I sell the house – if I sell the house.*

They crossed another tree-trunk bridge and then stopped by the rushing water to refill their bottles.

"Do you know why I'm coming to see her?" She said it guardedly, assuming he knew at least some of it.

"Nope." He didn't seem interested so she thought twice about launching into a long explanation that might take hours. "Do I need to know?"

"I suppose not. I just thought you might be curious."

"Nope." She nodded and smiled inwardly. *Definitely MYOBS.*

They sat by the water as it careered past them, frothing and tumbling over the rocks, disappearing down the mountain.

"So how long did you know Peter?"

"Until after the thing in the Balkans was over. In fact, the worst of it was already over when we got there but it trundled on till 2001, and then, when Colonel Jeffries retired, I took some leave and then got shipped out to Afghanistan; to special forces." *Special forces? SAS?* She felt her heart skip and her brain switch to overdrive. Michael had mentioned the SAS, two of Peter's men, Jackson and Rutherford.

She gasped inwardly and jumped up. He looked up at her bemused.

"You ... were with the SAS?"

"Yes." He drew the word out slowly but his face betrayed a creeping realisation that he might have overstepped some mark. He swallowed, the precursor to confession. "How's Leila?"

She stepped back and looked at her feet, trying to compute, trying to process the question, analyse the information, put two and two together and see how it all fitted. *Of course, it all fitted!* She put both hands to her head as if it hurt. *Just when you think you know everything,*

something, someone comes along and turns it upside down.
She looked at him and he raised his eyebrows in anticipation, but in anticipation of what, she couldn't tell. An answer to his question? She ignored it.

"Jackson ... or Rutherford?" she asked. He stood up and held out a hand.

"Simon Rutherford." She ignored the hand and glared at him.

"Why didn't you say?"

He shrugged.

"You didn't ask."

The rage was beginning to build inside her, but she remained calm.

"You didn't think I needed to know?" The words were slow and deliberate but laced with suppressed fury.

He shrugged.

"Nope."

She shook her head, bewildered and hurt, feeling a complete fool for failing to spot the obvious and, as ever, angry at being deceived.

"But I knew you'd find out eventually. I wasn't going to make a big deal of it. If those Chinese scum hadn't got in the way, you'd never have known anyway. I would have just stayed out of sight and you'd have been none the wiser." She shook her head, tried to find something to challenge his argument, negate his logic, make him contrite, but she couldn't. He was right. But she was still mad. She relaxed a little and took a deep breath. But she was seething.

"I wanted to meet you. I wanted to meet you both."

"Nah, you don't want to meet Jackson. He's trouble." As usual, he'd resorted to flippancy and she struggled to maintain her composure.

"I wanted to thank you," she said through gritted teeth.

"You're welcome." She wanted to hit him. She wanted to slap him so hard it hurt. And she wanted to hug him, and that hurt too. She sat down on a boulder.

"She's fine. Leila's fine." It sounded dispassionate and irrelevant, like a platitude. But she felt tiny and inconsequential and impotent; that she and everything she was, everything she had, her whole life, was incapable of functioning without the constant supervision and stewardship of others. Life's arrangements made for her, out of sight and behind her back, all with the best of intentions, the path cleared, her progress monitored and controlled so she could get on with the easy bit. Just living. She was torn between the overwhelming urge to break free and the urgent desire to convey her deepest gratitude. *I can't thank you enough, but, by the way, can't you all just MYOB?*

"Good. She's a terrific little girl. I know where she gets it from. Not her father, anyway." Jess thought her rage had subsided, but on hearing mention of Mo it burst to the surface again.

"Don't mention him!" It wasn't so much she hated being reminded of him, reminded of their relationship or his appalling criminality, or her folly in believing that Mo loved her and had rescued her from her hideous father, used and abused her in his own way, then committed the most heinous crime of all: taking her baby away. She knew all that and she had put it all behind her. It was that, yet again, her dark personal world had been penetrated, examined and analysed, turned over and shaken up without her knowing anything about it. That this guy may have known more about her husband than she did, and at the same time thought he knew a lot about her, made assumptions and formed opinions, when in fact he knew nothing, was vexing and left her totally exasperated.

"Sorry." He sat down on a boulder, picked up a pebble and flicked it lazily into the stream. She pursed her lips and rubbed a hand over her mouth, not trusting herself to say anything, fearing his response might just make things worse. She breathed in deeply, let out a long sigh and got to her feet. She walked over to where he was sitting. He looked pensive, flicking pebbles into the rushing water.

"No. I'm sorry." She put a hand on his shoulder and he looked up at her, and this time he wasn't smiling; he was studying her. She was suddenly conscious of her appearance. The cracked lips, the blotchy skin, the redness in her eyes, the greasy, lank hair, the filthy, streaked shirt and trousers. He squeezed her hand.

"I think we should be getting a move on."

CHAPTER 21

They walked on in silence, subdued, each with their own thoughts but, strangely, bonded now more than ever.

Jess couldn't shake off a new sense of impotence, a powerlessness she'd known in the past and now felt all over again, something she thought had been banished, supplanted by a nascent determination in the aftermath of Peter's death. During the few years she had known him, he had nurtured her into maturity, cultivating her self-awareness while secretly cementing the foundations of a secure and happy life for her and her children. Yet now, her new-found confidence had been undermined, her independence compromised unwittingly by people whose only motivation was to help.

On first hearing of the enigmatic former SAS soldiers who had rescued and returned her precious Leila, she'd simply assumed they were mercenaries, and although thankful for their efforts and keen to show her gratitude, she was equally content they remain in the shadows. But her encounter with Simon had been unexpectedly terrifying and violent. She'd been catapulted instantly into a dark, alien world, one in which, despite her own tribulations, she couldn't possibly survive alone. That the same person who could, without hesitation, initiate and administer such casual and gruesome violence to two vile criminals had also shown such compassion and commitment towards finding and shepherding a lost nine-year-old back into the arms of her grieving mother, was still something she couldn't rationalise. It wasn't just a job for him; it was a quest.

She remained in awe of his capabilities, and although constantly unnerved and wary of another demonstration of his apparently bipolar behaviour, couldn't think of anyone she would rather have by her side.

Simon Rutherford was in a new place. He watched this young woman, jaw set, head forward, striding out with renewed vigour and determination, and couldn't help but admire her spirit. He thought he had alluded to it by indirectly complimenting her through Leila.

Kidnapping and transporting a nine-year-old across Asia and great swathes of the Himalayas had been outside his normal comfort zone, but the kid had been a cutie. She'd been no trouble, once she'd begun to understand that not only was he harmless, but he was taking her home to see her mum. He'd been struck by her composure and her cooperation; there had been no tantrums, no tears, no resistance and, as far as he'd been concerned, the kid was great. He hoped he might see her again one day.

He didn't need or want to be praised for what he'd done. It was his job and it came naturally to him. He'd seen and experienced so many horrific things in his lifetime; the despatch of a couple of bandit scum was not worthy of a second thought. *Maybe I've been doing this for too long. Lost a sense of perspective.*

Jess's attitude to discovering who he really was had taken him by surprise. He'd said it was no big deal and he meant it, but he could see how far removed she was from his own dark, sinister world and how, having had the door to it opened, it might have been frightening for her. He tried to put himself in her shoes, imagine how he might have felt in her circumstances, but he had no conception. He had no family, no one who relied on him and no one to rely on. He had no obligations beyond delivering his latest assignment and that was the way he liked it. He knew no other way.

He'd been moved to hear about the death of Peter Jeffries. He'd been looking forward to seeing him again, but no sooner had the kid been successfully delivered to Kathmandu after four years of trying, the old boy had checked out. He had learnt long before of Janica's death, and it had affected him greatly. So young and so beautiful. But he had no knowledge of the disappearance of Lisa, whom he'd only known when she was a child. The colonel had been a giant. He'd heard about his exploits in the Falklands; and then in the Balkans he'd been a towering figure, a commanding presence eliciting absolute loyalty and commitment from his troops, guys like himself and that reprobate Jackson. The colonel hadn't deserved such heartache and trauma, especially after all he'd done for others.

And then, this woman. Jess. How did she know the colonel and how did she get hooked up with that scumbag from Karachi? And why was she busting her ass to meet up with the colonel's daughter, someone she'd never met, so far from home? He was not naturally curious, at least not about things that didn't concern him. Irrelevant facts clouded the mind, inhibited objective judgement, compromised attention and focus on the task at hand.

Nevertheless, and despite his instincts, he did want to know. He wanted to know because it involved the colonel and the people connected to him, and even if little else in life mattered to him, that did. Also, she intrigued him. He thought he'd sussed her out immediately, put her in a slot and moved on. But he knew now she was more than that; enigmatic, unpredictable and determined. He liked that.

***

The metropolis that was Chumtang hove into view. It started with a single farmhouse, not dissimilar to the ones they'd stayed in before, then became a steady succession of houses, barns, fences, huts, fields and rice terraces that, after a while, stretched out before them, spreading up and down each side of the mountain.

Metropolis was, of course, a relative term. This was no large city or conurbation, simply a small town that nonetheless stood out as significantly busier and more densely populated than any of the other places they'd seen along the trail.

A border post with one foot virtually in the People's Republic, Chumtang did most of its trade with its northern neighbours. This was supplemented by that in the opposite direction, serviced by the monthly mule train which ferried goods and supplies back and forth to the myriad villages in and around the Langtang Valley. The same mule train that had, five years earlier, carried the seriously injured and dying Lisa Jeffries to safety and ultimate obscurity.

Clouds had gathered over Chumtang and along with the inevitable aroma of wood smoke that hung over the town like incense in a monastery, the air felt thick, cool and clawing.

Footfall along the trail increased steadily as Jess and Simon walked the last kilometre to their destination, and although she nodded and smiled and said "Namaste" to many of the locals, she was surprised to find they were largely ignored. She'd not expected indifference from the townsfolk to the presumably rare sight of Caucasian trekkers.

"It's bigger than I imagined," she said. "It seems to go on for miles and it's quite spread out. I thought it was just going to be the odd hut or two."

"Yeah, well, you think it's a remote backstop but I guess the whole area becomes more populated the further you go into China."

"So, where's the Hilton?" She smiled at him and he looked at her, relieved that the silence between them was over.

"Ah, well. There's something I forgot to mention."

"What you mean is, there's *another* thing you forgot to mention. How many more are there?" She enjoyed ribbing him but he didn't seem to mind and joined in the joke.

"It was bought out by the Chumtang Hoteliers Co-operative and turned into a skanky row of huts with long-drop loos and cold showers."

"And what about the swimming pool?"

"Duck pond."

"So at least I can expect some crispy duck?"

"I wouldn't bank on it." They laughed and walked on up a stepped path criss-crossed on either side by side streets that led to more houses with barns, and cows, pigs and goats, standing around chewing in fenced fields and yards. Chickens ran around their feet, oblivious to the foreign visitors, pecking haphazardly at the stony ground for seed morsels, and dogs lay about dozing, yawning and eyeing them with disdain.

"Seriously. There is a hotel here, isn't there?"

"Leave it to your travel guide. Would I let you down?"

"Why do I get a bad feeling about this?" When he winked she wanted to slap him again.

They walked on until they came across two women sitting at the side of the path, huge bundles of straw trussed up like sheaves of thatch beside them. Simon addressed them and the three babbled on amongst themselves while Jess stood by watching. Finally, the women waved up the path ahead of them, ending the conversation with a toothless grin.

"It's up here, about two hundred yards. Traders Lodge. Come on." He set off with Jess scurrying behind, trying to keep up. She was pleased to be back in some form of civilisation, but given the less than hospitable reception they'd had so far from the locals, she wanted to stick close to him.

They arrived at a substantial two-storey building, a curved archway in the centre leading to an open courtyard at the rear, the building extending to two wings, the upper floors, accessible by a wooden staircase, featuring exposed walkways and railings.

They found the reception desk through a door in the right wing, the ground floor of which also opened out to a large dining area. A few surly looking men sat drinking tea and playing cards. A large brown dog of indeterminate mixed parentage, lying stretched out on the floor, eyes closed, twitched periodically. An elderly man with two days' stubble, wearing a black padded jacket and woolly hat, stood behind the desk, flipping through flimsy paper receipts and tapping on a battered old calculator. He looked up and scowled at them as they approached the desk, and then went back to his work.

Simon said something to him and after a moment, the old man sniffed, wiped his nose and grunted. Simon fished some rupees out of his jacket pocket, laid them on the counter and the man swept them up and reached under the desk before slapping two keys on the top, along with some grubby limp change.

"Come, madam. May I show you to your room? Do you have any luggage?" She took pleasure in slapping his arm and then followed him outside and up the stairs to the wing opposite. "I asked him for rooms away from the restaurant. I reckon once these trader boys start on the rice wine, it'll get a bit boisterous after dinner. Don't want them disrupting our beauty sleep, do we?" She shook her head. But she was inwardly calm and felt a comfortable serenity. They'd arrived at last. The place, although basic, looked better than anything else she'd seen since Kathmandu, and she prayed there was hot water to be had so she could finally shower and wash some clothes.

They reached the landing and walked along the wooden boards. Halfway along he stopped and handed her a key.

"Number seven for you, and" – he took a few more steps – "I'm here in eight." Another problem solved. They weren't sharing but he was next door. "Look. I think we've missed lunch but, to be honest, I could do with a bit of a lie down and then we can have an early dinner. Does that suit?"

"That suits me fine," she said, turning the rusty key in the lock and pushing open the door.

"I'll give you a knock at about five thirty."

"I don't have a phone or a watch so I've no idea what time it is."

"It's two fifteen. Does that give you enough time?"

"Plenty."

***

The room smelt damp and beige paint was peeling from the wall opposite, but she was astonished and delighted to find a door to an en-suite bathroom. Water had penetrated some rather haphazard wall tiling and the bathroom floor was awash, but that was a small price to pay for luxury such as this, and she wondered whether this was the sort of place for which the term "wet room" had been originally coined.

A cracked white basin boasted both hot and cold taps but no sink plug and was topped with a mirror and glass shelf supporting a used bar of soap and half a bottle of green detergent. The showerhead, inexplicably, was mounted on the wall above the toilet pan, next to a white plastic box that featured various pipes, hoses and unshielded electrical wires. She lifted the toilet lid tentatively and, although stained, she was relieved to find it contained only water and exuded a strong smell of bleach. The floor sloped down to a drain hole in the middle that lay submerged in a grimy puddle of grey water.

She turned on the hot water tap and was dismayed to find it freezing cold, but she let it run and after a few moments it started to warm up and she shivered with excitement and anticipation.

She found an incense stick in the bedroom and used it to lift the bathroom drain hole cover, poking it around in the hole until she lifted out a large clump of matted, slimy black hair, the remaining water bubbling and gurgling as it rapidly drained away. She grimaced at the stench and dropped the clump into the toilet, relieved that the flush worked first time.

She felt the desperate need to sleep but she resisted, deciding instead there was work to do, so she got up and pulled everything out of her rucksack. She found one clean shirt buried at the bottom and her spare trousers, which were creased but less dirty than the ones she had on, so she laid them on the bed.

She stripped off and had a shower. The pressure was poor but the water hot and it felt like the best shower in the world. She washed her hair with the green liquid and then dried herself on a small towel that was thin, scratchy and smelt vaguely of bleach. Reinvigorated, she dressed and fell onto the bed, stretching out on the top cover, hearing only the occasional shout, snippet of local banter and barking dog. Within a moment she dozed off.

***

The banging on the door startled her and she sat up, confused. "Jess!" It was Simon. She leapt up and opened the door. He had a white plastic bag in his hand and wore a different shirt. He looked like he'd at least made an effort to smarten up. "Time for dinner."

"God, is it that time already?" she said, flustered, trying to straighten her tangled hair. He leant against the doorjamb and held out a clenched fist. "What's that?"

"Present." She held her hand out and a gold-coloured shiny watch dropped into it. She looked at it, puzzled.

"Gucci?"

"Yep – only the best will do. Four quid's worth, that is."

"Thank you," she laughed, genuinely touched.

"Thought it might come in useful."

"Where did you get it?"

"Oh, some old bird out there on the street. Had to haggle, though. She wanted a fiver!" He held up the plastic bag. "Got your laundry?"

"They do laundry too?" she asked, amazed.

"Yeah. Twelve-hour turnaround. There's a bag in the bedside cabinet." She found the bag and stuffed all her clothes in apart from her jacket and fleece. "Right – time for that crispy duck!"

They dropped their laundry bags off at reception, paid a surly woman who had obviously taken over from the surly man and seated themselves in the restaurant area.

Even though it wasn't yet six, it was already busy and most of the tables were occupied, but they found a place opposite each other at the end of a long table flanked by a wooden bench on either side, near the kitchen door. Eight men, heads bent over steaming bowls, shovelled food into their mouths with chopsticks, stopping now and again to come up for air or make some debatable comment about something or other. The table was littered with beer cans, bottles of soy sauce and flimsy paper napkins a mere four inches square. She noticed most of the other tables were similarly populated and the canteen echoed noisily with the sound of robust chatter and continuous clanging from the kitchen.

"Fancy a beer?" She wasn't normally a beer drinker but looking around, there seemed little else on offer, so Simon hailed a man he presumed was a waiter and within minutes he'd brought them two small glasses, two large green cans bearing the name "Tuborg" and a couple of cardboard menus.

"Gosh," she said, looking at the beer, "I'll never get through all that."

"I'll help you." They chinked glasses, took a large swig and looked at the menus. They were greasy and stained and totally unintelligible. She looked up at him, seeking guidance.

"Ah!" he said.

"You speak the lingo, don't you?"

"Yes – I just can't read it. Never mind, what do you fancy: chicken, pork, curry, rice, noodles? I'm sure they've got pretty much anything back there."

"I'll have what you're having." She examined her watch. "Can I use your phone?"

"Sure, you can use your phone." He smiled, reaching into his inside pocket.

She dialled carefully, and as he ordered their food, he watched her eyes betraying a mixture of nervousness and eager anticipation, pressing the phone to one ear, a finger in the other to block out some of the extraneous noise. She spoke to home, five thousand miles away

"Sandy? ... Sandy? ... Hi! How are you? ... didn't expect to find you home ... Saturday? ... is it? ... no idea what day it is ... how's everyone?" He watched her eyes light up and she nodded as if in understanding as she spoke. "Really? ... that's nice. Well, give them my love and tell them I'll be back soon. Can you give Michael a message for me? ... Tell him I've met Simon," and as she mentioned his name, she looked up at him and he winked at her, "and he's looking after me very well ... yes ... I know ... no ... maybe the day after tomorrow. Okay? ... try and call you on the way back ... love to everyone. Bye." She handed the phone back to him.

"Everything all right?" he asked and felt uncomfortable at being disingenuous, because he already knew. He'd made a couple of calls earlier, one of them to Michael. He'd given him a thorough briefing on their situation and Michael had confirmed the girls were fine. He'd also called his man at the

Army Air Service and then the hospital to find out about Sujay.

"Yes, thanks," she said, "everything's okay. Can't wait to get back."

"I can understand that." As if reading his mind, she said.

"I wonder how Sujay is."

"I rang the hospital and checked. He's going to be fine. He'll be out by the time we get back. A few pints of the red stuff and some antibiotics is all it took."

"Oh, thank goodness," she said and took a swig of beer.

The food arrived. Jess could only guess what it was but she didn't care. She hadn't realised how hungry she was. They ate and chewed and chatted for a moment and then she caught him off guard.

"Tell me how you found Leila." He stopped shovelling and swallowed.

"Are you sure you want to know?"

"Of course I want to know. I want to know everything."

"Jess—"

"Please." She looked at him with a solemn expression. "It's important."

***

Major Colin "Jack" Jackson sat at a corner table in The Old Swan in Maida Vale, nursing three quarters of a pint of London Pride, watching the door. He looked at his watch with mild irritation and tapped the table with his fingers, then picked up his phone for about the tenth time in twenty minutes to check it for activity. No more texts since the last one ten minutes ago. "Running late, X." *Prick!* He sensed movement by the door and looked up.

"Where the hell have you been?" He didn't like to be kept waiting. Not for anything or by anybody.

"I'll have what you're having," grinned Captain Simon Rutherford, plonking himself down on a stool opposite. Jackson glared at him. "Er, okay, I'll get my own. Are you all right there?" Getting no response from his friend, he trotted off to the bar and returned a minute or two later with his pint, sipping the froth as he sat down again. "Sorry I'm late. Northern Line was buggered up."

"I knew there'd be a good excuse."

"It's not an excuse! It's a reason."

"Whatever," Jackson sighed. Si was always late and there was always a "reason".

"How are you, you old sod?" said Rutherford.

Jackson smiled at him. Forgiven as ever, he held out a hand which Rutherford shook heartily.

"I'm good. Keeping fit? Looks like it," Jackson said, nodding at his friend's middle. Rutherford looked down and patted his shirt front.

"Oh, working out now and then. Ready for the next big push. What's up?"

"How do you fancy Pakistan?"

Rutherford's face fell.

"Oh, please," he moaned, "tell me you're kidding. Tell me it's the South of France, or a Greek island, or maybe even Bangkok."

"Islamabad."

"Bollocks!" Rutherford took a swig of beer in protest.

"I knew you'd be pleased. It's for Peter Jeffries."

"The colonel?"

Jackson nodded.

"Remember that job we did a couple of years back, those two goons, little and large?"

"Oh yeah. The debt collectors. That was a hoot. Wonder if they ever got over it?" Rutherford flashed a mischievous grin at his colleague, who ignored him.

"Well, turns out it's all connected."

"What? With Colonel Jeffries? How?"

Jackson shook his head

"Too complicated to explain, but he needs us."

"How is he?"

"Not well, by all accounts. I haven't seen him myself, not for many years. Last time was his retirement do."

"Is he still with the gorgeous Janica? They had a kid too, didn't they?"

"They're dead."

"What?"

"They're both dead. His wife died of leukaemia and his daughter was killed in Nepal; that earthquake a few years back." Rutherford's jaw dropped open and he stared at his friend opposite.

"Oh fuck! That's terrible."

"Which is why we need to help him. We're looking for a six-year-old girl taken from her mother by her scumbag husband who's run off with her to Pakistan."

"So what's that got to do with the colonel?"

"Don't know. All I know is it's important to him."

"So the kid's Pakistani?"

"The father is, the mother's white." Jackson handed him a brown manila envelope. "Not much in there. A crumpled photo, well out of date, some names and addresses … bugger all, really. And they've been at it for two years already, got nowhere, so the trail's gone cold."

"Who has?"

"Local amateurs. I reckon they've just been letting it run and coining it in. No expense spared, you know."

"I don't give a shit. I'd do it for nothing."

"I know you would. We both would. I got the call from Brigadier Anders. The colonel got a bit fed up with the lack of progress and asked him to find us."

"He asked for us?"

"That's what he said."

"When are we off?"

"Friday."

***

"Michael said a lot of time had been wasted in the early days," said Jess, fingering her half glass of beer.

"Yeah, well, the first thing we did was pay a visit to the local boys in Islamabad. Turns out they were just bullshitting. Happy to fabricate reports to keep the client on the hook, always on the brink of a breakthrough, just needed a few more expenses, a bit more time, you know. They didn't even know whether they were looking in the right city. They spun it out for as long as they could. Jack and I put them right."

"What do you mean?"

"Fired them." He saw she was looking at him strangely. "We just told them politely to desist. We'd take over from there. Honest!"

"Okay. So then what?"

"Well, we knew his name, but that was it. Do you know how many Mohammed Khalids there are in Pakistan?"

"Lots?"

He nodded.

"But we had no idea where he was. Those goons were looking in Islamabad, but he could have been anywhere. So after a few weeks traipsing around the city, quizzing all the taxi firms, getting nowhere, Jack flew back home. To Wellingford."

"I lived there!" she blurted out, but then it sunk in. "Oh, sorry. You probably knew that." He nodded.

"We figured that his family probably knew where he'd gone, so we'd go ask them."

"You just knocked on the door?" He could see she was a little dubious.

"No! What do you think we are? Idiots?" She raised her eyebrows.

"No, Jack just staked them out for a while, watched them come and go, saw who was who, and he noticed there was an older kid, about seventeen or so, probably a brother. Figured he'd be the one who might keep in touch. Was always wandering around glued to his phone. So he nicked it off him."

"What?"

"Well, *he* didn't. He sub-contracted it to two guys on a moped. You know, the type who cruise around whipping phones out of people's hands while they're standing around in the street? Gave them two hundred quid to get the lad's phone. Took them a few days but they managed it."

"So you're well in with a bunch of thieves?"

"Hardly." He put on his best pained expression. "Are you complaining?" She shook her head.

"Had to get it hacked to get around the password, but once we'd done that, it didn't take long to find out who he'd been texting. And it wasn't big brother Mo."

"Oh," she said, suddenly deflated.

"But we got a few names and numbers and started to track them down."

"How?"

"It's very technical." She leant forward, interested. "Jack rang them up." She slapped his arm. "Oi!"

"Here, have some of my beer," she said, emptying the remains of her can into his glass.

"Well, one of the mobiles was foreign – you could tell by the ringtone – but Jack always hung up before anyone answered."

"Why?"

"Why do you think?" She shook her head.

"Because he wouldn't have sounded like Mo's brother and whoever it was he had rung would see they'd had a missed call, and if it was Mo, he'd probably he'd call back."

"And ...?"

"Bingo. The call came straight back and he left a voicemail. It was him."

"Wow!" But she looked puzzled. "Did that tell you where he was?"

"Not exactly, but at least now we had a number. And not only that; because we had his brother's phone, we had a picture."

***

Simon Rutherford stood by the window in his studio apartment in Islamabad and studied the photo and contact details Jackson had sent from Mo's brother's phone. The selfie was at least four years old, showing a teenager with one arm around the shoulders of an older boy, white shirt open at the neck, gold medallion and watch, big white teeth, coiffed hair. Mohammed Khalid. His thoughts were interrupted by a crunching noise followed by blaring horns, and he looked out of the open window down at the street below.

There'd been a minor collision between a taxi and a van, and the drivers were on the street shouting and gesticulating at each other while the cacophony of horns around them increased in intensity. The taxi had a generic illuminated sign on the roof but on the driver's door it bore the name of the company, Awami Taxi. He mulled a strategy over in his head for a moment and then picked up his phone.

He dialled the number Jackson had given him and it was answered in two rings.

"*Assalam u alaikum!*" Rutherford's Urdu was good and he knew that meant "Hello" but he needed to play the dumb tourist.

"Oh, hi. Er, is that Awami Taxi?" He could hear it was a car on the move.

"No, mate. Never heard of them. This is White Cab." *White Cab.* The voice was English, unaccented.

"Oh, I'm sorry. Must have misread the guidebook. Your English is very good."

"Ha! That's cos I am English. Sort of. Where are you going?"

"I need to go from the Serena Hotel to the airport." There was a pause.

"Say again?"

"Serena Hotel. The five-star?"

"Er, sorry mate, don't know it. Which city you in?"

"Islamabad." The voice let out a laugh.

"I'm in Karachi." *Karachi!*

"Oh. Sorry. I'm being really stupid. I'm reading the wrong page. Sorry to have troubled you."

"No worries." There was a click.

***

"So now you know he works for a company called White Cab and he's in Karachi?" She was looking excited now, desperate to hear the rest. "Were you sure it was him?"

"Pretty sure. I didn't want to ask his name in case he got suspicious, and I was afraid he might wonder how his phone got into a guidebook in Islamabad. But I didn't expect him to turn up in Karachi."

"So what did you do?"

"I got down there. It's a two-hour flight. The two cities couldn't be further apart."

"And what about Jack?"

"He flew out there and we booked into the Movenpick."

The waiter cleared away their bowls and said something to Simon.

"He's asking if you'd like dessert?"

"Er, no, but I wouldn't mind a lemon and ginger tea."

***

Jackson stood at the window in Rutherford's room on the tenth floor of the Movenpick, looking out across the Karachi skyline; a mixture of ancient and modern, shiny-new interspersed with slum and, in the distance, about half a mile away, the blue waters of the Arabian sea stretching to the horizon. He dialled the number and waited.

"Hi buddy, I need a cab." His American accent wasn't bad, thought Rutherford. Somewhere between Dallas, Texas and New York. In other words, nowhere. But it would do.

"Movenpick … Jinnah Mausoleum ... 'bout thirty minutes? ... Jackson … okay buddy … that's good." He hung up. "Easy peasy. We both go. Don't know how he's going to react when we pop the question."

"Yeah," agreed Rutherford. "Let's just be nice to the guy. Play to his sensitive side."

The switch from the air-conditioned luxury of reception to hot, humid and pungent hit them outside the hotel as they exited the revolving door. Chinos, striped short-sleeved shirt, baseball cap, small rucksack and cameras. Yankee tourists. A number of cabs drew up, disgorged their contents and moved on swiftly. Bang on time, a white Toyota bearing the name "White Cab" drew up.

The driver's window rolled down and they stepped forward. "Jackson?" asked Jackson and the driver nodded. He turned to look at Rutherford, who bore the same expression he felt. There was something wrong. The driver was at least thirty years too old. "Get in."

"*Assalam u alaikum*," said the driver, looking in the mirror at the two Americans in the back seat as he pulled the car away from the hotel and down the ramp.

"Yeah. Hi. How are ya?"

"I'm very well, sir. Jinnah Mausoleum?" asked the driver. He was clearly a local and Rutherford noticed the ID fixed to the centre console had a brooding photograph of a guy called Wahid Sajjadi.

"Yeah, that'd be great. Hey, are you the guy I called?"

"No, sir. I got the message from the office."

"Aw. Okay." Jackson considered this for a moment and exchanged glances with Rutherford. "He said his name was Mohammed."

"Oh yes, sir."

"D'ya know him?"

"We have many Mohammeds," said Wahid, grinning, and Jackson did his best to smile pleasantly back at him.

"It's just, er, he was an English guy and I thought that was, you know, kinda unusual round here." Wahid rubbed his chin with one hand. They were stationary in four lanes of traffic.

"We have no English Mohammed," he said after a moment, shaking his head. They looked at each other. *Fuck!*

"We have Tariq," he offered helpfully. "Tariq is English. Came maybe two years ago. From London." Jackson thought it best not to make it sound like an interrogation.

"Aw, okay." He nodded. "You got many drivers?"

"Maybe one hundred, one hundred twenty."

They both slouched down in the back seat, slumped in dejection. *It had all been going so well.*

***

They found the headquarters of the White Cab Company in Shah Faisal Colony Road, situated between a bakery and a hardware store. They sat in the kebab restaurant opposite, watching the traffic go by, and through two wrought iron gates they could see an open yard behind the White Cab building, but little activity.

"They'll all be out on the road, I guess," said Rutherford, chewing on some gristly lamb and flatbread.

"Well, they all have to turn up sometime. Question is, do we go in and try to find Tariq or do we wait until we spot him?"

"Could be ages. And we can't sit here all day every day, eating this shit, waiting for Tariq or whoever to show himself."

"What else can we do? I don't want to call him again. He's going to get suspicious, if he isn't already."

"Do you think that's why he didn't show up?"

"Maybe."

"We need a guy on the inside."

"That's exactly what I was thinking."

***

Simon had ordered himself another Tuborg and was eating a dessert that looked like a doughnut covered in a virulent orange custard while Jess sipped her tea.

"So how did you get someone on the inside?"

"Well, much against our instincts, we hired a local PI firm to send in one of their guys, Faisal, to apply for a job. It took two or three weeks before he started and then another couple of weeks before he came into contact with Tariq. Turned out he called himself Tariq Siddiqui, and Faisal confirmed he was the guy in the photo. Faisal got to know him and it turned out Mo, aka Tariq, was up to the same old tricks. One of his specialities was arranging, shall we say, young 'escorts' for foreign tourists."

"He was a pimp."

"'Fraid so. But much worse than that. Faisal said the girls were pretty much slaves. Homeless kids picked off the street, discarded by their families. No way of surviving otherwise."

"Thank God Leila wasn't one of them."

"Quite. But we didn't know that at the time. We got ourselves quite fired up thinking about Mo and how he might have been abusing his daughter and what we were going to do to him, so we were very anxious to get in there." Simon scooped the last of the Day-Glo custard off his plate and pushed it aside. Jess watched him wipe his mouth and hands with the tiny napkin, screw it up and drop it in the dish. She waited patiently for him to continue. "So I booked an escort."

***

Rutherford stood on the street corner in his American tourist gear, snapping the odd picture, checking his watch and pretending to study a crumpled street map while keeping one eye on the traffic. He had been there twenty minutes and was beginning to think the message hadn't got through, when a white car pulled in next to him. *White Cab*. The passenger window rolled down and Mohammed Khalid leant over, smiling, his gold jewellery glistening.

"Mr Abrams?"

"Are you Tariq?"

"Yes. You ordered a taxi?"

"Sure did." Rutherford reached for the rear passenger door and climbed in. The opposite door opened suddenly and Jackson got in beside him. "I brought my buddy. Thought we could have some fun together." Mo smiled through the mirror.

"No problem." He guided the car out into the traffic.

"How far is it?"

"It's only a few streets away. Very nice neighbourhood."

"Hey, you're an English guy," said Jackson in his best mid-western drawl.

"Born but not bred."

"What are you doing here?"

"Ah, you know, loads of hassle in the UK, easier to do business here." He tapped the steering wheel to the music that jangled from the radio. "And I understand you want to do some business?"

"Sure do."

The "very nice neighbourhood" was a filthy backstreet lined with potholes and abandoned cars, skinny stray dogs foraging around in upturned rubbish bins. Small children hung around on the pavements, bemused and barefoot in the dust, while older boys rode their bicycles hands-free and the occasional moped chugged past, three-up, with men or sometimes entire families on board. Mo stopped the car outside an open doorway that led down an alley to the rear of the three-storey building.

Jackson and Rutherford followed him down the alley, which opened out into a small courtyard. Rutherford looked upwards at the second and third floors and saw children, mostly young girls, peering down through grubby windows, waving limply. He caught Jackson's look: grim, dispassionate but resolute. Both looked around the courtyard, but there seemed to be no one else there.

Mo showed them into a room containing a desk with laptop computer, three chairs and a grey filing cabinet. An ancient ceiling fan whirled slowly above. An open door led into another room, but the building was quiet, with no evidence of human activity apart from the faces they'd seen at the window.

"Take a seat," he said. "Now, gents, what can I provide for your entertainment? Do you have any specific needs? We can offer you all shapes, sizes and ages, girls and boys." He grinned at them, his white teeth sparkling as brightly as the gold medallion dangling from his neck and the Omega on his wrist.

Two guys slid into view by the open doorway. Neither SAS men flinched, but through their peripheral vision they could tell they were big but unarmed. They had already decided that, circumstances permitting, they wouldn't waste time, nor, in the first instance, issue any threats. They each turned their heads slowly to check out the new arrivals. As expected, big ugly guys, open-necked shirts, jeans, but no knives or guns. Mo was talking again. "It's a hundred US each per hour …"

"We're not hiring," said Jackson, interrupting the flow. "We're buying."

Mo maintained his smile, affecting confidence he was still in control of the situation.

"No, no, no. We don't sell, we just rent."

"Ten grand." The words struck home and Mo paused, looking suddenly interested.

"Dollars," said Jackson, to avoid any doubt.

"Ten grand, for … what?"

"For one of your little girls," said Rutherford, joining in the conversation so he knew they were together on this. Mo grinned.

"Fifteen and you can take your pick." Rutherford nodded in agreement.

"We'll take Leila."

"I'm sure we can find you a Leila, that's ..."

"Leila Khalid, Mo. Your daughter." Mo's smile vanished and he flashed a look at his minders as he slowly sat back in his seat, hands on the desk. The SAS men watched him, calculating, thinking, inscrutable. Jackson watched Mo's hands in case they went for the desk drawer. Rutherford looked half right, keeping his attention on the men to his side. They each smiled at Mo pleasantly, relaxed but primed to defend themselves at the slightest movement or threat. Mo nodded slowly, feigning understanding.

"Why do you want her?"

"Her mum. She wants her back. And she's willing to pay." Mo snorted.

"I doubt Jess has the ability to pay."

"Fifteen grand US, in cash."

"Twenty," said Mo. They sat in silence for just a second.

"Done," said Jackson. Mo looked surprised and, for the first time, mildly flustered.

"Have you got it with you?"

"Is she here?"

"No! What kind of a father do you think I am?"

"We know exactly what kind of a father you are, Mo." Rutherford gave him a steely look. "Why else would you take her in the first place?"

"I don't need to explain myself to you," he hissed. "Now, have you got the cash or haven't you?"

"Where is she?"

"Bring me the money and I'll tell you."

Jackson sighed.

"I'm going to reach into my leg pocket, very slowly, okay?"

Mo barked something in Urdu to tell his minders to stay calm, as Jackson unbuttoned the flap of the pocket in the leg of his trousers. He pulled out a bundle of notes bound by a white strap and flopped it on the desk. "There's a grand. To show good faith. This is just business, Mo—"

"Tariq."

"Whatever. We're not here to cause trouble. We're just doing a job and we want the transaction to go smoothly. We don't really care what you get up to. We just want Leila and then we can be on our way."

"Where are you staying?"

"Movenpick."

Mo reached over and slid the money off the desk.

"Then I suggest you go back there and wait for me to call. One of the boys will take you."

***

Jess tried to picture the situation and a hideous image came to mind. A standoff between bad guys and good guys doing business over her daughter. Trading in children. Worse, the conversation had brought Mo back to life and she shuddered when she thought of him. How could she ever have got involved? How she could have been so stupid to fall for his charms? But then, he gave her Leila. It was just too much of a torment, too much to unravel in her head, too difficult to understand her conflicting emotions. *It all came right in the end. Didn't it?* Simon broke her concentration.

"So we went back and we waited and we waited, and after a couple of days, we called him, but he didn't answer. We couldn't help thinking something was wrong because we'd assumed he'd want to get his hands on the cash ASAP, so we were a bit suspicious at the delay. We got hold of Faisal and he said he'd seen Tariq behaving normally and doing his stuff. But he did say Tariq had a gambling thing going on, as well as a sideline peddling drugs to tourists, and that one day he'd seen him in a heavy conflab getting hassled by two guys in suits. Anyway, on the third day I got a text with the address of a hotel. Said he'd meet us in reception at eight."

***

"Hi guys," said Mo, standing to greet them and shake their hands. Jackson and Rutherford sat down on a plastic sofa in the grubby lounge area of the Hotel Fahran. A fat bloke with a moustache sat behind the reception counter watching TV and they could see the same two big guys from the other day loitering in the corner. "Have you got the money?"

"We've got the money. But not with us. Where's Leila?" Jackson was mildly irritated and not just with Mo. The text hadn't made clear why he wanted to meet, and he was concerned that by turning up without question, they'd handed some of the initiative to Mo.

"That's what I wanted to talk about. See, she doesn't live with me. I couldn't look after her myself. I wanted to and I did for a while, but what with, you know, the sort of work I do and stuff, it was just doing her no good." They both looked at him with disdain. *Bullshit.* "So I gave her to some foster parents and she stays with them, and I get to see her now and again whenever I can."

"So, where is she?" said Rutherford, clearly beginning to tire of this nonsense.

"Oh, she's quite close by."

"In Karachi?"

Mo nodded.

"Oh yeah. In Karachi." *Bullshit.* "And I've spoken to the foster parents and they're happy to let her go." He paused and the SAS men looked at each other, thinking the same thing.

"And ...?" said Jackson.

"It's just that they'd like a bit of compensation. You know, for their trouble. The heartache at having to give her up."

"Would they now?" They didn't believe a word of it. Mo was as transparent as glass. "How much?"

"Five."

"Then pay them and let's get on with it," said Rutherford. Jackson knew his mate was playing with him. He'd have done the same thing.

"Oh, no, no. We agreed twenty. The five is expenses." Jackson leant forward and Rutherford turned his attention to Mo's minders who were watching them, trying but failing to look casual and tough at the same time.

"I tell you what we'll do, Mo," he said quietly and Mo leant forward to listen.

"You tell us when and where to meet. Another hotel, perhaps. Public place. You bring Mr and Mrs Foster Parents along with Leila, and we'll give them their five grand and you your twenty and we can all shake hands and go home.

How's that?" He could tell by the moment's hesitation it wasn't what Mo wanted to hear.

"Okay. Okay, good idea." *Bullshit.* "Yeah. Okay. I'll set it up and call you in a day or two." He thrust out a hand but they ignored it. Mo grinned nervously and left, followed by his minders.

"What do you reckon?" said Jackson when they had left.

"I reckon we'd better be ready for trouble."

Jackson nodded.

***

A group of Chinese at the table opposite were playing mahjong while getting drunk on rice wine, the combined effects of alcohol and competitiveness spilling over into shouting and gesticulation. Simon watched them and Jess twisted her neck around. She shuddered. The guys were probably just horsing around, the way men do when they get drunk in a group and challenge each other to a trial of strength, but she was instantly reminded of the villains who'd attacked them a couple of days ago and she was grateful she had Simon with her.

"So then we had to wait for him again. But this time we were less bothered because we could tell he was anxious. Tell he really wanted the money and was desperate enough to risk jeopardising the deal to try and screw us for more." Jess could visualise the look. She remembered it well. When Mo had got himself into money problems he got panicky, and with her, it resulted in anger bordering on violence. She could see how, faced with two burly white guys with loads of money to spend, he'd be desperate to get his hands on it even though he knew he had nothing to give in return.

"He was lying about the foster parents in Karachi," she mused out loud, mainly to herself. "Leila was five thousand miles away. He just wanted to cheat you out of the cash." Simon nodded.

"Yep. We knew he was lying about something, we just didn't know what. So then we got another text. 'Meet me at the New Comfort Hotel.'"

***

They had two days to organise the withdrawal from the Mushran Bank. Michael Goodman had already transferred the funds but they'd left them there, knowing they'd be safer. The American tourists were big spenders, it seemed, and more than generous in their appreciation of the manager, who had seen to their every need. Now they had twenty-five thousand US dollars in thousand-dollar bundles stuffed into a rucksack which never left their sight.

They went to check the bizarrely named New Comfort Hotel, which boasted neither newness nor comfort as far as they could tell, and decided they needed to work out a plan. Rutherford would stay with Faisal in the car and hold the money; Jackson would meet them alone, and when he was satisfied Leila was there and the coast was relatively clear, he'd text Rutherford to join them. Faisal would stand by in the car and whisk them all away when the time was right.

At midnight, Jackson walked up to the double doors of the New Comfort Hotel carrying a rucksack over his shoulder, padded out with newspapers. The door was locked and although he could see the lobby area was dimly lit, there was no sign of life. He looked around him and plucked his phone out of his pocket. No messages. He heard a click behind him and the door opened, one of Mo's minder pals stepping back to let him in. As he passed, he dialled Rutherford's number and slipped his phone upside down into his top pocket.

He walked slowly into the lobby area, his body tensed and ready, expecting to be jumped, but there was no one there other than the minders. He was about to ask where Mo was when he appeared from a door behind reception. He looked sweaty and nervous and he skipped the pleasantries.

"Where's your mate?"

"Waiting in the car."

"Have you got the money?" he asked, nodding at the rucksack and wringing his hands together. He was agitated.

"Where's Leila?"

"Have you got the money?" It was almost a shout. Jackson tapped the rucksack with his spare hand

"You get the money when we get Leila."

Jackson turned his head as one guy came up alongside, the other taking up position in front of the main door. Despite the humidity inside, the guy next to him was wearing a jacket. He was big and blubbery and sweating profusely.

"I told you, Leila's with her foster parents." He was giggling now, a manic chuckle at a humourless joke. He nodded to the fat guy standing next to Jackson, who slipped his hand inside his jacket and pulled out a handgun, pointing it at Jackson's head. Jackson looked at it: a 9 mm Beretta lookalike. A locally made clone, but at this distance, just as deadly.

"No need for the pistol, Mo," he said slowly, head canted towards his shirt pocket.

"Insurance. Give me the bag," he said, holding out a hand and flicking a finger. Jackson stood and counted – *five, six, seven, eight* – and when the fat guy twitched his gun hand, he slipped the rucksack off his shoulder and handed it over.

Mo snatched it and feverishly unzipped the top – *nine, ten, eleven*. He stuffed his hand inside, looking for bundles of notes, and, not finding them, unzipped a side pocket, his panic growing. Jackson watched the fat guy. He moved a foot, adjusting his stance, and took his eyes off Jackson, momentarily distracted by Mo's rummaging.

Twelve! Jackson's hand shot out and grabbed the gunman's wrist, pushed the hand vertical and pressed his thumb hard on the nerve, causing him to shriek and release the weapon, and then, with all his bodyweight, brought his knee up between the guy's legs. The fat guy bellowed in pain, doubled over, and Jackson brought a fist down on his neck. He crumpled to a heap on the floor.

The other minder was only just beginning to react to the danger when the door behind him flew open and he was thrown forward. He turned, face contorted with fear as Rutherford grabbed his shirt collar, pulled his face towards him and headbutted him on the bridge of the nose.

His head snapped back, blood spraying in all directions as Rutherford put one hand behind his neck, bent him over and ran him into a concrete pillar face first. He hit the floor, legs and arms twisted and buckled beneath him, inert.

Mo hurled the bag at Jackson, but he swatted it away and jumped on him, got him in a headlock and walked him over to the reception desk. He slapped Mo face down and sideways on the wooden counter and twisted one arm up behind his back. Mo screamed in pain.

"Okay! Okay!" he wailed, chest heaving, saliva dribbling from one corner of his mouth onto the desk.

"Now," said Jackson through clenched teeth, "we said we didn't want any trouble, Mo. We just wanted the girl. Do you want trouble, Mo?"

"No, no! No trouble."

"Okay then, just tell us where she is and then we'll all go there together to see her. All right?" He jerked Mo's head up and slapped it down again on the counter with a bang. "All right?"

"All right, all right! She's in London," he said, sniffing, his words slurred, mouth twisted, one side of it pressed against the counter. "St John's Wood." Jackson narrowed his eyes.

"St John's Wood?" Mo tried to nod, twitching hysterically. "Where? Address?"

"Don't know!" wailed Mo, desperate not to incur their wrath. "Can't remember. Tudor Avenue or something. Name of Mahmoud Kayani. My mate Ahmed set it up. He's their driver."

"What's she doing there, scumbag?" hissed Jackson in frustration and banged Mo's head on the counter once more.

"Aagh! They gave me money. They wanted a kid."

Jackson's rage would have been almost impossible to contain, but a sudden noise behind them made them both turn to see four more guys coming through the front door towards them. Jackson let go of Mo, who slid off the counter onto the floor. He and Rutherford separated, clenching their fists in readiness. Jackson noticed Mo getting to his feet trying to escape but he didn't get far, his way blocked by three more heavies who appeared from a door behind reception. Mo stepped backwards towards the SAS men as this new set of villains approached them from both sides, two of them holding guns.

"Help me!" said Mo, panic-stricken, and it took a moment for Jackson to realise he was addressing them rather than the approaching men. Two of them stepped forward, grabbed Mo and held him, as a third, who was smaller and more smartly dressed, picked up Jackson's discarded rucksack and emptied the newspapers out on the floor. He nodded to the guys by the door, who sidled around the SAS men in a wide arc and followed their colleagues as they dragged a screaming Mo out the way they had come. "Help me!" came the plaintive cries until the reception eventually fell silent.

Jackson looked at Rutherford.

"What was all that about?"

Rutherford looked at Jackson and shook his head, and then his face fell.

"Shit! Faisal!"

They jumped over Mo's unconscious minders and charged out through the front door, sprinting fifty yards up the street. The car was where Simon had left it, Faisal still in the driver's seat. Jackson leapt into the back and opened the rucksack containing the money. It was all there. Faisal turned around, smiling broadly.

"Not all Pakis are bloody bastards, you know, Jack sahib!"

CHAPTER 22

The laundry was there as scheduled when they stepped outside their rooms the next morning. It smelt of detergent but was clean, ironed and neatly folded. Five dollars' worth. Jess treated herself to a full set of clean clothes and put the remaining dirty ones in the bag to take back to reception. Simon had said they'd stay another night, so there was time.

They drank tea and ate pancakes with honey, the Chinese opposite shovelling down noodles and rice, alert and talkative, apparently suffering no ill effects from the previous night's drinking session.

"I've been so busy thinking about what you told me last night I haven't given much thought to Lisa. Where are we going to find her?"

"I don't expect it'll be that difficult. We just ask around a bit. Someone will know her. It's not a huge place, just a bit spread out. Have you decided what you are going to say to her?"

She sighed deeply.

"No. I can't say I'm looking forward to it. The last thing I want to do is upset her."

"Fear of the unknown. That's all."

They started at the reception desk with the surly owner.

"European woman, twenties, looks a bit like my friend here but has a scar on her face, walks with a limp. They're sisters."

The owner shook his head without taking any time to think about it and went back to his calculator. They stepped outside, through the archway and onto the main street.

They walked through the village, passing people going about their business carrying bundles of grass or pushing trolleys full of vegetables, men flicking long bamboo whips at mules laden with gas bottles and heavy wicker baskets, the cowbells around their necks clanging tunelessly as they walked. Men and women were working in the fields on either side, prodding and poking at the rich brown soil with their hoes, forks and spades; small children hung around munching crispy snacks fished from plastic packets, while chickens, dogs and cats roamed freely. Simon asked a couple of people he thought might be able to help, but it seemed no one knew anything.

"You'd think Lisa would have been a minor celebrity," he said after a while. "There can't be many people like her around here." They walked on and they could tell they were reaching the village outskirts as the houses began to thin out, as did the number of people they met. "Let's go on another five minutes and then we can retrace our steps and explore some of the side streets."

The path began to deteriorate and the paving slabs gave way to dirt and rocks, signalling the end of the populated area and the beginning of open countryside. Ahead of them the valley opened up, revealing mile upon mile of rice terraces cascading down the slopes to join endless lush paddy fields that stretched into the distance.

Jess had begun to think the whole expedition may have been a waste of time and she felt increasingly despondent. She wanted more than anything else to be back home with her girls and she wanted an excuse to give up. She had a plane to catch and they didn't have much time left. She'd tried, she would tell Peter in her private moments, but she'd failed. She convinced herself that she would, after all, have to live with a cloud hanging over the heads of her and her family. So be it. Michael had been right. The chances were negligible, and having come all this way, seen the extent of the isolation and the remoteness of life in this far flung corner of the planet, it was inconceivable their two worlds would ever collide.

She stopped and leant on a rickety wooden fence that bordered the path and watched the cloud swirl around the towering, snow-capped peak of Shishapangma, 8,013 metres tall, which dominated the landscape, standing proud and majestic to the south-east. She looked down across a sloping wild flower meadow where a small stone house stood a hundred yards away, wispy smoke curling upwards from its thatched roof. In the fields around the house, goats grazed and chickens pecked, and beyond it a crystal-clear river glistened and sparkled in the sunshine as it danced its way down the valley.

Fifty yards to the right of the house she saw a bright white dome-shaped structure, topped by streams of multicoloured prayer flags that stretched to the ground, a large elliptical eye painted in blue on the side, its walls inset with prayer wheels – a small stupa, like the type she had seen in Kathmandu and in one or two villages along the way. And high above against the deep blue, circling effortlessly on the thermal currents, an eagle, vigilant and alert, guardian of its own domain. Simon rested his arms on the fence beside her.

"What are you thinking?"

She stood, quiet, the sun warming her face, her eyes squinting in the glare, her lungs pulling in the sweet, cool air until her chest could expand no more and she felt the spirit rise within her.

"It's here."

She walked back along the path until she found a break in the fence and the rough, grassy footpath that led through the meadow and down to the house. She walked slowly and rhythmically, relishing every step of the journey, her mind overtaken by a rare tranquillity, an awareness of calm and a growing enlightenment. As she approached the house from the right-hand side, a raised wooden platform came into view, and sitting on it, cross-legged, arms extended forward, hands turned upwards in supplication, was the figure of a young woman, long brown hair tied in a ribbon.

Jess continued until she was alongside the figure and then stopped, a distance of ten feet between them. She turned slowly to look at her, but the woman remained still, breathing slowly and deeply, eyes open but unseeing, unwavering in concentration.

Jess waited, unwilling or unable to interrupt, and after five minutes or so the figure bowed her head once, reached for the stick that lay before her, brought it up to a vertical position and, using only the strength in her arms, propelled herself to her feet. She wore a burgundy-coloured smock, streaks of orange and yellow on the sleeves, and black cotton trousers, baggy like culottes, revealing brightly coloured socks under open sandals.

She turned to look at Jess and her face was calm and benign, open and smiling, emanating a depth of goodness and kindness that filled her heart.

"I knew you'd come," said Alisha.

CHAPTER 23

Jess and Simon sat on a goatskin rug on the floor as Alisha poured boiling water from a blackened kettle into three tin cups before setting it back down on the open fireplace.

"Thank you," said Jess, and Simon nodded his thanks as they took the cups. Alisha crossed her legs and dropped to a seated position opposite Jess, with Simon at right angles, looking uncomfortable and confused, head switching from to the other and back again.

"I'm sorry I was not able to speak with you at my father's funeral. If I had, perhaps you would not have had to make such a long journey. But I am very pleased you did."

"I don't understand," said Jess. "Did you see me there? Did you have any idea who I was?"

"I saw a young woman with two small children. I asked Michael who they were and he was reluctant to explain fully, other than to tell me your name and to say that my father had made 'other arrangements'. I trust the little girls are not my half-sisters?" The question was direct and personal, but her smile so open and honest, there could be no possibility of misunderstanding or giving offence. However, Jess couldn't stop herself. She rushed to Peter's defence.

"God, no!" Then she realised she may have overreacted. "I mean, I was already pregnant when I met Peter. He helped me." She was aware Simon was looking at her and she turned her head to see surprise and confusion. He couldn't have known they'd be identical and now she'd have even more explaining to do.

"I wouldn't be unhappy if they were, Jess," continued Alisha, and Jess lowered her head, feeling some guilt and not a little shame.

Jess wrestled with her thoughts. She felt she owed Alisha an explanation even though Alisha had not yet given any sign she was inquisitive or looking for answers. And she soon realised that it was she who needed answers. That was why she had come, after all.

"I don't know where to start," she said sadly, suddenly tongue-tied. She had rehearsed this conversation from the moment she'd made the decision to come to Nepal, and now, none of it seemed relevant.

"We have time. I have no classes today so we can talk for as long as you need to find the things you are looking for."

"Classes? Are you still a teacher?"

"Yes. I teach the children English."

"No one in the town seemed to know who you were," said Simon, looking puzzled. "It's a miracle we even found you."

"I asked them not to help you, not to help anyone. If anyone came looking for me they should make no effort to direct them. I didn't ask them to lie; just to remain quiet."

"But why?"

"Because I thought there might be people who would want to use it for their own selfish purposes."

"Is that what you think about me?"

"No, Jess. I knew that good people would be able to find me themselves, or be guided here by good people." She turned her head towards Simon, the curiosity evident.

"Sujay was the one who brought me, but he got hurt. He had to go back. Simon here was on hand to take over." She didn't want to go into any detail. She didn't want to relive the nightmare of the attack.

"Sujay is a good person. I pray he recovers soon. He was the one who helped me remember who I really was."

"And who were you really?" Jess couldn't help the flicker of accusation creeping into her voice. Alisha was so calm and so measured and so totally disconnected it was unnerving. Worst of all, she seemed utterly dispassionate, especially so soon after Peter's death.

"Perhaps we might walk?"

Jess turned to Simon.

"Is that okay?"

"Fine by me. I imagine you two have a lot to talk about. I'll just hang around here."

Alisha got to her feet with the aid of her walking stick but Jess could see it was a struggle, and although Alisha tried to remain impassive, Jess could tell she was in pain. Jess jumped up and followed her out onto the porch and into the mid-morning sunshine.

"I think your friend Simon was quite surprised to see us together. We could be twin sisters."

"Yes, I think it came as a shock to us all."

"You knew?"

"Not initially. I saw a photograph of you and Janica. Peter had hidden it away."

"And what did you think?"

"I finally understood why he'd been acting so strangely. I wasn't sure why he was so keen to help me, and at the time I didn't know anything about him or you. He hadn't told me you were missing. I don't think he wanted to believe it. He just said, you were 'away'."

"Simon is your husband?"

"Oh no. I only met him a few days ago. I'm not married."

"But you have two small children?"

"Three."

"Goodness! You have three small children but no husband?" Jess looked at her and felt a sudden prick of resentment at the implied reproach. She hadn't come all this way for a lecture in morality. But why would anyone not be surprised? Sujay was. And anyway, she had misinterpreted Alisha's reaction. "That must be very hard for you." The smile said it all. It was a smile that saw the good in everything; sympathised with and forgave everything and everyone and conveyed nothing other than concern for her well-being. Jess wanted to explain how it had all happened, but it was too complicated and it would take too long. She hadn't come to explain herself; she'd come to listen.

Alisha stepped carefully down from the porch onto the ground, the stick in her right hand supporting a right leg that was stiff and awkward. Alisha limped while Jess walked slowly towards the stream and Jess felt the warmth of the sun on her head. She slipped off her jacket, throwing it over one shoulder, her finger crooked in the tab.

"We all thought you had died in the earthquake."

"Lisa died. Alisha was born."

"Is that what you believe?"

"Not literally, no. But the events of that day shaped us all, in one way or another. Changed things forever. Just as your being here has changed things." They reached the stream. Alisha crossed one leg over the other and lowered herself to the ground. Jess sat next to her, the eagle circling high, watching.

"I first learnt about the Buddha when I was at university. It did no more than intrigue me at the time and I would probably never have pursued it had I not lost someone very dear to me." Alisha maintained the smile but Jess could see it was different. She saw the depth of sadness wash over her; for all her apparent lack of emotion, Alisha was clearly still tormented by the loss of her mother. The contrast with her attitude to Peter was stark.

"I behaved badly towards my father and he got very angry. I see now that he wasn't angry with me, he was angry with himself. But the truth is, I refused to allow myself to be consoled. You know, Buddhists believe that the level of suffering we experience is a consequence of having behaved badly in a former life. I thought I was being punished for something I had done. I was looking for answers and for a way to repent my sins, although I had no way of knowing what those sins might have been. Through understanding the Dharma – that's the teachings of the Buddha – I learnt that the only way to break the endless cycle of rebirth, the perpetual suffering and dissatisfaction each new life brings, was to follow the Great Path."

Jess watched and listened in fascination as Alisha spoke in her gentle, rational and unemotional way but in terms she couldn't possibly understand. She wanted to interrupt her, to probe her with questions, challenge the self-indulgent delusions that seemed to have caused so much heartache to her father. But part of her recognised that Alisha had gone in search of an inner peace and, on the face of it, seemed to have found it. She felt the stirrings of admiration and not a little envy, and she wanted to hear more.

"Janica was the most beautiful person. She had grace and poise and tolerance in abundance. She was only twenty-one when I was born and I grew up alongside her, never separated. My father was often away during the first few years of my life, so when he did come home I saw this much older, rather severe-looking man in an imposing uniform, and he seemed like a stranger, or at best, a family acquaintance. Even at a very early age I think I may have resented him coming back, disrupting our idyllic existence, and we never truly bonded; not like I did with Janica, whom I regarded more as a big sister. And when I got older, I understood the significance of the age difference. I learnt that my father had been married before and I resented the fact that he had not waited for Janica, that he could have possibly given his heart to another. It added to the impression that he was not one of us, that he was separate.

"I was still very young then and it got better when he retired. I was fourteen when we moved to Chalton, and he seemed to soften and become more approachable. He was never one for physical contact, not one to pick me up and cuddle me, but I don't think I ever needed anyone other than Janica."

Alisha paused. Her gentle smile had not wavered throughout, her reminiscences, fond and genuine, but Jess could see she was gathering her strength, summoning up her energy and self-control.

"Janica became ill. We didn't realise it for a long time but she grew increasingly tired, and while she had always been slim, she lost weight, her beautiful skin developed marks and blotches, and streaks of grey began to appear in her hair. She never complained but when we eventually persuaded her to seek help, her leukaemia was well advanced. I watched her die a slow and agonising death, and all the while, my father remained rock solid, seemingly unmoved, incapable of showing any emotion as we just watched her slip away. I know now he was just trying to support us, remain optimistic despite the evidence and the certainty we all had that she would die, but it pushed us even further apart. I had to get away. Be alone for a while.

"I began to find the answers when I came to Nepal. It took a while, but I read the teachings and they gave me comfort, seemed to make everything clearer. I did speak to my father, on and off, just to tell him where I was, what I was doing and that I was fine, and despite the distance between us, or perhaps because of it, our relationship grew. The truth was, I was beginning to make peace with myself and I was able to look at him in a new light, understand that I was not alone in my suffering; we simply dealt with it in a different way. One of the guiding principles of the Mahayana strand of Buddhism is the quest to find happiness and contentment for others as well as yourself. I was coming to the conclusion that here was where I wanted to be, where I needed to be. It might all have been so different."

"Do you think you would have gone back to England if you hadn't been in Langtang?"

"I imagine I would have gone to visit."

Jess nodded in understanding. Lisa had found a new life for herself. Notwithstanding the terrible events at Langtang, Peter had probably lost his daughter anyway but in a way he might have been able to accept. He would never have stood in the way of Lisa's happiness, never have put his own interests ahead of hers, and if only he had known she was alive, he would have been saddened that they remained apart, but in the end, accepting and content.

"He blamed himself, and he never stopped blaming himself, right up to the day he died," said Jess.

"Then we definitely had something in common."

Jess could tell that, despite Alisha's composure and her enigmatic smile, Lisa was hurting,

"Is that why you came back?"

"Sujay spent two weeks with me here in Chumtang. He told me a story of a dashing army officer who had once gone in search of someone he loved, even though he knew it was hopeless. He described him to me and told me what he had said and where he had come from, and once the seeds had been sown, the memory came flooding back. I wanted to see him."

"But he died before you could re-establish contact." Jess remembered the day in the garden, the last day of Peter's life, when he got the news about Leila. And at the same time, Lisa was making her way back into his life. He just didn't know it. No one knew. "And then you came back anyway?"

"I had to say goodbye. I had to say sorry."

"He would never have accepted any apology. You could do no wrong in his mind."

"But instead of me, he had you."

Yes, me and my problems.

"Not instead, Alisha."

"But you brought him happiness in his final days."

Jess had never considered this before. She supposed Peter must have been content. Even when they found out she was pregnant he'd been kind and supportive; her condition had never been an issue for him. She always thought that, for him, having her there was better than having no one at all. But then she didn't know that he'd paid off all her debts, wiped the slate clean, nor that he'd set in train the operation to find Leila. All this consideration for her, never explicit, never mentioned, just a determination to help, to put things right, that was the sort of man Peter Jeffries was; a man who never sought recognition, or affection or devotion from anyone and expected no more or less from others.

"I think so. But I still owe him a debt of gratitude I can never repay."

"Perhaps you already did?"

They sat quietly in contemplation, side by side, at the edge of the stream carrying the crystalline waters down the valley. The sky was a deep blue with only fragments of cloud swirling around the snow-capped peaks of the mountains. Jess felt an inner calm, a release from the myriad thoughts that had tormented her, finding that however things might appear, the truth was never simple.

"Would you like to join me in meditation?" asked Alisha without turning her head, and Jess saw her eyes were closed, her expression serene, her arms resting on her crossed legs, the way they had been when she first saw her.

"I don't know how."

"I will teach you. It will help you get to know your own mind. The Buddha says the untrained mind is like an angry elephant, trampling over the happiness in your life, causing untold destruction and mayhem. Meditation can expand your awareness and so purify your mind." Jess copied Alisha's posture and closed her eyes. "Don't try and empty your mind. You'll find it impossible to think of nothing. Allow it to wander and allow your other senses to guide you."

Jess closed her eyes. After a while, the sounds around her slowly amplified to take up the space vacated by sight. She heard the wind whistling through the mountain peaks, distant and eerie yet beautiful and calming, the rush of clear water pure and life-giving, and in her mind she could see the eagle, perpetually circling, searching, watching. She saw her children, Leila and Sophie and Lucy, conceived through exploitation, ugliness and hatred, yet beautiful, laughing and smiling and loving, and the bitterness she had once felt gradually receded, replaced by gratitude for their being.

She saw Peter on the ridge, searching in vain for his own version of peace and then finding it by watching over her and bringing her a stability and peace she had never known before. And through the eyes of the eagle, she saw herself sitting on the ground, tiny and insignificant, surrounded by giants, vulnerable and defenceless in the face of the infinite forces of nature, yet susceptible only to the harm she might bring on herself through her own misguided mind.

She opened her eyes and turned her head. Alisha was looking at her, smiling in her own inimitable way. Loving, compassionate and considerate; the search of happiness and contentment for others a prerequisite for finding it for herself.

"How long have we been sitting here?" she asked, checking her fake Gucci and then feeling embarrassed at how quickly she had lapsed, reverted to the real world.

"Are you worried about time?"

"Simon might be getting concerned."

"Let's go back and have some food."

Simon was nowhere to be seen when Alisha and Jess arrived back at the house. Instead, there was a note pinned to the front door: "Gone back to the hotel, catch up later. S."

"I'll make us some lunch."

They sat cross-legged on the floor, ate fruit and rice with their hands and they talked. Jess talked about her life as a teenager, about her troubles at home and her marriage to Mo, his disappearance with Leila leaving her destitute and traumatised; her decision to abandon Jess and her renaissance as Alice, only to find her hopes of a better life quickly dashed and, just as she was about to end it all, her chance meeting with Peter.

"We loved that boat," said Alisha. "He used to take us out on day trips in the warm weather and we had picnics on the riverbank. What happened to it?"

"I ... we still have it. It's moored in its usual place but it hasn't been out for a long while. I'm not sure I could manage it." Jess was suddenly reminded that the boat and everything else Peter had ever owned was in her name now. She didn't know why she felt so deeply ashamed and unworthy, but she did.

She looked around her. Alisha's world comprised nothing more than the bare essentials of life. A range with open fire, a few blackened pots and pans, a bamboo basket containing fruit and vegetables and a small table with various jars and bottles. Cut into one wall was a niche housing a small Buddha, some fading flowers and a smouldering incense stick. A shelf held a number of books, mostly in a foreign language, and next to it, set against the wall, a narrow bed covered in blankets and goatskin. The only decoration was a large, colourful poster that was fixed to the wall above the bed, and Alisha saw it held her attention.

"That's the Wheel of Life. It illustrates the connection between those elements of a deluded mind which keep you in a permanent cycle of suffering and dissatisfaction. We believe that the things you experience in life are not pre-determined; they are a product of and caused by the delusions in your own mind. Our search for enlightenment, once found, will eventually lead us out of the endless cycle."

"There is no such thing as fate," said Jess absently, the phrase coming to her in an instant.

"I'll make you a Buddhist yet!"

"I don't think I'm cut out for it." They both laughed. "I'm not sure I can devote my life to any faith."

"It's not a faith, Jess. It's just a set of principles. The Buddha said that if some of his principles and teachings don't work for you, that's fine; follow the ones that do." Jess nodded although she felt she had a long way to go before even partly understanding. "Anyway, I would never preach to you. No one can make you a Buddhist other than yourself. You will know if and when it's right for you."

Alisha's words filled Jess with a warmth and humility that raised her spirits and lifted her self-esteem. In her short time with Peter's daughter many things had become clear in her mind, and she felt vindicated in having made the decision to find her. But she was reminded there was another purpose in her coming and time was running out. It seemed incongruous, here in a place where time and space seemed to have no relevance, that she should be looking at her watch, but her own world was waiting for her and it was a long way away.

She hunted around for the words. It seemed crude and vulgar to discuss matters of wealth, here in this place, with this woman who had nothing when she had everything. It risked debasing their relationship, defiling the bond she hoped they had so quickly formed.

"I wanted to ask you ..." she said hesitantly. "You came to say your goodbyes to Peter and then left. You came straight back here to resume your life alone in this remote corner of the world."

"I am not alone." Alisha looked puzzled at the assertion.

"I mean, you asked no questions about me, you simply disappeared again like you did the first time, and you choose to continue living here, like this." It wasn't coming out the way she wanted. It was beginning to sound like criticism and it wasn't what she meant. She needed to be brave. "Peter left everything in his will to me and my children."

"I know," said Alisha, as inscrutable as before.

"It doesn't belong to me. It belongs to you." Jess looked in the mirror that was Alisha, consumed with guilt for something she knew was not of her making, craving understanding and forgiveness for unwittingly purloining the birthright of another and conscious that in doing so she was putting her own family at risk. Alisha looked in the mirror that was Jess and the smiling countenance never once faded or flickered.

"Look around you, Jess. Not just here, but everywhere. I have no need for material possessions, nor, I believe, do you.

Otherwise you wouldn't be here. We reject the relentless pursuit of wealth, the insatiable desire to acquire physical objects; objects that delude us into thinking they will enrich our lives and make us happier, when in reality they only make things worse, creating further dissatisfaction and misery, thereby perpetuating the cycle. And so it continues. The Wheel of Life." She indicated the poster on the wall. "I am one of the lucky ones. I found another way. I found a way to break out of the Wheel of Life. I have not managed it yet, and I may not manage it in this life. But I expect to do it in the next. You may not realise it, but you are halfway there yourself." Jess looked up at her alter ego. Alisha was right, in one sense.

"You are willing to forsake that which countless others would sell their souls to own; not because you feel unworthy, although I have no doubt those feelings play some part, but because deep down you know there are far more important things in life. You did something I was not able to do. You supported my father through some of the darkest moments of his life, and you gave him a reason to live. You gave him someone to whom he could finally show his love and he did it in the only way he knew how: selflessly and unconditionally. There is no shame in accepting his gift. I know you will use it for the good of others."

Jess sat quietly, absorbing words she had never expected to hear. She had come to challenge Lisa, understand how she could have been so cruel to a wonderful man, her father, and let her know the pain she had caused. She had come to defend herself from any accusation, presumed or otherwise, that she had taken advantage of an old man's vulnerability. She had come to demonstrate her fierce independence, her reliance on no one and her determination to look after her own, regardless of what that might take. And she had come ready to hand it all back, renounce the pretender's rights in favour of the real heir, the real daughter.

Instead, Alisha had presented her with a new version of the truth; a truth that portrayed Peter as the main beneficiary of their chance encounter. He had been the one in need, and she, the one who fulfilled it. She was the one who had suffered the trauma of abuse and neglect throughout her life, despite which she had placed her trust in a man who, destroyed by self-inflicted, misplaced guilt and nearing the end of his own, had been given one last chance to make amends.

"Shall I make some tea?"

Without waiting for an answer, Alisha struggled to her feet, hobbled over to the stove and placed the heavy, blackened kettle into position. She reached underneath and pulled out a couple of logs and placed them carefully on the glowing embers. They ignited instantly.

There was a soft tap on the door. It opened and Simon's head appeared.

"I'm just making tea, Simon."

"Excellent!" he replied. Jess and Alisha looked at each other and, to his evident surprise and discomfort, they both burst out laughing.

CHAPTER 24

Jess and Simon ate dinner in the hotel canteen amidst the same cacophony of clanging woks, excitable Chinese traders and general ribaldry they had experienced the previous night.

"You sounded just like Peter." She was still laughing at the memory of Simon's return to Alisha's house. She guided a bundle of hot noodles into her mouth with her disposable chopsticks.

"Did I? When?"

"When you said 'Excellent'." She snorted again at the memory.

"Oh. I'm always saying that. Maybe that's where I got it from."

"It was his favourite answer to just about everything."

Two guys on the opposite table were having a major argument over a game of mah-jong and their mates were doing nothing to discourage the aggression.

"Did you and Alisha say your goodbyes?" asked Simon. She shook her head while she swallowed.

"She's got a class tomorrow. Eight o'clock. I said we'd drop by on our way. The school's that orange thatched building with the yard out front and the basketball net. We passed it on the way in."

Simon studied her closely.

"And did you find what you were looking for?"

"I found much more than that. I'm really glad I came. I would have spent the rest of my life hating her for something she didn't do."

"I can't get over the resemblance," he said, chewing on some pork belly. "You two are identical twins. Apart from the scar, of course. Without that I bet she'd scrub up really well." The comment brought her up short. She stopped shovelling and looked up at him but his head was turned away, doing his best to appear nonchalant, although his best wasn't very good. She narrowed her eyes and smiled at him and he caught her stare.

"What?" he shrugged. She hit him with her chopsticks. "Ow!"

"Don't get clever with me, Rutherford." She pointed her chopsticks at him threateningly and they both laughed.

"So, if we get a good start tomorrow morning, we may be able to get back to Langtang by the time it's dark and avoid another night in the shed."

"Bliss."

"After that, it's the usual ups and downs but on average it's down, so we should get back a lot quicker than on the way out."

"I can't wait to get home. It seems a lifetime ago I left Chalton. Can I call home?"

"You don't have to ask."

"It's only polite." She smiled at him as he handed her the phone and she dialled the number and waited, her eyes darting around in expectation.

Simon finished his meal and flagged down a waiter who brought him another Tuborg, while Jess chatted to the children and then Keira. "We're heading back tomorrow. I'll call you when I get to Kathmandu. Bye." She handed him the phone.

"Everything okay?"

"Usual chaos, but the adults seem to be bearing up under the strain."

"And are you coping okay?"

"It was difficult at first. I mean, when Leila came back. I was used to the twins but Leila was only four when Mo took her, and getting her back after five years away, well, she was a very different little girl, and we're both still coming to terms with it. And then no sooner is she back then I go off and leave her again." Simon sighed.

"There you go again. Beating yourself up. I don't think you came out here on a whim or because you fancied a bit of altitude sickness."

"No. I didn't. But I'm ready to get back." Jess handed the remains of her beer to Simon. Part of her was reluctant to revisit the subject, but she felt she needed to know. "You didn't tell me what happened after, you know, the business with Mo."

"Do you want dessert?"

"Go on, Day-Glo custard and all. Better get my strength up for the trek." He flagged down a waiter and mumbled something incoherent.

"Well, we regrouped back at the hotel. We didn't have much confidence that Mo was telling the truth, but we were pretty certain that he'd have exchanged Leila for the money if he had her, and making up a story about Kayani and his driver on the spur of the moment wasn't likely. It sounded plausible, but we didn't have Mo anymore and frankly we weren't sure whether we'd ever see him again."

Jess nodded. It sounded like Mo had finally reaped what he had sown. She couldn't help feeling some sadness, but reminding herself of all he had done to her and others, and what he had continued to do back in Pakistan, left little room for sympathy.

"But we did some checks on Kayani and quickly found out he was a big noise and, yes, indeed, he was resident in the UK. I went back to London to check it out and Jack stayed on in Karachi to keep his eye on the cab company. Faisal kept feeding him reports, but there was no sign of Mo, nor was there any sign of the bad guys in suits who'd been looking for him, so we figured it was a dead end. Faisal stayed on there for another couple of months and then we pulled him out."

The waiter dumped two plates of the unprepossessing orange doughnut concoction and they looked at each other like two people about to jump into the unknown.

***

Rutherford walked purposefully along the pavement opposite the Kayani residence, passing innumerable cars parked in the residents' bays along Tudor Avenue. He'd noticed the gates were closed, as usual, and there were always at least two cars in the driveway, meaning that the residents were coming and going, but so far he hadn't seen any movement.

He didn't stop. It would have looked suspicious, and he was sure that the cameras either side of the gate would pick up all movement within a wide arc, so he'd limited his viewings to one in the morning and one at night; a commuter going to and from work. After a week of no activity, he decided he'd have to find a more permanent place for a stakeout. The difficulty would be finding somewhere that was available to rent and afforded a good view of the house.

He'd already discovered the houses in and around the area started at five million pounds, so buying was clearly out of the question. Renting was also eye-wateringly expensive, and even if he could get clearance from Michael Goodman for the cost, the chances of a suitable place turning up in the near future were slim.

He'd been back in the UK for four months now and had got nowhere, and it bothered him. He still didn't know for certain whether they even had the girl as Mo had claimed, and although there was the odd reference to Kayani in the press, there was no evidence that he had any family with him, let alone some daughter he had bought as a plaything for his wife. But Jack had no more information from his end, so they relied on the fact that Mo was not interested in Leila, had simply wanted their money, and if he had chosen to lie about her location, he would have picked somewhere far less ostentatious to lie about.

In the absence of a suitable property from which to conduct surveillance, he sat, as he did most days, in his small hire car, parked in a side street around the corner from the house, fake resident's parking permit in the car window. He couldn't see the gates, but would see any car coming in or out and, if going out, see which way it had headed. He had followed the Range Rover two or three times, but it always had four guys in it, one of them Kayani, and they'd usually gone into the City or to a West End restaurant. The Porsche too had gone out, making the occasional visit to Knightsbridge, and had been driven by an expensively dressed woman whom he took to be Mrs Kayani, always with a woman companion. There was never any sign of children.

At around 11 a.m. the nose of a black Mercedes S Class appeared, driven by a woman, this time with two men in the back. He let it go and within a minute or two the Range Rover edged out and turned left, with only the driver on board. Rutherford fired up the Focus and set off behind it.

He followed the Range Rover from three cars back, lost it twice at traffic lights and then picked it up again as it headed up Finchley Road and onto Hendon Way. It pulled into the Brent Cross Shopping Centre car park and parked in a disabled bay. The driver got out and walked towards the centre.

Rutherford found a space, parked and jumped out. He'd lost sight of the driver but had already clocked the shaved head, dark suit and the black and gold aviators, and thought it would be relatively easy to find him again. It took him only five minutes. He was sitting in the window of a Caffè Nero, coffee on the table in front of him next to a folded-up Daily Mail, studying his smartphone.

Rutherford went inside, bought an Americano and sat at a table twelve feet behind, from where he could watch but remain out of sight. He pulled out his own phone and flicked the screen with a thumb to make himself look busy. He strained his eyes to try and see what the guy was looking at but he was too far away to see anything clearly. After about ten minutes a young white guy turned up, leather jacket, jeans and trainers, a pink streak in his blonde, slicked-back hair, carefully crafted sideburns, moustache and goatee. Approaching the table, he smiled broadly and went to embrace the driver as he stood up, who then looked immediately uncomfortable and gestured to his friend to sit.

The young man was unperturbed, leaning forward, eyes wide and smiling, chatting animatedly, although he kept his voice low and Rutherford couldn't hear anything. At one point he reached out and touched the back of the driver's hand and there was a second's hesitation before the driver drew his hand away and looked around nervously. The one-sided conversation carried on for another ten minutes or so until the driver looked at his watch, said something and the young guy sat back, smirking, doe-eyed. The driver stood up and put a hand on the young guy's shoulder. He reached up and squeezed it, and the driver walked out of the coffee shop. Rutherford followed. Out in the car park, the driver approached the Range Rover and, following ten feet behind him, Rutherford decided it was time.

"Ahmed!" he called, and the driver turned. *Bingo.* He could see the driver eyeing him suspiciously as he approached, one hand on the door handle of the Range Rover. Rutherford put a hand up as if he were greeting a long-lost friend.

"Who the fuck are you?" said the driver, taking off his aviators. Rutherford maintained his smile, careful not to react to the implied threat.

"We've got a mutual friend, Ahmed." He took another chance. "Mohammed Khalid?" Ahmed hesitated, just enough, a fraction of a second betraying the recognition. *Bingo.*

"Go fuck yourself." He turned back to the Range Rover.

"Who's your boyfriend?" Ahmed stopped and turned around slowly. Rutherford was still smiling, amicable, despite the aggression. "Must be really good working for someone as liberal-minded as Mr Kayani," he said. He wanted to wink but thought that might be overdoing the irony. He pressed home his advantage. "I mean, back home, that sort of thing's, you know, not really allowed, is it?"

He could see Ahmed weighing up the options. *Could he take me out? Here? In a public place? We're both big guys. Not likely.*

"What do you want, fuckface?" *Bullseye.* Rutherford put his hands up.

"Hey, a friend of Mo's is a friend of mine," he said with mock sincerity. "He just wanted me to find out how Leila was."

"Who?"

"Leila. His daughter. The one Mr and Mrs Kayani adopted?" He sounded earnest, keen to explain who he was talking about even though they both knew.

"Why?" No denial. *Ker-ching.*

"Because he's concerned."

"Well, you tell him not to be concerned. She's fine."

"Ah, well that's good. I'm sure Mo will be very relieved. Well, nice to meet you. Ahmed," he said, placing special emphasis on the name. Rutherford turned his back towards the shopping centre, hands in pockets. He heard the slam of a car door, the roar of the V8 and a squeal of tyres behind him.

***

Simon licked the spoon and put it back in the bowl with a flourish.

"Delicious!"

"So you knew she was there?"

"Ahmed pretty much confirmed it. But that was only one more box ticked. We guessed he wouldn't say anything to Kayani, not now his little secret was out, but we had no idea how we were going to get at Leila. I just thought now we had a foot in the door, we could work out a way of prising it open."

"Did you not think of going to the police? Telling them you had suspicions about an illegal adoption?" Simon gave her a look and she realised she was being naïve.

"Well, that wasn't our brief. That was for others to decide, although I think it would have been a waste of time. But we knew we were looking in the right place. We just needed an opportunity. And two months later, we got one. I'd been sitting there for days without seeing anyone coming or going, when Jack called me."

***

"They're back! The Kayanis. They're back in Islamabad."

"Oh, great," said Rutherford, cold, bored and thoroughly pissed off.

"No. It's good, Si."

"How?"

"Kayani's come back to make a bid for prime minister. I saw him and his wife on the telly meeting the press and a small crowd at the airport. He said how pleased he and his family were to be back home again." Rutherford was still confused.

"Why's that good?"

"Think about it. We know exactly where she is now, and if we're going to snatch her back, then it's better we do it out here than in London." Rutherford had to admit he hadn't worked out how he was going to snatch Leila in the UK and get away with it.

"You make it sound so easy."

"Yeah, well, at least it's progress."

"So where have they gone?"

"They've got a big place in Rawalpindi, beside the lake. That's his official residence."

"And how long are they going to be there?"

"Don't know. But the election's not for a couple of months, and if he wins, they'll stay here for good."

"And you think it's going to be a doddle kidnapping the Pakistani prime minister's daughter?" The phone went silent for a moment.

"Okay. I know it's a long shot. One step at a time."

"I'd better get back over there then." *Deep joy.*

"As soon as you can. See you in Rawalpindi."

CHAPTER 25

They were up at seven, had breakfast at quarter past, and then packed up their stuff and handed the keys in at the desk. There was no bill to settle; pay as you go, in cash, the normal convention. The surly owner smiled at them and waved his arms around effusively, finishing with a bow and a pressing together of palms.

"He's in a good mood," said Jess as they set off through the archway onto the path that was Chumtang High Street.

"Alisha is a highly regarded teacher. He's very pleased to have met her twin sister."

"Word gets around here, doesn't it?" And as if to prove the point, one or two locals greeted them with a bow and an occasional "Namaste" as they made their way along the path heading out of town. Jess felt clean and invigorated in her freshly laundered clothes and she'd been reluctant to surrender the relative comfort of the Traders Lodge in exchange for a few nights roughing it in teahouses, or worse. But she was fortified by the thought of getting home, seeing her girls again and, hopefully, returning to normal. As usual, she'd tied her hair back in a band and it was warm enough to be able to walk in her short-sleeved shirt, so unusually mild was the early morning weather.

They got to the school by 7.45 a.m. and many of the kids were already there, running around the yard, all in uniform; bright blue sweater and shorts for the boys, sweater and skirts for the girls. Jess judged their ages ranged from five to twelve but as the school seemed to comprise only two rooms, she wondered how they were divided.

Alisha saw them approach through the open window and came out to greet them, hobbling over with the aid of her walking stick. She wore a red smock over her baggy black cotton trousers and sandals, her hair tied back with a multicoloured scarf.

"Namaste," she said bowing.

"Namaste," bowed Jess and Simon in return. A number of children gathered round them, giggling shyly, fascinated by two more foreign faces. "I wonder what they're thinking?" said Jess. "Two of us, here together."

"Yes. Unusual enough to have one foreigner in their midst but two the same!"

"I'm going to wait for you by the path, Jess," said Simon, holding out a hand. "Alisha, it's been a pleasure seeing you again after all this time."

"May peace be with you, Simon," she said, surprising him by leaning forward and kissing his cheek. "I trust you will look after my sister?" He nodded and turned away. Alisha shouted something at the children and then followed it up in English. "Say goodbye to Miss Jess." The children complied, shouting and waving in unison. "Now, everyone inside, wait for me there," she said, and the kids dutifully scurried in through the front door.

"Do you think you'll ever come back?" said Jess, already knowing the answer.

"No." It was said without hesitation or regret.

"Then I shall have to come back here and surprise you one day."

"Don't, Jess. Stay and look after your girls. That's where you belong." Jess frowned. It couldn't sound like a rebuff, not from Alisha; it wasn't possible. "I will die soon," she said, her face smiling and impassive as ever.

"What do you mean?" Jess shook her head, unprepared for the shock, unable to hide her confusion.

"I have the same affliction as Janica. I know the signs and the symptoms. I shall die within twelve months."

"Oh, no. Are you sure?"

"Yes. I have lived through this once already."

"But if you came back with us, we could get you some help. Maybe it's not too late." Jess heard the pleading in her own voice and felt a desperate need to help her, make her better. But Alisha was unmoved, her mortality clearly of no great importance.

"I'm ready. I'm ready to come back. I'm ready for the awakening. I have learnt so much in this life that next time, I will find true enlightenment. I am looking forward to it." Jess wiped away the tears as they formed and ran down her face. The concept was alien and unfathomable and utterly terrifying for her, but she knew Alisha was telling her the truth as she saw it and it was clear the truth was not so terrible for her. She flung her arms around her and they held each other for a moment.

"Go in peace, Jess, and may you bring peace to everyone you meet. I know you're able to do that." Jess held Alisha's upper arms and looked into her twin's eyes, their faces an inch apart, tears cascading down her face, dripping onto her lips, the saltiness creeping into her mouth.

She put her hands on either side of Alisha's face, caressed the hideous scar, touched her nose with hers, and for a moment they were as one. She closed her eyes, kissed her sister gently on the lips and released her, turning away to where Simon waited. She strode straight past him, head down, without turning back.

***

"What was all that about?' asked Simon when he caught up with her. She had set off at a pace and although he knew she would waste no time getting back to her girls, it was a pace she couldn't sustain.

"Tell you later." Simon caught the tone in her voice and didn't ask again. They walked onwards and upwards for three hours, stopping only twice for water and a short rest before, after five minutes, she insisted they continue on. They passed the dreaded toolshed by eleven but the grumpy man with the gun was nowhere to be seen. It didn't matter anyway because she appeared determined to get back to Langtang before darkness fell.

Simon called a halt at one thirty and they stopped by a stream, unloaded their rucksacks and washed their faces in the cool water. He pulled bananas and apples out of his bag and handed her one of each.

"Is it something I said?" He never regarded himself as a sensitive soul, but he didn't like to see her like this. Something was eating away at her, festering, ready to boil over. He'd already seen both sides of her; the angry, argumentative, determined way she'd been the first day they'd met and the warm, generous, loving person he'd seen talking to her children on the phone; and if he was honest, he couldn't tell which he liked the best. He just knew that if she was anguished about something, he didn't want to be the cause.

"She's got leukaemia too. Just like her mother." Jess attacked the apple, as if trying to discharge some of her anger onto the fruit. "And she doesn't want any help. Stubborn. Just like her father!" *A bit like her sister too, methinks.* She looked up. "What?"

"That's tough. I didn't think it was hereditary. In fact, I'm sure it's not. It's in the genes. A genetic malfunction."

"Either way, Dr Rutherford, she'll be dead within a year." She was bitter, he could tell. He peeled back the skin of a banana and tossed it as far as he could down the scree bordering the stream. He realised this was no time for levity. Back in the army, it was something they had all learnt to use in order to survive. But it wasn't going to help her here.

"I'm very sorry."

Jess took another bite of her apple and sighed.

"No. I'm sorry. It's no one's fault. I don't mean to be stroppy. I'm just a bit, well, overwrought."

"But you did get to see her. You decided, against good, solid advice, that you needed to meet her. You were right and you must feel vindicated about that and glad you trusted your instincts." He wasn't sure where his new-found sensitivity was coming from. It just seemed natural, somehow.

"When I first saw her, she said she knew I'd come." She shook her head as if trying to clear the fog of conflicting thoughts rampaging around her head. "Is it possible? That it was all meant to be? Were there powers at work here that I just don't understand? Are these same powers at work now? God, it does my head in!"

"Are you asking me or God?" He couldn't help the lapse into flippancy.

"Oh. I've never been religious. Have you?"

"Nope. Although there have been a couple of times when I thought I needed a bit of divine intervention. Don't know if anyone heard me or I just got lucky, but I'm still here. It's all a bit mumbo jumbo to me, religion."

"I can't work it out." She was tormenting herself, he could see, but he knew it would pass as soon as she had something else to worry about.

"Then I suggest you don't even try. Focus on the stuff you can do something about. Like your kids." It was deliberate. He knew she would soften when she thought of her girls and she nodded, looked up at him and a semblance of a smile returned. He decided he liked the warm, loving Jess better.

"So Dr Rutherford is a philosopher too?" He shrugged, accepting the barbed compliment. "You know, an old woman told me something similar a long time ago, and I've never forgotten it."

"Well there you go. I'm as wise as an old woman. Jack would laugh his head off." He was pleased and relieved to see she was laughing too, and he noticed for the first time how intoxicating her smile was. "Come on. Time to get going."

They were back in Langtang by six thirty. It had been dark for the last half hour, but they'd been guided down the mountain by the lights of the town. The noise, activity and revelry of the trekkers and their guides and porters was a welcome release from the quiet seclusion of the trail.

He opened the door to the Panorama Restaurant and ushered her in. It was warm and noisy and steamy, the air filled with the aroma of cooking, the windows dripping with condensation, rows of benches and tables filled with animated travellers of all nationalities. They found a spot and dumped their rucksacks against the wall.

"I'll go and sort out the rooms. The place looks pretty busy to me so we'll have to take pot luck. Order yourself some food and I'll be back in a few moments."

"I'll wait," she said, and he nodded and stepped back outside into the chilly night air. She asked for a lemon and ginger tea and then people-watched, entertained by the porters who doubled up as waiters for their clients and the boisterous conversations of the trekkers, poring over maps and sharing photos. Her very first time out of her own country was to this weird and wonderful place and she would never forget it, for all sorts of reasons. Simon was back in a few minutes.

"Phew, that was a struggle," he said sliding in next to her. "Hungry?"

"Starved."

They ordered beer and dal bhat and apple fritters, and chatted to some Norwegians who, it seemed, spoke English better than they did, and when they had finished, Simon paid the bill.

"Come on. I'll show you to your room."

They crossed the courtyard and he unlocked the door to a room at the very end of the row. She breathed in deeply and stretched her arms but then shivered and wrapped her jacket around her, looking up at the night sky. It was clear and black and speckled with the wondrous light of a million stars. She noticed his outstretched hand, took the key and stepped into the room.

The teahouse was relatively new, as was everything in Langtang, but it didn't mean it was any more salubrious than the old. It featured the bare essentials of a double bed, a table and chair and a light bulb, and the stone floor glistened with condensation. It was damp and cold.

Jess sat on the bed and sighed, weary and washed out. Her body ached and although she craved a hot shower, she harboured no illusions she would find one here.

"Where are you?" she asked, dropping her rucksack on the floor.

"Er, I've got alternative digs. This was the last one."

"Where?"

"I'll find something. Goodnight." He turned away and attempted to pull the door shut.

"Wait! Get in here."

CHAPTER 26

They were only a day's walk from Syapru Besi where, they hoped, Mitesh would be waiting for them. Simon had called the hospital to find out about Sujay and they were relieved to hear he was conscious and recovering well; well enough to call his brother and tell him to go and pick them up. Jess was keen to hear the next part of the saga, so Simon talked as they walked briskly down the mountain on their way back to civilisation.

"So Jack and I were taking turns watching the Kayanis' place, but we just couldn't get near it. The best view turned out to be from the fifteenth floor of a filthy apartment block across the lake."

"Michael said you knew she was in there."

"Well, we bribed one of the agency cleaners but all he told us was that there was a young girl who fitted the description."

"But that's where you got your first glimpse of her?"

"That was a great moment, but we had no idea how to get into the compound. It was even harder than getting into their place in London. We needed them to bring her out."

"And eventually, they did."

"She turned up in Lahore with the Kayanis on the campaign trail, so I hot-footed it down there and checked into the same hotel. Found out which suite they were in and made my move."

"Do I want to know this bit?" She hated to think there had been any more violence, despite what Kayani had done to Leila. She didn't need to be reminded that although Simon had been heroic in rescuing Leila and protecting her, he was also a trained killer.

"What do you mean?"

"Michael told me you 'persuaded' the guard to 'step aside'."

"Oh, yeah. No, I just gave him a little tap. Honest. Anyway, you don't want to feel sorry for Kayani or his goons, they're not worth it."

"But how did you get her out?"

"I knocked on the door and shouted room service in my best Urdu. There was one woman in there, and once she realised I wasn't room service she started to scream, so I had to restrain her and take her phone away. I convinced her she wouldn't get hurt if she just stepped into the bathroom and locked the door."

"As easy as that?"

"More or less. I found Leila in one of the bedrooms. I talked to her, told her who I was and that I was taking her home to her mum in England. She didn't struggle at all. Just took my hand and followed me out."

"You charmer."

"Don't sound so surprised." He put on his hurt expression and she laughed at him. "We took a taxi to the Indian border and mingled with the crowds attending the border ceremony. I put Leila in the front seat to make it look like she was the driver's daughter and I played the dumb tourist in the back. It was all fairly chaotic but we crossed into India before the shit hit the fan, and ended up in Amritsar, where I have a good local contact."

Jess remembered Michael mentioning a girl called Juneeta and couldn't help playing with him.

"What was her name?" she asked innocently.

"Juneeta," he said without hesitation.

"Okay. And how do you know Juneeta from Amritsar?"

"Now that's a long story …" Jess smiled to herself. A girlfriend in every country. "But she was fantastic. We had to stay with her for a couple of weeks and she looked after Leila much better than I could have done. I don't know anything about kids. They frighten me a bit.

"You? Frightened by kids?" She laughed loudly.

They reached the last suspension bridge, a hundred feet above the raging river she and Sujay had crossed on the first day, and she knew they were not far from the town. One last climb and then down all the way; an hour at most. The climb was steep but they were below two thousand metres, and by now she was a seasoned trekker.

***

By three o'clock they were on the bus, and by seven thirty, back in the dust and smoke and filth of Kathmandu. They stopped by the hospital to check on Sujay. They found him in a busy ward with thirty other patients.

"I will go and see Miss Alisha as soon as possible. Before it's too late." He still looked weak and was connected to a drip.

"Only when you're fit again," said Jess, sitting beside him, holding his hand. "Please give her my love and best wishes."

"I'm sorry for letting you down, Miss Jess."

"Oh no, Sujay. I'll always be grateful for what you did. I promise to come back one day." She felt awkward making promises she wasn't sure she could keep, but she felt the need to say something to assuage his discomfort.

"You must bring your family. I would like to meet your girls and for you to see my wife and children."

"We'd love that."

Sujay turned to Simon who stood on the other side of the bed.

"Simon. I owe you my life."

"You're welcome, buddy. Keep trekking."

***

By eight thirty they were back at the hotel, Dwarika's providing the oasis of calm and serenity and luxury she had been craving for days.

She lay in the huge stone bath, submerged in hot soapy water, luxuriating in the heat and the fragrance, and was reminded of her bath at home, Lisa's bath, which she'd used on her first night at Chalton. She thought of Alisha; scarred and disabled, stricken by terminal illness and virtually alone, and she couldn't imagine how she would cope in similar circumstances. But Alisha had her Buddhist faith, and despite everything she'd endured, it was the foundation of her existence. It provided all the explanation she needed of life, death and resurrection. Jess hoped that when her time came, she could approach it with the same equanimity.

She wrapped herself in a soft, fluffy dressing gown and called home, pleased to hear the girls were on top form. She told Keira she was flying back the following morning and would be home by teatime. The clothes Sujay had made her leave behind were back in the room when she arrived, so she was able to pick something comfortable to wear for dinner; her favourite pink cashmere sweater over white jeans and black sandals.

Simon was waiting for her in the Fusion Bar. He was wearing an open-necked check shirt, khaki chinos and boat shoes, and he was clean-shaven; the first time she had seen him without stubble. It made him look younger. He stood up as she approached and for a second, they were lost for words. He recovered his composure.

"Gosh. Aren't you a sight for sore eyes?"

She looked away, mildly embarrassed, just like she had done all those years ago, and he saw it. "Did I say something wrong?"

"No." She said quickly, looking at him, studying his face.

"I got you a Prosecco."

They sat down and clinked glasses.

She'd guessed he was in his late forties but she'd never before had the nerve to ask. One sip of Prosecco was all it took to remove her inhibitions.

"I was trying to guess your age."

"Go on, then," he said, taking a large swig from his beer.

"You won't be offended?"

"Probably." But he was smiling. "Forty-eight. There, put you out of your misery."

"That's what I thought," she said, playing with him.

"And I'm guessing you're about twenty-seven, twenty-eight?"

"Don't you know never to guess a girl's age?" They clinked glasses and went to dinner.

CHAPTER 27

Mitesh took them to the airport. They ran the gauntlet of check-in, security and passport control before reaching departures, where they stood beneath the large screen that listed departing flights.

"There it is," said Jess pointing at the board "Dubai, gate twelve." But Simon was looking elsewhere and he took her by surprise.

"This is where I love you and leave you."

"What?"

"I'm on the Doha flight, en route to Malta. I have some business to do there."

"Oh. Really? I assumed you were coming back to London." She couldn't keep the disappointment out of her voice and it made him look uncomfortable. "Who's going to watch my back?" she said, in an attempt to make light of it.

"I don't think you've got much to worry about in Emirates Business Class."

"I can't thank you enough for what you did for us."

"You already did."

"Yes, I know. But it would be great if you came over to visit. I'm sure Leila would love to see you." He shifted his feet. "Look. I understand if you can't. I guess you have a busy workload, beating up bad guys and rescuing damsels in distress." She was gushing now and conscious of it. "Sorry. I didn't mean that the way it sounded."

"I know what you meant," he said, amused by her embarrassment. She wrapped her arms around his chest, he squeezed her shoulders and they kissed on both cheeks.

"Go on, then. Before I get all tearful," she said, waving him away.

"Bye, Jess. See you soon, I hope. Give Leila a big hug from me." He turned and walked away, leaving her feeling strangely lost and vulnerable again, but with a sudden thought.

"Simon?" she shouted, and he turned at the sound of her voice. "Your business in Malta. What's her name?" She grinned wickedly. He broke into a wide smile and her heart skipped.

"Theadora!"

***

Michael was waiting for her amongst the crowds in arrivals, holding hands with the most beautiful girl in the world.

"Mummy!" Leila ran up and threw herself at Jess, who dropped her bags and lifted her up high.

"Hello, sweetheart," she said, twirling her around and kissing her. "Goodness me, I've missed you." Jess was bursting with love and happiness for her eldest but wanted to know more. She put Leila down safely down on the floor and crouched down in front of her. "How are your baby sisters?"

"I've been looking after them for you."

"I'll bet you have."

"They were naughty once but I had a talk with them and now they are much better."

Jess hugged her again and looked up at Michael.

"I'm in trouble, I understand?" he said in his typically languorous way. She kissed him on both cheeks.

"What would I do without you?"

"Your own thing, I expect. But then, you do that anyway."

"Is everyone all right?"

"Yes of course, Keira and Sandy have had a great time. They're all waiting for you at Chalton." He grabbed the handle of her suitcase. "Come on. Let's go home."

***

Michael felt somewhat outnumbered, surrounded by seven women; Jess, Leila and the twins, Sandy, Keira and Emma, all seated around the long kitchen table, tucking into a casserole Sandy had prepared. But the guests were ready to go by eight, and although the girls had been given special dispensation, the twins were already worn out.

"I'd like to know how you got on with Lisa," said Michael as they embraced by the front door.

"You mean Alisha?"

"Yes, of course. I'm always getting names mixed up." She saw the irony in his statement but had no doubt it was meant to be light-hearted.

"There's nothing to worry about, Michael. Just as you said. I do want to share it with you. I just need a bit of time to come to terms with it all."

"You'll be a bit jet-lagged too, I expect."

"I'm just pleased to be back home."

***

Jess and Leila put the twins to bed and then they sat up on Jess's bed reading a picture book, though this time Leila did most of the reading. She had come on so much in a fortnight, Jess thought proudly. School beckoned.

"Do you remember Simon?" she asked at one point and Leila nodded gently. Jess could tell her daughter knew who Simon was, but she was hardly effusive. She hadn't discussed with Simon the circumstances of their long journey from Amritsar to Kathmandu; somehow they just hadn't got round to it. But having now been there herself, in the Himalayas, it shed a whole new light on how traumatic it must have been, for Leila especially, even with someone as capable and caring as Simon Rutherford. "Well, he sent you a big hug and he's going to come and see us all soon."

Leila looked genuinely pleased. But, Jess thought, she wanted to know more about what had happened and resolved to ask him when she got the chance. And then, in a moment of doubt, had to consider the notion that she may never see him again, that he would slip back into the shadows of his sinister world and disappear. She hated the thought of it, but had to concede it wasn't something she could control.

CHAPTER 28

"Come on! You don't want to be late on your first day," said Jess, chivvying the girls along before strapping them into the Range Rover and setting off down the drive. She was filled with fear and trepidation, not ready to entrust her family to strangers, not ready to leave them alone in the care of others, not ready to let go. But she had met the headmistress and some of the teachers and had found no reason to be concerned. She was particularly fond of Ellie, who looked after pre-school, recognising someone born to teaching and a natural with young kids. Despite her irrational fears, she'd concluded they couldn't be in safer hands.

But when they were met at the gate and she shook hands with the teachers and hugged the girls and watched them walk off hand in hand, her heart burst with love and pride and terror, all rolled into one.

She drove into Hareton to meet Michael, and Sandy showed her into his office.

"I know what it's like, Jess. Trust me. But they have to grow up sometime and you just have to let go."

"I know, Sandy. I just want to smother them with love. I can't bear being apart from them. And the house is so empty without them."

"It's only a few hours a day. Enjoy the freedom." Sandy closed the door behind her and Jess gave Michael a hug before sitting down.

"I hear you had an eventful trip," said Michael, master of the understatement.

"Simon saved us. I still have nightmares thinking about it."

"I've spoken to Sujay and sent your best wishes."

"Thank you."

"He's not back on the trail yet but he will be in a couple of weeks or so."

"Can we send him some money? I guess there are no benefits out there for people who can't work and I worry about him. He's got a family."

"I already have. I knew you'd want to."

"Oh, Michael," she said, suddenly weary with it all. "I keep telling myself how lucky we are but at the same time, I'm permanently on edge, fearful of the future. I can't seem to see where it is we're headed."

"Well, your priority is the kids, and mine, finding you a home you can call your own. How did you get on with Alisha?"

"She's dying, Michael." He looked shocked and upset as she told him. "I would do anything to help her, but she doesn't want it. She doesn't want anything she doesn't have and she doesn't have much. But then part of me thinks she has everything. How mad is that?"

"I'm afraid it's beyond my understanding."

"I think there must be a lesson there, achieving that level of contentment."

Michael closed the folder in front of him.

"So, nothing changes."

Jess nodded.

"As you said. But I was right to find her and see her. It was as if Peter were back with us. I could see it in her eyes. I hope he was watching us."

"I think we should start the ball rolling. Get Chalton valued, do some research on nice country cottages. Look to the future. It's going to be fine."

***

The girls settled into school and Jess settled into life at Chalton, the house now eerily quiet during the day. But she quickly established a new routine that involved the endless cleaning the house demanded, shopping and gardening, and she was easily able to fill the time between dropping the kids off at 9 a.m. and picking them up at 3 p.m., when the domestic mayhem returned.

It had been six weeks since her return from Nepal and she never stopped thinking about Alisha; what she might be doing that day and how she might be feeling. Whether or not she was still alive. She had unearthed the picture of Janica and Lisa, taken when Lisa was a baby, from Peter's desk, and set it up in the drawing room. And the photo of grown-up Lisa with her mother, which she had left by Peter's bed, served as a further reminder whenever she went in to dust.

She climbed into the attic and found several boxes of personal possessions: Peter's medals and army memorabilia, soft toys, books and bundles of letters he had written to Janica when he'd been away. She read one or two but was so quickly overcome with emotion she had to stop. But she also found more photographs: a young Peter in uniform, Peter and Janica's wedding day, Lisa's christening. She carried all the photos downstairs into the kitchen, sorted them out and took several of the larger ones into Hareton to be framed. Before long, there were framed photos everywhere around the house. She felt closer to them as a family than she had ever felt with anyone before.

***

It was Sunday afternoon when the doorbell chimed in the hallway. As usual, Sophie and Lucy were the first ones there, sprinting excitedly down the hallway, standing on tiptoes, struggling to turn the awkward and unwieldy doorknob and swing open the heavy wooden door. When Jess arrived a moment later, the girls were standing side by side, chatting with a large figure on his haunches. She knew who it was instantly and a warm feeling washed over her.

"How was Malta?"

Simon Rutherford looked up and then stood, rucksack over his shoulder, smiling broadly.

"Excellent. Warm and sunny and very relaxing. I don't think I've been introduced to these charming young ladies?"

The twins giggled and squealed in their inimitable fashion.

"This is Lucy with the blue ribbon and Sophie with the red ribbon. That's so you can you tell them apart. Girls? Say hello to Simon."

"Hello, Simon," they said as one, suddenly shy. Jess walked up and wrapped her arms around his neck and he kissed her on both cheeks.

"Simon!" Jess turned to see Leila running down the hallway towards them.

"Hello, princess!" Leila flew at him and he picked her up. She wrapped her legs around his waist and buried her face in his neck. "Goodness me, you're a bit heavier than last time." He swung her from side to side and then put her down and she grabbed his hand, dragging him down the hallway.

"Come on, Simon. I shall make you some tea."

They all had tea and cake and then went for a walk around the grounds and down to the river in the late afternoon sun, the girls laughing and shouting and leaping around chasing each other while the adults strolled and chatted about Nepal and Malta and boats and retired army officers.

"So you think you'll leave here?" he asked as they sat on the grass by the riverbank.

"It'll break my heart, but this'll never be my real home. It will always belong to Peter and Janica and Lisa, and anyway, it's far too big for us. It needs a real family to bring it to life."

"You are a real family!"

"Oh. You know what I mean."

"Yes. I know what you mean." She thought she sensed some regret in his voice.

"So when are you going to stop gallivanting around the world and do something sensible? Get a proper job? You're no spring chicken, you know!" she said, knowing he wouldn't be offended by the jibe. He wasn't.

"Thanks a bunch! I don't know. There isn't anywhere I can call home. And I'd really struggle to stay still for more than a few days."

"Sounds like you're constantly on the run." She knew she was probing, trying to get under the skin of the man, and she heard Peter's voice in her head. *MYOBS!* But she told herself she was genuinely concerned for him, so that made it all right to ask. But there was more to it than that. She had a friend for life and she hoped he felt the same way.

"Yes, I suppose I am. Something will turn up." She let it go. He clearly wasn't in the mood to elaborate.

"You'll stay for dinner?" It was less of a question than an instruction.

"If I'm invited."

CHAPTER 29

She put the girls to bed and returned to the drawing room. Simon was on the sofa near the open fire, flicking through *Good Housekeeping* while the smouldering logs glowed and crackled, emitting a toasty aroma and spreading a comforting warmth around the room. She sat on a rug on the floor facing him and he passed her a glass of red wine.

"Leila was very excited to see you. I've never seen her so chatty."

"She's a diamond of a little girl. The real deal. They all are. Take after their mum." She knew it was a gratuitously flattering comment, but enjoyed it all the same.

"We never got to talk about what happened after you and Leila arrived in Amritsar. You said that you had a girlfriend there … Juneeta, wasn't it?" Jess tried to make it sound casual and indifferent, that she had struggled to recall the name, when in truth she was already compiling a list that currently featured Juneeta and Theadora. She took a sip from her glass and noticed he was looking at her in that patronising way of his that indicated he could see straight through her.

"Juneeta is not a girlfriend. She is a friend who happens to be a girl."

"Oh, okay. Whatever." She shrugged and took another sip.

"She's married to Opinder and they have four children, Eshan, Navya, Prisha and Vivaan."

She tried not to react, but he had caught her off guard, again.

"Goodness. You must know them well?"

"Opinder and I served together in the Indian army. Well, I was there as a trainer. So whenever I go back I look them up." Jess smiled inwardly and struck Juneeta off the list.

"So she helped look after Leila?"

"Yes, I stashed her with them. I didn't know what to do with a nine-year-old, did I? Anyway, it was all over the news, Mrs Kayani blubbing on the TV about her daughter being kidnapped and her husband threatening severe retribution on the perpetrators, whom he claimed were supporters of his political opponents. Heads were going to roll and throats were going to be cut; that was a given."

"Oh my God."

"So, because we weren't far from the border there were lots of police around the town. Kayani had a fair amount of support in the Punjab, especially from the ruling party, so it suited the authorities to try and help. It meant that we had to keep our heads down for a while."

***

Rutherford climbed the wooden steps to the Chaudhary apartment on the first floor and rang the bell. Opinder opened the door. Six foot four, lithe, not an ounce of fat, bushy beard and bright blue dastaar tight on his head.

"Simon, sahib. Come in, please." They shook hands in the short hallway and Juneeta came out from the kitchen area wearing a multicoloured sari, an orange sash over her shoulder, wiping her hands on a tea towel. Simon bent and kissed her cheek.

"How's my little princess?"

"Oh, she's fine," said Juneeta, rocking her head from side to side. "She's very quiet, though. Her big eyes are always watching."

"Look, I think it's time we got going. I can't impose on your hospitality any longer. You have to think about your own safety."

"It's no problem, Simon sahib," said Opinder, holding both hands up. "Leila is no trouble for us."

"Yeah, I know, mate." Simon touched his friend's arm. "And I'm really grateful. And I am sure her mother will be too."

"Does her mother know where she is?" asked Juneeta. After all, she was a mother herself, her empathy total.

"I don't think her mother knows anything. My bosses decided the less she knew the better. To be honest, there's still no guarantee we can get her home. Look, the town's teeming with pilgrims here for the festival. There'll never be a better time to merge in with the crowds and slip away under the radar."

"But where will you go?" asked Opinder, clearly troubled by the notion.

"Nepal."

"What? But that's at least eight hundred kilometres. Why go there?"

"Because I'll never get her out of an Indian airport. The security is too good. If I can get her to Kathmandu, I'll be able to use my influence and wangle a passport."

"You mean buy one?"

"Of course."

"So when are you leaving?"

"Day after tomorrow. The buses will be heading back east stuffed with pilgrims and we are going to be on one of them. Juneeta, can you do me favour? Go shopping tomorrow and get Leila some clothes: walking boots, fleece, trekking jacket, trousers, you know the sort of stuff. Warm weather outdoor gear, plus a rucksack. Get a selection of shoe sizes and see what fits. You won't be able to take her with you so you'll have to try them on here and see what works. Don't get cheap stuff. I don't know how far she is going to have to walk." He handed her a bundle of grubby notes. "Here's fifty thousand; that should be enough. Keep the change. Can I see her?"

Juneeta nodded and took the money, and Rutherford followed her into the sitting room. The TV was on full blast and Leila was sitting on the floor playing with the two youngest, Prisha and Vivaan. "Leila, honey?" said Juneeta. "Simon is here." Leila showed no reaction, appearing not to hear. Simon moved over to her cautiously and dropped to his haunches.

"Hey, princess. How are you doing?" But there was still no reaction or acknowledgement. "We are going to go for a bus ride soon. Just you and me. We're going to see your mum. Would you like that?" Nothing. "Your mum … Jess?" Leila stopped and looked up at him. The name meant something to her. Rutherford put his hand awkwardly on the top of her head and gave her hair a soft rub.

"Will you have some dinner with us, Simon?" said Juneeta.

"Thanks, but no. I have some things to do. I'll call you tomorrow and fix up timings."

***

The fire had died down a bit. Jess leant over to the wood basket and threw a couple of logs onto the embers. They began to smoulder immediately. She moved away from the fire but remained on the floor, putting her back to the sofa alongside where Simon was sitting. She reached for her wine and took another sip as the logs caught and new flames licked up around them. Simon sat back, legs crossed, one arm stretched across the arm of the sofa, wine glass in hand. The clock ticked languorously in the hallway.

"What are you thinking?" he asked, and for a moment she didn't answer.

"I'm thinking. I know what's coming. I've been there. I know how rugged, remote and isolated, how primitive it is and how cold it can get at night. And I'm wondering what's going through the mind of a forty-eight-year-old soldier with no experience of children, and how he thinks he's going to transport a nine-year-old across hundreds of miles of inhospitable terrain. And I'm wondering what's going through the mind of a nine-year-old for whom the last five years have been one nightmare after another."

"One step at a time."

"What do you mean?"

"Well, if you have a mountain to climb or a seemingly impossible problem to solve, you break it down into tiny pieces and you do each of the pieces one at a time."

"That simple, eh?"

"If you try and think through all the potential obstacles and hurdles and pitfalls and risks, you'll never get anything done. You'll give up before you've even started." Jess understood that only too well. She was sitting here now, listening to this incredible story, knowing at the same time that it wasn't incredible at all, because it was all true; humbled again by the prodigious efforts of all those involved in Leila's return and realising that she had played her own part. She had climbed her own mountains, taken on the impossible, risked everything to find her own way in the world, and if she hadn't done that, she wouldn't be here now.

The warmth of the fire and his company, the all-embracing blanket of security she felt with him there, made her feel soporific and heavy-eyed. Or maybe it was the red wine taking hold. She thought she had better hold back for a while, but she took another sip anyway.

***

Rutherford called and Juneeta confirmed Leila was all ready for travel. He said he would come and collect her at exactly 7 a.m. the next day.

The doorbell rang and Opinder answered it.

"Holy shit!"

"Put your jaw back, mate." Simon stepped into the hallway. He wore a multi-pocketed safari jacket, khaki cargo pants and heavy walking boots and carried a large rucksack over one shoulder, none of which was worthy of reaction or particular comment. It was the orange dastaar tied tightly around the head, the black eyebrows, tanned skin and black bushy beard that did it.

"Simon, sahib. Have you converted at last to the only true religion?"

"What do you think? Will I pass?"

"As long as you don't have to say much, you'll pass. Juneeta?" he called, and his wife appeared from the sitting room. She looked quizzically at the stranger and then put a hand to her mouth in shock.

"Oh, my goodness! Simon?"

"'Fraid so. Simon Singh to you."

"How … did you …?"

"Film make-up. Backstreet Bollywood make-up artist did it. I figured a young mixed-race girl accompanied by a big white guy was going to look a little suspicious on the bus to Dharamshala."

"You're probably right. How's your Punjabi?"

"I can do enough to get by. Where's my little princess?"

"Leila!" called Juneeta. Leila dutifully appeared, trussed up in her new outdoor gear, hair tied back, looking subdued and slightly bemused. Rutherford went over to her, knelt down and looked into her eyes.

"Hi, princess. It's just me. Simon. Do you like my fancy dress?" he asked, trying to sound enthusiastic but getting no response. He tried again. "Are you ready to go for a ride on the bus?" Nothing. He stood and turned to his friends.

"I owe you both."

"Anytime, my friend. Go safely. I will lend you my God for a while." The men hugged and he kissed Juneeta.

"Come on, princess. Let's go for a walk." She took his hand and they walked out of the apartment and into the swirling masses of Amritsar.

They queued at the bus station along with thousands of other travellers arranged in hundreds of neat lines, as smelly, smoky buses rolled in, filled up and rolled out again. Their turn came, he showed the driver their tickets and lifted Leila onto the bus, taking a seat near the back. He pulled a banana out of his rucksack, peeled it and offered it to her but she wasn't interested, so he reluctantly ate it himself. He offered her some water but that was similarly ignored.

They'd left the house only an hour ago and it was a four-hour drive to Dharamshala. He wondered how he was going to keep her entertained and found himself praying to Waheguru, the Wonderful Lord, the one and only God, that she would remain calm.

The bus was full both inside and out, the roof stacked three-high with assorted bags and suitcases, chickens in baskets and, inside, even a small goat. It bounced, clattered, grunted and roared its way out of town, and he was relieved to see Leila taking great interest in whatever she could see through the dusty windows. Had he been alone, he'd have spent most of the journey asleep, but he didn't dare take his eyes off her, observing her watching intently, her lips moving from time to time in response to the things she saw, as if speaking a silent language to herself.

After a couple of hours, the bus stopped and everyone piled off, either to relieve themselves or stock up with provisions from the roadside traders. Rutherford felt he needed to ask, desperately hoping she'd decline.

"Toilet?"
She nodded.
Great.

He took her hand and led her off the bus, leaving their rucksacks on the seat. A queue of women waited outside the toilet block so they joined the end, hand in hand, but he felt awkward and conspicuous. A woman who looked about thirty stood in front of them, and by the time they'd reached the door of the toilet block, he'd rehearsed his Punjabi.

"Madam. Is it possible that you can help my daughter?" The woman turned, looked down at Leila, smiled and said in English.

"Of course. Are you English?"

"Oh. Yes. Is it that obvious?"

"Your accent," she said nodding and then looking at Leila. "What is your name?"

"Leila. She doesn't say much," said Simon, hoping upon hope she didn't suddenly decide to start speaking. They went inside and he dashed quickly into the gents, then stood outside waiting anxiously, working out a contingency plan if everything went wrong. It didn't.

The woman brought Leila back out, he thanked her profusely and they got back on the bus. He offered her an apple but she shook her head and pointed to a banana. He started to peel it for her.

"No!" The people in the seats in front turned around and he smiled feebly at them as Leila took the banana out of his hand and peeled it herself. She finished it in four or five huge bites and handed him back the skin, still chewing. He offered her the water bottle and she took a long drink, placing the bottle in the seat netting in front of her. Rutherford smiled to himself. *Maybe we're going to be okay.*

The bus pulled into Dharamshala Interstate bus station at three thirty in the afternoon. Rutherford had originally planned to carry on to Palampur and stay there overnight, but Leila was looking tired and a little tearful and he thought it better he didn't push her too hard on their first day.

He was worried they might look conspicuous but the town was full of tourists, many of them there to visit the

Dalai Lama's residence, so they didn't appear out of place. He took the little girl by the hand and they walked together down to the Gurudwara Road where he found the taxi service he was looking for. He'd researched the route carefully back in Amritsar and already discovered there was no bus service between Dharamshala and Palampur, taxi being the only available option. They went inside and he booked a taxi to take them to Palampur the next day, then walked up the Gurudwara Road into the centre of town.

In a side street, he found the Suwanna Guest House and took a twin room with private bathroom at the top on the fourth floor. He checked in with Jack on the satphone.

"How's it going, Si? Have you got the package?"

"Fine so far, Jack. I won't tell you where I am, save to say I'm making progress and I'm on schedule. Just checked into a hotel and I'm going off for some dinner soon. Anything happening out there?"

Jack had an update on the drama from Pakistan.

"That politician bloke, Kayani, has still got an APB out all over the border and some of his guys have been causing trouble at the opposition headquarters. A few of them got beaten up and one of them didn't make it, so it's all getting a bit frantic."

"Terrible thing, kidnapping. Imagine that poor little girl. She must be frightened to death." He looked across at Leila who was sitting patiently on one of the beds, watching him.

"The Indians are on the case too, but they seem to be concentrating on the border area, train stations and airports. I don't think she's gone anywhere. I bet she's still in Lahore. What's the news where you are?"

"Haven't seen it yet. I'll check the TV. Call you in a day or two." He hung up and gave Leila a big smile, but she failed to reciprocate. "Hungry, princess?" Nothing. "Fancy a pizza?" She nodded. *Bingo.*

Remarkably, they found a Domino's and he watched her wolf down a Diavola, complete with chilli and pepperoni substitute, all by herself. There was a TV fixed to the wall high up in the corner but it was small and nobody was taking much notice. He saw the story come up briefly, accompanied by a photo of Leila, but it was a poor likeness and she was wearing a brightly coloured shalwar kameez, an ornate traditional dress, a far cry from the bland trekking gear she now wore.

At six thirty he took her back to the hotel but then, with increasing disquiet, wondered how he was going to put her to bed. He removed her jacket and boots and showed her into the bathroom. He gave her a toothbrush and a small tube of toothpaste and a towel, and waved awkwardly at the toilet and basin. She stared up at him blankly and was still staring at him as he backed out of the bathroom, closing the door behind him.

She reappeared five minutes later.

"Done," she announced and he sighed with relief, encouraged that she was beginning to respond, albeit in monosyllables. But it was short-lived. He pulled back the bed covers and gestured for her to get in, but she just looked at him. He tried again.

"Are you not sleepy?"

She nodded.

"Well, go on then, get yourself snuggled under."

She stared at him and he wondered how the dispassionate stare of a nine-year-old could make him feel so uncomfortable. He suddenly got the message. "Ah okay, princess." He turned his back on her and sat on the opposite bed, picking up a magazine he had bought earlier. After a minute, he heard the light rustle of clothing and the squeak of bedsprings and eventually plucked up the courage to turn around. Her fleece and trousers were on top of the bed and the blanket was pulled up to her chin. He went over to her bed, leant over and touched her forehead.

"Goodnight, princess." Nothing. She turned over to face the wall and closed her eyes. He drew the curtains and turned out all the lights apart from the one by his bed.

He couldn't do much about washing his face in case he dislodged the fake beard or smudged his fake tan, but he brushed his teeth and washed his body as best he could. He put his clothes back on, checked the door was locked securely and lay on the other bed. It was only 7 p.m. and he wasn't tired yet. He craved a beer but he couldn't leave her, so he read the magazine until he got bored and lay back, eyes open, thinking, planning. It would be a long night.

The next morning, they did the undressing routine in reverse, and when he heard her say, "Ready," they picked up their things and checked out. He found a local bakery with a café where they ate stuffed paratha and drank marsala chai for breakfast, and by nine they were in the taxi, heading out of town.

"How far to Palampur?" he asked Ranesh, the driver.

"Just one hour," he replied but he was not the talkative type and Rutherford was just as pleased. He sat Leila directly behind the driver so he didn't have a permanent view of her through the mirror. He didn't want to take any chances but he knew that as time went by, they were getting further and further away from trouble.

***

It took them three more days to get from Palampur to the Nepalese border, via Shimla and Srinigar and Almora, each leg of the journey taken by taxis in various states of decrepitude. Leila seemed to buy into the hotel and travel routine, repeating favourite words such as "toilet", "drink", "hungry" and, more often than not, "no", the latter usually indicating displeasure of some sort.

His objective was Dharchula on the banks of the Sarda River, the natural border between India and Nepal, the border crossing comprising a suspension footbridge that citizens on both sides could easily cross without showing passports. The only difficulty he saw, and it was not insignificant, was that, despite the casual nature of border control, he didn't look like a local, with or without his Sikh disguise.

They checked into the Haldwani Hotel situated on the banks of the river and he had a good view of the border crossing from their room. He'd discarded the dastaar and beard when they got out of the taxi and had done his best to clean off most of the face paint in a local restaurant, but he looked especially filthy, and when she saw him, Leila's expression confirmed it.

He left her watching TV and had a shower, the first for four days, and, wrapping a towel around himself, returned to find her asleep on top of the bed. Relieved he didn't have to worry about exposing himself, he foraged around in his rucksack for fresh clothes and got dressed. He watched the bridge and the steady stream of foot traffic and bicycles moving in both directions, and although there were border officials on the Indian side, no one seemed to be challenged or stopped. But he doubted whether a European man accompanied by a young Asian girl would be able to cross unimpeded, not least without some exchange of currency, and he needed to find out.

He called Jackson.

"He's dead," came the crackly distorted voice down the line.

"Who is?"

"Kayani. Blown up in a truck. Some lunatic cast his vote early." Rutherford's mind flipped into overdrive but his friend had already done the thinking for him. "I don't think it's going to help you in the short term. He certainly won't be looking for you anymore, but just as the story was going cold, it's right back up there at the top of the news agenda.

The accusations are flying around like bullets and it's all kicking off. I think you need to stick with the plan and hoof it across the border."

"I think you're right. Look, I need to go, the phone is about out of charge. Call you when I get across."

He pulled the phone charger out of his bag, connected the phone and rammed the plug into one of the wall sockets. There was a flash and a bang and he pulled his hand away.

"Jesus!"

He picked up the phone and checked it. It appeared unharmed, but there was no charging icon on display and it showed only one bar. He carefully extracted the charger plug and tried another socket. Nothing. "Shit!" And then he noticed Leila looking at him. "Sorry, princess. That's not very nice."

"Shit," she said. He didn't know whether to laugh or cry. He rubbed his forehead.

"Pizza?" She nodded with glee.

***

They stayed at the hotel another day and had their laundry done. He toured what few shops there were to try and find a compatible phone charger but without success, so he bought her some comics in the local store and she watched TV while he kept watch on the crossing and eventually formulated a plan.

"Indira?" he asked the girl on reception, Leila next to him, holding his hand.

"Yes, sir. Can I help you?"

"I wonder if you could do me a favour?"

"Yes, of course, sir. If I am able."

"My daughter would love to cross the river tomorrow and see the Nepalese side. Would you be willing to take her?" Indira looked at Leila and then back at Rutherford, and he could see her confusion. "My wife's Indian. She's in New Delhi. I brought Leila here to see some of the Himalayas."

"But you can take her yourself, sir. You just have to show your passport."

"Yes, that's the problem. I didn't bring Leila's passport because I didn't expect us to cross the border. I have to carry mine around with me all the time, naturally." He waved it in the air. Indira looked uncertain. "Thing is, if I try to take her across, they'll want to see her passport, but if you do it, no one will blink. I'll go across separately and meet you on the other side, and then we can have a quick look and come back." He smiled, as if pleased with himself, which, in a way, he was.

"I don't know, sir," said Indira looking uncomfortable.

"Ah, okay, I understand if it's too difficult." He looked down at Leila and made a sad face. "Sorry, princess, it's just not going to be possible." Leila said nothing. "I know you really wanted to go across and see Nepal, but Indira says you can't." Indira shifted her feet and put her pen down.

"Maybe I can do something."

"We'd be very grateful," said Rutherford, winking, leaving the girl in no doubt she'd be well rewarded.

"What time would you like to go?"

"Tomorrow morning. About eight?"

***

Indira was waiting for them and was surprised to see them wearing their rucksacks.

"We'll check out now, if that's okay? When we get back across we'll get the bus straight to Pithoragarh. It'll save time." He handed over the key and Indira quickly ran off the bill; just under ten thousand rupees. He gave her twenty and she hunted for change. "No – please keep it. And thanks for your help."

She smiled in gratitude at the extremely generous tip.

"Thank you, Mr Rutherford. Are you ready to go?"

Outside, the weather was cool and misty, so Indira pulled her woollen shawl over her head and tossed the ends over one shoulder.

They stood outside the front door of the hotel where Rutherford could see the entrance to the crossing fifty yards away. There were two border guards wearing military-style fatigues; camouflage pants tucked into shiny black leather boots, baseball caps and, inevitably, pistols on their belts, watching a steady stream of locals crossing the bridge, pushing trolleys laden with goods, children and animals in tow, most people on foot, some on bicycles and scooters. The guards chatted to each other, standing in a slovenly fashion, bored and restless, arms folded.

He crouched down to speak to Leila and rubbed a finger down one cheek.

"Now, princess, we're going for a walk across the bridge to the other side. Do you understand?" Nothing. He tried again. "Is that okay with you?" Nothing. "Indira here is going to take you and I'm going to follow in a few minutes." He stood up again and Leila looked up at him as if she was about to burst into tears. She threw her arms around his waist. "Hey, princess. It's okay. I'll just be a few minutes, promise."

"Come on, Leila," said Indira, clutching her shawl. "Let's go and look at the river." Leila released her grip and took Indira's hand and she led her up the road towards the crossing. Leila looked back, forlorn, and Rutherford waved. To his astonishment, he sensed a lump in his throat. *Get a grip, Si!* He watched them stroll past guards who appeared totally disinterested in another woman and child amongst the crowds crossing into Nepal. He waited till they were fifty yards across and set off.

The first guard saw the foreign trekker when he was just ten feet away. Rutherford strode up to them.

"Namaste," he said, not intending to stop, but one of them held out an arm. The other stood, hands on hips, one hand covering the handgun.

"Passport?" He flicked a finger towards Rutherford who feigned confusion and, although knowing exactly where his passport was, made a show of patting and feeling around various pockets until he found it. He handed it over, smiling, and turned his head casually as if to take in the view.

The first guard flicked through the pages, holding up the photo page to check the likeness, rubbing his chin as if he were considering something relevant but saw the Indian visa and handed it back.

"You need visa for Nepal." He said, pointing at the other side. Rutherford nodded.

"Yes, thanks. I know. I'll buy one over there." They all knew no one was manning the Nepalese side so he'd be able to get in without paying, but even if there were, it was a mere formality. The guard waved him on, unsmiling, and he set off at a brisk pace, losing himself amongst the locals.

Halfway across, Indira had noticed that the little girl kept turning round, looking anxiously behind her, apparently concerned about leaving her father. She tried to comfort her.

"It's okay, Leila, your Daddy will be coming soon."

They walked on a few steps.

"He's not my Daddy," said Leila.

Indira stopped and looked down at her.

"What did you say?" She frowned, but getting no answer, bent over and shook Leila's arm.

He was fifty yards in but fifty behind Indira and Leila when he saw they'd stopped at the halfway point. Indira was bending over, talking to Leila, and she looked agitated. He quickened his pace and reached them in a few seconds. The bridge was only two metres wide so they had to move to the side to allow the passage of locals in both directions. Indira looked up at him and he could see she wasn't happy.

"What are you doing?" she said, flustered and anxious. He shrugged, not knowing quite what her problem was. "You are not her father!"

"I can assure you I am responsible for her." Indira let go of Leila's hand and turned to him, angry and panicky.

"She says you are not her daddy! And her mummy is not in Delhi!"

"That much is true. Look, Indira, I'm taking her back home to England. That's where she belongs."

But before he could do or say anything, Indira shoved him aside and set off back the way she had come, pushing and barging her way through a stream of people, bikes and goats.

"Help! He is kidnapping a girl!"

Simon had to think fast. They were in the middle of the bridge at the lowest point and due to the elevated ends, he could easily see past the crowds to the Indian side and the border guards, suddenly alert to the commotion.

"Help!" he heard her cry again.

He grabbed Leila's hand and dragged her through the throng, weaving and swerving to avoid the human and animal obstacles moving in both directions. More cries came from behind them.

"Stop! Stop!"

And then, a shot, and there were screams all around. The people coming towards them who could see what was going on behind all stopped in their tracks, mouths agape, then swiftly turned and started running back the way they had come. Others coming from behind pushed him in the back, trying to get past. He looked behind him. One of the guards was running across the bridge towards them, gun in the air, the other dragging Indira back to the border post. Another shot. More screams. An old woman in front of them was pushed and fell, and others tripped over her, landing in a heap, creating an instant human pile-up. He grabbed Leila around the waist and tucked her under his arm, leapt over the writhing mass of bodies and into clear space, all the while assuming the soldier pursuing them wouldn't aim at anyone for fear of hitting the wrong target. Two more shots. More screams.

He checked behind him briefly. The soldier was stuck at the halfway point, trying to climb over the pile of bodies. They were fifty yards from the Nepalese side, crowds streaming out frantically into the road to escape the mayhem and running away in all directions. He got to the end of the bridge and set Leila down on her feet, gripping her hand. There was no sign of officialdom, and although he'd thought fleetingly the Indian soldiers wouldn't venture across and risk a diplomatic incident, he dismissed it. If they thought someone was kidnapping an Indian national, they wouldn't hesitate.

He looked left and right up the main road. The traffic wasn't heavy but what little there was had stalled as a wave of people, bikes and animals fanned out in all directions from the bridge, and amidst the screams, blaring horns and screeching tyres, he saw a red Toyota pickup, six men sitting sideways on the loading deck. Its horn blasted and the driver gesticulated to an old man struggling to drag a recalcitrant goat out of its way. The engine roared again and Simon lifted Leila and ran towards the back of the moving truck.

"The Indian soldier is crazy! He's shooting everyone! Help me!" The men in the back swivelled their heads to the bridge and saw a soldier three quarters of the way across shooting a pistol in the air. The two at the back leaned forward and hoisted Leila aboard but the Toyota was gathering pace and Simon had to hold onto the tailgate, running faster and faster, realising he would never be able to keep up.

Then there was a burst of shouting and banging on the back of the cab and the truck slowed, and Simon leapt over the tailgate, landing on his back on the ridged metal floor next to Leila, between the legs of the six men. The truck accelerated up the hill.

Simon looked back to the chaos at the Nepal border and saw a white car with a blue flashing light screech to a halt and two armed police jump out. Another passed the Toyota from the opposite direction, sirens wailing, stopping at the bridge in a cloud of black smoke, the images and sounds disappearing as the truck rounded a bend and sped out of town.

***

Jess couldn't help it. She put a hand on his knee and looked up at him from her position on the floor. She'd had no conception of the difficulties he'd faced and the danger they'd been in. If they'd been caught, he'd have been thrown into prison and Leila presumably returned to the Kayanis, or worse, given that by then Kayani was dead, deposited in a children's home somewhere. The whole project would have fallen apart. She shivered.

"How did Leila cope with the drama on the bridge?"

"Cool as ice. Didn't bat an eyelid. But she did give me a big hug in the back of the pickup and wouldn't let go until we got out."

Jess pursed her lips, still fearful of latent trauma suddenly manifesting itself in Leila's behaviour. She recalled the incident in her bedroom in the first few days, and although there'd been no repetition, she was ever vigilant for the first signs. The best she could hope was that the whole experience had been character-building. *Hell of a way to build character.*

"So, once in Nepal, it was plain sailing?" Jess knew she was being flippant, but it reflected her strange relief that the end was in sight, and even though she knew exactly how it ended, she still wanted him to tell her.

"Not quite. The hounds were loose."

She rubbed his leg absent-mindedly, as if it were her own, preoccupied by the images in her head.

"I knew it was only a matter of time before the police realised we'd got away, and there were only two roads out of town so they were bound to give chase. They now had a description of us both and we'd be quite conspicuous, so after a few miles, I said my thank yous to the boys in the truck and we hit the countryside."

"How far did you still have to go?"

"Oh, only about a thousand ks."

"What? On foot?"

"No. We walked the first twenty kilometres or so and I came across a disused barn, so we holed up there for a few days. I had stocked up on snacks and fruit and there was a stream nearby for water. Just wanted to lie low. Figured the Nepalese would give up after a while, provided, of course, they didn't make the connection with the Kayanis."

"And you had no phone?"

"No. Dead."

"So, what did you do? How did you spend the time?"

"Just ate and slept mainly and chatted a bit."

"Did she say anything?"

"Not much. She preferred Urdu to English but I tried to wean her off it." Jess could picture the scene, see the terrain, the mountains, feel the heat and the cold and the altitude, and was almost overcome with emotion thinking about them, thinking about her beautiful young daughter, exposed to such hardship, and thinking about him, being with her, looking after her.

"Did she mention me? Did she know she was coming home? Did she even know where home was?" She said it wistfully, almost as an afterthought, not sure if she wanted to know the answer but at the same time desperate to know whether Leila had any understanding of what was happening and whether she had expressed any joy at coming home; to her.

"It's difficult," he said, trying to choose his words carefully. "Remember I didn't know you either, so we had nothing in common. But she did talk about school and she did mention her bedroom and Tinkerbell on the door and she did say that her Mummy was nice and looked after her, and her Daddy wasn't nice and was away all the time."

"Did she talk much about him?"

"No."

"What about the Kayanis?"

"No."

"Did you see the scars?" She turned to look at him.

Simon hesitated, but he judged it wasn't a trick question and he nodded.

"It was unavoidable. You know what it's like. I had to help her do all sorts of things."

"You were her father. Her protector."

"She's an amazing little girl."

"I know," Jess whispered, her voice cracking. *That's the wine again*. She wanted to rush upstairs and hug her, make sure she was still there, check it wasn't a dream and she wouldn't wake up and find herself in a tent, or worse, back in Wellingford, alone and afraid. She suddenly realised she was stroking his leg and drew her hand away abruptly, embarrassed at her mistake. He didn't react.

"So, when we got moving again, we came across a road and flagged down a van that took us to a town called Amarghadi, which is up in the mountains at about two thousand metres. After that it was a mixture of treks and taxis, guesthouses and teahouses, you know the sort of thing, trying to stay away from populated areas while minimising the effort."

Jess knew exactly what he meant and what they were going through.

"We got to Pokhara in about a week and I managed to get a new charger for the phone. I called Jack and told him we were on the last leg. We flew from there to Kathmandu in a small plane. No passports required. And then we spent a week or so in a hotel there while I got her a nice new dress and a passport."

"You just 'got her a passport'?" She had recovered her composure enough to remain fascinated by the dark underworld in which Simon seemed to spend most of his life.

"Yeah." He said it as if getting a fake passport in a foreign country was common knowledge. "You just take a photo, splash a bit of cash and there you have it, Nepalese national, UK visa, the works. And you know all the rest."

The clock struck eleven.

"My God. We've been talking for hours," she said.

"Time to take my leave."

She looked at him, alarmed.

"Where are you going?"

"I'll call a cab. There's a Travelodge outside Hareton."

"No! You must stay here. You can have Peter's room. You can't leave now. Please."

He frowned at her.

"Are you sure?"

"Of course I'm sure!" She knew she sounded animated, so she tried to calm herself. "Please. Stay?" He smiled and nodded in submission and she jumped to her feet and placed the fireguard in front of the rapidly dying embers.

She checked the doors were locked and led him upstairs and along the corridor to Peter's room. Inside, she drew the curtains.

"Happy families," she heard him say and turned to see him holding the framed picture of Janica and Lisa. She could sense the sadness and resignation in his voice, and again, she was reminded how lucky she was.

"Shall we check on the girls?"

He dropped his bag on the bed and followed her back along the corridor. They stopped halfway and gently opened the door. The room was bathed in the soft orange glow of a nightlight as they tiptoed silently around the three little beds.

Jess leant over and kissed each of them on the head. They didn't stir. He followed her through a door in the corner of the room and they emerged into a huge master bedroom lit by one bedside table lamp.

Simon was momentarily disorientated. They'd entered the girls' room from the corridor and exited through another door into what he assumed to be Jess's room, inside which were two other doors in opposite corners.

"That's so I can always keep them close," she whispered, gesturing to the door they had just come through. "I'll always hear them if they wake up."

He felt he should go back, but wasn't sure which was the way out. She walked around the bed and switched on the second table lamp and he followed her, intending to say goodnight. She stood with her back to him, and he could see she was shaking. He put his hands on her shoulders and she turned and looked up into his eyes. She stepped forward until she was close enough to touch him, then raised herself up on her toes and slid her arms around his neck. She pulled herself up towards him and kissed him on the mouth.

They stood, lips barely touching, sensing each other's breath, until she released her hold, stepped back and met his eyes. She slowly raised both arms until they were vertical. Simon hesitated but took her cue and lifted her cashmere sweater up and over her head and arms, dropping it on the floor next to her. She stepped forward, carefully unbuttoned his shirt and pushed it back over his shoulders, running her hands around his smooth chest, grimacing faintly at the scars and blemishes; souvenirs from a lifetime of conflict.

They undressed each other slowly, one garment at a time until there was a pile at their feet. She pressed her body against his and he held her tightly, his cheek resting on her hair. After a moment's embrace she turned and slid under the duvet. He climbed in beside her.

They lay side by side; she, with the duvet pulled up to her chin, he next to her, aroused but uncertain, his mind running through the options. Had she had too much wine and too much emotional fallout from the saga of Leila's escape? Was she giving herself to him? Payment for services rendered? A show of gratitude? It wasn't necessary and he didn't want it, despite how much he wanted her. But he could tell she needed him now as much as ever, and he saw a new side to the extraordinary young woman lying next to him; still submissive, vulnerable and helpless despite the absence of any threat. Maybe he intimidated her, frightened her? He couldn't tell, but he steeled himself to stay calm and composed even though all his hormones were screaming at him to do otherwise.

She turned on her side and snuggled up to him, one arm across his chest, head pressed into his neck, one knee crooked over his thigh, and he wrapped an arm around her shoulder in support. He felt her breathing through the rise and fall of her chest and the exhalation of warm breath onto his, and he disciplined himself to stare at the ceiling in silence. Then after a moment he sensed a cool dampness on his chest. She was crying, shedding tears that trickled down his skin, moist and tingly, and he increased the pressure on her shoulder.

She whispered, falteringly, barely audible.

"Thank you for bringing my baby home."

"You're welcome," he whispered.

"Thank you for saving me."

"You're welcome." A tiny river of her tears flowed down his body.

"I don't know what to do."

He sighed deeply and kissed her head.

"You don't have to do anything, Jess."

***

She brought him tea at six, while he was still asleep, put the mug down on the bedside table and walked round to her side of the bed. She'd already checked on the kids and they were still spark out, so she climbed back on top of the duvet and arranged her silk dressing gown over her legs. She sipped her tea and watched him breathing, thinking about their night together.

She mused it hadn't been their first; they'd already shared beds in toolsheds and teahouses, but last night had been especially intimate, if unconsummated. He'd neither exploited her vulnerability nor taken advantage of her distress, even though she'd have been a willing participant. She hadn't been with a man for years and hadn't thought anything of it. She hadn't missed it, but moments like last night, moments of intense tenderness, had always been rare for her. What little she did remember of those first few months with Mo had been relegated to the furthest recesses of her mind, subordinated and subsumed by the surfeit of trauma that had preceded it and would inevitably follow.

She had to accept also the possibility that Simon didn't want her and was simply being polite and protective, a character trait he'd already demonstrated in full. She knew he'd be highly experienced and had various women friends spread across the world, all of whom, no doubt, were more sophisticated and independent than she.

She hoped most of all that when he woke, neither of them would be consumed by embarrassment or awkwardness. After all, they hadn't done anything. On cue, he snuffled and turned and looked at her, bleary-eyed.

"What time is it?"

"Well, I did have a solid gold Gucci once but it broke down on the third day out, so I've no idea. About six, I think. I brought you some tea."

"Oh, thanks." He rested on one elbow and knocked it back in two gulps, falling back on his pillow, a forearm covering his eyes. She watched his chest rise and fall steadily, and seeing her protector, her rock, her guardian lying close to her, it invoked a profound feeling of peace and security.

She felt a stirring deep inside, a growing certitude of purpose. She placed her mug on the bedside table and shuffled over to him, snuggling up under his arm, resting one hand on his chest.

"You said last night you didn't know me."

He lifted his arm away from his eyes.

"Did I?"

"When you were with Leila, and before you met me, you had no idea who I was, or what I may have been feeling."

"Yes, that's true."

"Do you know me now?"

Without waiting for an answer, she slid the duvet down. When it was clear of his thighs, she swung one leg over him and sat up, straddling his waist. She stared at him intently, confidently, and he remained motionless, their eyes locked together, as she untied the belt of her silk dressing gown and slipped it off her shoulders.

She leant forward and kissed him gently, then reached back through her legs and guided him in. She sat back, slowly releasing her weight, and she felt the heat and the pressure surge through her lower body. He closed his eyes and exhaled loudly as his head tilted back onto the pillow.

She slowly and methodically worked herself up and down and she felt his hands on her hips, assisting, guiding, refining the sensation, while watching his face, eyes tightly closed, lost in the moment. And when his breathing began to increase in pace and depth and his body eventually convulsed, she slowed and stopped and watched him gather his senses and come back down to earth.

She kissed him again and then lifted herself off him, swung her legs off the bed and walked calmly to the en suite, closing the door behind her.

***

Jess stood under the torrent of hot water, body tingling inside and outside from a myriad sensations. She was filled with a strength of mind that, in the context of what she had just experienced, was unique to her.

She felt emancipated and empowered – a free spirit – and it felt good. The steaming hot water burnt her skin until her shoulders were pink, but she didn't want it to stop. She wanted to heighten the stimulation, the heady mix of extremes; the pain, the pleasure, the exhilaration. And she wanted to relive and perpetuate the feeling of ecstasy.

For the first time in her life, she had initiated the intimacy they had just shared. For the first time in her life, she had taken control instead of being controlled, and to her astonishment it felt perfectly natural. Instead of subjugation and subordination came fulfilment and honesty and partnership, and it was a revelation.

She had given herself to him willingly and unconditionally, but he hadn't taken, he had received, and in so doing bestowed on her a profound sense of self-worth and contentment. And from her new, elevated position of enlightenment, the world became clear, her role in it defined and the confidence in her ability to play it, resolute.

She didn't know how long she'd been in the shower; ten minutes, fifteen? But the glass was opaque with condensation and water droplets, and the air thick with steam. She washed her hair and scrubbed her body down with a shower puff and reluctantly, at last, turned off the flow.

She wrapped herself in a heavy towelling robe and went back into the bedroom, rubbing her head with a small towel. The bed was empty and Simon's clothes had gone. She smiled inwardly, thinking about the last half hour, hoping he felt as relaxed and soothed as she did. *Don't fret about stuff you can do nothing about!*

Her thoughts turned abruptly to the kids. She needed to get them up, get them breakfast and get them to school. Back to work. She stepped into a long cotton skirt and slipped on a clean cashmere sweater, found her slippers and went into the girls' room. Her heart skipped. The beds were empty.

She raced through the door opposite and turned into the corridor, almost colliding with the wall, ran the twenty feet to landing and swung her arm around the top baluster, careering down the spiral staircase two at a time.

"Leila! Sophie! Lucy!" she screamed, almost losing her balance in the panic to get down, to find them, to see them safe.

As she hit the bottom step, she heard a squeal coming from the kitchen. She lost her footing on the stone floor and almost went down but recovered and bounded into the kitchen. She stopped, breathless, taking in the scene.

Leila was at the head of the kitchen table, Lucy and Sophie sitting next to each other on one side, all of them still in pyjamas, bowls of rice krispies in front of them, spoons huge and ungainly in their tiny hands. Simon, fully dressed, sat opposite the twins, tea cosy on his head.

The twins were laughing hysterically at Simon pulling a funny face while Leila looked on, smiling but composed. He saw the movement by the doorway and turned to see a frantic, panting Jess, a squirm of embarrassment slowly forming on his face.

"Mummy!" screamed Lucy, "Simon's a teapot!" and both twins laughed and squealed. Leila put her hands over her ears.

"You are being too loud," she admonished them, "eat your breakfast," and her young sisters dutifully complied.

"Morning, Mum," said Simon, still wearing the tea cosy sideways, doing a passable Lord Nelson. "Or is it afternoon?"

She stomped round to his side of the table, stood behind him, hands on hips in mock rage and pulled the cosy down over his eyes, which set the twins off again.

"Quiet!" shouted Leila.

"I'm glad to see someone is in control of things down here," said Jess, breaking into a smile. She walked around the table, kissed Leila and the twins and, giving Simon a look to indicate his turn would come later, filled the kettle.

He removed the cosy and replaced it over the teapot.

"Just filling in for a few moments while you got ready."

"Did you find everything you needed in Peter's room?" she asked. It was a facile and transparent attempt at subtle, adult conversation, intended for little ears, but it was also naïve.

"Is Simon sleeping in your bed now?" asked Leila with apparent innocence, leaving Jess lost for words and feeling awkward. He rushed to her assistance.

"I've got to go away now. But I'll be back again. Soon."

The adults smiled at each other and she put her hand on his arm. The kettle boiled and clicked.

"Right!" she announced. "Who wants more tea?"

***

She dropped them off at school and was home again by ten past nine. Simon had already said his goodbyes to the girls, lifting each one in turn and swinging them around, promising to come back soon and bring them something nice from his next trip. She'd asked him to wait at the house until she got back and as he had plenty of time, he agreed.

"I've called a cab. It'll be here in a few minutes."

They stood in the hallway, suddenly awkward with the anticipation of parting, each searching for the right words.

"So, where to next?" asked Jess, trying to sound casual.

"Gibraltar," he said, with an air of formality.

"Business?" she asked. He nodded. She paused. "What's her name?" she asked with mock innocence. He looked up sheepishly at her.

"Maria."

She nodded and grinned widely. He grinned back.

"I'm going to miss you," she said.

"Nah, you'll have forgotten all about me in five minutes. I can see you've got plenty to keep you occupied. Plenty of people to worry about."

"But you will come back and see us soon?"

"If I'm invited."

"You're invited." She stepped forward and hugged him and stole a quick kiss. They heard the sound of tyres on gravel and he turned his head to the door.

"Time to go. Bye, Jess. Take care."

He picked up his rucksack and walked outside into the cool autumn air. She shouted after him as he climbed into the car.

"Please be careful. I know the sort of things you get up to. I don't need anyone else to worry about!"

He waved and she waved back, and she watched sadly as he disappeared out of sight.

CHAPTER 30

They fell back into their routine: dressing, breakfast, school run, washing, ironing, cleaning, gardening, school run, playtime, TV, dinner, bath and bed. They went shopping at the weekends, saw Michael and Emma from time to time, went for a picnic or lunch with Sandy, her husband Brian and Keira, and had them over in return. There was little or no communication with anyone else. She often thought of Alisha and Sujay but accepted that in more ways than one they were worlds apart. Part of her was saddened not to stay in regular touch with Simon, but she knew his world was so far removed from hers, it was probably for the best.

For the time being, and for the foreseeable future, the focus was on the girls' schooling and the plans to sell Chalton and move elsewhere. The house had been valued at two point eight million pounds, and although the estate agent had conducted several viewings, none had resulted in a sensible offer so she resolved to remain patient and let things take their course. In an idle moment she'd tried to look for smaller properties on the market using Peter's old computer, but she wasn't skilled enough to work it properly and gave up in frustration. She was in no rush and would take advice as and when she needed it.

At 3 p.m. she parked the Range Rover in her usual place, fifty or sixty yards from the school, and wandered up to join the other parents waiting to collect their kids. She'd exchanged the odd pleasantry with a few whom she'd come to recognise, but for the most part people kept to their own little groups and did no more than pass the time of day.

She waited at the school gates, anxious as ever to capture a glimpse of the girls, relieved as ever to see the twins hopping and skipping across the playground, hand in hand with their big sister in control. She waved but they couldn't see her, preoccupied with their own thoughts and excitement.

"Alice?" She heard the voice and the name but it didn't register for a moment. "Alice?" The name repeated, louder, persistent. She turned her head, still puzzled, recognition slowly dawning. A woman, about thirty, blonde hair, comfortably built, jeans and trainers and fleece, hand in hand with a small blonde boy, was smiling at her, quizzically. "It is you! Alice!" She stepped forward and Jess frowned. "It's me! Jade. From the pub?"

Jess shook her head as the years peeled away. The Navigation. *Cask Ales, Fine Wines, Home-Cooked Food and Free Moorings.* Jade, the Aussie waitress, her trainer, her colleague, her friend, but plumper, older, different hair and with a child. She struggled to find the words, twisted her head to see her girls getting close, felt the need to be polite. She smiled woodenly.

"Jade! How are you? I didn't recognise you there."

"Aw, different hair, that's what did it. How's it going? Great to see you!"

"Great to see you too." In a way, it was. They'd been friends until that terrible day, her last, when she'd made her escape from ... the mess. And in a way, it wasn't. She didn't want to remember, didn't want to be reminded of things she'd rather forget. She twisted her head around. The twins. How could she ever forget? "I haven't seen you here before."

"Aw, Ben's just started." She rubbed the little boy's head. "How was your day, sweetie?" Ben squirmed and looked away, shy. Jess nodded vacantly.

"So," she mumbled, lapsing into the obvious, "you live around here?" But Jade was looking past her, over her shoulder. Jess turned and crouched to hug the twins.

"Yeah, in the next village. Fotherham. Who are these little beauties?" she gushed. "Oh my God! Alice. Aren't they just a delight?" Years in England had done nothing to temper the Australian's accent or her mannerisms. Jess smiled with pride.

"This is Lucy and this is Sophie. Say hello to Jade and Ben."

"Hello Jade and Ben," chimed the twins as one. Leila stood behind them, detached and wary. Jess leant over and pulled her to her side.

"And this is Leila." Jade did a poor job of hiding her surprise.

"Hi, Leila." She frowned, clearly thrown off balance, searching for a suitable response. "Aw, Alice, we must get together. Have a good chinwag and catch-up."

"Why is she calling you Alice?" said Leila, deadpan, staring at the strange woman.

"That's Mummy's other name!" piped up Sophie, stomping her foot in exasperation at Leila's ignorance. Jess decided to bring the encounter to a close.

"Yes. Yes. That would be nice," she said, trying to be non-committal. She needed to get away and gather her thoughts. But Jade always had been, and still was, irrepressible.

"Let's have lunch. Tomorrow. In the coffee shop. One o'clock. We can have a good talk before we pick up the little rascals." She rubbed her son's head again. Jess searched in vain for an excuse, but she didn't have one other than she'd rather not, which was the truth, and though she couldn't bring herself to speak the truth, she couldn't see beyond it. She smiled.

"Okay. Coffee shop. One o'clock tomorrow. Bye."

"Great to see you, Alice. Bye."

Jess led the girls to the Range Rover, relieved to see Jade and Ben walking the other way. As she walked, she kept turning her head and saw them climb into a battered old Fiesta and drive out of town.

As she drove the girls back to Chalton, the twins shouting and screaming in the back, Leila sitting pensively between them, she tried to put it out of her head, but she remained disturbed. It had been a terrible moment in her life; as terrible as her experiences with her father and her husband, but at the time made worse because at The Navigation she'd been lulled into a false sense of security. The new life she'd just started to build, cruelly torn down and trampled on. But then, Mo had done the same thing. She should have known. However, it was all water under the bridge, and through those trials she'd found Peter and he'd found Leila and everything was all right again.

She'd liked Jade. There was no reason they couldn't be friends again, and she didn't have any others, so that was a good thing. Despite her initial misgivings, she warmed to the idea and decided she'd try and make the best of it.

***

Jade parked the Fiesta in the car park behind The King's Head in Fotherham. They manoeuvred themselves around a stack of empty barrels and went in by the back door. She led her young son through the deserted kitchen area and out into the bar where her husband was in his usual spot, sitting at a table with a coffee and a newspaper.

"Hi, hon! Hey. You'll never guess who I saw today?"

Dave Morley, looked up, disinterested as ever.

"Hello, mate," he said to his young son. "All right?"

CHAPTER 31

She left the Range Rover in her usual place at twelve forty-five. It was only a ten-minute walk past the school and up the High Street to Sarnies, the village coffee shop, and she needed the walk. She had toned down her attire, having yesterday seen Jade looking decidedly scruffy and driving a battered old car, so she thought jeans and a plain shirt were more appropriate. For the same irrational reason, she wanted to keep the Range Rover out of sight.

Jade was waiting for her at a table by the window and she noticed with some irony her friend had obviously made an effort for their lunch date, smartly dressed in jacket and trousers. Jade stood up and hugged her, but Jess felt stiff and awkward.

"Hi, Alice. Aw, I can't tell you how nice it is to see you. I want to know everything," she gushed, and Jess felt a wave of despair. The coffee shop was three quarters full, mostly ladies lunching, and Jess wondered how, in such a small village, the place was not only so popular, but where all these people had come from.

"It's great to see you too," she said. "How long have you lived in Fotherham?" She'd driven through the village several times but never stopped so didn't know it well.

"About a year. Love it. It's perfect." They were interrupted by a waitress who handed them some menus. "What about you?"

"I live here in Chalton, have done so for about five years."

"So straight after you left the pub?"

"Yes, that's about right."

They decided on sandwiches and mineral water.

"Those girls of yours are just beautiful. How old are they?"

"About four and half."

"And the older one, Leila wasn't it?" Jess nodded. "Is she ... yours?" Jade's hesitation was transparent and revealed her inevitable and obvious confusion about Alice having an older child who was clearly of mixed parentage. Jess was reminded why initially she had been so reticent about meeting, but here she was, and the questions would keep coming so best she try and answer them.

"Yes. I was married before I met you, but my husband left and took her away. But later, I got her back." *Five years later.*

"Aw Jeez, that must have been terrible. You never said at the time. I always thought there was something troubling you, you know." Jade nodded to herself in satisfaction. "And then you got married again?"

"No. I don't see the twins' father anymore."

"Strewth, Alice. How do you manage?"

"I manage." *I live in a three million pound mansion and drive a Range Rover and have more money than I can possibly spend!*

The waitress brought their food and drinks and Jade tucked in. She'd ordered a portion of chips on the side and Jess wondered uncharitably whether Jade's loss of figure was post-natal or carbohydrate driven. She decided the best way to divert attention from herself was to ask Jade about Jade.

"So, what brought you to Fotherham?"

"The pub. The King's Head. Me and my old man run it."

"Oh. Really?" Jess tried to sound interested but wasn't. She could visualise Jade in the pub, but it brought back bad memories. Jade was looking at her knowingly, as if she could see through her, or maybe she was holding something back.

"Jeez, Alice. You'll never guess."

"What?"

"Well ..." Jade took a big bite of sandwich and a handful of chips, and Jess knew this was the precursor to a long story. "Remember the day you left ..." *How could I forget?* "... well, shit hit the fan big time." She stopped for a second to swallow and Jess could feel her own heart beating faster. "Trish and Dave had this massive row. About you." She nodded towards her and Jess took a breath, trying not to react.

"Well, I know you and Dave had a thing going, and that's fine. He tried it on with all us girls and we all told him to piss off. But he really fancied you and I can understand, you know, having a little frisson of excitement about the boss, and perhaps falling for his charms. He was a bit of a charmer, Dave. And obviously Trish found out, and that's why you were fired. I mean, I heard her coming in and out of your room in a major strop and then attacking him in the kitchen, chucking pots and pans and crockery at him. It'd be hilarious if it weren't so tragic. Still, we can all laugh about it now." She chuckled and stuffed her mouth with chips.

Jess wanted to scream.

We can all laugh about it?

She couldn't bear to hear it. Jade was so wrong, and even if she had a way of putting her right, she didn't have the will. *I had a "thing" going with him?* But Jade was in full flight.

"Well, Trish chucked him out the flat. Wouldn't speak to him. And he had a gash over his eye where she'd hit him with a plate. He was in a terrible state!" She glugged some water to wash down a mouthful of sandwich and took another bite. Jess had lost her appetite and just stared down at her plate, wondering under what circumstances she might feel sorry for Dave Morley.

"So he ended up in your old room because it was the only place left, and I felt a bit sorry for him, you know. So I went in to see if he was all right and" – she smiled wickedly – "you know, one thing led to another, and we..." She winked at Jess who simply stared at her blankly.

"You and Dave?" Jade nodded enthusiastically while still chewing. "But ... I thought you hated him?" She was confused and bewildered, and although she didn't want to hear about it, she wanted to understand.

"Aw, it was just a one-off, you know. And I thought if his missus has chucked him out then, you know, fair game!" Jess didn't know. "And then, next thing I know, the regional manager comes round cos Trish won't work with Dave and wants him out, tout suite, so while they're getting divorced, they ship him off to run some other pub miles away cos all they want is to settle things down. So Dave suddenly disappears.

"Well" – she wiped her mouth with a paper napkin and took another bite – "everything goes quiet for a while and then he calls me and asks me if I'll go and work with him as assistant manager and it's loads more money, and it's a no-brainer, so I tell Trish and she goes ape-shit, but you know, I tell her it's nothing to do with her anymore, and next thing, I'm off."

Jess knew it couldn't have been as simple as that but had no interest in challenging Jade's version of events, and anyway, Jade looked so pleased with herself for apparently asserting her independence, she wasn't going to disabuse her.

"Where was the pub?"

"Carnhill. Near Cambridge." Jess had no idea where it was, but it sounded far enough away. "Real dive. Grottiest pub in the estate, but we made a go of it. Got the sales up." Jess's instincts were beginning to bother her and were fuelling something deep down that was making her feel queasy. She wanted to change the subject, but she knew there was more to come and it wasn't going to be good.

"So ... you and Dave ran this grotty pub and then you left and came to Fotherham?" she asked tentatively, but she sensed palpitations. Jade was grinning at her.

"Can't you guess?" The wickedness was back and she flashed her left hand where something sparkled. "Dave's divorce came through and we got married and they gave us The King's Head. In Fotherham!" She finished with a triumphant flourish of napkin.

The air seemed to have been sucked out of the room; there could be no other reason she found it difficult to breathe. She had just been told by this woman that her husband, her nemesis, the rapist father of her beautiful babies, was living and working in a pub three miles from where they were sitting. She wanted to scream, sweep the contents of the table onto the floor, overturn the furniture and slap Jade so hard she'd be prosecuted for assault. But Jade was still talking.

"He sends his regards. I told him I saw you yesterday and we were having lunch." Jess instinctively swung round to face the entrance, expecting him to swagger in, lascivious grin, sneering, strutting, drooling over her. Her flesh crawled. "But he's busy at the pub. I had to get lunch off!" she laughed. "Not that Tuesday lunchtime is the busiest session. But he said we should meet up. Have a foursome?"

"That won't be possible," said Jess, too quickly.

"Aw, yeah. Didn't know you were, you know, by yourself. Well one day, maybe."

And then another thought came to her.

"So, Ben is …"

"Dave's and mine. Can't you see the resemblance?" Jade was bursting with pride, like any mother would.

"Yes. I can." She needed air. "Jade, sorry. But I have to go and do something before school. Do you mind?"

"Nah, we can do this again sometime." Jess reached for her purse. "No," said Jade, putting a hand on Jess's arm. "My shout. You can get the next one." Jess nodded, they embraced awkwardly and she fled the coffee shop.

She sat in the car, alone and quiet, a sanctuary of sorts. She couldn't stop her hands shaking, her heart thumping or her head pounding, weighing up the implications of her worst nightmare suddenly turning into reality.

She tried to calm herself, look at it rationally. What threat did Dave Morley pose to her? Jade had said he "sent his regards" but what did that mean? Maybe he was shocked to find out that the woman he raped five years ago lived close by, and not only that, she now knew where he lived. Maybe he just wanted to stay away? Then why suggest they "get together and have a foursome"? An olive branch? Did he want to say sorry, make amends? Jade couldn't possibly know exactly what happened between them. "*I know you and him had a thing going.*"

But that wasn't the way Jess saw it. She saw the evil of a man who had manipulated her, forced her to do what he wanted, threatened to ruin her unless she submit to his carnal lust. Psychological pressure; a precursor to rape. The thought she might bump into Dave Morley again was repugnant and repulsive enough, but, above all, she had to keep this monster away from her children.

Then a thought came to her. She could threaten to go to the police and accuse him of rape, because that was what it was. But she could hear the questions. Why did she leave it five years? Why didn't she go to the police at the time? She couldn't even imagine explaining that one. *Because I was used to it. Being abused. That's why.*

She realised it was for her children that she was most fearful. They must never know. At the moment, he had no way of knowing he'd fathered any children, and he need never know, must never know. Logically, the last thing he needed was to find out he had two other kids; not only would that be extremely damaging to his own family, he might think she would come after him for maintenance. She knew she wouldn't and clearly she didn't need it, but he didn't know that. The more she thought about it, the more she realised that Dave had much more to lose than she did, so provided she never laid eyes on him, she could live with it, and maybe, just maybe, that would suit him too.

But she couldn't live with seeing Jade every day and keeping up the pretence that Alice and Dave had just had a "fling". She would just have to tell Jade that it was nice seeing her again, but that she'd moved on and didn't want to rekindle old memories. And she'd have to accelerate the house-moving project. It would be better if she put distance between them.

She picked up the kids at three. She saw Jade walking towards her but was able to rush off with just a wave. She'd pick her moment in the next day or two and politely but firmly, end it. They all had their own lives to lead, and that was that.

***

Dave Morley was sitting in his favourite place when his wife and son got back at three fifteen.

"All right?" he mumbled without looking up from the sports section. He was bored, fed up with life, fed up with the fact that his wife seemed to put on a pound or two every week and fed up with the burden of family responsibilities. He looked up at her. "Nice lunch?" he sneered. *I bet she went for the chips again. She's turning into a real lard-arse.*

"Yeah. Great." Ben, go up and get changed, there's a good boy." Ben trotted off without a word from his father. "Alice sends her best."

Dave scoffed, knowing she'd made that one up. There was no way Alice was going to "send her best". He knew something about Alice that Jade didn't, and he had no doubt that Alice was feeling pretty nervy at the moment, wondering whether he was going to come after her.

He was still pissed off that he'd had to do the lunchtime shift so his wife could go and pig-out somewhere else, but at least it gave him the chance to have a chat with that new Lithuanian waitress, Irena, and give her a bit of "training". Maybe life had its compensations.

"So what did she say when you told her we lived here?"

291

"Aw, she was surprised, you know. Thinking about it, she looked a bit shocked."

"I'll bet she did," he sneered, pleased that the bitch might be a bit wound up.

"What do you mean? I thought you two got on all right. I mean, I know you got your leg over, Dave, but that doesn't mean we can't be friends."

He closed the newspaper with a slap of the hand, barely concealing his annoyance and frustration.

"I'll tell you what that bitch did. She fucked up my marriage and my career."

Jade looked at him and her mouth dropped open.

"Aw, thanks a bunch, mate." She put her hands on her hips and shifted her weight in preparation for yet another row. "Sorry, me and Ben not good enough for you?"

He spotted his faux pas immediately.

"No, no. That's not what I meant."

"Well what did you mean, Dave?"

He racked his brains for a plausible explanation, a suitable compliment, something to get himself out of his self-inflicted problem.

"Look, it was a very difficult time for me. If it hadn't been for you, well, I don't know what I would have done." That was the best he could come up with and he embellished it with a look that demanded sympathy. It was true; he didn't know what he would have done if he had thought about it, but it wouldn't have been this. "Anyway," he said, going back on the attack, "the bitch owes me twelve hundred quid."

"What?"

"She owes me twelve hundred quid!" he repeated for emphasis, his voice rising to a falsetto. "She nicked it."

"What? Alice stole twelve hundred quid off you?"

"Yeah!" He stood up. "While me and Trish were going at it in the kitchen, she buggered off and took a wad of money off the bar, and then disappeared." Jade was still looking confused. "Trish left it there, stupid cow, and that bitch Alice walked off with it."

"Why didn't you call the police?"

"If you remember," he said, ladling on the sarcasm to make the fat tart understand, "I was suffering a bit from concussion and blood loss while trying to dodge flying bloody kitchen knives. I didn't notice till later and then Trish chucked me out. Then, when she found out, she said she'd deal with it but she didn't. Just fucking blamed me." He wiped his mouth to clear some spittle that had formed during his rant. "I've a good mind to go down there and tell her what I think."

"No, Dave. Don't do that. We don't want no trouble. We don't want people seeing you getting all wound up in the street, shouting at a young mother and kids. Word'll spread and folks might stop coming in."

"Yeah, well. She'd better not come in here while I'm around." He stomped off to the coffee machine and poured himself another cup. Jade left him to stew.

Dave was twitching. He was twitching because he hadn't stopped thinking about Alice since his wife had mentioned seeing her. He remembered their little dalliance fondly. He remembered the excitement he felt at the time and the way she had first quivered at his touch and then cracked and smouldered when he put her under pressure. He'd never worked her out.

He wondered what she looked like now. Apparently she had three kids and one of them was a bit of a Paki so she obviously wasn't fussy about the sort of blokes she had, and by now she was probably a lard-arse too. But he could still smell the perfume, see the make-up, sense the fear and the vulnerability, and it turned him on again. He still lusted after her. He'd have to go down to the school and take a peek.

***

Jess rehearsed her speech in bed that night. She didn't want it to sound rude or unfriendly, but she had to make it clear that she didn't want to pursue an old friendship. Yes, that was the best way. She anticipated responses and had answers to them all; she just had to be firm but polite. It would be difficult, but it was necessary.

***

She planned to say something the next morning, as soon as the kids had gone in and she could have a minute or two alone with Jade, but they got held up in traffic and only just got there as the bell rang, by which time and Jade and Ben had already gone. She was partly relieved that the moment had passed, but having convinced herself to confront Jade, she wanted to get it over with as soon as possible. She would get back early this afternoon and make sure she saw her before the kids came out.

At ten to three she waited alone outside the school gates as other parents gradually appeared. She nodded and smiled at one or two, nervously watching the street, and then saw Jade walking towards her purposefully. She looked less than her ebullient self; arms folded, face set, mind preoccupied. She came straight up to Jess, no welcoming smile, no greeting and certainly no contact. Jess waded in.

"Jade ..." she started, but a hand came up.

"Alice, I don't wanna hear it." She looked upset and nervous. "I know what happened and I think it's wrong, but it's all ancient history now as far as I'm concerned. So the less said about it, the better. All right?"

"Well, if you ..." Jess tried to respond although she wasn't sure what she was responding to, and before she had a chance she was interrupted.

"I think it's in everyone's interests to just leave it be, and we go our own separate ways. For the kids' sakes. Okay?"

It hadn't gone according to plan. It never did. But the same result had been arrived at without her having to say anything. She wasn't sure why Jade was upset. Maybe something Dave had said to her? Maybe he'd confessed? Maybe he'd done the decent thing? Whatever. She just wanted the problem to go away.

"Okay, Jade. I understand." Jade turned abruptly and stood ten yards away, waiting for her son to appear. Jess turned away, saddened but relieved, a potential new friendship destroyed before it had even started. *Time to move house for good.*

The girls arrived, the twins excitable as ever, Leila controlled and calm as usual, shepherding her little flock, vigilant and wary.

***

Dave had parked in the side street opposite where he could see the school gates, and he saw the brittle exchange between Alice and his wife from fifty yards away. Alice had her back to him so he couldn't see her face, but he could tell from her figure she had kept herself well, and next to Jade, she looked positively fit.

He saw them separate abruptly and then, within a second, two little blonde girls and a mixed-race kid came out, and he watched Alice hug them and lead them up the path in the opposite direction to Jade and Ben. He leapt out of the car and scurried down to the main road, following them at a distance.

Other kids and parents were walking the same way but thinned out progressively as they jumped into the line of parked cars, until only Alice and the three girls were ahead of him. He kept his distance and then saw them stop by a brand new Range Rover. His jaw dropped open.

The car's lights flashed as she pulled the back door open and shovelled the kids in. Heart racing, he quickened his pace and got to the car just as she closed the back door.

"All right, Alice?"

She froze. He sounded just the same. She was sure he was about to tell her how much he appreciated her, tell her he was going to give her a bonus, tell her that she ought to be nice to him or else.

"Go away, Dave." She strode around the front of the car to the driver's side.

"Nice motor, Alice. That must have cost a bit."

"I've nothing to say to you. Now go away!"

"Aw, come on, Alice. How many blokes did you have to shag to get that, then?" He put his hands in his pockets and leant forward, making a show of peering into the back. "Two or three. I reckon," he said, chuckling at his own wit. He walked towards her.

"Stay away. Or I'll call the police." He frowned at her, feigning hurt and confusion. "Tell them what you did." She inadvertently snapped her head to look in the back of the car. The girls were still, quiet, watching, apprehensive.

"What I did?" he said, turning serious. He sensed something in her voice and in her posture and he looked at her. She presented very well, was nicely scrubbed up. She was turning him on again and he was enjoying it.

"You stay away from the girls. They're mine! You hear?"

Two blonde kids. Same age as Ben. The penny dropped and he was thrown off balance for a moment, lost for words. She yanked open the door, climbed up into the driver's seat and the V8 roared into life. He stepped back swiftly onto the pavement and watched her swing the car round in a U-turn and speed up the hill. *Holy fuck!*

***

"Mummy?" Leila had helped put the twins to bed and was now drying up dishes in the kitchen. "Who's that nasty man? The one after school?"

Jess had tried to hide her anxiety and although she was sure the twins hadn't noticed anything untoward, Leila was not stupid. She thought about trying to brush it off, but her eldest was experienced beyond her years and she didn't deserve to be told any lies, even if Jess had the ability to tell them.

"He's someone I used to know a long time ago. He's not a nice person and I don't want to see him again."

"Is he Sophie and Lucy's daddy?" Jess shook her head, not in denial, but in admiration. *What am I going to with you, Leila? You're far too clever for your own good.*

"Yes," she nodded. "But they don't know that and I don't want them to know that. It's just us, okay?" She pulled Leila up against her and held her head against her body. "We don't need anyone, do we? We just need each other. Just us."

"Just us."

CHAPTER 32

Dave was in his normal place for a Tuesday evening, behind the bar, lording it over his domain. There were a few diners in the restaurant, but this was one of the quietest days of the week and they could get by with Jade and Irena, plus two in the kitchen. They'd do no more than fifteen covers this evening, plus a few diehards in a bar that would otherwise be virtually empty.

Except, of course, for old Trevor, who was in the same spot he occupied every night, perched on his personal barstool facing the main door, from which he could monitor the comings and goings over a single pint of Jenkins' Best, eked out over the course of an hour.

Dave was quite happy to chinwag with Trevor; football, politics, international relations, race, religion, the price of oil. Trevor had opinions on everything and was right about everything too. Dave had learnt quickly not to bother arguing with Trevor, because Trevor didn't acknowledge any opinion that deviated from his own. Trevor knew everything and everyone, and tonight was Trevor's lucky night.

"Can I get you another, Trev?" asked Dave, looking at the last inch in Trevor's glass, knowing full well what the answer would be.

"Oh no, no. One's enough for me," he grunted. "Got to get back. See what the missus is up to."

"On the house?" said Dave, similarly certain of the response.

"Oh! Oh, well," said Trevor, quickly draining his glass and handing it over. "Don't mind if I do. Is it your birthday or something?"

"Nah, just looking after my best customers," said Dave, smirking. He wasn't used to giving booze away except under special circumstances. But Trevor would pay in kind. He poured another pint and set it down.

"Thank 'ee kindly," said Trev. He took a big swig of beer.

"You've lived here a while, ain't yer?"

"Man and boy. All me life."

"So you know everyone round here and in Chalton?"

"Just about. Seen 'em all in this life. Seen 'em come and go."

"There's a woman lives in Chalton. Young, drives a big flashy car … Range Rover; three kids, one of 'em's" – he looked around and leant over to Trevor, lowering his voice – "a Paki. Do you know what I mean?"

"Paki?"

"Shh, not so loud."

Trevor thought hard for a moment and then lifted his finger in the air.

"Yeah. I seen 'em. Tasty bit of scrumpet. Fancy her, do yer?"

"Nah, course not." Dave was beginning to wonder if asking Trevor had been a good idea. "Just looked a bit odd around here, that's all. Out of place."

"She's the lady of the manor," announced Trevor. "Chalton Manor. The Jeffries's place." Dave had heard of it. "Yeah, old man Jeffries died a few months back, left her there. She was his housekeeper, you know. Had a couple of kids as soon as she arrived and then, as soon as he's in the ground, the foreign kid turns up. Don't know what that's all about."

"So who else lives there?"

"No one, as far as I know."

"What, just her and three kids?"

"Yep."

"So where's the father?"

"Well, gossip was old man Jeffries, you know, put her in the club, but I don't think that's right."

"Why?"

"Because she's the spitting image of his daughter, that's why. He weren't like that. Not the colonel. He were a gentleman."

"So where's his daughter?"

"Disappeared. Lost somewhere in them Himalayas. Never seen again. No, no. Them kids weren't the colonel's. I reckon the girl was well gone by the time she got here."

"Weird," said Dave.

"Nowt so queer …" said Trevor, and took another swig.

***

Dave Morley was nothing if not resourceful and ambitious, and he was proud of it. He could spot an opportunity when he saw one, and the more he understood about Alice, the more the semblance of a plan took shape.

It had been clear from her reaction to seeing him that she was not about to respond favourably to his advances, and he regretted that. He would have quite happily let bygones be bygones, kissed and made up, and seen where a renewed acquaintance might take them. But he guessed that would be pushing water uphill, and anyway, he had a better plan; one that might encourage her to be more receptive, more amenable to his needs.

He couldn't be absolutely sure he was the father of the little blonde girls but the timing fitted, they bore a slight resemblance to Ben and she had let the cat out of the bag by being too quick to keep him away. He'd absolutely no interest in pressing his rights – he needed more kids like a hole in the head – but he was fairly sure it wouldn't come to that.

He wasn't sure how he was going to break it to Jade, but he guessed she'd come round when he explained, and if she didn't, well, she could make her own choice and take her chances elsewhere. The priority was to test the water and see how hot it was. He relished a challenge, especially one that involved sniffing around young women, and he couldn't wait to get started. He'd go and explore tomorrow morning.

The new girl, Irena, tottered by with an armful of plates, smiling nervously at him, concentrating on her balance. He gave her a wink, his eyes zeroing in on her tight little bottom as she walked past. *Steady boy. One at a time.*

***

Jess was gardening at the back of the house, deadheading the cosmos in the raised beds surrounding the patio, just like Peter had taught her. They were well into autumn, so there was not much life left in the spindly stalks, but she guessed she might tease out a few more flowers before she'd have to pull them up.

She loved being out in the fresh air and, weather permitting, she much preferred to potter outside, clipping and tidying, to being indoors, ironing and dusting; important enough tasks but better kept for rainy days. She bemoaned the decline and loss of Peter's vegetable patch, being unable to maintain it along with all the other things she had to do, and she'd resolved to get the kids involved and start it again in some small way. It was something useful they could do together.

But now her priorities had changed. She'd called the estate agent and told him to reduce the price by two hundred thousand to get things moving. He'd tried to talk her out of it, encourage her to be patient, but she was having none of it. She knew she was running away, but there seemed no alternative and the strategy hadn't changed; just the urgency with which it had to be deployed.

She heard a car on the gravel drive and walked around to the front of the house to see who was calling unannounced on a midweek morning in September. The blue Mondeo pulled to a halt and Dave Morley got out, grinning broadly.

"Nice gaffe, Alice. I'm impressed."

She felt her heart rate soar and she began to shake.

"Go away, Dave. I never want to see you again!" He ignored the comment. He stood ten feet from her, assessing the house like a prospective purchaser, and then let his eyes fall on her, her body taut and erect, arms folded, petulant and defiant, but also fearful.

"I notice you're selling up. Worth a few quid, this place. Hope you're not leaving on my account?" She didn't answer. She fumbled in her back pocket and pulled out her phone, holding it up towards him.

"If you don't leave now, I'll call the police."

"And tell 'em what? I ain't doing no harm."

"You're trespassing." It sounded limp and she cursed herself for appearing pathetic, because it wasn't working. His grin hadn't faltered.

"Your house is for sale and I've come to view it," he said, spreading his arms wide before his smile dropped, just a bit. "And I've come to see my kids."

She felt a wave of fear and nausea well up inside her, each breath coming more quickly as she fought off the urge to scream, to run at him, attack him and claw his eyes out. Anything to make him go away and leave her alone.

"They're not yours!" It was a lie, of sorts. She knew he was the biological father, but that was all. He'd had no role in their lives so far and he'd have no role in their future. The twins were hers and hers alone.

"Oh, I think they are," he said winking at her. "You can't fool me, Alice. I can tell. Anyway, I got rights. I want to support them. I want to fulfil my responsibilities as a loving father," he announced pompously, his disingenuousness self-evident.

"If you come near me or my family again, I'll report you to the police for assault" – she hesitated before summoning up the courage to spit out the words – "for rape!" But to her dismay and frustration, he just put his hands in his pockets and chuckled.

"Get out of it. I really like you, Alice, and I really like the girls, and all I want to do is be a part of your lives. Again." The threat was real and explicit. "You can't deny me my rights."

She dialled furiously on her phone and put it to her ear.

"Police? There's a man here harassing and threatening me ..." He put his hands up

"Okay, okay. I'm going. But you'll be hearing from my lawyers." He pointed at her as he backed towards the car. He got in the Mondeo, swung it around the drive and out of the main gates.

"Michael, yes. I'm sorry," she said into the phone. "I need to see you, urgently."

***

Jess sat opposite Michael in his office, teacup in hand, head down, exhausted at having related the story of The Navigation, the Morleys and now the hideous revelation of Dave's reappearance.

"So he is the father?"

"Yes. But he has no right!"

"In the eyes of the law I'm afraid he might, Jess."

"I won't have it. He's got to be stopped."

"Well he hasn't done anything yet apart from upset you, and I know that's horrible in itself, but if he is the sort of character you describe, then it may just be he's having a bit of cruel sport at your expense."

"I want him locked up. I want to sell the house and get away from here." She was calm but determined and seething.

"Well, we can do something about the latter, but getting him locked up? I think that's a long shot, Jess. Whatever he did to you, it was a long time ago, and it's going to be impossible to prove."

"I have the evidence." She was raising her voice and she knew it.

"I'm afraid the existence of twins alone is not evidence of sexual assault." She deflated, sagging in her chair. She put the cup back on the saucer and rubbed her forehead. "I think you should try and forget about it. Tell me if he contacts you again. We may be able to scare him off with a stalking charge; apply for a restraining order. Meanwhile, we'll give the house another push."

***

There was no doubt she had taken it badly, but he'd talked her round. Jade had initially responded to the announcement that Ben had two half-sisters with a typical Aussie expletive, followed up by two or three slaps around the head and a severe bout of weeping.

But he'd been able to persuade her to look on the bright side. There was nothing to lose and everything to gain. He intended to demonstrate to everyone his determination to do his duty and they'd all be the better off for it.

Even though he'd been seduced, tricked and deceived, his responsibilities weighed heavily and Dave Morley was going to carry them out, whatever it took, whatever the cost.

***

A week later, she was back in Michael's office. He read the letter twice before putting it down and removing his glasses. He sighed deeply.

"Can he do that?" asked Jess, already knowing the answer.

"Yes, I'm afraid he can. Anyone can apply for paternity rights, and if you resist and he demands a DNA test, then we both know what the outcome will be. Are you sure he's the father?" She glared at him, about to explode. "Sorry" – he put his hands up – "that was insensitive."

"I'm going to threaten a rape charge."

"Jess, we've been through this."

"I don't care! It's the truth. I'll tell them everything that happened. The truth will come out."

"Do not underestimate how difficult that's going to be," he said gently, trying to mollify her, lower her expectations without sounding patronising. "If you get the police involved, it might get very distressing for you. They'll have little to go on other than your word, and they'll be very reluctant to press charges without evidence or witnesses. They'll be obliged to pursue your claim, but they'll judge it to be futile and, I regret to say, try and get you to drop it by whatever means they can."

"What do you mean? Aren't they on the side of law and order? On the side of good people? Of doing what's right?"

"I think you'll find that to keep their numbers up, they'll prioritise the easy cases, and they'll look at this and decide it's not an easy case. They can't be seen to be dismissing it out of hand, not in the current febrile environment, but they'll do their best to discredit you and your arguments and you might come out of it worse off than before."

"So what do we do? We can't just do nothing."

"Well, the first thing to do is to write back to his lawyers and rebut the claim. At the same time I think we should threaten a counterclaim for sexual assault and see if it's enough to warn him off. But that means your having to provide me with all the gory details. Step by step, what happened, when it happened, who was there, who saw you, if anyone; the whole story, blow by blow. And you might find that too distressing."

"Do you think it'll work?"

"I have to say it's a long shot. But it's worth a try."

***

She tried to behave normally for the girls' sake, and for the most part the twins were oblivious their mother was suffering from a deeply worrying situation that threatened to spiral out of her control.

Leila, astute and perspicacious, quietly and surreptitiously performed small tasks to ease the burden on her mother when she seemed lost in her own thoughts. She was still too young to understand the circumstances or the exact cause of her mother's distress, but she knew it was something to do with a nasty man and wasn't surprised by that.

Jess recognised her eldest daughter's rapidly growing maturity and pondered over the parallels between her and Peter's family; wondered if Lisa and Janica's exceptionally close relationship was just an age thing or had been stimulated by circumstance. She also wondered how the relationship between all four of them might develop once the twins got a bit older and the knowledge of the past became known to them. She prayed that they would always be as close as they were now but had to accept that all people change over time, and not always for the better.

But there was no doubt in her mind that Leila was growing into a companion, becoming more like a sister than a daughter, and in a few years from now their age difference would diminish and cease to be relevant. By which time, she hoped, all this trauma and misery would be behind them.

CHAPTER 33

They sat in the reception area of Laker, Neal and Robson, a twenty-partner firm with offices in a modern building situated in a modern business park. The contrast with Michael's modest, traditional office in a Georgian townhouse could not be more stark and, for Jess, more intimidating.

They'd arrived five minutes early and the receptionist had called it through, but fifteen minutes later they were still waiting.

"Are you okay?" asked Michael, sensing her nervousness.

"Yes. I just want to get it over with. What's keeping them?" she said, her impatience evident, her anxiety difficult to hide. "It's just rude."

"Tactics, Jess. She'll be here in" – he looked at his watch – "ninety seconds." He was out by ten.

Pauline Robson, in pin-striped suit and high-heeled court shoes, sashayed across the marble floor to where they were sitting and gave them her most affected rictus grin.

"Mr Goodman and Miss Jeffries," she gushed, "so sorry to have kept you. Pauline Robson." She held out a limp hand to Michael as if she expected him to kiss it, but he took it and shook it briskly. "I was just getting a last-minute brief from my client," she drawled, ignoring Jess completely. "Please follow me." She swivelled on the spot and strutted off in the opposite direction, waggling her bottom as she went. Jess looked at Michael, noticing a raised eyebrow.

She showed them into a meeting room furnished with an oval table and four chairs, one of them already occupied by Dave who was studying his phone.

"This is my client, Mr Morley," she said to Michael, but Dave didn't stand and Michael made no attempt to reach out a hand. "I believe you two have met?" she said, acknowledging Jess's presence for the first time. She gestured to them to sit, smoothed her skirt behind her and sat down next to Dave in front of a new manila folder containing several papers. Jess judged her to be fifty or so, with short dark hair severely swept back and wearing little or no make-up, a pearl necklace and matching ear studs the only adornments, her left hand devoid of rings.

Jess looked up at Dave and saw he was grinning at her, relaxed and calm, supercilious. He put his phone down and rested his hands on the table. Pauline Robson arranged her spectacles on her nose and casually studied the papers in her folder.

"Now, Mr Goodman. No doubt you've discussed with your client our letter of the fourteenth in which we set out on behalf of our client, Mr David Morley, his claim against Miss Alice Jeffries for access rights to his two young children?"

"Ms Robson …"

"Miss."

Michael cleared his throat

"Miss Robson. You will have noted from my reply dated the seventeenth that my client wishes to be known as Miss Jess Jeffries."

"Yes, I did notice that. What is your client's real name, may I ask?" She said all this without looking once at Jess and it made her feel she shouldn't even be in the room, which was probably the intention.

"My client once used the name 'Alice' but that was a long time ago."

"I see," said Miss Robson, with a hint of disdain, and hastily scribbled something on her pad. "Well, I've read and discussed your letter with Mr Morley and I have to say we are somewhat shocked and dismayed by the very serious and flagrantly inaccurate allegations contained therein. Needless to say we refute these vile accusations unreservedly and will require you and your client to undertake never to repeat them."

Dave smirked at Jess and she struggled to remain calm.

"Jess stands by her allegations and is quite prepared, if necessary, to repeat them in front of a police officer." Michael had already made it clear to her that this would be an idle threat, but she had insisted. He was right.

"Mr Goodman, you and I both know your client has no prospect whatsoever of getting the police to press charges on something so" – she made a pretence of searching for the right word – "fanciful. If your client persists with these outrageous claims, we shall issue proceedings for defamation. Furthermore, I should warn you Mr Morley is considering reporting your client to the police for theft."

"Theft?" Jess couldn't help blurting it out, her anger building. Michael put a hand on her arm. Dave smirked. Pauline Robson raised her head slowly, peering down at her over the top of her spectacles.

"On the day you left The Navigation, you stole the sum of twelve hundred pounds. Do you deny it?"

Jess took a moment, trying to work out where this had come from, and then the realisation dawned on her. *The money on the bar.* But it was too late; her hesitation was faintly damning and she felt Michael stiffen.

"I paid the money into their bank an hour later!"

The woman smiled at her disdainfully.

"So you admit you took it, then."

"I gave it back!"

"Mr Morley has no record of that."

"Well I'm sure his ex-wife does." She knew her voice was rising in pitch but she couldn't control it.

"How convenient. Anyway, the appalling allegations you have made against Mr Morley are nothing more than a pathetic attempt to distract from the real issue, which is Mr Morley's statutory right to have access to his children."

"Never!"

The woman pursed her lips in distaste at Jess's attempt to look and sound defiant.

"Mr Goodman, if I may, I should like to ask your client some questions about the time she was at The Navigation working for Mr Morley, and in particular, the day she walked out without giving notice, taking twelve hundred pounds from the till. Mr Morley has given me his version of events and I think you may find them ... illuminating."

Michael looked sideways at Jess to check she was happy to proceed. She nodded grimly.

"I also think it will be a useful means of setting out the facts as we know them. It is no more or less than that which the police would do, were your client to carry out her vile threat to repeat her scurrilous accusations, and it may help her understand why the course of action she is pursuing is futile."

"Go ahead."

"Thank you. Miss Jeffries, I understand you worked at The Navigation for Mr and Mrs Morley for a period of approximately four weeks. Is that correct?"

"Yes, about that."

"And where were you living at the time?"

Jess shrugged

"I wasn't living anywhere."

"You mean you were homeless?"

"I suppose so."

Jess dropped her head. She didn't want to go into the history; the story of her life.

"And is it not the case that Mr and Mrs Morley took you in, gave you employment and accommodation despite your not being able to provide any references?" Jess nodded. "Trusted you, in fact?"

Jess remained silent. She knew the Morleys had exploited her circumstances, kept her off the books and used her as cheap labour, but at the time she was content with the arrangement; it was far better than being homeless, but she didn't have the energy to try and explain.

"And how did Mr and Mrs Morley treat you?"

"What do you mean?"

"Were they cruel to you? Did they criticise your work? Refuse to pay you? Did they make life difficult for you, such that you wanted to leave?"

"No. Not until …" She shuddered, not wanting to think about the events again, but there was no choice.

"Not until what, Miss Jeffries?" The woman's tone was officious, supercilious and smug, but Jess was relieved she hadn't attempted to delve into her past.

"Not until he tried to touch me."

"We'll come on to that. So why did you take advantage of their good nature?"

"I didn't!"

"Why did you try and seduce Mr Morley?" It hit her like a punch.

"What!?" Jess looked across the table at Dave, astonished at how anyone could tell such lies. She returned the woman's steely gaze, the raised eyebrows that challenged her to explain. But the woman went on.

"Is it not true, Miss Jeffries, that, on the day you left The Navigation, you attempted to seduce Mr Morley while his wife was out?"

"NO! Of course not. He groped me!" she shouted, pointing a finger at Dave who flinched momentarily in response.

"The truth is you plastered yourself with perfume and make-up and flaunted yourself in front of him."

"No! It wasn't like that at all."

"But you were wearing perfume and make-up?"

"Yes. Mrs Morley gave it to me."

"And she told you not to wear it while you were working?"

"Not at the time." She was flustered, trying to remember the chronology of events. "She gave it to me and I wore some the next day to show her I was grateful, and she said I smelt and looked nice but that I should remove it before lunchtime."

"And did you?"

"Did I what?"

"Did you remove it?"

"No."

"I see. So you were asked to remove it but you disobeyed." The woman was forcing her into a corner.

"I didn't have time. No sooner had Mrs Morley left the pub, he had his hands on me." She poked a finger at him again.

"So Mrs Morley had left the building, leaving you alone with Mr Morley."

"Yes."

"And you took the opportunity to take advantage of him."

"No!"

"Mr Morley paid you a simple compliment and you reacted by pressing yourself up against him."

"NO! I was minding my own business when he came up behind me and groped me."

"So you say. Did you ask him to desist?"

"Yes. I asked him not to … to put his hands there."

"Put his hands where?"

"On me. Around my waist."

"But that was your intention, wasn't it? Your intention was to draw Mr Morley in?"

"No!"

"And then, when you succeeded in drawing him in, you spurned him."

"What?"

"You drew him in and then asked him to desist. I think the phrase is 'playing hard to get'."

"That's not true!"

"And then you asked him for money." Jess shook her head in bewilderment. And then the memories came back to her. *Where's my bonus?* The woman was looking at her. She knew.

"Did you ask Mr Morley for money?" she demanded.

"No! Well ... yes, but ..."

"Which is it, Miss Jeffries?"

"Yes, but not like that."

"Like what?"

"I was just trying to get rid of him."

"I cannot see how asking Mr Morley for money when he was allegedly 'groping' you was likely to achieve the result you claim to have wished." Jess took a breath and tried to calm herself. She spoke slowly and carefully in an attempt to make herself understood.

"Earlier that week, he said he wanted to give me a bonus and I turned it down at first, but he insisted and then, when I said okay, if you really want to, he put his hands on me and I thought he was trying to ... you know ... wanted to ... touch me."

"You thought he was trying to buy sex."

Jess looked up, startled. It was crude and direct and she imagined being in a police station with a male police officer asking the same question. She shuddered.

"Yes."

"So, after you'd thought about it, you spotted the opportunity to make some extra cash?"

"No! When he tried again, I just said the first thing that came into my head. Just to get rid of him."

"So, you asked him to pay you and he agreed. Then what?"

"He said, 'Okay, I'll get your bonus,' and he went off."

"And what did you do?"

"I didn't do anything. I was too afraid to think. I didn't know what to do. Then after a moment or two I decided I'd just go back to my room and shut myself in for a while."

"And did you?"

"I tried but he was back in an instant and he grabbed me again. Waving money at me. Grinning." She looked at Dave and for the first time he looked a little unnerved.

"So, you waited for him to come back?"

"No! I was confused. By the time I'd decided what to do he was back."

"And how long was he away?"

"I don't know! A minute or two."

"And then he offered you the money and you accepted it?"

Jess hesitated. She knew where this was going, how this was being portrayed, and she felt the same shame and revulsion she had felt afterwards. Shame at her inability to protect herself, not thinking any of it mattered. Not making the link or rationalising the sequence of events. How it would look to the casual observer. Not understanding the consequences.

"Yes."

"And then you offered yourself to him."

"No! I tried to stop him. To push him away."

"Why? You'd already taken the money. The contract was sealed. Or were you just being a tease?"

She could hear him now. *"I know your sort. You're nothing but a tease."*

"No. I tried to stop him because I knew it was wrong."

"You knew what you were doing was wrong?"

"I wasn't doing anything! It was him!" She stabbed a finger at Dave without looking at him. "He threatened me. He said if I wasn't nice to him, he'd throw me out, and I couldn't bear the thought of being out on my own again." The ghastly woman was twisting everything to make it look as if she'd planned and initiated the entire incident. Jess dropped her head and sighed. "I had nowhere to go."

"And did you think it unreasonable that your employer should require you to behave responsibly?"

"I did behave responsibly. I didn't do anything wrong."

"Mr Morley's judgement" – she looked down at her notes – "was that you had behaved very badly indeed. Overstepped the mark. That you looked and smelt like a low-grade prostitute with behaviour to match." The slur hit home.

"That's not true!" Jess knew she was losing the battle and tried but failed to keep the pleading out of her voice. The appeal for understanding. There had only been two of them there. There were no witnesses. It was her word against his but he had this harridan on his side; this woman who was able to manipulate and misrepresent the facts to suit her case. It was far more difficult for Michael to defend her in the same circumstances.

"So then you invited Mr Morley to your room." Jess remained silent. The woman pressed on. "You invited Mr Morley into your room, undressed and engaged in sexual intercourse with him."

"No." She sounded subdued and broken.

"No?"

"He undressed me."

"But you didn't resist." A statement. A fact. No, she didn't resist. She'd let him do what he wanted. Just like she'd let the others do what they wanted. That was her place, to do what men wanted.

"No."

"You didn't say stop. You didn't say no."

"No."

"You allowed him to undress you and have sexual relations with you without uttering a word of resistance, without hitting back or scratching or fighting him in any way?"

Jess remained silent as the tirade continued.

"And you only stopped when Mrs Morley came back unexpectedly and found you."

Jess nodded, broken.

"And, having been caught in the act, you ran away, stealing twelve hundred pounds."

The lie demanded a response.

"I didn't steal it!"

"I think we've been through that." Pauline Robson removed her spectacles and placed them on the folder in front of her. "So, what we have here is" – she presented the fingers of one hand and started to reel off the facts again, one finger at a time – "you wore provocative make-up and perfume. You attempted to seduce Mr Morley in order to make money. When Mr Morley responded in the way you had planned, you feigned resistance and then demanded money in return for 'giving in' to his advances, which is what you'd intended all along.

"You took the money and then pretended to resist in order to heighten his desires and no doubt give yourself some perverse satisfaction. You invited him to your room and allowed him to undress you. You willingly participated in sexual intercourse and would have continued to do so had you not been discovered by the unexpected return of Mrs Morley. Realising the game was up, you fled the premises, taking money that didn't belong to you, and left the Morleys angry, confused, frustrated, their marriage in tatters, and twelve hundred pounds worse off." For effect, she took a pause for breath, her aspirations towards a seat in the judiciary clearly evident in the presentation of her case and, especially, the summing up.

"In the circumstances, no reasonable person could conclude that you were anything other than a prostitute and a thief, that the sex was entirely consensual and pre-planned, and any suggestion that this might be remotely regarded as 'rape' totally implausible, outrageous and a vile slur on the unblemished character of my client."

Jess, head down, breathing deeply, felt the stirrings from deep inside. The same feelings she'd once had on a riverbank, in torrential rain, in the midst of the most violent thunderstorm, when her only shelter had been ripped from her hands and lost, the last semblance of protection blown away; everyone and everything conspiring to destroy her, leaving her with nothing other than her own spirit. Now this woman was trying to destroy her, trying to take from her all she had, like so many had tried to do before, and ultimately, they'd all failed, because ultimately, the truth would out. She lifted her head slowly and looked at the strutting, pouting, gurning monster in front of her. Her voice calm, measured, barely audible.

"Have you ever been raped?"

"I beg your pardon?"

Jess exploded with rage and smashed one hand down on the table so hard the room shook.

"Have you ever been raped!?" she screamed. Pauline Robson recoiled in fear and horror; fear at the unexpected outburst, abject horror at the affront, and terror at the sudden and unpredictable change in the girl's character. Dave and Michael both sat back instinctively, similarly shocked by the transformation.

"How dare you?" Pauline Robson pumped herself up, nerves fuelling a rush of pomposity. "I have never been so—"

"Well I have!" shouted Jess, interrupting her, thrusting a hand in the air spreading three fingers and stabbing them at her assailant. "Three times! I know what it is. You have no idea. I suggest you go try it and then maybe you might be able to talk from experience!" She stood up abruptly, pushed back her chair, tipping it onto the floor. She leant over the table, two hands supporting her weight, staring at Dave who recoiled in fear.

"You will never see my kids." The menace in her tone was unmistakeable and unambiguous, and she watched him cower in front of her. She turned and strode out of the meeting room leaving the door wide open, as wide as the three mouths she left behind.

CHAPTER 34

They sat quietly in Michael's car, parked in a supermarket car park, Jess supporting her head on one hand, pressed up against the window, Michael tapping the steering wheel aimlessly.

"Tell me about the money."

She didn't want to talk about anything. Not The Navigation, not Dave Morley, not that ghastly woman and certainly not the money. She just wanted to get back, collect the girls from school and pretend nothing had happened. But she knew it wasn't possible. She let out a deep sigh.

"I forgot all about it, Michael. I'm sorry."

"I could have deflected that one, if I'd known." Jess recognised the slight admonishment, the frustration he felt at being made to look ill-prepared and ineffectual. It was not something she'd ever seen in Michael before and it upset her. She couldn't afford to lose his trust; she had so much invested in it.

"I guess I'm still so naïve. The things that matter to me are not the same things that matter to everyone else. I still don't expect people to try and take advantage, even though it seems like it's been that way all my life. When will I ever learn?" They both knew the question was rhetorical.

"I was shaken to the core about what Dave did to me. Especially when I thought I was just getting back on my feet again. I enjoyed the job, got on well with everyone, had a place to stay and some money in my pocket, and I never had to talk about Jess or what had happened to her. I never imagined something like that would happen to Alice. And when it did, I just thought, well, here we go again. The place wasn't a sanctuary. Wasn't a new start for Alice. It was just another chapter in Jess's disastrous life.

"I did ask him for money. But not for that." She twisted her face in distaste. "It was genuinely meant to distract him. It was so stupid. I see now exactly how it looks. But he put me under so much pressure, made me feel like I was the one to blame, called me all sorts of terrible things, and I just crumbled.

"And it was just like my father and just like Mo. It was the same thing all over again. I was the common denominator, the constant. I was made to feel like I was the problem, not them. That's why I just gave in. Let him do whatever he wanted. Get it over with. I gave in to them all. I thought that was what I was supposed to do.

"But when Trish came back and looked at me as if I was mad, something snapped. I had to get away. I threw the money on the bed. I knew it looked like money for sex, even though that was never my intention. I felt dirty and disgusted with myself."

"How much was it?"

"I don't know; a few twenties."

"So what about the twelve hundred?"

"As I was leaving, I heard Trish and Dave screaming at each other in the kitchen. The money was sitting on the bar, in a plastic wallet with a paying-in slip. She was supposed to have taken it to the bank."

"So you decided to take it for her?" She could tell he wanted to believe her, but she could also sense the scepticism from the tone of his voice.

"No. I don't know what I was thinking. I just saw it and I'd just been attacked and I wanted to retaliate, so on impulse I just picked it up. I got a lift in the laundry van, and the next thing, I'm fifty miles away."

"So then what?"

"Well, I felt really guilty afterwards. I've never stolen anything, Michael. Never. It was so out of character, so when I got dropped off in Newhampton I went straight to the nearest bank and handed it over. I admit I kept twenty, but they owed me a lot more than that and it was all the money I had in the world."

"So he's making that bit up? About the theft?"

"Well, I don't know. I suppose it looked like theft to them and it would have taken a day or two before they realised the money had actually been paid in. Jade told me that Trish threw him out immediately, so maybe he never found out the money was paid back."

"But she'd have a record? His ex-wife?"

"I suppose so. It was five years ago, but she wouldn't have forgotten something like that." She rubbed her forehead. "Oh God, what a mess."

"It's a sideshow, Jess. Whether he knows it or not. It's just another fact Pauline Robson is using to press his case."

"How can she be so horrible?"

"She's just doing her job. Sometimes we lawyers have to be like that."

"You're not like that." She looked at him. It was inconceivable that Michael Goodman could be horrible to anybody.

"If I have to get nasty to protect you ..."

"But what are we going to do? I won't let him near the kids."

Michael sighed.

"Well, I don't think we're going to get anywhere making threats. But you can see how it'll play out if we go to the police. It'll be the same again but ten times worse. It'll be extremely traumatic and totally futile. She was right about that."

"But what about Trish? She knew. She knew what he'd done."

"Did she witness you ... in the act?"

"No, but she knew what had happened." And then her heart sank, remembering the words. Remembering Trish's words and her own response.

Did he force you? No. I let him.

"Maybe we can contact her and ask her to be a witness."

"Forget it, Michael." She knew she'd destroyed her own case; damned by her own honesty, her own state of mind. There was no way of proving rape. If only she hadn't asked for money. If she had just walked out there and then, the moment he first touched her. But then she wouldn't have two beautiful daughters, Lucy and Sophie; just like if she hadn't married Mo, she wouldn't have Leila.

"Michael, why do I love my children so much?" It sounded rhetorical, but he had an answer.

"You're their mother. How could you not?"

"I mean, how can I love so much something conceived in hate?"

"That's the way you are, Jess. And they're innocent."

"And I'm going to protect them."

"And I'm going to help you." He put a hand on her shoulder, and she leant over and kissed him on the cheek. "Come on. I'll run you home."

***

Pauline Robson and Dave Morley took a comfort break and then reconvened their meeting in her office over coffee. She was still smarting from the outburst by that little trollop and it showed in her mannerisms; constantly touching her hair, fiddling with her pearls and flicking through papers, trying to expunge the memory of the last few moments of a meeting in which she had been so outrageously insulted, her composure shattered and, most crucially, her dignity soundly trashed.

Dave sat opposite. She was a stuffy old tart, he thought. Except when Little Miss Stroppy wound her up. What Pauline needed was a good seeing to. He tried to imagine what it would be like, how she would look scrubbed up and wearing something skimpy, and the thought of it got him aroused. He'd have a go, given the chance. Teach her a bit. Probably never had it before. He was looking vacantly at her, his imagination out of control, not realising she had asked him a question.

"Mr Morley?"

"Oh, sorry, Pauline, I was thinking about something else," he chuckled.

She seemed to bristle at the unauthorised use of her first name, or perhaps she could read his mind; he wasn't sure which. Either way, he relished the imaginary flirtation, the deliberate provocation, and he felt his arousal intensify.

"I was suggesting we follow up with a letter rebutting her accusations just so they are in no doubt about the futility of their case. And then—"

"Nah, I wouldn't bother with that."

She looked at him disparagingly.

"Mr Morley …"

"Dave." He smirked at her.

"Mr Morley," she went on. *Stuck up bitch. The things I could do to you.* "If you will please allow me to finish. I shall, at the same time, demand a DNA test to prove parentage, a precursor to an application to the family courts for a child arrangement order to have you formally recognised as the father of the two children, thereby securing your access rights."

"Nah, as I said. I wouldn't bother with that." She removed her spectacles again and gave him a look of disdain, bordering on contempt. "Waste of time."

"Mr Morley. If we are to succeed in getting you access to your children, we have to follow the correct procedure."

"Pauline," he said again deliberately to provoke a reaction, which it did, in the form of a curled lip. "I need two more kids and another nagging mother like I need a hole in the head."

Pauline Robson sighed and slumped back in her chair.

"Then why, may I ask, have you started proceedings in the first place?"

"She's loaded."

"Excuse me?"

"Alice. Jess. Whoever. The tart's loaded. She's got a huge house and acres of land and a flash car. She's rolling in it!"

"And your point is?" she asked guardedly, but her tone suggested she knew exactly what his point was.

"Tell her I'll give up my rights, waive 'em or whatever the correct legal term is, and promise never to darken their doorstep again. All I ask in return is a promise from her not to mention the 'R' word again."

"And?"

"And a bit of compensation for the trauma and disappointment I'll feel at being parted from my daughters. You know … giving them up."

Pauline Robson looked at Dave Morley with ill-disguised contempt.

"You want to sell your paternity rights? You want to sell your half of the children to their mother?"

"Nah. Not sell. Not as such. She gets what she wants and I get what I want. It's perfect, innit?" She put down her pen and sighed.

"And do you have a figure in mind?"

"Oh yes."

CHAPTER 35

Jess picked the girls up from school, gave them all a big hug and took them home for tea and cake. She'd caught a glimpse of Jade and Ben outside the school gates, but she and Jade continued the pretence that they didn't know each other, and that was fine by her.

She wondered how much Jade knew; what story Dave had given her. Whether Jade too regarded Alice as the scheming, man-eating, money-grabbing tart she was made out to be by her husband and that witch of a lawyer. And in particular, whether Jade knew Ben had two half-sisters.

Above all, she wanted to put it out of her mind. Attending to the girls' every need was top of her agenda and would normally have been the perfect distraction, but every time she looked at Sophie and Lucy, she saw an image of Dave. It had never bothered her before. He had totally slipped out of her consciousness, but now he was back, making vile assertions about her and demanding access to the twins. It was all too horrible to contemplate.

And when she'd put the children to bed and sat up alone with a glass of wine, or lay in her own bed unable to sleep, she could think of nothing other than that repulsive man, touching her, touching her children, defiling their innocence, poisoning their lives with his lies.

Michael had told her there was nothing for either of them to do in the meantime except wait. He expected to receive a letter in the next couple of days from Laker, Neal and Robson setting out their demands and once he got that, they'd plan what to do next.

She'd already ruled out going to the police. Michael didn't have to convince her that her story was simply not credible; all the evidence was against her, none of it in her favour. If she thought she had any chance of winning, any chance of getting him put away, or even succeeded in keeping him away from her family, she'd happily endure the harshest interrogation, the deepest humiliation and the profound shame that would accompany it. But she didn't. She had no chance and she knew it.

But she wrestled with one question she hadn't been able to answer for herself. Why would a man like Dave Morley, with all his vulgarity, his tasteless humour, his arrogance and complete lack of sensitivity, deign to accept parental responsibilities for two families? In the normal world, a single mother would have tracked down the father, demanded maintenance, and, on the basis of DNA evidence alone, it would have been granted. The circumstances behind the twins' conception would be utterly irrelevant and open neither to question nor debate.

Maybe she was the one he wanted. Maybe he wanted to carry on as he had left off, despite being married to Jade and having a small son of his own. Maybe he just wanted a bit on the side. The thought was repugnant, but anyway, she judged there were cheaper and easier ways to inveigle himself into her affections; by saying sorry, for example, not by going straight to expensive lawyers. But the more she thought about it, the more it became clear.

If Dave was the same repulsive monster she'd always thought, then he could have no inherent desire to take responsibility for another family. So, if he didn't want that, what did he want?

***

The call came two days later.
"I've had a letter."

Jess put down her iron and sat down at the kitchen table, pressing her phone to her ear.

"Do I need to come in and see you?"

"It's very long-winded, but I can tell you what it says. It goes into great depth explaining the procedure by which they will be able to prove parentage and apply to the court for the requisite order and proposals for access rights, et cetera, et cetera. Just Pauline racking up the bill, I suspect."

"Nothing we didn't expect?"

"Except, they've given us a get-out clause."

"What does that mean?"

"It's what I always thought, Jess. He has absolutely no interest in being the father of twins."

"But he is the father."

"Yes, we all know that. But he also knows that you don't want anything to do with him. He also knows, or thinks he knows, that you're well off." She let the thought sink in and it all dropped into place. How stupid.

"Money."

"Precisely. He wants money. He's prepared to walk away, sign a self-restraining order and promise never to come near you or your family ever again."

"Provided we pay him."

"They call it compensation."

"How much?" It was the only question that mattered, if it mattered at all. There was a way out and she would take it. She would willingly give up everything to keep her children safe. It only mattered that they had something left to live on and the speed with which this whole sorry saga could be concluded. It was of no relevance how much he wanted; he could have it all.

"Two hundred and fifty."

"Thousand?"

"Each."

"Half a million?" She rested her forehead on one hand and considered it. For three seconds.

"Pay it!"

"Jess ..."

"Pay it, Michael. Get rid of him. I want rid of him."

"Jess, hold on. You have to think this through."

"Why?" She knew she was getting wound up again and she hated it, but here was an escape route and she had to take it now before it closed up again.

"They don't want that much. That's just their opening bid."

"How do you know!?" she said, increasingly frustrated at his calmness. *How can you be so calm?*

"Think about it. You know and I know he has no interest in the kids. He's already got a family. You told me what he's like, and from the brief encounter I had with him last week, I can believe it. He only ever wanted money and he'll take a lot less. They expect us to haggle with them."

"I'm not haggling over the price of my children!" she shouted.

"I'm sorry. Poor choice of words. What I mean is, if they assume we've already drawn the same conclusion and are ready for them, then they'll assume we'll make a counter-offer. If we just accept their figure, they'll see how weak we are, how desperate we are and how deep our pockets are, and ask for more."

"I'm sorry if I sound desperate, Michael, but that's because I am," she said. She had calmed herself, for the moment.

"I suspect half of that sum is still a huge amount of money to him and that's the amount he'll settle for."

"So what are you suggesting?"

"I propose we write back, acknowledge parental rights, consider offering him access—"

"NO!"

"Consider offering him access," he repeated calmly, "but suggest that if he would like to waive his parental rights in perpetuity, we are prepared to offer him the sum of one hundred thousand pounds."

"What if he says no?"

"He won't. We'll settle at two, two fifty at the most."

"And what if we don't"

"Then we're no worse off than before."

"I don't know, Michael. I'm worried."

The voice came back. Calm, measured, confident and soothing.

"Jess, trust me. We have to take control of this. They've shown their hand. We now know what he wants and we know how badly he wants it. No matter what you might think about the threat he poses, he won't carry it out. He doesn't have anything to use against you other than your own fear."

"Let me think about it."

"I'll draft a reply and call you tomorrow."

***

He was right, of course. As usual. She'd lain awake for days worrying about it and eventually she had to acknowledge it was fear that had taken hold, fear that was driving her decisions. She had the financial resources to deal with the problem. She had the resources even to pack her kids into the Range Rover and take them away to somewhere he wouldn't find them, another part of the country, Australia, Canada even.

And now she had proof that all he wanted was money, it seemed to make it a lot easier. It was the least worst of all the options and if she could be sure she would never see him again, it was worth it. She was still determined to sell the house, and this business with Dave now made it inevitable they'd move further away from Chalton to ensure she never bumped into him or Jade by accident or otherwise.

But her fear wouldn't go away completely. She knew what he was and what he could do, and whatever legal agreement he signed, she didn't trust him to stick to it. As soon as he'd blown all the money, or at least had the appetite for more, he'd be back, and she couldn't bear the thought that she might have to fight him all over again. She needed a guarantee he'd disappear. The trouble was, she knew there were no guarantees in life. Ever.

Above all, and despite how financially secure she was, she didn't feel safe or in control, and by extension, she feared for the safety of her children. Peter had once made arrangements that he thought would guarantee their safety and security, and now even that wasn't enough. She wondered what it would take, how much it would take to do that. And she wondered what would have happened had Peter still been alive. Despite Michael's help and support, and his pledge to continue supporting her, she still felt alone. Still felt there was someone missing.

She looked at the bedside clock. It was eleven thirty. She noticed a pale shadow on the wall by the door adjoining the two bedrooms. She sat up.

"Leila? What's up, darling? Can't you sleep?"

Leila wandered over and climbed into bed next to her, and they cuddled up together.

"You can't sleep, Mummy. I know you can't sleep."

"I'm fine, sweetie. Just not very tired."

"Are you thinking about that nasty man?"

"No, of course not." *That's a lie. Don't tell your children lies.* She kissed her daughter's head and squeezed her. "He is a nasty man but Michael has told him to go away, and he will."

"Was Daddy a nasty man?" *Oh God. No lies.*

"No. Daddy was a bad man."

"Are all men nasty and bad?"

"No, sweetie. Not all men. Michael's a nice man."

"Was your daddy a bad man?" Jess winced. There was no way she could explain that one. Not yet.

"Ooh, that's a story for another day. I promise I'll tell you all about it. Mm, when you're fourteen. Okay?"

"Okay."

They lay quietly for a moment, both of them wide awake, both of them thinking. There was something Jess needed to know. She'd never brought up the subject, partly because she feared it might be too distressing for Leila, but mainly because she was afraid of the answer. But here and now, it seemed the right time.

"The man with the belt. He was a bad man, wasn't he? Tell me about him."

Leila took in a deep breath. Jess held hers.

"Mm, I shall tell you when I'm twelve," she announced with aplomb. Jess blinked at the unexpected answer, but she took comfort that she could sense no latent trauma, no element of denial or delusion. Just a young woman, ahead of her time, emulating her mother.

"Okay, sweetie. Or any time before then if you want to."

"Simon's a nice man," she declared, and Jess smiled, a prickling sensation at the back of her neck. Her daughter had a gift, a sixth sense. An ability to think beyond the superficial, conventional senses that seemed to guide and influence everything her mother did. A sixth sense, not just to recognise Simon as a nice, good man, but one that also recognised that her mother, deep down, had been thinking the same thing. She wondered what he and Maria were doing right now and wished he were here instead.

"Yes, Simon's a nice man."

***

Jess was not the only one having sleepless nights. The same subject had been keeping Jade awake night after night, and despite her intrinsically forthright character, she hadn't found the right opportunity to discuss it with her husband. Until last night.

They had a rare night off and went to dinner in Oxford, leaving the pub in the hands of barman Marius and head chef

Faroukh, and Ben in the care of young Irena. Dave had noticed Jade wasn't being her ebullient self, so he wanted to tell her about the meeting he'd had at the lawyers and put her mind at ease.

Jade was surprised to find herself in such an upmarket establishment. On the rare occasions they did get out, it was only ever to a Chinese or Indian, so the French fine dining Fleurs D'Amour was a real treat. It was so unlike Dave to be flash with the cash, but it was considerate and sensitive and she appreciated it.

She took a sip of white Burgundy and looked at him, but he seemed distracted, his eyes darting around the room, watching the waiters and waitresses the way people who work in hospitality always do when their roles are reversed.

"So, go on, tell me!" she pressed him.

"Ah, well, it was all a bit difficult. Difficult for me, anyway," he said and she could tell he was dispirited. She reached across the table and put a hand on his.

"Aw hon, it'll be okay. We can get through this."

Dave gulped back his beer. He'd start on the wine next. He was driving, but he needed it, and in his head he was already celebrating.

"It's just that I feel so responsible. I know I was stupid. I was gullible and she played me for a fool. She got what she wanted, and now look at her."

"I never expected that of Alice. She seemed such a nice, quiet girl."

"Yeah, well, she fooled us all then. She waited till Trish had gone out and then virtually jumped on me. She wanted babies. No doubt about that. She's a nutcase! God knows how many times she tried that on with other blokes. She did the same to that old bloke who owned that big house she's in. Witch."

"That explains why she came out of nowhere. Wouldn't say where she was from."

"Yeah, but the worst thing was she was also a thief."

"Yeah. You said." Jade sat back, still reeling from the astonishing revelation about kind and gentle Alice.

"Trish comes back because she's forgotten to take the bankings and then leaves it on the bar. So while I'm trying to explain to Trish what she'd done, the bitch grabs it and does a runner. Twelve hundred quid!"

"I know. I still can't believe it."

"You'd better believe it. Anyway, we had it all out. I told her to pay it back or else I'll go the police."

"Pay it back to Trish?"

"Nah. Back to me. It's my money. Anyway, Trish got the pub. And, it covers us for, you know, the distress of it all."

She smiled at him and lifted her glass.

"Is that why you've brought me to a posh gaffe?"

"That's not all though." He shook his head, put on a serious face. He looked down at his hands and she was suddenly concerned for him, worried he had something on his mind.

"Aw, hon, you can tell me."

"Well, I know I was stupid and I let her take advantage and I never guessed it would end up like this, but the fact is, I'm the father of them two beautiful young girls." He paused and then said quickly, "as well as a beautiful boy. And I feel a terrible responsibility towards them. Not to her, you understand? The bitch!" he spat out the words. "Nah, I wanted to do right by them. It weren't their fault their mother's a tart."

"No. I'm still amazed. Alice was never like that. Even when I met her last week she seemed the same as ever. You know, quiet, unassuming, nervous even."

"That's the way she does it. Puts on the little girl lost look, reels you in, and wham, your life's turned upside down forever."

The waiter arrived with their starters and she took another sip of wine. It was having a suitably soporific effect, but it didn't stop another rush of insecurity washing over her. She reached out a hand again.

"Aw, hon. You've no regrets though? About the way things turned out?"

"Course not! Course not. I just feel a bit used."

"I understand, love. I told you, we'll get through this. Together."

"What would I do without you?" he said, his voice cracking for a moment, and she welled up, wanting to hug him and make it all better, but before she got the chance, he was off again.

"So, there I am, pouring my heart out, telling her that I want to do my duty for the girls as well as my own family, and she's having none of it." He shovelled in some paté and toast and wiped a hand over his mouth. "Says she wants nothing to do with me and neither do the girls."

"Oh, no!"

"Yeah. Here I am, saying I'm ready and willing to pay for their upkeep, you know, maintenance. I understand my duties and responsibilities, and she just throws it back in my face. Says she doesn't need any of my money because she's got loads of it herself!"

"That's outrageous. What sort of mother—"

"And on top of that, she says she never wants to see me again."

"Aw, Dave. That's so cruel. How could she be so cruel?"

"I dread to think how them little 'uns are going to turn out."

Jade had been studiously extracting snails from shells while concentrating on her husband's outpourings but she made a great show of looking aghast.

"I'd never have thought that of her."

"No, well you ain't heard the worst yet."

"What?"

"Well, you won't believe it. The bitch offers me money to go away!" Jade was still chewing but her jaw dropped open in surprise. "Can you imagine? She's putting a price on those kiddies as if they were a commodity! Like something you can buy and sell. Bloody disgusting, that's what that is."

"What did you say to her?"

"Well, I was lost for words. I was so upset I didn't know what to do with myself. I repeated my offer, said all I wanted was to do right by the kids. And then I thought of you and little Ben and how understanding you'd been, and I thought maybe we'd let bygones be bygones and say it's all water under the bridge, and for the sake of the little 'uns we should be nice to each other and maybe have an extended family and that."

Jade stopped eating for a moment. Stopped chewing and breathing and her heart joined in the pause. *An extended family? What's he talking about?* But before she finished analysing the scenario in her head, he was off again.

"But she got angry and swore at me and threatened me, and I thought to myself, I don't want this bitch coming anywhere near my Jade and my Ben. Fuckin' lunatic!"

"Dead right, mate. She needs to be locked up, by the sounds of it."

"So what do I do? I do the decent thing. I say I'll give up the girls. I say I'll stay away and not bother her, provided she stays away from my family. And I don't want any of her money neither."

"And what did she say?"

"She says she wants it all done legal, and to make sure it sticks, she's going to pay me off."

"Oh my God!"

The waiter cleared away their starters and Dave poured himself a glass of wine. He took a long draw, emptying half of it in one go.

"So. I says to myself, this is war. So be it. I went into bat for you and Ben, cos you're all I care about. She gave me a figure and I refused, and I kept refusing. I drove a really hard bargain, Jade, and I beat her into submission and in the end, she gave in." He took another swig of wine and sat back in his chair, satisfied.

She waited. Waited for the announcement, the big denouement. She held her arms out and looked at him with raised eyebrows, and when he didn't respond, said in exasperation.

"Well? How much?"

"How much do you think?" She sighed. *He's enjoying this, the prick.*

"I dunno. Tell me!"

"Fifty." He still looked smug.

"Fifty quid?" she said shaking her head.

He leant forward and looked her straight in the eye. She took a swig.

"Fifty. Grand."

He'd waited till she was in mid-slurp before saying it, and she almost choked on the Burgundy.

"What? Fifty grand? Oh my God, Dave. I can't believe it!"

"Yeah well, babe, you'd better believe it. She's paying us fifty grand. That's for you, me and Ben. My family."

Jade jumped up, ran around the table and flung her arms around her husband, kissing him heavily, smothering him with garlic breath, and he tried but failed to avoid spilling wine down his shirt. "All right, all right," he said, trying to fend her off. "There's people looking."

"So what, Dave. We've got fifty grand!"

"Shh. Keep your voice down. Don't want the whole of Oxford to know."

"When do we get it?" she asked feverishly, unable to contain her excitement.

"As soon as we sign the docs. A couple of weeks maybe."

"Aw Dave, I do love you," she gushed, tears forming. "I love you for being kind and considerate and wanting to look after them little girls, and wanting to look after all of us."

"I did it for you and Ben, doll."

They clinked glasses and he knocked his back in one.

"Oi! Another bottle of this, mate!"

CHAPTER 36

Michael was right, of course. They settled on two hundred and fifty thousand; a quarter of a million pounds. There had been a time when a sum like that was beyond her wildest dreams; a lottery win to most. Yet, she'd never got used to her wealth. She didn't spend any more than she needed to spend and most of that was on the upkeep of the house.

The car was an indulgence, of course, but that had been Emma's idea, not hers, and although she'd have bought a car of some description to ferry the girls around, it would have been far more modest. She had to admit, though, she felt safe and secure in it and that was the important thing.

But a quarter of a million? She wouldn't miss it. She was conscious she was giving away the girls' inheritance and, however far into the future that might be, she still felt guilty. But she took consolation in the thought that she was doing it for them, in order to keep them safe, and, after all, wasn't that why Peter had left it to them in the first place? It was regrettable, but it was the right thing to do.

Michael said he would have to liquidate some of her assets and that would take a week or so, but she exhibited no interest in how he did it, just signed the requisite bits of paper as and when required. He'd agreed a completion date with Pauline Robson three weeks hence, which would give them time to draw up the necessary contracts and get the funds together, and although Jess wanted it to be quicker, Michael had got assurance from his opposite number that, until everything was finalised, her client would neither come anywhere near the house, nor communicate with her in any way.

So, with at least some of the weight off her mind, she tried to live life as normally as possible. She and Jade studiously avoided each other at school times, and it now seemed much easier to do after once catching a glimpse of Jade looking at her strangely; a weird mixture of contempt and smugness which surprised and disappointed her. *Oh well, she picked Dave, so they must have something in common.*

***

A week had gone by and, as lawyers racked up fees, documents were drafted, argued over and redrafted, lives rearranged and reorganised to steer the hapless participants through the next stages of their complicated lives, the world moved on regardless. And despite the combined intellect applied to the matter, which gave it a gravitas and importance way beyond its intrinsic worth, no one, least of all Jess, could see through its superficiality; until someone did and the call came.

Michael asked to see her and, by arrangement, he turned up at the house the next morning. She showed him into the kitchen and they sat opposite each other at the kitchen table with some tea. Pleasantries over, and assuming he simply needed more signatures, she felt relaxed and therefore unprepared for what he had to say.

"I decided to bring this over personally, Jess. I thought it only right and proper." She tensed. Given the many terrible things that had happened to her over the years she was no stranger to bad news, and her instinct told her that this was something bad. "I had an email yesterday. From Sujay."

"Sujay in Nepal?" she asked, although it was more an expression of surprise rather than a question, and she sat up, anxious.

"Yes."

"Is he all right? Did he get the money?"

"Yes. On both counts. But I think it's best if I just let you read what he says."

Michael slid four pages of stapled-together A4 across the table and crossed his hands. She looked down at the paper and scanned the headings. The subject line contained the words "Miss Alisha". She felt a wave of foreboding. Her eyes dropped to the text of the message, which was quite short.

Dear Miss Jess,

I wanted to write to thank you so much for the money you have sent. I was in the hospital and not able to work for three weeks and I became worried that my wife and children would struggle without having any money. It was very kind and thoughtful of you, especially as I let you down on that terrible day. I am most humbled that you should think of me like this and I offer my sincere apologies that I failed in my duty to protect you from harm. I am very grateful also to your friend Simon, who saved my life, and I hope you will send him my best wishes when you see him again. I hope it has not put you off visiting my country again and I hope very much to see you soon so that I can thank you personally.

"Oh God. I never imagined he might feel guilty about anything. It wasn't his fault. I must write to him," she said, visibly moved by his letter and saddened he felt the way he did, but relieved that, so far, the email had been quite innocuous.

"They're obviously a very proud people," said Michael, "and, as a professional, he thinks he could have done better. But … there is more." Reluctantly, she turned the page.

The other reason I am writing is that I received two letters from Miss Alisha, both in her own handwriting. One of these is addressed to me, thanking me for helping Colonel Peter all those years ago and also for finding her. The other is addressed to you. Mr Goodman asked me to open and scan the letter so you can see what she says. I have not read it, because it is not mine, but I believe my own letter contains similar information. Thank you again for all you have done for me.

Best regards,
Sujay Bahadur Gurung

Jess looked up at Michael in wary anticipation, but he remained impassive.

"Sujay called me to say he had Alisha's letter for you and he would post it. I was nervous about what might be in it and concerned that it might never get here, which is why I asked him to scan it. I hope you don't mind."

She turned the page over. A slightly skewed image of a letter, handwritten on modest, lined notepaper, occupied the centre of the page.

Dear Jess,

I hope you and Simon managed to find your way back to Kathmandu without too much difficulty and that you had a satisfactory flight back to England. I prayed for your safety every day.

A few days after you left, I sat on the decking looking out over the mountains, eyes closed, legs crossed, just as we did together, trying to imagine the scene at Chalton the moment you were reunited with your daughters. It brought me a deep joy and a profound inner contentment. The sort of thing we Buddhists like the most!

At this very moment, and as I write, the sun is going down over Langtang Lirung, the river below continues its relentless journey to the sea and that seemingly tireless old eagle circles interminably overhead. I often wonder what he is looking for but then I realise I already know. The same thing as the rest of us!

I am very grateful you took the time and trouble to come and visit me. I know you may have had certain expectations that were not realised, but I hope that what you discovered about me and my father and Janica will have provided you with some peace. It was only after you left that I tried to imagine what you thought of me, of my disappearance and my apparent lack of concern for my father. I fervently hope that you might look upon it in a new light and appreciate we were all victims of events, most of them outside our control.

Similarly, there were some things within our control which, for whatever reason, either through human weakness, misplaced loyalties or simple misunderstanding, we were unable to influence or articulate, and to the extent that we all realise this now, we may be able to avoid the same mistakes in the future.

Despite any preconceptions you may have had about me, I hope now you believe that I truly loved my father as much as I now know he loved me. I shall always be indebted to you for the sacrifices you made in order to convey the depth of love my father had for me, and I feel comforted that, in my absence, he was able to share the same love with you. That fact alone creates a bond between us that cannot be broken.

It may surprise you to know that you ably demonstrated some of the characteristics of a person steeped in the Dharma. The lack of interest in material wealth; the generosity of spirit in leaving your children to travel halfway around the world to meet someone whom you may have judged harshly, in order to return something you felt belonged to them; your passionate desire to convey the love of another, to another, to bring them peace and contentment; and finally, your earnest attempt to persuade someone to seek salvation, at your own expense. All of which behaviour is consistent with the bodhisattva; one who places the welfare of others before their own.

I am bound by the Dharma to resist temptation wherever it arises, which is one reason I shall not express any desire to make you into a Buddhist! That isn't who we are. You will find your own way, adopt those teachings and principles you feel are appropriate to your own life and use them. Anyway, as I said to you before, I need do nothing to try and convince you as, without realising it, you are already halfway there.

The other reason I shan't seek to influence you is that, by the time you read this letter, I shall already have passed from this life. My condition deteriorated rapidly after I returned from England, and since you left, I have been preparing for the transition, which will come within the next few days.

I imagine you may be distressed to hear this, but I urge you not to be downhearted. I have been waiting for this moment all my life, and now it is upon me, I am filled with a contentment that borders enlightenment, and when the time comes, I shall finally have achieved the awakening.

And it is to you that I direct my thanks and my love that, through your kindness and equanimity to me and my father, you were able to steer me along this last stretch of the path I was following. I know you have the strength to extend the same love and consideration, not only to all those close to you, but also to those for whom you may harbour feelings of fear, anger or pain.

I have my suspicions that, through your own indomitable spirit and with the help and love of your children, you yourself may be fortunate enough to achieve the awakening first time round.

Good luck and best wishes Jess Jeffries, my sister. You deserve nothing less.

Lisa Jeffries

Jess slowly laid the paper on the table and lifted her head to see Michael watching her.

"Have you read this?" Her voice was so distant and detached it could have come from five thousand miles away.

"No, may I?"

She slid the paper back towards him, got up and stood by the window overlooking the garden. She could hear the rush of the trees outside, and beyond that, the distant howl of the wind around the mountains, the rush of water in the stream, and she could see Alisha sitting in meditation on the decking and the eagle soaring, circling above. She felt a profound sense of well-being and serenity, an inner peace and calm and an unbridled optimism that belied the tears flowing down her cheeks. She heard the rustle of paper and Michael's sigh.

"Goodness me. Thank you for letting me see something…so private."

"It's not private between us. We have no secrets. Thank you, as always, for looking after us."

"You're the nearest we have to family, Jess, the nearest Emma and I have to a daughter. We'll always be there."

She pulled a small handkerchief from under her sleeve and wiped her eyes, then walked around the table and wrapped her arms around him. He held her awkwardly and patted her back.

"There's nothing to do, is there?"

"No. I guess not. Will you go back to Nepal one day?"

"Maybe. When the girls are older. It would be a wonderful adventure for them."

"I think Peter would have been proud of you both," he said.

"Don't start me off again, Michael Goodman!" she said, slapping his arm.

"Yes, ma'am."

***

From a mind recently obsessed with and tormented by the unexpected return of Dave Morley into her life, the fear and anxiety it created had now been supplanted by a new calm and optimism that, in the end, everything would turn out all right.

The letter had been heart-breaking yet profoundly beautiful and uplifting. She could still not subscribe fully to the teachings of Alisha's faith and doubted she ever would, but she aspired to the principles it propounded and was still perplexed as to why some of these principles seemed to come naturally to her. She knew the day she left Chumtang that she would never see Alisha again, but as with all the dear and departed, she would be forever in her heart, along with their father, Peter.

But sitting alone in Chalton Manor while the girls were at school, or later on when they were asleep in bed, she had little to occupy her mind other than the matters at hand and the future and what it might hold.

And as for the "awakening", she had no conception of how that might be achieved or what it would mean. Life for her had always been a search for the truth, taking the path that promised least but invariably led her to the light.

She knew that she had to go on and she believed Alisha had shown her the way.

CHAPTER 37

The canal looked the same, as did the sign, the tables and chairs on the patio and the narrowboats moored alongside. The Navigation hadn't changed a bit, or at least it didn't appear so, five years after she had made her getaway in the laundry truck.

She didn't even know whether the pub was under the same management. She could have asked when she'd made the reservation, but she wanted to go back anyway; prove to herself it wasn't such a hellish place after all, expunge the bad memories and replace them with new, optimistic ones. And she needed to know.

The girls had been excited to go for a drive but as always the twins' attention span was limited, and after twenty minutes, Leila had turned on the video screens in the back to keep them occupied. It took them two hours to get there, and although Jess was relieved they'd made it without any major tantrums, she was not looking forward to the return trip. She judged, however, that once fed and watered, the twins would probably spend most of the way back sound asleep. At least she had Keira and Leila with her to help.

She and Keira lifted them down one by one from the back of the Range Rover and she led them all hand in hand across the car park and through the restaurant entrance. They were greeted by a young waitress, white shirt, black skirt, black apron, holding a tablet screen, who ticked off her name and showed them to a table away from the bar area, near a window with a view of the canal. *No reservations book anymore.*

Jess didn't recognise the girl nor any of the other staff on duty but cast an eye around the place and struggled to find much else that had changed. She couldn't resist running a finger along the window ledge to see if there was any dust or grime and, finding little, judged the standard of cleaning acceptable.

They ordered traditional pub grub; full portions for Leila and the adults and small plates for the twins.

"Is it possible to speak to Mrs Morley?" asked Jess of the waitress who'd taken their order and was now tucking the menus under her arm.

"I'm sorry," she said looking disconcerted. "I don't think we have a Mrs Morley here."

"Trish Morley?"

The girl's eyes lit up.

"Oh, you mean Trish Roberts? The manager?"

"Yes, that's right." *She's moved on, then.*

"Mm. She's a bit busy right now. Can I tell her who's asking?"

"Yes, of course. Tell her it's Alice. I used to work here. Years ago."

"Oh, that's cool. I'll let her know."

Jess felt a sudden rush of nerves and part of her wished she hadn't come at all, but she took a deep breath. It was done now. There was no going back. She had no idea how she might be received after all this time; no idea what opinions Trish might have had or still have about her or the disastrous day she left.

"You used to work here?" asked Keira. "What, before the twins were born?"

"Yep. I used to wear a uniform, clean the floors, serve tables."

"Oh wow! It must be weird coming back."

She actually had fond memories of most of it and she was pleased she had, despite what might happen next. She didn't have long to wait.

She caught a glimpse from the corner of her eye; the waitress standing at the end of the bar with a woman in a blue shirt, chatting and pointing in their direction. The woman had blonde hair, not black, and it was still short, but there was no mistaking the posture. She approached their table and as she got closer, Jess turned to look, spotted the large, dangly earrings and stood up.

"Well, well, well. Look what the cat dragged in," said Trish Morley Roberts, hands on hips, studying her carefully, looking her up and down. "On yer holidays?" she said brusquely and then her face burst into a wide grin. "Come here, Alice," she said, holding her arms out, and the two women embraced fondly. "Where have you been? I could do with some help!"

"Nice to see you, Trish. I wasn't sure whether I'd be welcome or not."

"It's called hospitality, love. Everyone's welcome. Well, almost everyone." They both laughed, knowing exactly who she was talking about. "And who do we have here?" said Trish gesturing around the table.

"This is my friend Keira."

"How do you do, Keira?"

"Hi."

"And this is my daughter Leila" – she saw the beginnings of a frown – "and these are my daughters, Sophie and Lucy." Trish's mouth dropped open.

"My, you have been busy," she said, beaming at the children in front of her.

Jess decided just to come out with it.

"Sophie and Lucy were born nine months after I left."

Trish's head turned slowly towards her as she computed the meaning, her mouth dropping open even further than before.

"Oh. Goodness me. Well, I didn't expect that."

"Maybe we can have a chat, after we've had some lunch?"

"Yes, of course," she nodded. "I'd like that, Alice."

"Jess. My real name's Jess."

***

After lunch Keira took the girls outside to the play area and they amused themselves on the swings and the slides while Trish and Jess had coffee together at a discreet table.

Jess told her all about her life before she'd arrived at The Navigation and how, after she'd left, she had been rescued by Peter, both of them unaware she was carrying Dave's children.

"I always knew he was a philandering bastard. I did love him once. But I knew what he was like. I just didn't know he would take it that far. I'm really sorry, Jess."

"You mustn't be. It's not your fault."

"You seem to have had a fair bit of man trouble yourself."

"How can I have any regrets? Look at them." They both stared out of the window at the children playing.

"You're very fortunate."

"I know." But Jess had other things she wanted to say.

"Trish. I saw Dave the other week. Him and Jade."

Trish let out a puff of air.

"She's welcome to him. She doesn't know what she's let herself in for."

"They've got a little boy. Ben. Same age as the twins ..."

"Jesus Christ!"

"... and they run a pub three miles away from me."

"Oh. That must be a little awkward."

"Well, he found out about me and the twins, put two and two together and now he's demanding money to stay away."

"The shit. How much?"

"A lot. But that's not your problem; it's mine and I'm dealing with it. The thing is, he accused me of stealing money. From here." Trish frowned, trying to remember.

"Oh yeah. The twelve hundred. Yeah, how could I forget? If I hadn't forgotten to take it to the bank, well, who knows …"

"Who knows indeed. I did take it."

"Yes, I assumed it was you and I was really pissed off, but then it turned up in the bank so I thought nothing more about it. So you paid it in?"

"Yes. I don't know why I took it. I was stressed and I had nowhere to go and I didn't have a penny, but as soon as it sank in, well ... I'm not a thief. It was just a moment of madness. I paid it in at Newhampton as soon as I got there."

"There was twenty quid missing," said Trish, smirking.

"Yes, I know. I'll give you it back."

"No you won't! And lunch is on the house."

"You don't need to do that."

"Yes, I do," she insisted, and they smiled at each other.

"Thanks. I just needed to know. That's all. And I needed to know you had no hard feelings. About me."

"No, of course not. I always felt responsible for what happened. But in a weird way it all turned out for the best." Trish leant over and put her hand on Jess's arm, stroking the cashmere.

"You've done well for yourself. I'm pleased for you."

"I just got lucky."

"Favours the brave, apparently."

"I don't think I'm brave."

"Oh, I think you are, Jess."

***

She was tired for once. Tired in a pleasant way, and she looked forward to bed. But she treated herself to a glass of wine once the girls were asleep. Her decision to go back and see Trish had been a good one, and she felt vindicated. She'd made another friend for life, or rather, she'd rediscovered a friend she didn't know she had.

It was highly unlikely that she would ever have to call Trish to corroborate her story, but she'd be able to brief Michael and, if he felt inclined, he could speak to Trish to remove any doubt he might have about the money. She now understood Dave and his lawyer were just using it as a stick to beat her with, to make her feel like she was the villain and he was the victim, so that she'd give in to their demands.

More than anything, seeing Trish again had removed any lingering doubts in her own mind that, in some way, she herself had been to blame for the incident at The Navigation. Trish could never be regarded as an impartial witness and it changed nothing, but it gave her peace of mind and that mattered.

But after she'd read Alisha's letter, she felt different inside, and going to see Trish had just been the beginning. She was forming a different view of her world, a different perspective on the things she feared the most, and was beginning to realise that a lot of it was just in her head. A lot of it was borne out of ignorance; supposition, presumption and misguided impressions of the things around her. She'd started to challenge her preconceptions and her conclusions and finally see things in a different light, and when she looked at them again, she saw something new; something less daunting, less fearsome.

She went to bed. She wanted to visualise her new world, so she closed her eyes and used her imagination, let her mind focus on the possibilities, and although she was deliciously tired, it was an hour before she finally dropped off.

CHAPTER 38

It was Monday and so, back to school. She delivered the girls as usual, Jade ignored her as usual and, as usual, she drove back home to start the washing. The documents would be coming through any day now and the problem that had plagued her mind for almost a month would finally be resolved.

But it wasn't a usual Monday. She had other plans. She filled the washing machine, set it going and climbed back into the Range Rover. There was something she needed to do, and she needed to do it now.

She steered the huge machine into the car park at The King's Head in Fotherham and parked it opposite the blue Mondeo she recognised. She noticed Jade's battered little hatchback alongside and was relieved. She didn't want to be alone with him, and anyway, she needed them both to be there to hear what she had to say. It was only ten-thirty so the pub would be closed, but she had no doubt the management would be up and about.

As it happened, the front door was open. She ventured in slowly, looking left and right, and then a familiar sight came into view. Dave; seated, coffee, newspaper. He looked up when he sensed movement and she moved slowly towards him. She remembered the first day they'd met at The Navigation, the clammy hand, the leer, the lascivious grin, and she felt a shudder of revulsion. *It's all in the mind. Look at it from another's point of view.*

"You're not supposed to be here."

"I'm sorry. I know you're closed."

"No. I mean I've been told not to contact you and I think it should work both ways."

"Well. I think that was for my benefit. And I wanted to talk to you. And Jade."

"She's not here," he said curtly, standing up and walking around the table towards her. She felt his eyes on her, looking her up and down, and she had to concentrate hard not to let it unsettle her. "What do you want?"

She was instantly thrown off balance. It wasn't going according to plan. She needed Jade there and she needed to do it at her own speed, and now he was harassing her. But before she could say anything there was movement behind him.

"What's she doing here?" Jade wandered into the bar and stood next to her husband, a brown leather bag over her shoulder.

"Thought you were going out."

Jade looked at her husband suspiciously.

"I am. In a minute."

Jess smiled in relief and tried to sound calm and composed.

"Well. I'm glad you're both here. I have something to say, you know, before we sign any contracts."

"And pay up?"

"Yes."

"Jade knows all about that. No secrets in this house," he said, trying to sound confident and defiant but instead sounding guarded and unsure of himself.

"I wanted to clear the air. Jade, you and I were once friends and I want us still to be friends and I want Ben and the girls to be friends. I know it's hard for you to accept what happened, but that was back then and this is now, and we're all different people." Jade nodded in apparent understanding. Jess looked at Dave, who appeared to be considering her words carefully.

"I have fond memories of The Navigation, don't you?" she smiled in reminiscence. Dave chuckled stiffly.

"Yeah, but that's all water under the bridge."

"Exactly," said Jess, raising one finger to emphasise the point. "Whatever mistakes I may have made, I hope they can be forgiven and we can move on in a civilised way like grown-ups. I can't live with the thought that we'd be enemies."

"We're not enemies, Alice … I mean Jess," said Jade. We just want what's rightfully ours. Don't we, Dave?"

"Yeah. That's right. We're giving up something precious and we need to be compensated," he said, straightening his back and lifting his chin.

"Well, that's the problem, you see. I don't care about the money. I had nothing before, and if I had nothing tomorrow, that would be fine. I'd manage. I'd still have my kids. I understand if it's worth more to you. I mean, two hundred and fifty thousand pounds is life-changing to most people." Jade's eyes opened wide and her jaw dropped.

"What?"

"The money," said Jess, "the figure we agreed." Jade turned her head slowly to look at her husband who had gone white but continued to stare stiffly ahead.

"Two hundred and fifty? You said fifty. Why did you say fifty?" Dave swallowed but said nothing, frozen, thinking. "Why did you say fifty?" she screamed, her face inches from his.

Jess stepped back. She hadn't expected this, but then, it was no surprise. Dave eventually managed to get his mouth into gear and a few words tumbled out.

"It … was originally fifty … then I thought, that's not enough, so I went back for more."

"Liar!"

"No. No, doll. That's the God's honest …"

"You filthy lying scumbag!" Jade stepped back and swung her bag at his head, but he fended it off with one arm.

"Leave it!" he shouted

"No, you leave it, you bastard. Conning me and Ben out of two hundred grand!" She snarled at him and in response he bent forward, baring his teeth, stabbing a finger at her face.

"It ain't your money! I'm the father of them kids," he shouted back at her, pointing a finger at some indeterminate place outside. "Now get out and leave it to me!"

Jade hesitated for a moment, then stomped off muttering expletives and slammed the door behind her. Jess had watched the exchange in genuine shock. This was not going well, but maybe it had made things even easier?

"I suppose you think you're clever, eh?" he said angrily, hands on hips.

"I don't know what you mean." She was nervous because he looked angry and it made him unpredictable.

"Why did you tell her it was two fifty?"

"Because it's true?"

"You shouldn't have told her anything. It ain't her money, it's mine. I'm the father of them kids, not her."

"I'm sorry. How was I supposed to know what you told her?"

"You stupid cow!" he shouted. He rubbed his chin and shook his head. "Okay. Okay. I'll sort it out. Just you do your side and I'll do mine. Okay?"

"Well, that's what I was trying to tell you." Jess was genuinely fearful now and she rubbed her hands together instinctively, her palms moist and cold. She'd seen Dave angry again. Angry in the same way he'd been all that time ago in The Navigation, threatening her, forcing her to do his will, and here he was again, totally wound up, standing over her, looking at her, leering.

"What?"

But there was no going back. Not now.

"I've decided that we should all be friends. It's best for the children that they know who their father is and that you should be able to see them whenever you want." Whatever colour had returned to Dave's face quickly drained back to white.

"What are you saying?" He said it with a menace she recognised only too well and she knew she was pushing him all the way to the edge.

"I'm saying that we shouldn't sign any silly contracts."

"And what about the money?"

She shook her head.

"It's wrong to put a price on a child's happiness. I won't do it. I'm not going through with it." She looked at him and saw he was sweating and breathing heavily, and her own heart was beating loudly in her ears. She waited for a response. She got one.

"Bitch!" he shouted. He took a step towards her and she backed up in fear but they were both distracted by a noise behind him. Jade stomped back into the bar clutching a holdall.

"Where you going?" he said.

"I'm out of here. Me and Ben."

"Oh no, you're not," he said grabbing her bag, and as the two of them wrestled and tugged and shouted at each other, Jess turned and ran out of the pub to the car park. She fired up the Range Rover and put her foot down. The beast lurched forward, rear tyres spinning as she twirled the wheel, frantically trying to keep the car in a straight line.

Dave finally overpowered his wife by slapping her so hard she fell backwards against the bar, hitting her head on the front edge and dropping to the floor in a heap. He grabbed his keys and burst out of the front door just in time to see black tyre smoke swirling around the car park and the back of a Range Rover disappearing up the High Street.

Inside, Jade, groggy and groaning, crawled across the floor to where she had dropped her bag and pulled out her phone.

The Range Rover slid to a halt on the gravel drive and she leapt out, plucking her phone from her pocket. She used one thumb to dial while feeding the key into the front door lock with her other hand. He answered almost immediately and she could tell from the background noise he was hands-free in the car.

"Michael!" she said, still panting from the exertion and the fear. "I've told him I'm not paying. I've told Dave."

"Calm down, Jess. What's happened?" She stepped into the hallway and closed the door.

"I went to see them and told them I'm not going through with it. He's not getting a penny."

"And how did he take it?"

"Not good."

"I wish you'd discussed this with me first."

"Nothing to discuss, Michael. I made up my mind. I tried to reason with him but all he ever wanted was money. Well, we're moving anyway. We'll just move far enough away so he can't get to us. No more giving in."

"Okay. I understand. Hang on, there's another call …" The phone went silent for a minute. "It's Pauline Robson in a panic. I'll call you back." The line went dead.

She heard the sound of an engine roaring outside, followed by tyres skidding on gravel. She opened the door and saw Dave Morley jumping out of the Mondeo, slamming the door and marching up to the house. She redialled while pushing her back against the door, but the call went straight to voicemail. Then, without warning, the door flew open and she was thrown back into the hallway, the phone flying out of her hand as she tried to keep her balance.

Dave Morley stepped into the hall and she backed into the drawing room, terrified. He walked towards her, fists clenched as if ready to attack, his shirt wet with sweat, his face twisted in rage. She continued to step back and he followed her, watching, leering.

"If only Trish hadn't come back, I'd have given you a good seeing to," he snarled. "I can't believe the way you just lay back and took it. Didn't struggle one bit. I wanted you to.

I wanted you to scream and shout and dig your nails in. Fight back. Would have made it all the more exciting."

Her heart was pounding. Just like at home in her bed with her drunken father all over her; just like three in the morning in her bed, on her face, pinned down by her vile husband; just like in The Navigation when she was on her knees in submission; and just like in Nepal, with murderers and bandits standing over her, screaming. She felt like she was back there, at altitude, the oxygen somehow sucked out of the air.

"I knew you didn't want it. You did it because I made you do it and you gave in. You're pathetic, that's what you are." He stabbed a finger at her.

"You raped me, Dave Morley," she shouted back at him, but he just grinned at her. It seemed to excite him even more and he kept coming towards her, but she'd reached the end of the sofa and her way back was blocked.

"You call that rape? That weren't rape. That were just a man taking what he needs, taking what's his. I was the boss and your job was to be a good girl and do as you were told. You were a good girl, Alice. Weren't ya? But you thought you was too good for me. Nah. That weren't rape. Let me show you what rape is."

Before she could react he leapt towards her, one hand gripping her throat. His other grabbed her by the hair, and he dragged her onto the floor where she landed heavily on the rug, with him on top of her. She clawed at the hand around her throat but her nails were too short to do any damage, and he slapped her face with the back of his other hand which made her head spin, and she screamed as she looked into his red eyes, white mucus foaming around his mouth, showering her with flecks of spittle. Her skirt had ridden up past her knees and he pressed his legs between them, pushing them apart, and she writhed and screamed as he used his free hand to unbuckle his belt and open his jeans.

"No!" She tried to scream again but her breath was constricted and her chest tight from the lack of air and the weight of his body, and he banged her head on the floor and continued to wrestle with his pants until he'd got them down beyond his buttocks and then reached up under her skirt. And then a sound; an echo in the distance, getting louder and louder. Someone calling her name.

"Jess! Jess! My God! Get off her!" A shout from above.

Michael Goodman was on top of Dave, one arm around his neck, red-faced, grimacing, struggling, and their combined weight was crushing the life out of her but he still had one hand around her throat, the other ripping her clothing and tearing at her skin, and she tensed her body in anticipation of the ultimate assault. And then, in her oxygen-starved haze, Michael rolling off to the side with a crash and another shout and Dave, saliva drooling through bared teeth, a long string of nasal mucus dangling over her face, leering at her like a demon possessed, his expression suddenly turning to surprise.

Simon Rutherford had one hand between Dave's thighs, the other around his neck, and lifted him bodily into the air, holding him aloft like a weightlifter before crashing him down horizontally on the oak floor like a wrestler hitting the canvas. Dave hit the floor face first, twitched violently and passed out, jeans around his knees, buttocks exposed.

Simon dropped to the floor next to the squirming, writhing figure, lifted her up into a sitting position and rearranged her skirt. He held her in his arms and she twitched and screamed and wept as her body shook and convulsed. He looked back at the door.

"Call the police!"

Pauline Robson hesitated momentarily before a second instruction broke her trance.

"NOW! And get the paramedics too."

She fumbled hastily with her phone and went out into the hallway, passing Jade Morley who stood by the door, shaking uncontrollably, struck dumb with fear. Michael lay on his back, head under the coffee table, groaning.

Simon rocked her back and forth like a mother with child and kissed her head. She opened her eyes and saw him.

"Hey, lovely lady. Long time no see."

"How's Maria?" she whispered.

"Tell you later."

CHAPTER 39

They sat in the kitchen as the last remaining paramedic packed up her case and left, her colleagues having already taken Dave away on a stretcher accompanied by a police officer and a forlorn Jade.

The police and paramedics had arrived quickly, but the police were keen to take statements as soon as possible before anyone's recollection of events became blurred. They'd been there for over two hours and there was no inconsistency in the statements. There was no doubt what had happened.

Jess sat alongside Simon, holding his hand, his jacket around her shoulders to stop her shivering, while Emma poured tea into four mugs. Michael was nursing a nasty gash on his forehead and now sported a white cotton bandage.

"Really sorry about that, Mike," said Simon. "I didn't mean to manhandle you, but it was the quickest way."

"That's quite all right, Simon," said Michael, wincing "I understand."

"I think you were very brave," said Emma, bristling with pride at her husband's heroics.

"Best left to the professionals, that sort of thing. Are you sure you're okay, Jess?"

"Yes, thanks. I'm fine. I just don't understand how you all got here."

"I was already on my way over here when you rang, and then I got a call from Pauline. She said Dave Morley's wife had called her in a panic saying you'd had a row and she thought he'd gone after you. I told her to get over here and I'd meet her. I then called you back to warn you but your phone went to voicemail."

"I was trying to call you to tell you Dave was here, but yours went to voicemail too. You must have been on the phone to Pauline. And then he burst in."

"Well you didn't hang up, so the whole conversation between you and Dave was recorded. All that stuff about The Navigation and, of course, the entire incident here."

"That's going to be pretty convincing evidence, I would have thought," said Simon, squeezing Jess's hand. She smiled weakly at him.

"Yes. But what about you?" said Michael. "Where the hell did you come from?"

Simon looked at them, puzzled, and spread his hands as if having to state the bleeding obvious.

"Gibraltar."

Jess went upstairs to shower and change. The hot water helped her relax and wash away the filth and degradation she felt at having had Dave's hands all over her.

Her mind was still buzzing from the events of the day. No one other than her and Dave could possibly have known for certain what had happened that day in The Navigation. Without the evidence, and despite what her friends might say, some would always harbour a doubt that her version of events was true and complete.

But Dave's unwitting confession, recorded by chance on voicemail, was evidence that five years ago he had forced her; forced her to submit to his demands for sexual gratification, and assaulted her. Raped her.

And yet, even with the evidence of his confession, their understanding could never be complete. She hadn't fought him off and no one but her would ever know or understand why she hadn't, except that by his own admission it might have made things worse. She knew, however, that her acquiescence had been born out of her past, a symptom of the abuse she had endured at the hands of her father and her husband, all of which had conditioned her to believe that such actions were normal, inconsequential and, ultimately, to be tolerated.

On that day, she'd made a decision that submitting to him was the lesser of two evils; preferable only to being homeless again, preferable to starting all over, sure in the knowledge that the same fate awaited her wherever she went. *There's no such thing as fate!* The Wheel of Life.

But regardless of the confession, there was clear evidence of his intentions today, as well as witnesses to him carrying them out, and she shuddered again. Shuddered at what might have happened if Michael hadn't turned up, and of course Simon, who'd rescued her again. What would she do without him?

She had gone to see Dave and Jade bearing an olive branch, of sorts. She had already determined that once the house was sold they would move far away, and so the chances of him pursuing her and the children would be greatly diminished. She had assumed that, once he learnt that there was no money, he would lose interest. She hadn't anticipated how obsessed nor how violent he would be. And in approaching him at all, she had been mindful of Alisha; consideration for others even though you feared they might do you harm, one of the characteristics of Buddhist teachings. If there was one teaching that didn't work for her, it was that one.

She thought about Jade and what this would mean for her and Ben. They were largely innocent in all of this, and in all likelihood, the marriage was over and Ben would be without a father for several years. She'd been saddened to see Jade apparently as motivated by the money as her husband, and dismayed at the antagonism she had displayed towards her erstwhile friend. But she couldn't know what Dave had told her, and in all probability he'd poisoned her mind with his lies. If Jade hadn't already discovered Dave's penchant for lying then she had now, and now she'd been a witness to his appalling attack. But she had to thank Jade for raising the alarm, as without that … she shuddered again.

She resolved to try and see her to put the record straight and offer support to her and Ben, but then considered that would be difficult, especially if, as she suspected, there was going to be a trial; something she wasn't looking forward to.

But there was much else to look forward to. Another new start in another new place. She knew it would come; she just hoped it would come soon.

Michael had already asked Sandy to pick up the kids from school for her, so they'd be home soon and then domestic mayhem would start all over again, so she turned off the water and wrapped herself in a soft white towel.

She dressed in her favourite cashmere sweater – *thanks Lisa, for letting me wear yours all those years ago* – and skinny blue jeans, satisfied they still accommodated her figure, and dried and brushed her long brown hair till it shone.

Downstairs, everyone had gone except Simon, who was still in the kitchen, flicking through a newspaper.

"Better?" he asked, standing and smiling warmly at her. She floated across the floor without breaking step and fell into his open arms, resting her head on his chest.

"I need to thank you all over again."

"You're welcome." He kissed her head then released her and they sat down next to each other. She swept her hair back over her head

"Tell me about Gibraltar."

"Warm, sunny, monkeys, you know."

She slapped his arm.

"Maria?"

"Oh. She's gorgeous. I absolutely love her to bits. I'm sure she and Carlos will be very happy.

"She and Carlos?" she said frowning.

"Yeah. They got married."

"You went to a wedding?"

"Yeah. Didn't I mention it?"

"You said you had business with Maria."

"And I did. I gave her away. Her dad and I were in the army together, in Afghanistan. But he didn't make it."

"Oh, that's very sad."

"Yes. So what did you think?"

He knew exactly what she'd thought, and she knew he knew and, suitably embarrassed, she slapped him again.

"I hate you, Rutherford!"

"What did I do?"

"Well, what about Theadora?"

"What about her? Can't a son go and visit his eighty-three-year-old mum without getting the third degree?"

She was lost for words again. She moved over and sat down on his knee, wrapped her arms around his neck and hugged him.

"So where are you off to next?"

"Nowhere. Nobody wants me. Getting too old for this game."

"You're forty-eight."

"Forty-nine."

She looked into his eyes and their lips almost met, but there was a clatter from the hallway, the sound of high-pitched squealing and a shout from Leila. Jess stood up abruptly.

"Sophie, Lucy! You must be more quiet," said Leila, in charge as usual. All three children burst into the kitchen, followed by Sandy.

"Simon!" they all shouted at once and he went down on his knees for a group hug.

"Hello, princesses. Have you missed me?"

"Yes!" they shrieked in unison.

"Right," said Jess. "Better get the kettle on."

***

Later, Simon played games with the girls as Jess prepared dinner, which they ate noisily, like many a real family, around the kitchen table, and afterwards they all helped with the washing-up and drying. Eventually, the kids went to bed, as exhausted as the grown-ups.

Jess and Simon closed the bedroom door behind the girls and wandered down the spiral staircase into the hallway. He stopped at the bottom of the stairs and looked down the hallway towards the front door.

She saw him looking pensive. She put her arms around him and then craned her neck to kiss him gently on the lips.

"Will you please stay?"

"If I'm invited."

"You're invited."

Printed in Poland
by Amazon Fulfillment
Poland Sp. z o.o., Wrocław